THE GOD OF WAR

ALSO BY CHRIS STEWART

THE FOURTH WAR

THE THIRD CONSEQUENCE

THE KILL BOX

SHATTERED BONE

THE GOD OF WAR

CHRIS STEWART

THOMMAS DUNNE BOOKS / ST. MARTIN'S PRESS  NEW YORK

This is a work of fiction. All of the characters, organizations, and events portrayed in this novel are either products of the author's imagination or are used fictitiously.

THOMAS DUNNE BOOKS.
An imprint of St. Martin's Press.

www.thomasdunnebooks.com
www.stmartins.com

Design by Dylan Rosal Greif

Library of Congress Cataloging-in-Publication Data

Stewart, Chris, 1960–
The god of war / Chris Stewart.—1st ed.
p. cm.
ISBN-13: 978-0-312-28956-0
ISBN-10: 0-312-28956-1
1. Air warfare—Fiction. 2. Laser weapons—Fiction. 3. Air pilots, Military—Fiction. 4. Terrorism—Fiction. I. Title.

PS3569.T493 G64 2008
813'.54—dc22

2008001807

First Edition: April 2008

10 9 8 7 6 5 4 3 2 1

To Major Dave Ellis, who taught me how to fly and fight.
"Post Tenebras Lux"
After darkness, light.

ACKNOWLEDGMENTS

None of my work would be possible without the support of my agent, Ted Chichak, and the exceptional people at Thomas Dunne Books/St. Martin's Press. All of them are experts in their trade and I will always be grateful.

Much thanks to those friends in the military and intelligence communities who are willing to take the time to listen to my unending questions and answer when they can. Buck, special thanks to you.

By the end of the decade, fighter aircraft with laser pods or turrets could be in test flights. The age of laser weapons has nearly arrived. No science-fiction here: Lasers as weapons are in the final stages of development, and plans for their integration into combat forces are proceeding.

—*Air Force Magazine* (December 2002)

Once fully developed, solid-state lasers could shoot down mortars and artillery shells, explode ordnance in enemy depots and even wipe out ballistic missiles 500 miles away. They would strike with incredible speed and could be retargeted instantly . . . the lasers will not be visible streams of light. Instead, targets will simply explode.

—*Oakland Tribune* (October 2003)

Compared to the chemical lasers now in use by America's military, solid-state lasers would be compact and efficient—perhaps running off the engine of an Army Humvee or an Air Force F-16.

Solid-state lasers would also be deadly. In a recent demonstration at Lawrence Livermore National Laboratory—one of three sites of research on a solid-state laser—a test-fired laser emitted 400 pulses of light in two seconds, drilling through an inch of steel.

—CBS Broadcasting (October 2003)

Lockheed Martin is tailoring a laser for the F-35 Joint Strike Fighter that could be ready as early as 2010 for demonstration and the start of a full-scale development program.

An advantage of a directed-energy weapon is that it can shoot indefinitely and is limited only by the ability to cool it, and it's covert. "There's no huge explosion associated with its employment," a Lockheed Martin official said. "A foe would be left largely clueless trying to analyze what happened and why. . . ."

A Defense Science Board study last year said that several technology breakthroughs have moved high-energy lasers on fighters into the realm of the possible. Among them was increased electrical power-generation capability achieved under the "More-Electric Aircraft Project." The DSB contends that aircraft systems will be able to provide one megawatt of power in less than five years. Other rapidly developing technologies allow smaller packaging of systems. These include advanced solid-state lasers, chemical lasers with electro-regeneration of chemicals and fiber lasers.

—F-16.net (April 2004)

The U.S. military has been developing a gunship that could literally obliterate enemy ground targets with a laser beam.

The laser could have tremendous repercussions on the battlefield, particularly in urban warfare in such countries as Afghanistan and Iraq. "It's the kind of tool that could bring about victory within minutes," an official said.

Officials said Advanced Technology Laser was being developed through the Pentagon's Advanced Concept Technology Demonstration program. Should the tests in 2007 prove successful, the Pentagon was expected to approve full-scale development of the airborne tactical laser.

—*Insight* magazine (January 30, 2006)

Discrimination and proportionality are essential elements in the "law of war." And yes, a laser could do a better job of discriminating, but the power it would bring to the battlefield may blow any sense of proportionality right out the door.

—Senior Pentagon official

Ares: Son of Zeus. Also known as the God of War.

THE GOD OF WAR

PROLOGUE

"You've got to try and understand the magnitude of what I'm proposing," the military officer began. His voice was low and husky, and he spoke with confidence. "First, the city is home of the Black Stone of the Kaaba. One point two billion Muslims consider the Black Stone the most holy object on earth. It existed before the prophet Mohammad, even before Jesus Christ, even before the first man. The Black Stone was Allah's gift to Adam; it came directly from paradise. From Adam to Abraham, from Jesus Christ to Mohammad—all of their prophets have touched or held the Black Stone.

"Believe me, sir, there is nothing in the East or the West that compares. No temple, no mosque, no Holy Grail or Shroud of Christ even begins to come close to the sacred stature of the Stone. Because it is so sacred, it is strictly forbidden for non-Muslims to behold the Black Stone. They can't even be in the same city where the Black Stone is housed. Beheading is the sentence for any nonbeliever who walks through the city doors.

The second man was silent, pulling on his thin beard. He was fat and smelled of garlic, cumin, and sweat. His eyes were pale and translucent, and he never seemed to blink. Everything about him reeked of brutal power and greed.

The officer wet his lips, uncomfortable with the silence. "Consider this," he went on, "several years ago an Air France 747 ventured within the city's no-fly zone. Within minutes the Saudi Royal Air Force had four F-15s on its tail. They came to within a few seconds of shooting it down. Four hundred people, blown right out of the sky. They would have done it and not apologized, wouldn't have given a second thought. Such is their sacred duty to protect the Holy City that protects the Black Stone of the Kaaba.

"And while the Stone is the primary explanation for why Islam considers the city so holy, there are several more. The *Masjid al Qaeda Haram* contains a miraculously preserved set of footprints created by the great prophet Abraham's feet. The Angel Gabriel appeared to Ishmael in the city. Allah would send his Great Prophet there.

"These are the reasons the world's Muslims turn to face it when they pray, why millions of destitute and poverty-stricken Muslims sell every possession they have to finance their pilgrimage there. It is a pillar of their life just to *touch* the Black Stone. Once they have done that, their lives become complete. Life becomes the enemy. Death is welcome to them then."

The fat one shifted, moving his eyes to stare at the far wall. "It is a courageous thing you offer, but perhaps not the best option now."

The other man leaned toward him. "How many lives have been sacrificed to protect the Black Stone? How many wars have been fought to keep the city safe? Not enough, any Muslim would tell you, for no price is too great to defend the Black Stone."

The dark-haired man fell into silence, his evil eyes burning bright. "The people of Islam have been promised the city will never be destroyed or defiled," he answered slowly.

The other man only stared. Prophecies of religion didn't mean much to him. "Give me the word," he finally whispered, "and we will see if that's true."

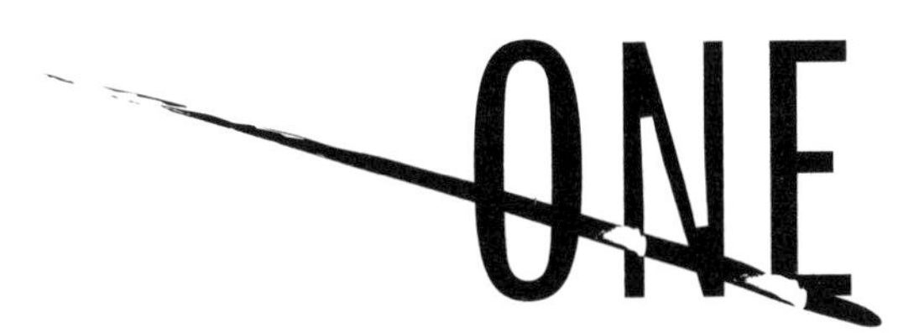

UPPER BITTERROOT MOUNTAINS
CENTRAL IDAHO

The man masked his power very well.

He looked to be about fifty, though he was almost ten years older and clearly in good shape, with long legs and well-defined arms. He had dark hair with tints of gray and a small tattoo of a star on his shoulder, which would have shocked three hundred million Americans had they known.

Everything he had on was new: his logging shirt was pressed, his jeans stiff and clean. Even his waders glistened, smelling more like fresh rubber than fish. He stood eleven feet from the rocky bank. The late morning sun had finally broken over the mountain peaks, glistening on the whitecaps as they rolled over the boulders in the stream. The man cast the artificial gnat, a Rio Grande King (dark red tail, hand-tied in a small room off of the Lincoln Bedroom at the White House), the same way he did everything else—deliberately. No beauty, all power. Pulling back his arm, he jerked it forward while snatching his wrist, floating the leader, fine as human hair, out before him. The artificial gnat lay on top of the water, caught the current to wash over a large rock, then was pulled upriver in the backwash to hover in the shade of stone.

There he let it linger.

A native cutthroat trout was hiding in the backwash behind the stone. The man hadn't seen it yet, but he'd sensed the tiny ripple and knew it was there, resting in the null area where the water pooled. The cutthroat wasn't a monster—eight, maybe ten inches is all—but large for this stream, which meant he'd been smart enough to survive in the river awhile. Which meant he would be hard to catch.

But the man was going to catch him and he smiled again as he cast.

The gnat caught a sudden current and was spit into the main stream again. The man let it drift downriver, pulled out a little more line, then took in the slack and cast again.

Forty feet behind him, the small stream spilled down a rocky bank and poured into the Salmon River with a constant roar. Above his head, the wind blew down from the Rocky Mountain peaks. Thirteen thousand feet up, there was still a lot of snow, most of it piled in the glaciers that had been there for ten thousand years. Two hundred meters downriver, the Forest Service campground had been completely taken over by his men. Three huge helicopters had been towed across the grass to the shade of the old pines. The choppers were unmarked, dark green and black, with odd-shaped bubbles behind their main rotors to hide the antennas of the top-secret communications gear stuffed inside. The camp's main lodge was crowded with his men, but the fisherman stayed away from them as best as he could, choosing to stay in a tent by himself, twenty meters back in the trees.

As the man cast again, he caught a shadow to his right. The agent hadn't moved in almost three hours, and he was impressed. Still, though, he mumbled. "Two thousand miles I come, to the most isolated river in the lower forty-eight, *and yet I can't be alone!" Not even for a moment! Not even out here!*

Providing security in the mountains was a nightmare, and he felt bad, knowing it was hard on his security forces, but he needed time alone, time to feel the presence of no one but the mountains and the wind, to look at the sky and imagine he was the only man on the earth, to smell the pines and hear the river and simply be by himself.

He glanced at the agent in the trees, then turned back to his line.

The gnat was sucked into the backflow again, and he saw a shadow in the water. "Come on, you little bugger," he whispered. "It's you and it's me, baby. Man against nature. Now who's going to win?"

The shadow rose and then fell. He tugged lightly on the line, a subtle move of his fingers that pulled the tiny gnat across the water, seeming to give it wings. "Come on, you little wise one, come on."

The shadow started rising.

"Good morning, Mr. President," a man shouted from behind him.

The shadow dropped out of sight, falling beneath a large stone. The president swore, his face angry. He didn't even turn around.

Not alone for ten seconds! Not even out here.

"Mr. President," the national security advisor called to the president again.

The Secret Service agent in the trees dropped to his knees. Behind him, another agent emerged from the shadows to stand in the sun.

Patrick Abram reluctantly turned around.

The NSA stood uncertainly on the edge of the bank. He wore dark jeans, a white shirt, and black loafers, as authentic a Western look as the Massachusetts boy could muster. The president ignored him and cast again. The

NSA waited a full two minutes, then took off his shoes, rolled up his pants, and waded knee-deep. The water was ice-cold, fresh off the glacier. This would be a short conversation; the water and the president's demeanor made that pretty clear.

"The Chinese have wrapped up Angry Tiger," the NSA said as he moved to the president's side. He stood back, allowing enough room for the president to cast.

The president glanced in his direction. "And?"

The NSA cleared his throat.

"Keep it short, John. I've got a fish waiting."

The NSA adjusted his weight, his feet already turning numb. "Bottom line, Mr. President, is the Chinese could kick our teeth down our throat. Regular army forces could be in the capital of Taiwan before we could grab our bathrobes and climb out of bed. Two weeks, maybe three, and it would be over, I'm afraid."

The president grunted. "That's not what I wanted to hear."

"I understand that, sir. But let me remind you again: the Chinese started their military buildup in earnest in the midnineties, picked it up after 9/11, really kicked into high gear after we went into Iraq, and have been rolling ever since. They have built a true blue-water navy that can protect their oil tanker lanes from the Persian Gulf to their own eastern shores. The new *Luyang II* Aegis-class destroyers passed their sea trials with flying colors in the first two weeks of Angry Tiger. They've got the missiles, the warheads, the fighters and bombers, and now—"

The president cut him off. "The KC-40s?"

The NSA looked away, embarrassed. The dull ache in his feet felt like nothing compared to the red burn on his face. "Yeah. We finally saw them. They used them to refuel their fighters over the Gulf of Taiwan."

The president stared, then carefully cast again. "So the Chinese have developed an air-refuelable fighter *and* an air-to-air tanker *right under our noses*. They've developed two completely new weapons systems, and *we didn't even know!*"

The NSA shook his head bitterly. He'd been wrung out over this issue for months and had nothing more to offer in his own defense.

He knew his days were numbered. He read the morning papers, same as everyone else.

The president frowned, wiping his hand across his jaw. "Have you talked to Edgar?"

The NSA pressed his lips at the mention of the chief of staff's name.

Edgar Ketchum. Doorkeeper to the president. Flaming Sword at the Gate. Saint Peter could only hope to be as efficient controlling access to heaven as Ketchum was at controlling access to the president. The NSA would rather drive toothpicks under his nails than talk to the president's chief of staff.

The president watched, seeing the hesitation. "Brief him," he told the NSA. "Tell him everything. He and I will talk later on."

The NSA nodded and tightened his jaw. "Of course, sir. But as you must know we still—"

"What I know, *Mr. Feldman,* is that for the past thirty years our military has been unmatched anywhere in the world. But that is no longer true. The balance of power has shifted. Shifted on *my* watch, and that's a hard thing to take."

The NSA leaned again against the current as President Abram fell silent.

Taiwan wasn't the only problem that he faced now, he thought, not by a long way. The Chinese were now as interested in secure oil as they were in Taiwan. They were as interested in expanding as the old Russian Army was. And the opportunity for mischief had now spread far and wide. From the Southern Pacific, through the China Sea, across the Indian Ocean to the Persian Gulf, the Chinese had developed the navy and the air forces to control that half of the world, the only part of the world that was experiencing double-digit economic growth, that contained the two fastest-growing economies, two emerging superpowers. Now a dozen Chinese ports had been built from Beijing to India, across Bangladesh to Iran. A dozen air fields. Tactical and strategic aircraft. Aircraft carriers. Nuclear missiles from Russia on a par with anything the United States had.

Abram grunted. "Angry Tiger has proven they could take down Taiwan in less than a week. General Shevky called it the most impressive military exercise he has ever seen, quite a compliment coming from the chairman of the U.S. Joint Chiefs of Staff, I would say. They have proven they have the missiles to soften up the Taiwanese defenses, the landing craft for two hundred thousand soldiers, the submarines to protect them, the air forces to land their paratroops, and the C-four and satellites to control the battlefield."

The NSA didn't answer. His mind was already somewhere else. He would sit on the board of a couple corporations, nothing where he had to make any decisions, just throw around some advice, something that paid well, a little travel, but didn't require too much thought. He wouldn't wait for the president to fire him. He'd give it two weeks, let things settle down at little, then submit his resignation on a Friday night, just before the weekend news cycle went into hover mode.

The president glanced at him, noting the far-off look in his eye. "Hide our capabilities, bide our time," he said, bringing the NSA back to the present, his shame and his feet aching in the cold stream. "Isn't that what the Chinese always said? But they don't hide it any longer. And their biding is done. They'll go after Taiwan. And we can't stop them! There's not a thing we can do."

The NSA didn't answer. His feet and legs were aching so badly he wondered how much longer he could stand.

The president looked at him, noticed him shaking, and cast once again. "I have three choices," he said. "One, we sit on the Ares and no one knows. One day soon, we will have to use it, but it will be already too late.

"Two, we leak its existence and let the chips fall where they may. But leaking the story means the results are unpredictable, and worse, beyond our control. Maybe it's enough to dissuade them. Maybe it's not. We really don't know.

"Three, we have a coming-out party that will shake up the world. We reveal everything about the Ares, show them all its power. Then the fighter becomes a deterrent that will keep them in line."

"But sir, by revealing its capabilities, we also compromise—"

"We compromise nothing! We've been through this before. But if we show them exactly how deadly this new fighter can be, they will have to think very carefully before loading up their amphibious ships and sailing off to Taiwan."

The NSA took a step against the current. "Alright, sir," he said.

"Peace through deterrence. That's the smart thing." The president teased his line, slipping it across the pool of water behind the rock one more time. "I'm as certain of this, Mr. Feldman, as I've ever been of anything. Our enemies can't be deterred if we keep our ace in the hole. Yes, we could destroy them with the Ares, but is that really what we want? Isn't it better to show them what they'd be dealing with than to surprise them in war? If it comes to war, Mr. Feldman, then we will have already failed. I don't want that to happen, not when there is another way."

The NSA nodded. They had argued before; the generals and politicians had been arguing for months now. And maybe the president was right. Either way, he didn't care.

The president turned and faced him, dropping his vintage fiberglass pole to his side. "I've been watching those Chinese snakes for almost seven years. They've been stretching their muscles, hoping to impress the world. Now it's my turn to stretch. I want to put on my own show. I want you to set it up for Paris, just like we discussed. We're going to roll out the Ares. And I want to be there when we do."

HANGAR 115
AÉROPORT DE PARIS–LE BOURGET
PARIS, FRANCE
THREE WEEKS LATER

It was a fine airport, one of the city's largest, but its extreme proximity to downtown had forced it to be restricted to only small business jets. Still, every two years Le Bourget Airport became the center of the aviation universe when it hosted the Paris Air Show, the most prestigious aviation event in the world.

The president stood by a small metal doorway on the side of the enormous aircraft hangar. Behind him, a group of heavily armed French police stood in a semicircle, their backs to the metal building, their snub-nosed machine guns held anxiously at their sides, as if expecting an imminent attack. Looking at them, the president wasn't impressed. "Window dressing," he scoffed quietly as he shook his head.

The president glanced beyond the line of French officers to the dark suits and dark SUVs lined up across the tarmac. American Secret Service agents. Real men with real missions who didn't have to ask permission to shoot.

Thank you, messieurs, but the United States is capable of taking care of its own, he thought as he glanced at the line of French policemen again.

His own security force, more than two hundred strong, almost all of them unseen, had complete control of the area by now; they had already swept the entire north end of the airport parking ramp, taken control of the outer perimeter of the field, the flanks of the runway, and the inside of the hangar. Military attack helicopters, overhead fighters, satellite data-linked portable bunkers, armored personnel carriers, dozens of black and blue SUVs hiding .50-caliber machine guns, shoulder-fired antiaircraft missiles and rocket-propelled grenades, communications gear, chemical warfare suits—the list of men and equipment that was dedicated to protecting the president went on and on. President Abram knew the French officers could have been holding water pistols and he wouldn't have been any less safe. But the French prime minister had insisted, and so the president had acquiesced.

He glanced again beyond the French line of troops. Four Secret Service agents were standing behind the soldiers, close together, watching him carefully. His chief of staff stood ten feet to the side, but he stayed in the background, a few steps away from the line of French troops.

This was a private moment, one the president had been looking forward to, and Ketchum was smart enough to stay out of the way.

The president turned for the hangar. The chief of his personal security detail opened the door and led the president through. Security Operations 101; POTUS was *never* the first one to enter a room.

There was a four-inch steel railing at the base of the metal door, and the Secret Security agent nodded toward it as the president stepped inside. Abram stood for a moment. Outside, the sun was shining brightly, reflecting off the smooth cement, and he had to pause a few seconds to allow his eyes time to adjust to the dark.

The main doors had been rolled shut. The enormous space was lit by large fluorescent lights suspended from the high ceilings on long metal rods, but there weren't any windows to let in the sun. A pair of Secret Service agents stood in each corner. Behind them, dozens of U.S. military police waited for the moment when the Secret Service would release responsibility for the area back to them. Yes, the new fighter would soon be unveiled to the world, but until that time direct access to the aircraft was being tightly controlled. Motion, laser, sound and heat sensors, armed sentries, security codes and passwords—all were being employed to protect access to the jets, ensuring that no one could get within a hundred feet of the aircraft who was not supposed to.

Edgar Ketchum followed the president into the hangar but remained by the doorway, always checking his watch.

Ketchum was obsessed with managing the president's day. In his mind the administration wasn't just running a nation, it was writing history, building a legacy. Because of that, there were enormous demands on the president, which meant enormous demands on him too. The president didn't have a half hour that wasn't scheduled for the next five months or so, and Ketchum wondered at the wisdom of this whole Paris Air Show. But the president had insisted. And so they were here. Powerful as he was, Ketchum wasn't the boss, as the president reminded him almost every day.

The president listened to the crack and pop as the steel hangar walls expanded in the afternoon sun. The cement floor was dark gray, freshly painted and perfectly clean.

He took a deep breath.

After all the years of waiting, it was time for his private tour.

He looked toward the back of the hangar.

Both of the aircraft were there.

He stared at them a moment, a shiver running down his spine. The fluorescent lights glinted off the dark canopies. The beak-shaped noses slanted downward. At the rear of the aircraft, the twin dorsal fins canted outward at seventy degrees. The engine inlets were hidden deep in the bellies of the jets, and the canopies were deeply tinted to absorb any reflections from the sun.

The president saw the general waiting under the shadow of one of the wings, and he started walking toward him, letting the metal door close behind him with a clang.

General Hawley stood alone by the first aircraft's landing gear. The president's footsteps echoed through the enormous metal hangar as he walked, and the general stepped toward him and snapped a perfect salute.

Abram raised his fingers to his eyebrow, then extended his hand. "Robert, good to see you."

Major General Robert H. Hawley took the president's hand in a bone-crushing grip. "Mr. President, always an honor, sir."

The two men nodded at each other, a hint of self-congratulation in their smiles.

The president walked to the front of the jet and stared, his eyes shining. It was the first time he had seen the aircraft, and he was clearly in awe. General Hawley watched him carefully, noting the look on his face.

Yeah, the Ares could do that. The fighter made everyone stare.

The president didn't say anything as he studied the jet, then slowly moved around the aircraft, sometimes touching the skin, sometimes stepping back to look up. He walked around the gear, the twin jet exhausts, then the left wing and nose. It was a surprisingly large aircraft, especially for a fighter, long and narrow to house the enormously powerful electric generator and laser. And it sat high up on the gear, almost too high for him to reach up and touch the wing. Coming to a stop at the front of the aircraft, he peered at the cube of clear glass suspended underneath the cockpit. The tip of the laser. He touched it. It was warm.

He took a quick breath and stepped back. "She's beautiful," he pronounced.

There was more truth in his comment than the general would have liked to admit. The sad reality was that the new fighter had become more than his mistress. Like many military families, the general's wife and two children had paid the price of his eighty-hour work weeks and the endless months he'd been gone. His wife, a former Miss Nevada who was almost as proud of her brains as she was of her looks, got tired of being lonely and took off with the kids, leaving him with four-thousand-dollar-a-month child support payments and a huge, empty house. A lousy price to pay. If he could live his life over, he wouldn't make the same mistake. Forget the whole general thing, forget the obsession with power. He would have been satisfied making lieutenant colonel, flying every day and being home with the kids.

But that was water under the bridge now, and he tried not to think about it anymore.

Regrets, he had learned, were the deepest secrets a man ever kept.

Hawley turned to the beautiful fighter. "Sir, I want you to know how proud I am of this jet," he said.

The president nodded. After all of these years, he couldn't have been more satisfied. He touched the aircraft again, wanting to claim part of it for his own. "You know I used to be a navy pilot," he said.

No kidding! the general thought. The president had spent eight years and two campaigns pointing that out every chance he got. No way could he be accused of being weak on defense. *I was a freakin' naval aviator. I hate America's enemies as much as anyone else.* It was a pretty good impression to leave on the American electorate, and especially important for a moderate governor from a liberal northern state. And the fact that he hadn't ever flown anything more sophisticated than a prop-driven navy trainer didn't get mentioned a lot. But that didn't seem to matter much; in the public's mind all military pilots were studs and they didn't need to know the details any further than that.

And that was just fine with the general. He didn't care if the president had spent his four years in the navy peeling potatoes, painting ships, or cleaning heads. He didn't care about the president's politics either—liberal, moderate, or conservative—none of that mattered to him. Professionally, he wasn't allowed to care. Personally, he simply didn't, but on one central question—the funding, design, and creation of the Ares—he and the president were of one mind.

Hawley stepped to the president's side. He was three inches taller than the president, something that bothered both men, and he unconsciously slumped his shoulders to appear less imposing to him. A religious runner who took leave every year to run the Boston Marathon, Hawley was thinner than the president but just as smart and determined. And worse, just as proud. Indeed, the two men were very much alike: driven, ambitious, and willing to sacrifice anything for their goals.

The general touched the composite skin of the fighter. "Sir, I'd like to explain to you what your money has bought."

"That's why I'm here, Robert. And as you know, I don't have much time."

Hawley glanced at the Secret Service men in the corners of the hangar, then lowered his voice. "The official Air Force designation for this aircraft is the F-38. Some call it the Thor, some the 38-Special. Officially, the SAP . . . I'm sorry . . . the Special Access Program, or Black Box funding designation, has been Fighter Integrating Strategic Technologies, or FIST, but Ares is the name which seemed to have stuck." Pointing to the cube of hard crystal underneath the nose of the fighter, he continued. "The heart of the Ares is, of course, the laser gun. I won't go into the technical descriptions, Mr. President, the Nd:GGG neodymium-doped gadolinium-gallium-garnet, which are the waveguides for the laser, the Nd:glass and energy absorption, the power generation and all. I know you don't have the time, and no offense, but you wouldn't understand it anyway. Neither do I, at least not completely. There are probably less than ten people in the world who really understand the technology behind this gun. But it's a real crowd-pleaser, President Abram, believe me. I've seen the strike test, and trust me, this is one incredible gun.

"Officially, the laser weapon is called the SSHCL-105B. It is a solid-state heat-capacity laser; one hundred kilowatts of savage power. To give you an idea what one hundred kilowatts really means, consider this; four years ago the best thing we had was a laser in the ten-kilowatt range. It was large as a dump truck, but those ten kilowatts still produced a five-hundred-joule pulse in a two-second burst, enough, sir, to vaporize two inches of tempered steel. Ten kilowatts. Two inches of steel. Times that by a factor of ten, now, and I think you can begin to understand just how powerful this laser gun is. Plus, we reduced the length of the burst to less than one thousandth of second. That's a lot of heat, Mr. President, in a very short amount of time."

The president nodded. Most of this he already knew. "The aircraft doesn't carry any missiles?" he asked.

"No sir. No reason. The laser will shoot down enemy fighters far better than a missile can. It's a speed-of-light kill versus a Mach 1 approach." The general lifted both hands, forming symbolic scales. "Seven hundred miles an hour. Three hundred and eighty-six thousand miles a second. I don't know. You tell me." He raised one hand a few inches. "The advantage seems pretty clear.

"But it's also important to remember that, unlike the movies, the laser doesn't make things explode. It simply burns a hole in them or cuts them in two. The velocity of the targets is what tears them apart. If there is fuel to ignite, there is an explosion, yes, but the laser doesn't shoot down enemy fighters by exploding them, sir. Same with ground targets. It can burn a hole in a battleship to tear it apart, but it doesn't blow it up. That's just movies, sir.

"Because of this, we thought it prudent to include the capability to carry conventional weapons. The F-38 can carry two one-thousand-pound, satellite-guided bombs for nonexplosive targets—you know, buildings, runways, things like that. But far and away the preponderance of its targets will be hit with the gun."

The general paused, waiting for a question or comment, but the president was quiet, so he went on. "Simply building a laser gun, sir, wasn't the only technological challenge we had. Size and weight. It always comes down to those. Several years ago we successfully built a one-hundred-kilowatt gun, but it was so big and heavy we could barely stuff it inside a modified 747 commercial aircraft. Worse, it was a chemical laser. Toxic, dangerous, and only good for one blast. That one burst of heat required enough poisonous chemicals to kill half the population of Manhattan. Not a good option, sir, as I'm sure you'd agree.

"But then, a little more than three years ago, we had a breakthrough with the Nd:GGG crystal technology. The result is what you see here: a solid-state electrical laser gun, small enough to fit inside the new fighter yet powerful enough to burn through a warship. Computer controlled, it can identify and destroy dozens of targets from hundreds of miles away. And it only requires an easily producible amount of energy to accomplish the task—"

"Okay," the president interrupted as he glanced at his watch. "You're going too deep for me, Robert. Give me the bottom line. What can our baby really do?"

The general nodded and smiled and answered carefully. "The no-exaggeration, no-crap bottom line is pretty simple. The Ares can identify and assassinate a world leader from three hundred miles away. He's walking to his car, and suddenly he has a hole in his head. There's no flash of light, no zap, just poof, a wisp of burned flesh, and he's gone. The bottom line, Mr. President, is the Ares can identify and track up to fifty-eight airborne targets and shoot them out of the air instantly. One hundred percent accuracy. And it could do it a hundred and sixty miles before the enemy fighters are even within range of firing their guns. The bottom line, Mr. President: the Ares can take out an entire naval battle group, the carriers, escorts, and destroyers, before they could launch a single jet.

"Simply put, Mr. President, the F-38 is far and away the most powerful and dangerous weapon system ever put in the air. It is a *transformational* weapon, for it has the capability to change military doctrine and tactics for the next fifty years. A single F-38 has the destructive power of a hundred other fighters. And precise as a pin. And since the laser light is invisible, the fighter can strike dozens of targets without being detected, circling safely from hundreds of miles away. And it can kill an unlimited number of targets, for it never runs out of ammunition or bombs. The only thing it needs to reload is another burst of power from the generators hidden in the belly of the jet. In addition to the deadly potential of the laser, the F-38 has demonstrated capabilities beyond anything envisioned before—super-cruise, stealth, sixth-generation guidance systems. Basically, we took our most modern fighter, the F-22, an incredible weapon system itself, made it larger to give it a much longer range, modified it a little, improved it a lot, integrated the laser, and now here it is. And everything I have just told you is one hundred percent accurate. Completely demonstrable, as we will prove during tomorrow's air show."

The president couldn't help it and he broke into a smile that spread ear to ear. "You guys at the Skunk Works are to be congratulated," he said.

"Thank you, sir."

"Tomorrow we fly it. Tomorrow, we show the world."

"Yes, sir, we do."

"Alright then. As you know, all of the Group of Eight leaders are in Paris for the week."

The general nodded. He knew that, of course.

"In addition to the Group of Eight leaders, a Chinese military delegation will be at the unveiling."

The general nodded again.

"I want things to go perfectly. You understand that. There can't be any hiccups or surprises. I want to make a statement and I want it to be clear. I want our allies to know that we have the strength to defend them and our enemies to know that we will use that strength to further our will."

The president hesitated, staring at his friend. "I want this jet to blow their socks off. I think you know what I mean."

The general nodded confidently, then placed his hands on the jet. "Believe me, Mr. President, we're going to blow off a lot more than that."

For a long moment the two men stood in silence. Then the president turned to Hawley, who was staring at the jet, and saw the look of pure joy in his face. This was the general's baby. This was his life's work. He had sacrificed everything to build it, and now the Ares was here. "Alright then," he said as he glanced down at his watch. "Tomorrow we will do it."

Hawley nodded slowly. The president pressed his lips with pride and touched his shoulder, then turned for the hangar door.

General Hawley watched the president walk away. He knew the president was nervous; he had seen that in his eyes. Both men were nervous. They had worked so hard and taken so many chances to get to this day. As he watched him leave, Hawley remembered something the president had once said. "Reagan brought back the B-1s. Bush I unveiled the F-117s. Every good president needs a significant weapons system or a war on their watch. If we can make the Ares a reality, history will be satisfied."

Having spent the last ten years working at the Pentagon and the White House, Hawley understood the mind of a politician about as well as he understood anything. Abram was claiming the Ares for his legacy, but that seemed fair to him. Still, the truth was that the technology built into the F-38s had been in development long before Abram had come to office. Some of the research dated back to the sixties, when military scientists had first begun trying to build the holy grail of all weapons, a practical laser gun. A generation later, when the technology began to look more promising, Bush II had pushed hard for a battle-proven laser weapon. The other breakthrough technologies built into the new fighter—the stealth, the thought-controlled weapons systems, the advanced avionics, and jet engines capable of supercruise—were also technologies that had been in R&D for at least thirty years.

But Abram had been the man who fought to bring them together. He'd been the man who had seen the vision, who'd really understood what incredible power the new fighters would bring. He'd been the man who'd made a commitment to the program, funded, and supported it, even through the lean years when the technology of the laser weapon was still very much up in the air.

More important, he had successfully (and amazingly) hidden the program from Congress, where it certainly would have been leaked to the press. If it had been leaked, the scrutiny would have been unsustainably intense, crushing the project under the weight of the enormous dollars involved. There would have been quarterly meetings with the Congress, hearings and stories and demands from the press. There would have been semiannual reviews with the Pentagon and their contracting officers, followed by chaos and riots when they saw how much the president intended to spend. If they had tried to build the aircraft in the open, it would have taken thirty years to get the funding approved.

After all, *eighteen billion dollars* was a fair amount of money for *two* jets.

Had they stretched a few ethics to birth this fighter? Perhaps just a few. Had they broken any laws? Almost certainly not, for executive orders and privilege were very powerful tools. A lot of things had changed over the past dozen years that allowed the president incredible latitude when it came to any issue surrounding national security. But still, a few brooms might have been kept busy sweeping a little dirt under the rug.

And although the Ares had not come gently into the world, it was here now, and that was the only thing either one of them cared about.

The money had been well spent. It was impossible to estimate how much these new fighters were worth, for the Ares had the power to literally change the world.

General Hawley knew that. The president knew.

Soon, everyone else would know it, too.

THREE

PARIS AIR SHOW
AÉROPORT DE PARIS–LE BOURGET
PARIS, FRANCE

At exactly 4:00 p.m., the hangar doors rolled open. The crowd, three hundred thousand citizens—aviation lovers, elected officials, reporters, consultants, military officers, and defense officials from all over the world—stared in awe as the sleek, black fighter emerged from behind the rolling doors. The pilot was already in the cockpit, the canopy down, the two engines screeching as the new fighter began to taxi toward the crowd. Behind a black curtain at the rear of the hangar, the second F-38, the only other one in existence, stood ready in case the primary fighter had a mechanical malfunction of any sort.

The crowd was held back by a thick, red rope and hundreds of security guards. As the Ares started moving, an American announcer's voice boomed over the public address system, though he was barely understandable above the roar of the jet engine exhaust. *"Ladies and gentlemen, honored guests, the United States Air Force is proud to present the most advanced and lethal aircraft ever built. The F-38, code name Ares, was built in utter secrecy at a highly classified facility in southern Nevada . . . "*

The fighter moved forward, heading directly toward the center of the crowd, then suddenly turned, its nose gear never straying more than an inch from the center of the yellow taxi line. The canopy windows were deeply tinted to avoid reflecting the sun, and the observers could not see through the dark Plexiglas, though they caught an occasional glimpse of movement from the pilot inside.

"The Ares is piloted today by Colonel Gene 'Hangman' Ray, United States Air Force. Colonel Ray has logged more than two hundred combat missions in Kosovo, Iraq, and Afghanistan. A twenty-three-year Air Force veteran, Colonel

Ray is one of the senior test pilots for the F-38 and has logged almost three hundred hours in the Ares."

The F-38 stopped midcrowd, giving them a good look, then began to move again, heading toward the east end of the airport for takeoff.

Moving toward the runway, the pilot checked the flight controls. As he stirred the stick, the aircraft's leading edges, trailing slats, tails, rudders, and nose canards moved together. There were so many moving parts on the skin of the aircraft that it looked as if it were alive, stretching its muscles like a giant insect getting ready to fly.

The announcer went on. "*Capable of identifying, tracking, and targeting an incredible but highly classified number of targets at one time, the Ares can destroy enemy fighters a hundred miles before they even know it is there.*"

The black aircraft moved quickly across the white cement. The airspace within twenty miles of Bourget had to be closed to all air traffic and, as the F-38 moved toward the runway, the controllers in the tower were busy making sure that all of the airspace was clear.

As the F-38 rolled, the pilot pushed the engines into afterburner for half a second to test the igniters. At the back of the aircraft, the exhaust burner cans closed, then shot open as the afterburners ignited, sending a shot of two-thousand-degree exhaust spouting from the back of the jet. The hot fumes of burned fuel created visible heat waves that stretched across the cement.

"*Supercruise allows the pilot to fly supersonic using only cruise power, something fighter pilots have dreamed of for more than fifty years.*" The announcer's voice seemed to fade behind the scream of the engines and noise of the crowd. "*Able to hit targets literally at the speed of light . . .*"

The American fighter stopped short of the runway for its final pretakeoff checks. The timing was perfect. The announcer completed his script. The pilot was ready to go.

The president of the United States was sitting in a glass-enclosed stand at the front of the crowd. The other leaders of the G-8 nations sat beside him, lined up like a group of anxious students out on a field day. The end of the runway was a little less than a mile from the presidential stand and, in the distance, the fighter's paint blended in almost perfectly with the trees on the horizon. Near the back corner of the reviewing stand sat the leader of the Chinese delegation, a dark and sullen look on his face. It looked like he wished bitterly that he was back in Beijing.

"*Now sit back, ladies and gentlemen,*" the announcer finally said, "*as you witness the most incredible flying demonstration of the twenty-first century.*"

The Ares' twin engines roared and the fighter taxied onto the runway. The pilot stopped and held the brakes while pushing the throttles up to just below the afterburner range. The F-38 squatted, straining against her brakes, then shot suddenly forward, the engines shattering the air.

The American fighter accelerated down the runway. Twelve hundred feet from the point at which it had released its brakes, the pilot lifted the front wheel into the air. The fighter rolled nose-high for a couple seconds, then the wings lifted as well. The pilot snapped up the gear and nosed over, accelerating down the runway only five feet above the ground. At the five-thousand-foot marker, just as he was approaching the center of the crowd, the aircraft was accelerating through four hundred knots, and tiny white vapor trails began to float off of each wing. Six seconds later, still accelerating, the air flow over the blended wings began to approach the speed of sound and a soft, floating pillow of vapor formed behind the cockpit as the moisture in the air condensed in the heat of the transonic airflow.

The batlike aircraft passed in front of the crowd, its engines roaring, the gray paint standing out against the blue sky. Approaching the end of the runway, the aircraft hit .96 Mach and the pilot jerked back on the stick, pointing the nose straight up in the air. Keeping both of his throttles in afterburner, he climbed with astonishing speed.

The crowd stared, their jaws open. The aircraft climbed so quickly, it simply didn't seem real.

A scattered layer of puffy clouds hung in the sky between ten and twelve thousand feet. Seconds after takeoff, the F-38 shot through a large gap between the clouds, still vertical, an arrow piercing the sky. Three hundred thousand people stared in awe. Reaching the clouds, the pilot rolled the fighter onto its back, let the nose drop to the horizon, flew upside down for five seconds, then rolled wings level again. Bright blue sky shined behind the scattered clouds, but the aircraft never reflected the rays of the sun.

The president stared upward, his heart slamming in his chest. *What . . . an . . . amazing . . . machine!* His mind reeled. He laughed to himself, then shivered, almost bursting with pride. American determination, what a beautiful thing!

He looked around. The other leaders stared up. Some mouths hung open. All of them squinted in surprise. He glanced back at the Chinese general. *You haven't seen anything yet,* his eyes seemed to say. *Wait until you see the Ares use its laser. Watch it destroy half a dozen targets in the time it takes you to blink. Then imagine half a dozen of these fighters waiting for you over the Gulf of Taiwan!"*

The president gloated a moment, then turned his eyes back to the sky.

The Ares pilot turned the fighter back toward the crowd, heading west, then jammed his throttles into afterburner again. He accelerated, aiming to fly directly overhead.

The president waited. What a great way to start the show.

The fighter continued toward the crowd, then, nose dropping, it descended suddenly, like a rock from the sky. It leveled off at five hundred feet, continued toward the crowd, building speed, then shot over the airfield like a black bullet from a gun.

A thunderous sonic boom crashed over the field as the American fighter pushed through the speed of sound. The boom rolled across the crowd with unbelievable power, forcing three hundred thousand people to slap their hands to their ears. The president felt the ground shudder as the force of the shock wave hit him square in the chest like a huge hammer, and he took a step back as the reviewing stand shuddered, pushed by the force of the wave. Half the people fell over, holding their hands to their ears. The children started crying, their parents holding them tight. Behind him, in the enormous parking lot that had been set up on the other side of the road, the president heard the sound of falling glass from the broken windshields that had been shattered by the boom. Car alarms started blaring. An older lady kneeled over, blood trickling from her ears. A siren started wailing in the distance, then fell silent.

The president looked up at the sky, but the fighter was gone. He looked left and right. The aircraft was not there. He winced in confusion, then scowled at General Hawley. Idiot pilot! What was he thinking? Breaking the speed of sound! Did he realize that he had just blown out every window within three miles of the field? Half the population of Paris had just been rolled to the floor. He had asked for a good show, but he had not asked for *this!*

The sonic boom rolled away, and the crowd began to recover, standing again. Some clapped their hands in excitement, but most of them only stared.

The president searched the sky one more time. "Bloody eh!" the English PM muttered in disbelief at his side. The president saw the expression on the French prime minister's face and looked quickly away. Behind him, General Hawley jammed a finger to the side of his jaw, listening to the tiny receiver he had stuffed in his ear. His face turned pale as his Adam's apple bobbed like cork on the sea.

The president glared at him with rage in his eyes. Pushing away from the others, he stomped toward the general and hissed, "Where is the aircraft. What in the world is going on?"

Hawley shook his head and stepped back, clenching his fists at his side.

The president took another step forward until their faces almost touched. "Where's my aircraft?" he demanded.

The general lifted his hand as he listened to the radio, then spoke into the microphone with a growl.

The president's lead Secret Service agent also listened on his radio, then surged forward, pushing the European leaders aside. Three other Secret Service agents suddenly appeared at his side. Surrounding the president, they pulled at his arm. "Come with us, sir," the lead Secret Service agent said.

The president resisted, turning to the general instead. "Where's my aircraft?" he demanded, his voice icy with rage.

The general only stared, his jaw set in fear.

He instantly knew what had happened.

The Ares had run.

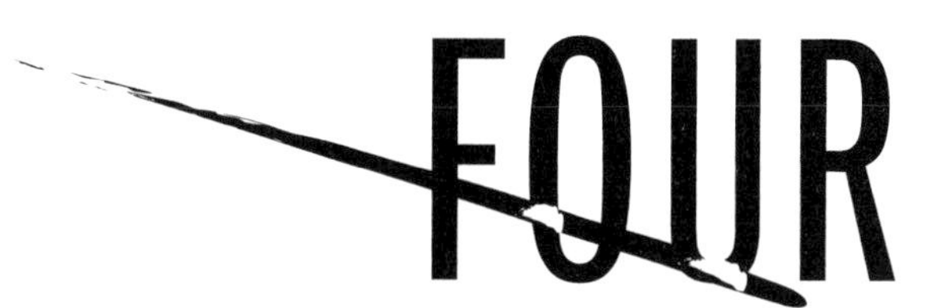

FOUR

It took less than twenty seconds for the U.S. Secret Service to move the president off the reviewing stand, shove him into a waiting SUV, and speed him away from the center of the enormous crowd. A line of security vehicles formed around the president's SUV as it moved across the tarmac, sirens blaring, tires screeching, headlights flashing as they rolled. The Americans left the European leaders standing, their eyes wide in fear.

The other leaders watched as the president of the United States was swept away. There was some kind of danger, but they didn't know what it was, and they were left standing, staring at each other, unsure and confused. Seconds later, their own security forces moved in, following the U.S. Secret Service's lead.

Speeding away, President Abram sat in the back of the huge SUV, surrounded by his personal security guards. An evacuation lane had already been cleared (the Secret Service always had a preplanned escape route) and the presidential caravan accelerated to one hundred miles per hour as they moved away from the crowd, the lead driver steering toward the access road on the south end of the runway. Inside the lead vehicle, the head of security, code name Piper, took control. Like a general in battle, he commanded his troops.

"What's our destination?" he demanded.

"Stand by!" another agent said.

The Secret Service had spent fifty years and a million man-hours trying to envision every conceivable threat to a president, but in all their planning, they had not thought of this.

The radios were silent; a sense of confusion was in the air. "Are you heading to the Bird?" the lead driver demanded again. No one spoke for a painful five seconds. "What's going on up there?" Piper's voice was rising now.

Having watched the Ares disappear, the aviation agent sitting in the control tower had a much better idea than anyone else about what was really going on. With the aircraft gone, knowing it was armed and capable of an attack, he had been the agent who had initiated a piñata, or a general alert, meaning there was an unspecified hazard, not a direct danger to the president, perhaps, but enough of a threat to require the Secret Service to improve their position until they knew what was really going on. "The Ares is gone," he quickly explained to the others. "It's loaded with weapons and the laser. Keep POTUS away from Air Force One and head somewhere more secure."

After twenty seconds of discussion, the decision was made. They certainly couldn't send the president up into the sky with his aircraft, and sitting in the 747 at the end of the runway might be the worst place to be.

"Okay, okay," Piper frantically instructed the caravan, "make it the C-Cock. I'll coordinate with the French police to clear traffic lanes as we go."

The Central Emergency Contingency Observation Center (CECOC) at Le Bourget International Airport was a secure building a little more than a thousand meters from the base of the tower. Already relatively sophisticated, it had been recently upgraded and outfitted even further in anticipation of the president's visit, with video and communications links to fire, rescue, weather, maintenance, security, administration, support, legal affairs, mortuary services, the city police, state militia, and local military bases. The command post had been designed with one thing in mind: to effectively deal with any emergency the airport might encounter, from a terrorist attack to a hostage situation, from a hijacking to foul weather or the crashing of a jet.

Minutes after the disappearance of the Ares, the president of the United States, surrounded by his Secret Service protectors, was escorted from his black SUV across a wide sidewalk to the side entrance of the CECOC, where a metal door with no doorknob was being held open for him. A bulletproof ceramic umbrella was held over his head, and he kept his head low as they moved toward the brick-and-cement building. Once inside, the group of men moved quickly down a narrow corridor, descended three flights of stairs, down another corridor, and through a set of double steel doors. Stopping in front a vault-like structure, they found a French officer waiting for them. He pressed his palm against a scanner, entered a code, and the metal door opened on its hydraulic arms.

Entering the command center, the president wasn't surprised to see dozens of FBI, CIA, DoD, NSA, and DIA agents were already there, and he frowned at the noise—voices calling over each other, a dozen ringing phones, flashing computer screens, a loudspeaker calling for some unknown French officer to report to the controller's desk. The room reeked of chaos, and the president shook his head.

President Abram watched as General Hawley was escorted into the command center. The general had obviously been running, and he spoke into a small cell phone, nearly out of breath. When he saw the president, he whispered, "Gotta go. I'm there now," and flipped the phone shut.

The president walked toward him. The general stood his ground, waiting, the two silver stars on his shoulders reflecting the bright overhead lights. His light blue shirt was impeccable, but there were growing sweat spots under each arm. His face was pained yet determined, and he took a deep breath.

The president came to a stop a few feet from him. The general's personal aide, a young colonel, took a deferential step back, and the other men and women in the command post gave them plenty of room. The president studied the pained look on the general's face, then leaned toward him. "Robert, are you okay?" he quietly asked.

Hawley straightened himself, brushing a hand through his short hair. Tall and handsome, he looked like a warrior—Roman nose and clear, dark eyes. But he had taken a wound here, and he looked at the president in shame. "I'm fine, sir," he shot back, anxious to put any question aside.

The president hesitated, then glanced around the room. "Okay, Robert, now tell me, why am I here? Why haven't I been taken to Air Force One, where I have command-and-control capability as well as my traveling staff?"

Hawley shook his head. "I'm sorry, Mr. President," he answered quickly, "but that would be a very bad idea, sir. Under the circumstances, Air Force One may be the very last place you want to be. On the runway, in the air—either way it would be incredibly vulnerable—"

"Vulnerable to what?"

The general swallowed, his Adam's apple straining visibly in his throat.

"Tell me," the president demanded. He kept his voice even, but he blinked half a dozen times as he spoke.

Hawley's jaw tightened. "Sir, we've got a . . . ah, a little problem with the Ares."

The president scoffed. That was painfully clear. The aircraft had taken off, flown back over the base, blown out a couple hundred windows, then climbed and disappeared. Seconds later, he had been shoved inside his blast-proof SUV.

It didn't take a genius to realize something was going on.

"I don't have time to explain right now," the general said, his face showing hints of panic. "I will explain the instant I can, but right now I need you to authorize an S&D mission."

"An S&D mission? I don't even know what that is!"

The hydraulic door slammed behind the president, and Abram turned to see his chief of staff rush into the room, two bodyguards and a couple aides following him. Edgar Ketchum glanced furiously around the command center, glaring at the French officials scattered among the U.S. men. Though only of average height, the chief of staff walked with long and powerful strides. Bald, wire glasses, heavyset, he had heavy eyebrows and glaring eyes that could burn a hole through bare skin. He rushed toward the president, his old college roommate, and stood at his side.

General Hawley ignored him, though he turned his shoulders slightly to square up to the man. Ketchum pressed his lips together and set his jaw as the two men stared at each other, shooting noxious looks back and forth. It was plain to everyone who watched that there was bad history between them.

The three men were silent until the COS leaned toward the general. "What has *happened* to our jet?" he demanded.

Hawley didn't flinch. He didn't work for him, he worked for the president. "President Abram," he began, ignoring the chief of staff, "right now we don't know where our fighter is."

"You don't *know!*" Ketchum cut him off with a hiss. "You've got a freakin' eight-billion-dollar aircraft that just freaking disappeared. In front of three hundred thousand people, including every single world leader that we care about. Are you kidding me, Hawley?"

Hawley stared at him. "No sir, we don't."

The chief of staff lost it. *"But it's your pilot!"* he screamed, the veins on his forehead protruding from his head.

The room fell into deadly silence. A few eyes turned toward the men, though most looked away, embarrassed to hear the COS scream. Even the phones seemed to fall silent as Ketchum's voice echoed off the concrete walls. The COS focused on the general, his lips drawn and tight, his last words hanging like a foul smell in the air.

No one cursed around the president. He forbid it completely. So *freakin'* was about as foul as the chief of staff ever got. But still, Hawley was taken aback by the venom in his voice, and he stared at Ketchum. No way was he going to take any crap from this man. He didn't know what had happened to their aircraft, but he knew what he had to do now, and he was running out of time. He glowered at Ketchum, then turned back to the president. "Sir," he said calmly, "everything was Ops normal as far as we knew. The pilot was following the script perfectly until three minutes after takeoff, at which point he was supposed to descend and accelerate for the first high-speed pass."

"High-speed!" Ketchum sneered. "The idiot nearly blew out our ears."

"It was supposed to be a low-level pass, Mr. President, a fifty-feet, Mach point-nine overfly of the airfield. High speed, yes, but certainly not faster than the speed of sound. But as you saw, at that point the pilot broke away. He made a supersonic pass over the airfield, heading west, and was gone."

"Gone!" the COS staff cried before the president could cut him off.

"Charlie," the president said, turning toward his aide. Ketchum finally faced him. "I want you to go get me a Coke."

"You what, Mr. President?"

"I want you to get me a Coke. And while you are out there, I want you to drink one of your own before you come back, okay?"

The chief of staff stuttered, and the president nodded his head. Ketchum bit his lip, then stepped back, motioned to one of his bodyguards, and turned away. The bodyguard went for the soda but Ketchum remained only ten steps away, close enough to still hear what was being said.

The president turned back to the general. "You say the Ares is gone?" he asked softly. "What exactly do you mean?"

Hawley shifted on his feet. "What I mean, Mr. President, is we have no idea where it is, but I need an S and D mission now! Once we have given the alert fighters their orders, then I will have time to explain, but every second right now is one we can't waste."

"You want us to authorize a mission against our own jet."

Hawley didn't hesitate. "Yes, sir, I do."

"You're going to shoot our own pilot!"

"We might force it down, but I wouldn't count on it, sir."

The president stared at Hawley. "General, there's no way I'm going to authorize your mission until I know *exactly* what is going on with that jet."

Hawley swallowed. He had a painful knot in his throat, and frustration was rising like a burning geyser. He started to say something, then changed his mind. Turning to a colonel at the control console, he said, "We've only got a few hours of daylight."

The colonel nodded anxiously.

"After that, we will lose him."

Abram took an angry step toward him. "Daylight? You will lose him? What are you talking about?"

Hawley shook his head at the president, then turned back to the colonel and spoke in an unwavering tone, "Launch the F-15 alert fighters. Tell the French to get their birds in the air, and get our alert fighters up at Lakenheath in the air as well."

The colonel stared at him, uncertain, then picked up a secure telephone.

The president stepped forward, an incredulous look on his face. "You can't do that without my authorization!" he said, his voice dripping with pride.

Hawley shook his head. "Actually, Mr. President, the regulations clearly state that I can."

The president stared, a look of disbelief on his face. Hawley's gut churned in fear as he stared at the president, the most powerful man on the earth, a man who could ruin him—no, destroy him—with a simple stroke of the pen. But none of that mattered. He had no choice anymore. The young colonel was waiting, a painful look on his face.

"Do it! Launch the fighters!" Hawley told him, then slowly lowered his eyes.

CAFÉ DE PARIS
ALONG HIGHWAY A104
TWENTY KILOMETERS NORTHEAST OF PARIS

He was obviously American, and worse, almost certainly military. His hair was short, like lots of European men, but far less stylish—close-cropped sides, hanging bangs, the kind of cut a military commander might have loved but a decent girlfriend would have certainly found *embarrassé*. And there was something more than the tight sideburns that indicated he was military, something subtle yet unmistakable in his body language, his expressions, and the way he met everyone's eyes.

Dépourvu d'humilité.

Arrogant.

The American sat alone at a small table near the back of the outdoor café, shaded by the hanging vines, his back toward the *L*-shaped brick wall that separated the café from the alley and shops to the east. He spread his arms across the round table, taking up lots of space.

As if *he* was important.

"*C'est toi qui t'en occupes!*" the headwaiter scoffed, a little too loud but in French. "*You* serve him!"

"Oh, no, Louie, I had the last one. This one is yours."

The American lifted his eyes from the menu and looked across the small café, then folded and set it on the edge of the table, clearly indicating he had made up his mind.

The waiters pretended they were busy wiping glasses and discussing business as they set out racks of red wine. The café was almost deserted, as it was too early for dinner and too late for lunch (who else but an American would eat at this time of day!), and difficult as it was, they ignored him, all the time arguing in French about who would have to wait on him.

"You get him."

"Stinking Americans. I don't care how much they tip."

"Look, why don't we just throw some fatty meat on the broiler. You know he'll order a burger with fries and a Coke, so let's get it over with."

The American watched and listened, a blank stare on his face.

"Look at him." A waiter laughed as he watched out of the corner of his eyes. "Staring at us like a child hoping for a treat."

"If we refuse to wait on him, do you think he'll go away?"

This went on for several minutes until the younger waiter was forced to walk toward him. "Monsieur," he said, putting on a fake smile, *"avez-vous arêté votre choix aujourd'hui?* Have you decided for today?"

The American smiled dumbly.

"Parlez-vous français?"

The American only stared.

The waiter almost snickered. This one was dumber than most. "Sir, what might I serve you?" he asked in acceptable English.

The American looked relieved. "You speak English. Great. What do you recommend?"

The waiter smiled slyly. "We have excellent burgers, monsieur."

The American nodded eagerly. "Perfect," he said.

The waiter pressed his lips in a sarcastic smile.

"With french fries," the man added.

The waiter paused, then wrote on his pad. "Will that be all, monsieur?" he asked.

"No, I also want a Coke."

The waiter looked up from his writing, his hands moving nervously. The American stared, a knowing look on his face. "Of course, sir," the waiter answered uncomfortably.

"And make sure the meat is well marbled. You know, something with a little fat."

The waiter's eyes moved down to the table, noting the sinew and muscle on the American's arms. A small tattoo on his bicep. Eighty-second Airborne. A shield with two crossed swords. He shifted his weight anxiously. "Very good, sir," he muttered quickly, flipping his notepad shut as he walked away.

"Hey, Francis," the American called out to him.

The waiter turned slowly. "Monsieur?" he replied.

"Et s'il vous plait, un drapeau blanc . . . excusez moi, j'entende une serviette blanche de la table?" His French was halting but understandable, and the waiter flushed, his ears burning red. Partly embarrassed, mostly angry, he huffed and walked away.

"And please bring me a white flag . . . I'm sorry, I mean a white table napkin," the American had said.

The waiter shook his head. It was easy to hate the Americans. Way too easy sometimes.

U.S. Air Force Major David "Jesse" James watched the French waiter walk away. He was a little disappointed at having to order a burger. He'd wanted the chicken almond salad with raspberry vinaigrette, but after that setup, how could he resist? But a burger wouldn't taste all that bad, anyway. And it would match his mood. Heavy. A little bland.

The major wasn't beyond a little self-pity and, sitting alone in the café, he had a little time to feel sorry for himself. He sighed, looking at his surroundings. It was beautiful: the ivy, the crowded sidewalk, the ancient rock-and-stucco flower shops and art boutiques, the bakeries and butchers, each of them containing flower-box apartments on their second floors. Beyond the last of the white-clothed tables, near the street and to the west he could see five blocks to the end of the neighborhood, where the stone fences and green pastures lined two forks in the road. It was a picture-perfect village, a couple hundred people, not large enough to even be on the map.

Taking it in, he felt a familiar disappointment. He used to love France; all Americans did. His great-grandfather was French. It was an easy place to love, but he simply wasn't comfortable here anymore.

A lot of things had changed. Old friends. New competitors. Times had shifted many allegiances, and everyone saw the world in a different way.

Taking a sip of bottled water, he let the bubbles wash down the dryness in his mouth, then glanced at his watch.

16:04. A little after 4:00 in the afternoon. The flying demonstration would just be getting under way. He sighed again in frustration. He wanted to be up there, at the controls of the most perilous fighter the air force had ever put in the air: The Ares. A 100-megawatt laser. Supercruise. Superstealth. A deadly light from the sky.

He should have been up there, slamming around the controls, screaming and diving and touching the tips of the clouds, demonstrating the accuracy of the laser and the power of the jet. He should have been the pilot for the air show; he was far and away the most qualified. And after years of working in utter secrecy, of living and flying in the most remote and desolate locations in the United States, after years of frustrating testing and development and not being able to tell even his closest air force buddies what he was working on, after years of enduring the lousy Nevada desert and the ghost towns that surrounded Tonopah, the top-secret test base where they had developed the Ares, the time had finally come to unveil the jet. And he should have been at the controls; as the chief test pilot, he had more time in the F-38 than anyone else, hundreds of hours more than the man who was flying it today.

But his commander, Colonel Ray, had stepped in and stolen the show.

The major stared at his watch, remembering the timing on the demonstration script:

4:00 P.M.— *The president of the United States arrives at the reviewing stand.*
4:03 P.M.— *The announcer's narration begins.*
4:06 P.M.— *Hangar doors roll open. Narration continues.*
4:10 P.M.— *Aircraft begins to taxi. Stops in front of VIP stand.*
4:12 P.M.— *Ares taxies forward to press galley, delays, allows time for photos and video, taxies to end of runway.*
4:17 P.M.— *Announcer narration ends. F-38 takes off, climbs, then descends and accelerates on airfield for first low-level, high-speed pass . . .*

The major almost shivered, feeling the excitement of flying in front of the crowd. A fighter pilot wasn't that much different than a Hollywood star, always demanding a little attention and fighting to show who was best, always wanting to thump his chest and say, "Hey, look at me!"

Now Colonel Ray was getting all the action.

But that was okay, the major tried reassuring himself. No biggie. It was only one flight. One flight in front of three hundred thousand people. And the president of the United States. And every European leader. And the entire world press. It was only the first public demonstration of the world's most powerful flying machine.

No biggie.

Major James swallowed another mouthful of water, trying to push the disappointment out of his mind. He was whining and he knew it, and he tried to laugh at himself. Petty and childish. He was embarrassed about how he felt.

Enough feeling sorry, he thought. A good burger was coming, with fries and a Coke. He was the chief test pilot on the world's slickest flying machine! He had two weeks in France, courtesy of good ol' Uncle Sam, not a whole lot to do, and a little money to spend. Take it all together and it was pretty hard to complain. He stared out at the cobbled street and finally forced a smile.

Ten minutes later, the young waiter appeared with his plate. Jesse thanked him in French, doused the fries with salt, asked for some Tabasco sauce, making the waiter cringe again, then dug into his burger. He took a huge bite, showing no French finesse, a red-blooded American eating a hunk of red meat.

Major David Jesse James was a man who had taken a very unusual route to get into air force pilot training.

Born and raised in South L.A., Jesse knew the streets. His father, a thick-necked and rough-handed longshoreman, got off work at two, was into the Ugly Goat by three, drunk by five, home by eight, and in bed by nine. Jesse could count on one hand all the good times he had ever spent with his dad.

His mother was a startlingly young and beautiful Mexican girl who must have been drunk, Jesse thought, when she married the old man. She held on as long as she could, then headed back to Mexico, where she married a whole lot better the second time around. With her new husband, a wealthy German businessman who'd retired on the Mexican Riviera, she'd found everything she wanted, and Jesse now had a little brother and sister running through some mansion built near the sandy beaches of Playa del Carmen, though he'd never met them and probably never would.

Still, his mother had been a powerful influence on his life. "There is nothing in the world, *nothing,* like the U.S.!" she had told him on the day that she left.

"Then why are you leaving, momma?" the young Jesse had cried, tears of fear and loneliness streaming down his nine-year-old face. The thought of living without his mother was simply too much to endure.

"This is your place. It isn't my place. This will never be my home. But this is yours, you belong here"—here her voice had grown cold—"so don't you even think about following me to Mexico. Your future is in America. Don't you ever try to follow me down there."

So he'd struggled along, sometimes with the old man, sometimes alone, living in and out of different foster homes. Then, despite a 4.0 GPA out of a high school where it was anything but cool to be smart, despite a half-dozen scholarship offers, Jesse turned away from college. At seventeen, he was more interested in fighting than in learning. The army was for him.

The night before he was ready to sign his enlistment forms, the old man had pulled him aside. "Don't do it, Jesse," he demanded. "The military ain't the kind of place for men like you and me."

Jesse stared at his father and almost laughed. Even at seventeen, he knew he was nothing like his father. "Gotcha, Walter," was all he said as he stood up and walked away.

The next day he signed the papers. Three weeks later, he was gone. He got selected for Airborne, eventually rose to staff sergeant, and spent the next three years hunting terrorists in the mountains of Afghanistan.

Tired of eating mud and living in tents (and very weary of the blood), he had separated from the army and got accepted to Boston U., part of a military outreach program that most of the professors clearly hated. Graduating in three years (proving his 4.0 out of high school hadn't been a gift), he had entered the air force with a pilot training slot.

At the age of twenty-four, Jesse was a hotshot pilot who would have happily given his life for his country or the opportunity to fly really fast jets.

Jesse smashed his burger, pressing down the bun, and took another bite. Then something caught his attention and he looked toward the street.

She entered the flower-filled café alone, looked around quickly, then selected a table on the other side of the restaurant and sat down with her back to the ivy-covered wall.

SIX

Jesse tried not to stare but couldn't take his eyes off her.

The waiter brought her a cup of tea without asking, and they laughed for a time before he disappeared. She gazed intently at the porcelain cup, completely lost in her thoughts. Jesse stole a glance in her direction every chance that he could, trying hard not to make it too obvious. Deep dark hair, thin and silky, hung halfway down her back. A long neck, thin and elegant. He felt his stomach tighten up.

Come on, boy, hold on, he whispered to himself.

She lifted her face and he quickly diverted his eyes to his plate.

Nothing's going on here. I'm just eating my food. I'm not staring at you, baby. At least I'm trying not to . . .

A few seconds passed before he dared look at her again. She was lifting her steaming tea while looking at the empty space somewhere beyond the rim. He summed her up again. Beautiful skin. Dark complexion. She was partly Arab or Persian, he would have bet anything. She lifted her face enough that he could see her eyes. Green, oh so green . . .

She smiled at him coyly.

He nodded, his best attempt at sophistication, while feeling very uncool. Yes, he was one of the world's greatest pilots, trusted with an eight-billion-dollar jet. Yes, he had stared down death in combat with nothing but ice in his veins, yet she had turned his guts into jelly with only one smile.

He dropped his eyes and stared at his burger as if it were the most fascinating thing on earth. He took a bite, his mouth dry, then grabbed the menu and studied it intently.

Anything to keep from looking over at those eyes . . .

Someone pulled back the chair at his table. He looked up. She was there.

"*Monsieur,*" she said, her speech slow and careful. Definite Farsi accent. She was Persian. He had called it right.

"Yes," he stammered slowly.

And that was it. Nothing else. He continued to stare, his face a foolish blank.

She hesitated, waiting for an invitation, then turned as if she might leave.

Jesse almost panicked. "Would you like to join me?" he quickly asked, pointing to the chair.

The young woman hesitated. "Oh no, *monsieur,* I think I might be intruding. You appear to be . . . ah, preoccupied."

"If I acted that way, I apologize. Please, would you like to sit down?"

She let her eyes move around the restaurant, then said, "*Oui, monsieur.*" The same beautiful voice. He stepped around the table and pulled out her chair. She sat with a grace that couldn't be taught, all her weight leaning forward, dainty and fragile on the edge of her chair. She was still holding her tea, and Jesse motioned to his plate. "Could I order you something?"

"No, I'm fine. Thank you."

Jesse tried really hard to keep his eyes under control. But that face. And those green eyes. His stomach fluttered again.

"My name is Petrie Baha," she said as she rested her arms on the white tablecloth.

Jesse extended his hand across the table. She stared at it a moment, then awkwardly extended her hand as well, only letting him touch the tips of her fingers before pulling it back. "David James," he said, feeling the tingle of her fingertips on his palm.

"It is *Mr.* James then, not monsieur?"

Jesse nodded uncertainly. "I'm American," he said, hoping that was not bad.

She smiled, white teeth and full lips. "I thought so," she answered.

"Really. Why is that? Do I have that ugly-American look?"

"Ugly American? I don't think I know what you mean. But yes, there is something about you Americans that is pretty easy to recognize."

He waited, but she didn't explain and he didn't press.

"What do you do here in Paris?" he asked.

"I'm a student in the international program at the Université de Paris."

"Studying to be . . . ?"

She looked away. "I don't know yet. I've got a couple options. It kind of depends on my dad."

"Your father? I don't get it. Does he—"

Petrie waved her hand to change the subject. "Do you speak French?" she asked.

"A little."

"Where did you learn it?"

Jesse hunched his shoulders. "I don't know. I have this thing for languages, it seems. I grew up speaking Spanish and English. Took French and Italian in high school and college. Picking up another language just seems to come easy for me."

She nodded. "That's very good."

He sipped at his water. "You are French?"

"Yes, David."

"Please, call me Jesse."

"I'm sorry, my mistake, I thought you said—"

"No, you are right, my name is David, but I usually go by Jesse."

"It is a . . . how you say it, an alias? You are a mystery man. Someone running from the law?" She was clearly teasing and he instantly liked her more.

"I guess not," he answered simply. "Just a nickname. Nothing more."

She thought a minute. "Jesse James." Then she smiled. "I get it. The cowboy. You are a cowboy, Jesse James?"

He shook his head. "No, I grew up in L.A. Never been on a horse in my life. Jesse is a nickname I picked up a long time ago. It's a long story and not interesting." The last thing he wanted to tell her was about his military background. He had learned long ago that European women weren't impressed by military men. This time he changed the subject. "You are French, but you are also . . . ?" His voice trailed off. He wasn't sure how to ask about her ethnicity without saying something rude.

She sipped at her tea, keeping her eyes on him. "My father is Iranian. My mother is French. They met in New York, of all places, when my father was working for his government, my mother for the U.N. We moved back here to Paris when I was a little girl."

Jesse played with his fries. *"Te dissent Anglais très bien."* He tried, but he butchered the French, and the correct pronunciation suddenly escaped him now. "You speak English very well," he repeated in English.

She shook her head. "I'm only okay. I am much better in Farsi and French."

"I see," Jesse answered. "And that's why you wanted to talk to me, to practice a little of your English, am I right?"

She blushed and looked away. "Is that okay?"

He appeared a little deflated.

"I have so many friends who think they are good at English," she went on. "All French people think that they are, but the truth is most of them are so terrible I can hardly understand what they say. You know how it is; the French people are proud, and they . . . I guess I should say we . . . are offended to have to admit that English is the universal language now."

"Please, I'm flattered," Jesse replied. "But yes, to be honest, I was a little surprised. Most Muslim women I have met are less outgoing and extremely reserved."

"What makes you so sure I am Muslim?" she answered quickly.

Jesse made a face. "I'm sorry, I guess I just—"

"Am I to assume you are Christian? Might you not be Jewish, maybe Buddhist? Maybe nothing at all."

"Of course you're right," Jesse offered apologetically, his heart skipping a beat. "There are Iranian Christians, Iranian Jews. I was presumptuous and I'm sorry."

"It's okay," she offered easily. Jesse saw she wasn't angry and began to relax. "And you are right anyway, I'm a little unorthodox, I guess. Half Persian, half French. And yes, I'm a Muslim, but like Christians, or Jews, there are degrees of orthodoxy, degrees of commitment. My father is very . . ." She hesitated. Jesse saw a pained look cross her face. "My father is very orthodox," she concluded.

Jesse nodded. "I see."

There was something more to her story; he could see that by the flash of pain in her eyes.

The two were quiet a long moment. They'd already talked religion, about their families, touched on Muslim culture—what was next? What other hot-button issue could he bring up to spoil this introduction?

She glanced awkwardly at her hands.

"Are you sure I can't get you something?" he asked.

Again, she shook her head. The long silence returned.

Jesse knew he wasn't very good in such situations. He'd been shy since he was a little kid. Growing up like he did, it engendered one of two attitudes, arrogance or shyness, and Jesse defaulted to the second when it came to girls.

Petrie sipped at her tea. It was cool now, no longer wafting steam into the air. "You are a soldier?" she wondered aloud.

"How did you know?"

She hunched her shoulders. "A lucky guess."

"Really?"

"Well, perhaps I also heard the waiters talking."

Jesse glanced to the back of the restaurant. None of the waiters were in sight now. "I hope you might be willing to look past any disparaging remarks you might have heard."

She sat back in her chair, relaxing just a bit. "Did you really ask one of them for a white flag?" she laughed.

Jesse looked around, embarrassed. Yes, she was Persian, but she was a French citizen as well, and like anyone else, she was surely proud of her country. "It was a hasty gut reaction—" he started to explain.

Petrie raised her hand. "It's okay, Jesse James, you don't have to defend yourself. Sometimes we Europeans can be a little . . . how do you say the words . . . a little full of our judgments."

She immediately cringed. She knew that wasn't right.

"Judgmental," Jesse offered.

She nodded vigorously. "Yes, yes. And see what I mean? I need all the practice I can get. If I had said that with one of my friends, they would have accepted it as right."

Jesse bit a fry just for something to do, anything to keep from staring at her. "No, your English is very good. You have nothing to be apologetic about. And you know, it's too bad, but true, that not enough Americans can speak a different language."

"Your mother is Spanish," she asked.

"Latino. Does it show?"

"Well, perhaps just a little in your eyes. But here in Europe we are more keyed to people's background, I think. Take this neighborhood for example; within a few kilometers of here you have pockets of Muslims, Spaniards, Albanians, North Africans, and Poles. We don't integrate as well as you do in the United States. So we are more keyed to our ethnicities. Some say that is good. I don't agree. It brings us many problems, I think."

"But how did you know it was my mother who was Latino?"

"Easy," she explained, "your first language is English, not Spanish. If you had a Spanish father, it would have been the other way around. The father most often determines what the children will speak. At least, that's the way it is here. I assumed it is the same in the United States."

Jesse bobbed his head in an exaggerated motion of "maybe yes, maybe no." "It kind of depends," he answered. "Depends on the family, the parents, where they live . . . you know, lots of things."

Petrie seemed to shrug, unconvinced. "So, Mr. James, tell me about yourself. What brings you here to Paris? Surely you aren't traveling alone?"

"Business," he answered casually. After years of working on the secret F-38 program, he was so conditioned to not talk about his job that it never even occurred to him to say any more.

"You are not here on your honeymoon?" she teased with a gut-crushing smile.

"Oh no," he answered quickly.

"So . . . just business then?"

"Yep. Nothing interesting, I promise."

She smiled at him shyly. "Are you certain, Mr. James?"

Waiting for an answer, she reached for her purse. Jesse kept his eyes on her while putting another cold fry in his mouth. Opening her handbag, she pulled out a cell phone. Jesse hadn't heard it ring, but still she flicked it open, touched a few buttons, then flipped it shut again and returned it to her purse.

He followed her motions to the handbag.

A flash of beveled metal. A hint of silver.

She had a gun in her purse!

He frowned, his heart accelerating, his mind spinning into high gear. There were more handguns in any average-sized town in west Texas than in all of Europe. Paris had more registered prostitutes than registered handguns on the street. Carrying a weapon was much more than just unusual. And it was unheard of for a woman to be armed.

Jesse smiled to himself as he sat slowly back in his chair. *Miss Baha . . . Miss Baha . . . you're a student, I don't think.*

Petrie looked up suddenly as if she had read his mind, saw him staring at her handbag, and quickly closed her purse.

Her green eyes flashed as she pushed a strand of hair from her face.

If she knew he'd seen the handgun, she pretended not to know. "You interest me, Mr. James," she said with a coy smile. "You have a reason for being here in Paris that you aren't telling me about. You are too quiet and unassuming about the things that you do. If you're a liar, you're not a good one, and that makes me wonder about you."

She smiled as she said it.

Oh, so French. So direct.

She extended her legs and Jesse felt her brush his ankle with her feet, but she kept her bright eyes on him and he couldn't help but smile as he thought, *There are a few things about you, Miss Baha, that make me wonder, too.*

SEVEN

Jesse heard an automobile engine rev and looked up to see a Porsche 911 GT-2 pull into a tiny parking spot on the other side of the road. It was a beautiful car, brilliant silver, deeply sculpted door panels, aerodynamic design, two hundred thousand dollars of adrenaline and speed. Like any man, his jaw dropped and he stared. The driver tried to pull into a parking space that was too small, leaving the back half of the silver sports car protruding out on the narrow road.

Jesse was clearly disappointed when the driver climbed out of the car.

He was a huge man, slow and brooding, all steroids and meat. Black shirt, black jeans, heavy work boots. It was like watching an alcoholic guzzle a bottle of ten-thousand dollar wine, like watching a sixteen-year-old graffiti expert grab a can of spray paint to touch up a Renoir.

The guy was smoking. Jesse cringed. Smoke on the leather! Did this guy have *no* class?

As he stepped from the GT-2, the driver was surrounded by his friends, young punks who emerged from the side streets to kiss up to him.

Petrie saw him, then sank down in her seat.

"You know him?" Jesse asked.

She nodded quickly, keeping her eyes on the table.

"A friend of yours?"

"Not anymore."

She turned, glancing over her shoulder. "I'd better go," she said.

She stood quickly. Jesse stood as well. "Hey, wait a minute," he said, disappointment on his face.

The thug kept his eyes moving and quickly found Petrie in the back of the café. He watched her a moment, looked at Jesse, then turned back to his friends.

Jesse noticed the look on Petrie's face as she grabbed her purse. "You got a problem with him?" he asked, motioning in the direction of the street.

She shook her head. "Nothing. Really, it's nothing. But I do have to go."

Jesse reached for her shoulder. "Are you okay?" he pressed, glancing toward the Porsche driver again. "Because, if you're not, if there's anything I can do to help you . . ."

Petrie pulled away. "I'm fine." She was indignant now, her eyes defiant and proud, and he saw a flash of determination he had not seen before. She didn't need some American cowboy to ride in on a white horse. She reached into her purse and pulled out her car keys. "Thank you for taking the time to talk with me," she said, forcing a more friendly tone. "It was a pleasure to meet you, Jesse. Maybe we'll meet again."

Not likely, Jesse thought. He just didn't spend that many afternoons hanging around Parisian cafés. "Petrie, I'm here for a couple weeks. I'd like to see you again," he said.

She shook her head. "Thank you, Jesse, that's sweet, but it might not be a very good idea."

"You are seeing someone?"

She laughed. "Certainly no."

"Then come on, Petrie. I mean, if your father would object or there are some cultural or religions reasons, I understand. But I'm not asking you to . . . you know . . . I'd just like to get together for lunch. Practice your English, my French."

She hesitated, her eyes always moving. "Okay," she answered quickly. "Give me your cell number and I'll call you."

Jesse hesitated. "I've got a good memory," he told her. "Give me your number instead."

She smiled and then told him. He repeated it once but did not write it down.

She put both of her hands on his arms. "Thank you, Jesse James, for being willing to talk."

"It was purely my pleasure."

"I'll call you," he shouted as she walked away, embarrassed by the overly eager tone in his voice.

She waved good-bye, then walked past the café tables that extended to the sidewalks and turned left, down the street.

Jesse watched her until she was out of sight.

The Porsche driver watched her as well.

EIGHT

CECOC COMMAND CENTER
LE BOURGET AIRPORT
PARIS, FRANCE

Hawley reiterated his order to the colonel. "Do it. Launch the fighters. Send them west," he said, his voice cold and determined as stone.

The president of the United States leaned into General Hawley, almost touching his chest. "You can't do this," he hissed.

Hawley nodded grimly, an apologetic, almost repentant look on his face. "I'm sorry, Mr. President. I have failed you already. Please, I don't want to fail you again."

Abram frowned and stared at Hawley. The problem was, of course, that he *trusted* him.

Hawley saw the softening of the president's eyes, sensed the opening, and leaned toward him. "Mr. President, sir, let me get the alert jets in the air, then I will tell you everything once the interceptors have been launched. Then, if you don't agree with my decision, you can call the jets back. I will resign on the spot, sir, and we can do it your way."

The president hesitated. "You say—"

"Give me two minutes, Mr. President, and you will know everything."

The president stared at him and grimaced, then slowly nodded his head.

The next four minutes passed in a chaos of panicked questions, heated exchanges with the president's chief of staff, frantic demands and counterdemands between U.S. and French officers, unanswered questions and wild guesses based on information so incomplete that it made everyone sick. When it was over, it came down to the general's gut-instinct decision and some hurried telephone calls.

At one point, General Hawley had turned to the president, his hands over a telephone receiver, his shoulders hunching as if pleading somehow. Every eye turned to the president and a heavy silence filled the air. The president nodded, a determined look on his face, and the general spoke again into the secure phone.

A red light came on in the corner of the command post as the launch call went out. Hawley put the phone down and nodded. It was done.

The two men stood before a large plasma screen that showed a security feed from a video camera mounted on the top of the airport tower at Bourget Airport, one of more than a dozen that looked out on the field. The camera focused on a hangar just in time to see its enormous metal doors begin to roll open. Four American fighters taxied out, and Hawley breathed a sigh of relief. The camera zoomed closer as the fighters accelerated toward the end of the runway. The phone rang again and Hawley snapped it up, keeping one eye on the video screen. It was the French Air Force officer at Avord Air Base.

Avord, a base in central France, was used to house and support two squadrons of French Boeing E3-F AWACS, but General Hawley knew that half a dozen French Mirage fighters had been deployed there to provide security for the G-8 conference and the Paris Air Show. It was to the commander of the Mirage fighter group that he was talking to now.

"How many jets you got on alert?" he demanded, then swore in reply. "Alright, only two. How are they loaded?" He paused. "Miracle II air-to-air missiles and cannons." He shook his head. The French Miracles were miserable air-to-air missiles even when they were new, and now they were thirty years old. Same for the Mirages—sexy airplanes in the eighties, not much of a fighter anymore.

He thought of the Ares. Supercruise. Impossible to detect on radar. More maneuverable and faster than any other fighter on earth. It was like sending a go-cart after a Lamborghini. But they were all the French Air Force could give him and they would have to do.

And there was one thing that he had on his side: The sun. If they could just get close enough to visually locate the Ares, shoot at it with their missiles or guns, or set up a wall to intercept it, then the daylight might save them.

He glanced at the clock. Three hours before sunset. Three hours to locate and shoot down the jet. Once it was dark, it was over.

"Okay," he said, speaking into the secure phone to the French squadron leader. "Get those jets in the air. Keep them together. Have them head west, toward the English Channel. I'll get back to you with a game plan as soon as I can."

Hawley grunted and hung up the phone.

Truth was, he had no game plan. The Ares had incredible speed and intercontinental range. They didn't know where it was heading, what the pilot intended to do, and only had a handful of fighters to locate it and bring it down.

Still, if the Ares was really heading west . . . if it had not changed direction . . . the birds out of Lakenheath could meet it, his own birds could chase it . . . they might be able to surround it . . .

But that was it. That was the game plan. He pushed his hands through his hair.

The president was waiting, staring at the huge plasma screen. The digital screen—wide, bright, and full color—showed a close-up of the four American F-15s that were waiting short of the runway at Bourget while orange-vested weapons specialists pulled their arming pins and removed the red flags attached to the safety bolts on the missiles under their bellies and wings. The fighters were ready to go.

The general loved the F-15s. He had a couple thousand hours in the jets, almost five hundred in combat. He'd been shot at, he'd been hit, and the babies had always brought him home. The F-15 Eagle had shot down more enemy aircraft than any other fighter in the world; their kill-to-loss ratio was about 30–0, and the advanced medium-range air-to-air missiles (AMRAAMs) they carried were as good as anything in the air . . . The general quickly corrected himself.

Not anymore. He shook his head, realizing he was kidding himself. Go-carts and cap guns were all that he had.

He felt a heavy weight of blackness in his chest. He knew it was likely he was sending these pilots to their deaths. The Eagles were going out as the hunters, but that would change the instant the Ares pilot discovered they had come after him.

CAFÉ DE PARIS
ALONG HIGHWAY A104
TWENTY KILOMETERS NORTHEAST OF PARIS

Jesse noticed the 911 driver on the other side of the street. Sipping his Coke, he took stock of the man. Expensive watch. Lots of diamonds. Too much gold, too much flash. Jesse instantly recognized that ol' Guido didn't make his living selling flowers or working for the government. Drugs. Probably hashish. Maybe opium from the East. The western districts of Paris were flooded with illegal narcotics, and the insatiable demand created a ring of vicious Italian and Turkish cartels with loads of money to spend. This guy was a mover in that world, there was no doubt in his mind.

Jesse studied the stranger's pocked face and artificial smile, some very expensive dental work showing through his thin lips. Guido stood on the sidewalk as he talked with his boys. A couple of cars started honking, unable to get by the back of his Porsche. He left them waiting a few minutes, then climbed into the 911, fired up the engine, and backed up, disappearing behind the brick wall to Jesse's left.

Jesse thought of Petrie as he watched the street, feeling lonely. Glancing at his watch, he dropped fifteen euros on the table, then turned for the street, walking toward his rental car that was jammed into a tiny parking space half a block up the road. The cobbled street was narrow, wide enough for two horse-drawn wagons but barely wide enough to let two cars pass by, and the sidewalk was covered with awnings over almost every shop. Cars, most of them tiny European SmartCars or Fiats, with a few BMWs and Toyotas mixed in, were all parked on the north side of the street, jammed so closely together it was hard to understand how the drivers had maneuvered them in.

The silver 911 was now double-parked in front of his car. Guido was sitting on the bumper, surrounded by three of his thugs in their early twenties, with hanging clothes and shaved heads.

Jesse approached his tiny rental and unlocked the door, then stared at the stranger, who pretended not to see him and kept talking with his boys. Taking out a pack of American cigarettes, he pulled one out with his lips, lit it quickly, and threw the match not far from Jesse's feet.

"Pardon," Jesse said, motioning to his car, "you've pinned me in here and I'd like to leave."

The man ignored him as he pulled another drag on his smoke.

"Pardon," Jesse said again, motioning to his car. "I've got an appointment. Could you move your car, please?"

The man huffed as if severely offended. "I'll be on my way in a minute," he replied in heavy English, his voice low and gravelly from years of sucking smoke. Turning back to his friends, he mumbled something and the four men laughed again.

Jesse counted to thirty while leaning against the side of his car, then saw a row of ugly key marks that ran from the Fiat's front fender to the rear body panel. He bent and studied the scratches. Some cut all the way through the paint to the metal underneath. He shook his head and swore. It would require an entire paint job. What a stupid thing to do!

Guido was watching him, holding a set of keys in his hand. He tossed them up and caught them, flashing his porcelain teeth.

"Nice," Jesse sneered, pointing down at his car. Guido tossed his keys again.

"It's a rental," Jesse said. "It won't cost me anything. Surely you knew that. Or are you really that dumb?"

The stranger took a step toward him. "You talking to me, friend?"

Jesse raised his hands in a frustration, trying to keep his emotions in check. He wasn't going to get in a fight. Not with this guy, over a rental car. He was an officer of the U.S. government, not some drunken tourist wandering through the red-light district in Amsterdam. It was his responsibility as an officer to keep the situation in check. He had never been afraid of a fight in his life, and three years of army combat training hadn't been wasted on him, but he knew that he couldn't ever let it go that far. He shook his head in disgust, leaned against the old Fiat, and took a deep breath.

Finally Guido walked toward his Porche, stopped in front of Jesse, and leaned into him. "That girl you were talking to, she don't like you," he sneered. "Don't ever try and see her. For your own sake, listen to me and leave that one alone."

Jesse stared at the huge man, feeling his hot breath on his face.

"Do what I tell you." He sneered again. "This is a mess you don't want any part of."

The man spit, then walked around to the driver's side and climbed into the Porsche. Firing up the engine, he screeched his tires and drove down the street.

Jesse watched the Porsche disappear, then pulled out his cell phone and dialed the number Petrie had given him.

"*Oui,* Jesse," she said after only two rings.

"Just testing," he said at the sound of her voice. "I'll call you later, okay?"

"Okay, Jesse." She laughed and hung up the phone.

Jesse got in his car and maneuvered through traffic away from the village. Getting to the outskirts, traffic began to thin out. Four kilometers from the village, he heard a chest-thumping boom that rattled the windows on his Fiat and sent him looking to the sky. He searched left and right, then figured out what it was and shook his head. Sonic booming was a real no-no anywhere over land, but especially bad over a heavily populated area such as Paris. Problem was, in the Ares, it was so easy to do. *Colonel Ray.* He almost smiled. *What have you done, my friend*?

Half a kilometer later, he slowed down and merged onto highway A1, which went almost straight south into Paris. Le Bourget Airport was a little more than twenty kilometers away. He relaxed a bit.

His cell phone rang in the seat beside him. "Major James," he quickly answered.

"Jesse, this is Hawley." The caller sounded out of breath. "Where are you? Get moving! I want you back here right now."

"What's up, boss?" he asked.

"I want you here in ten minutes." Jesse could tell General Hawley was talking as he ran. Then he picked up the sound of sirens in the background and a noisy crowd. "Get to the CECOC at de Gaulle," Hawley instructed. "An escort will be waiting."

The phone went dead. Jesse stared at it, confused, then flipped it shut with one hand and tossed it in the seat beside him. Pressing on the accelerator, he moved into the far lane.

NINE

CECOC COMMAND CENTER
LE BOURGET AIRPORT
PARIS, FRANCE

As General Hawley watched, the four American fighters taxied from the hammerhead and accelerated down the runway, five seconds between them, then lifted into the air. They took off as four separate fighters then slipped toward each other immediately after they had sucked up their landing gear, forming a single formation. Following their leader, they turned to the west and kept climbing, pulling their noses into the sky.

The secure telephone buzzed again and General Hawley jerked it from its cradle. "Hawley," he answered.

It was the French officer at Avord. He listened, aware the president was hearing every word. Behind the president, the COS paced, fidgety and on edge.

"Yes, yes!" Hawley answered after listening only a second. "I will have written authorization for you within three minutes. Now, please, Dauphine, get your alert jets in the air."

Hawley grunted and hung up. Ketchum was standing at his side now, a small notepad in hand, ready to pounce like a starving rat on bad cheese.

The fighters were launched. The immediate pressure was off. Hawley finally had a couple of minutes to talk to the president.

Abram moved toward him. "Alright, Robert," he said. "I gave you your Search and Destroy mission. Now I want to know everything."

"Thank you, Mr. President," General Hawley said, a look of gratitude on his face. The plasma screen blinked beside him, then switched over to a feed from Air Traffic Control, showing the flight of four fighters climbing and flying northwest. Hawley forced himself to ignore it and focused on the president. "Sir, there's a small conference room," he pointed toward the back of the command center. The president nodded and followed him, his COS close behind. The Secret Service agents watched, one of them staying close enough to post outside the conference door.

The three men entered the room. A small table, a single telephone, and four rolling chairs were inside, but they all remained standing, Ketchum off to one side.

"Okay, where's my aircraft?" the president began.

Hawley shook his head. He didn't know.

"Surely you can track it!"

"Sir, you have to think back on your flying days. Remember, all aircraft—civilian, military, even Stealth fighters—carry a special radio transponder which constantly transmits special codes to Air Traffic Control. They call it a squawk and this squawk, or code, carries a special four-digit identification number which is assigned by ATC. With this code, the controllers are able to instantly know where an aircraft is, what altitude, airspeed, direction of flight, everything essential to monitoring and controlling the movements of the ten-thousand aircraft that are up in the sky at any given moment in time.

"Our Stealth aircraft also carry transponders, sir. In fact, it is even more essential for Ares pilots to use their squawk than it is for other jets. Without the transponders, ATC would never be able to locate and track the jet. Raw radar coverage is entirely incapable of detecting our Stealths. Upon takeoff, the Ares pilot initiated his squawk just like he was supposed to do, but right after he completed his supersonic pass, he turned off his transponder. Once he did that and flew away, he utterly disappeared."

"So let me understand this," the president said. "You're telling me the Ares rolls out of the hangar, takes off, and is stolen right out from under our nose."

Hawley nodded.

"I'm sorry, Robert, but I just don't get it. How could this happen?"

"We don't know, Mr. President, at least not yet."

"Do you think Colonel Ray stole our fighter?"

Hawley bristled. "No sir, I don't. I absolutely guarantee you Colonel Ray is not piloting that jet."

The president touched the general's chest. "Then *who* is up there in *my* aircraft?"

"Mr. President, this will take a little time. We're checking all of the security cameras—the hotel where the pilots were staying, the checkpoints along the road. We've started talking to people, but it's only been a few minutes since the Ares disappeared. This much I can assure you: there are too many security procedures in place for us not to know soon."

The president scoffed. "So we have enough security procedures to find out who took our aircraft but not enough to stop them from stealing the jet in the first place. Good. I'm pleased to hear that." He was losing the battle to keep himself under control. "Three hundred thousand people," he stammered, "every foreign president and prime minister. Do you know how hard they must be laughing? Oh yeah, and the Chinese are going to be *really* impressed. Maybe they'll come over and steal a couple of our fighters for themselves!"

The president was almost screaming. Then he stopped suddenly, took a breath, and held it before gently letting it go. He raised his hand to Hawley and slowly turned away.

Hawley waited, his face frozen.

The president turned around. "Okay, our new fighter is gone. We don't know who the pilot is? We don't know what his intentions are, where he is headed or what he intends to do?"

"At this time, we have no idea, sir."

"It might be a matter of extortion. Holding the jet hostage and demanding ransom. Maybe they simply wanted to embarrass the U.S., you know, make us look like incompetent fools. Heaven knows they did that. Mission accomplished, boys. Or maybe they want to take the fighter somewhere, tear it down, and study it so they could build one of their own."

"All those are all possibilities, Mr. President, but I don't think for a moment that's what we're dealing with here."

The president stared and then swallowed. He'd already considered the other options. He wasn't stupid. He'd thought of them the instant he saw the jet fly away. "What are you saying?" he asked.

"What I'm saying, Mr. President, is we have to assume the worst-case scenario and make preparations for that. We have to assume the pilot's intentions are hostile, that he has a target in mind. The pilot could not have done this alone. It would have taken a very sophisticated group of individuals to pull this thing off—fantastic planning, lots of money, a coordinated effort and plan of attack. And I don't think they would have gone to this effort just to make us look bad."

"So you understand now, Mr. President, why we must bring that aircraft down. It's a very ugly option, but it's the only option we have. If we don't . . . if they go after a target . . . well, I think you understand. They could strike anywhere, any target; civilian airliners, government buildings, nuclear power plants, military assets—the list is infinitely long—and we only have until sundown to find the Ares and destroy it. After that it will be hopeless."

The president of the United States stood silently in front of the tactical control screen. The large screen was split into four equal squares that showed different inputs from the various air traffic control centers, most of which was jumbled symbology that he didn't understand. Behind him, he heard the rising voices of the French airport security and military officers. Yes, it was an

American operation, and yes, they had agreed to a subordinate role in the security plan regarding the president's visit to Paris, but this was their country, their command center, and they were beginning to insist on exerting some type of control. The president listened as General Hawley talked to the French officers. He was polite, even deferential, but he still held his ground. The F-38 was an American fighter and it was crucial for the United States to maintain tactical control.

Hawley spent a few minutes with the officers, explaining his plan and asking for their support, but he didn't give an inch when they tried to push back. Though he said it nicely and in different words, his message was clear: *Thanks for your help. Now please stay out of the way.*

After talking with the French officers, the general returned to the president's side and the two men stood a moment in silence. The president felt isolated, not having his national security staff at his side. He was used to having a hundred aides, a dozen generals, his national security advisor, the chairman of the Joint Chiefs, the secretary of defense, CIA and FBI chiefs—all brilliant advisors at his beck and call. Even as he stood there, he knew his COS was on the phone, calling and coordinating with the national security staff back in D.C., but for now it was only him and Hawley, and he felt a sudden crash of loneliness that he couldn't explain.

He shot a look at one of the half dozen clocks on the wall. Less than twenty-six minutes since the Ares had disappeared. It seemed like it had been hours.

Glancing at Hawley, he noted the calm look on his face, but the president knew it was an act—no, not an act, a role: General Quaalude. He was playing his part, but he knew that General Hawley was boiling inside. They had been friends for years and, though it was subtle, he recognized the hard look in Hawley's eyes. He had seen it once before, when the first top-secret prototype of the Ares had crashed into the mountains west of Tonopah. The president had demanded a briefing. Watching the general explain the loss of the prototype and its pilot, the president had seen the same empty stare, the look of loss and responsibility, as if Hawley had been shot in the heart. No good commander could remain unemotional when he lost one of his men, and though the president didn't know yet what had happened to Colonel Ray, it wasn't impossible to make a reasonable guess. The colonel wasn't at the controls of the stolen aircraft, which meant he was certainly dead.

He watched Hawley a moment, then turned back to the plasma screen. "Explain it to me," he said, nodding to the symbology before him. General Hawley pointed to a three-hundred-mile ring that ran around Paris. "This outer ring is our estimate of how far the stolen Ares could have flown since we lost it," he began. There was a dark wedge on the northwest quarter of the ring. "Based on the aircraft's last known heading, which could have changed, of course, this is the area we are mostly likely to find the aircraft in."

Pointing to a small, yellow triangle that was moving northwest, he continued. "These are our guys, the four Eagles which we launched from Bourget. As you can see, they are staying together, but in a couple minutes, when they cross over the English Channel, they'll do a tactical split and set up a wall between the mainland and the English Coast. But the problem is, sir, they are chasing a much faster aircraft and will likely never catch it." He pointed to another symbol that was circling over southern England. "These are our F-15 interceptors out of Lakenheath Air Force Base in England, sir. If the stolen fighter is making a break to get out of Europe, and if the pilot has chosen the shortest route, then these guys are the most likely to catch him. They are ahead of the fighter now, waiting for him. They are our best hope."

The general then pointed toward a green triangle that was also moving north but was still on the south side of Paris. "And these are our French friends, Mr. President, four Mirage fighters going stones to the wall. But as you can see, it looks like they'll be too late. By the time they catch up with our Eagles, they will nearly be out of gas. Now, they might trap the Ares from the back end, but if they don't get that lucky, I doubt they'll be any help at all."

The president watched the data relay from Air Traffic Control. "So what's the plan then?"

Hawley stepped back and rested one elbow on his palm, holding the other hand to his chin. The room was busy around him, the sound of hurried voices and telephones ringing, but he kept his voice low. "I wish I had something brilliant or dramatic to tell you, sir, but it's pretty simple. First, we're sending out a notice-to-airmen, or NOTAM, a kind of an all-points bulletin to all aircraft in the vicinity, asking them to keep their eyes open for the missing jet." The general nodded toward a technician two desks away. "Bring up all civilian traffic," he told him. The plasma screen shifted, then was suddenly crowded with a hundred radar hits. Hawley motioned to them. "Civilian air traffic, sir, airliners, private aircraft, corporate jets, and such. There are, what . . . maybe a hundred aircraft between us and the coast. Once the NOTAM goes out, they will be instructed to look for the stolen fighter. That's a couple hundred sets of eyeballs, which is a very valuable thing. Yes, it's old fashioned, but it's the best option we have."

The president lifted an eyebrow. "Best or the only?"

Hawley hesitated. "Both, sir, I'm afraid."

The president only nodded.

"So we estimate where the stolen fighter is heading," Hawley continued, "based on its last known position, altitude, and heading, then put out that information in the NOTAM and hope we can find it, sir."

"You don't sound overly optimistic."

Hawley thought a long moment. "We have the world's most advanced fighter, designed to be completely invisible to radar and IR detection, with a revolutionary weapon capable of blowing all of our guys out of the air faster than you can blink, faster at cruise speed than our Eagles are at full power. It will be a challenge. But I think we've got a chance of locating the fighter and forcing it down."

The president exhaled slowly. "Sounds like we need a miracle."

Hawley nodded grimly. "That would be nice right now."

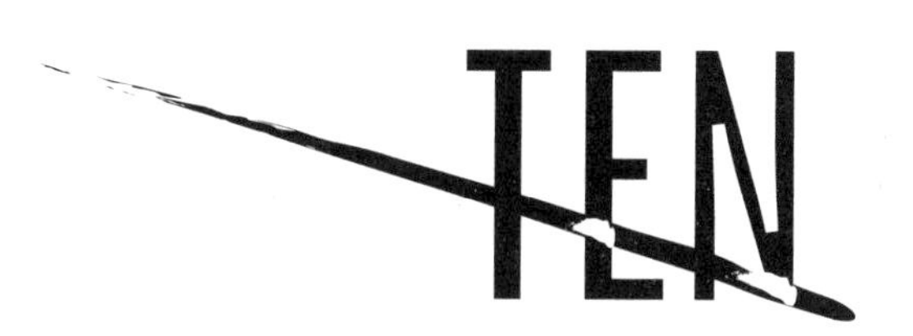

TEN

HOWL 44 FLIGHT
OVER SOUTHERN ENGLAND

The four American Eagles flew in tactical formation, half-a-mile spacing between them, aircraft two and three positioned two thousand feet high and on the right side of their leader, number four high and on the left. The pilots talked to each over the secure radio and communicated data between them using a sensitive black box they called Al, a highly classified system that allowed the four fighters to share information regarding their heading, altitude, airspeed, fuel remaining, weapon and system status, the location of friendly land-and-air forces, threat locations, and status—everything required for the pilots to understand what they called "picture," or "situation awareness," or "what-the-hell's-going-on."

To fly a supersonic fighter aircraft in combat requires a pilot to sort through information overload. An incredible number of variables has to be taken in and processed, much of it at the same time, while the pilot tries to think in five dimensions, taking in the three elements of space as well as speed and time. It is nearly impossible to even gather all the information, let alone process it, prioritize it, then make an adequate decision while leaving time to react.

One in a hundred people can learn to fly the air force way. One in five hundred could learn to fly a supersonic fighter. One in a thousand can do it in combat, against other superbly capable pilots, and not have their heads blown off.

All of the American Eagle pilots were those one-in-a-thousand.

But the F-15s they flew were just not up to task. Getting old was difficult for people and fighter airplanes alike.

Its roots dated back to the early days of Vietnam War, when the need for a superior air-to-air fighter became painfully evident. At fifteen million dollars apiece, the F-15 Eagle was easily the most expensive and sophisticated fighter ever built, at least up to that time. All-weather capable and extremely maneuverable, the Eagle had been designed to be the fastest, meanest, most powerful piece of steel in the sky. Their mission: maintain air superiority by kicking Russian pilots in the teeth.

Soon after its introduction, an Eagle set the world time-to-climb record. Other climb and speed records followed. With its twin Pratt and Whitney F100 turbofan engines (later updated with the more efficient and even more powerful F100-200s), a combat-loaded F-15 could climb to an altitude of 65,000 feet and reach a top speed of 1,875 miles per hour. Mach 2.5. A pilot-pleasing speed to be sure.

But powerful as the Eagle was to fly, it was the advanced avionics package that really set it apart. It was the first fighter in the world that was capable of look-down, shoot-down capability, the pulse-Doppler radar system allowing the pilot to look downward and see through ground clutter well enough to detect, identify, and track a low-flying target. And the Eagle was also the first aircraft to allow BVR combat—Beyond Visual Range—the ability to detect, identify, and fire on a target beyond what the pilot could see. And there were other innovations as well. HOTAS, or Hands On Throttles And Stick, allowed the pilot to manipulate primary avionic functions, including arming and firing his missiles or cannon, without taking his eyes off the target or his hands off the stick or throttles. When life-or-death situations sometimes came down to fractions of seconds, the ability for the pilot to do this proved to be a huge advantage. Other avionic systems in the package proved to be technological breakthroughs as well. The radar fed target information to the central computer for effective weapons delivery. During close-in dogfights, the computer could automatically guide the pilot's eyes to the target through the head-up display. In addition, the F-15's electronic warfare system provided warning and automatic countermeasures against enemy missiles.

Through continual avionic and engine upgrades, including the Tactical Electronic Warfare System, Hughes APG-70 radar, and the Advanced Medium Range Air-to-Air Missiles, for more than a generation the F-15 Eagles maintained their status as the best fighter in the world.

But the times were a-changin'.

And the Eagle's time had now passed.

The pilot in the lead F-15 was a major who was scheduled to be promoted to lieutenant colonel in four months and twelve days. A solid man, thirty-eight, with a wife and three kids, he was an Air Force Academy graduate who sometimes drank too much, loved his wife, went to church when she made him, and was completely satisfied with a middle-class lifestyle as long as he could fly jets.

As he flew he kept his head on a swivel, looking over both shoulders at his wingmen to check their six, then turned back to search the airspace in front of his fighter. The formation was at 31,000 feet (altitude is airspeed and airspeed is life), 540 knots, and heading almost due west. He turned the formation in a gentle circle as they waited for their instructions. The English Channel was twenty miles in the distance, the White Cliffs of Dover glimmering dimly in the late afternoon light. The channel was choppy and dark. It looked bleak and cold, especially from altitude. The sky was partly cloudy, heavy with haze and humidity, low stratus clouds at two thousand feet, and a few cumulonimbus clouds above that. Visibility was pretty good for this area, but that didn't mean it was great, for it seemed visibility over southern England was always terrible. The formation leader could see five, maybe six miles, but then everything washed out in the haze. He stared through his HUD as he flew, his heart racing, questions and fears running round in his mind.

Why were they up there? He still didn't know. Ten minutes before, he and the other pilots had been watching TV in their alert shack back in England when they had been scrambled and sent south (the first time they had ever scrambled in that direction), then told to loiter and wait for further instructions. He had three other fighters behind him, sixteen missiles between them, four cannons, lots of gas, but no target to go after, *and he didn't know why*. He was in a rage. He wanted more information *now*.

Then his radio crackled and he listened up. It was the guard channel, the open frequency that all civilian and military aircraft were required to monitor every moment in the air. And it was an American voice, his English perfect, not the heavily accented international controller who had been there before.

"Mayday, Mayday, Mayday, this is Paris Control on 121.5 and 243.0. This is an emergency message for all aircraft within three hundred miles of the Paris Terminal Control Area. Repeat: all aircraft, this is an emergency message for all military and civilian aircraft within three hundred miles of the Paris TCA. Le Bourget Aerodrome reports the likely hijacking or theft of an ultrasecret American fighter. The target was last seen flying northwest, toward the English Channel, at approximately twenty-thousand feet, sustaining eleven hundred knots . . ."

The F-15 pilot swallowed, his throat suddenly bone dry. You got to be kidding! 1,100 knots! No way! Some fighters could fly that fast, but only for a few seconds before they burned all their gas. *This dude was sustaining 1,100.* It had to be a mistake!

"It is estimated," the controller went on, "the target will penetrate International Air Defense Identification Zone sometime in the next four to six minutes. Suspect target is a gray fighter aircraft. Forty-three-foot wingspan.

Twin Delta tails. Embedded engines. Dark gray, almost black. Subdued insignia and tail numbers with a small U.S. flag."

The radio went silent and the lead F-15 pilot stared ahead again.

He shook his head. He didn't believe it! *This* was too weird!

"All aircraft," the controller broke in again, "Paris Control is requesting assistance in locating suspect aircraft. All pilots and crew members, keep your eyes out. Advise any possible sightings to me on one-two-three-point-five or two-four-four-point-eight. Repeat, all aircraft are requested to assist in locating the suspect hijacked or stolen aircraft."

There was silence, then the controller added in a far less official tone, "Come on, give us a hand here, ladies and gentlemen. This baby is superfast, superdangerous and, if you haven't figured it out already, completely invisible to radar. You are the best hope we have here and we really need your help."

The radio fell silent.

The lead F-15 pilot swore, constantly turning his head. He'd heard the stories in the squadron bars. *The spookity-spook aircraft crash at Tonopah wasn't an F-117. A new fighter was coming, something developed in total secrecy. Faster, badder than anything ever seen. And it had a new weapon. They called it the Ares. . . .*

It was true. There was a new fighter.

Now it had been stolen.

And they were supposed to bring it down!

He stared at the cold waters before him.

How could they possibly find it, one tiny aircraft in so much airspace?

Then his radio crackled on guard frequency once again. "Paris, this is Air France 1146 on guard. We've got the aircraft in sight. *It is right off our nose!*"

"State your position!" the controller shot back.

The airline pilot read his coordinates, his voice strained and high. He was approaching the English side of the Channel, not more than twenty miles from the F-15s. "He's right there before us, a little higher now," the French civilian pilot cried. "The idiot almost hit us. Now he's right off our nose. He looks like thirty-four, maybe thirty-six thousand feet, heading north . . . no, he's breaking, he's breaking, he's turning west now."

The lead Eagle pilot jammed his stick to left, rolling the fighter up on the side, the g-forces pushing him in his seat. He pushed against the crushing force of gravity as he turned his head, straining to see to the west. The sky was a light, gun-barrel blue. Clouds. Haze. Dark water, gray sky. He moved his eyes constantly, searching, straining, looking for anything. He resisted the impulse to glance down at his radar, knowing it wouldn't do any good, but fifteen years of training were making it extraordinarily difficult to resist. He saw a couple airliners below him, a small Cessna on his right, but no fighter . . . no fighter.

"Tally on the target!" his number-three said, her voice calm and cool and ready to fight. "Gray fighter, eight o'clock. Low now. Descending."

The lead F-15 racked his aircraft almost to its back. His body fell against the ejection seat straps as he hung there, almost upside down. He strained as he looked over his shoulder and down, jamming his head against the ejection seat.

Then he saw the aircraft.

"Tally on the target," he said.

ELEVEN

CECOC COMMAND CENTER
LE BOURGET AIRPORT

Major James was escorted into the command post, a French lieutenant at his side. He had grabbed a leather bag from the backseat of his rental car and already washed up and changed into his military uniform, a dark green flight suit with pilot wings and bronze maple leaves on each shoulder. He pushed away from the French officer as he passed through the metal door, then stood without moving, taking in the chaos.

He could feel the emotional electricity that crackled in the air. Tension and confusion showed on every face in the room. He searched for someone he knew, wondering why he was there. Then he saw the only two men he recognized, General Hawley and the president. His heart started slamming like a hammer as his mouth went instantly dry. They were toward the back of the room, huddled together, the president looking at some kind of radar screen. There seemed to be an invisible barrier around the president that the other officers in the room seemed reluctant to break as they all circled around him.

Jesse stared a long moment, unable to move. As a military officer, he was hyper-geared to be respectful of authority, and the greatest authority he could ever face was standing just across the room. And though he was dying to walk up to Hawley and find out what was going on, he couldn't. Not with the president there. One didn't approach or talk to the president until one was told.

So he stood for thirty seconds, then slowly moved toward them, stopped a dozen steps away, and waited for Hawley. Sensing his presence, the general made eye contact, gave the smallest nod of his head, then turned back to the president. Jesse took a step back and waited. From where he stood, he couldn't hear most of what they talked about, but he caught a few words.

The Ares. Interceptors out of England.

His heart hammered once again.

The fighters are closing on the target . . . ?

He glanced behind the two men to the relay from Air Traffic Control. It wasn't the same Combat Tactical Control screens he was used to working with, not nearly as detailed or intricate but still familiar, and he recognized most of the symbols—lots of air traffic, a couple of fighter formations that seemed to be converging . . . but no target.

His head started spinning. There were too many dots not to start drawing lines. The sonic boom, the sudden call from General Hawley, the president huddled at the CECOC, the ATC relay showing a combat intercept . . . Jesse staggered back and tried to swallow but he couldn't force the spit down. Even as he stared at Hawley, he knew. He turned to the president. Yes, it was obvious.

Another minute passed before the president walked away from Hawley and the general pulled him aside.

"Sir, please tell me this isn't what it seems!" Jesse whispered as the two men huddled together near the ATC screen.

Hawley glanced around. "I don't have much time," he said.

"What happened at the air show? What happened to our Ares?"

Hawley was leaning against a large, metal desk crammed with red binders, classified communications plans, and a couple of diet Cokes. He lifted a can, swirled it, realized it was empty, and threw it in a wastebasket already overflowing with trash.

Jesse waited, watching him closely. "Sir . . . ?" he prodded gently. "Have we lost our jet?"

Hawley nodded gravely.

"But it's out there, isn't it, sir? It didn't go down. We actually . . . lost it?"

"Yes," Hawley answered. "Everything was going according to the script. The aircraft took off, made one high-speed pass, blew out all the windows, and then, poof, it was gone."

Jesse looked over the general's shoulder to the tactical screen, studied it a second, then swore. His hands were shaking, his face drained and pale. "It was what? Hijacked . . . stolen?"

"We don't know. It's only been a few minutes and we haven't even *started* to sort this thing out."

"What about the pilot, Colonel Ray?" he asked.

Hawley glanced at the president who was standing a dozen steps from them and shook his head. "He was last seen this morning." Hawley took a few seconds to tell him everything that had happened since the Ares had taken off. It didn't take long; there was not much to tell. Jesse asked in a whisper, "What do you want me to do, sir?"

The general nudged his shoulder toward the tactical screen. "The Lakenheath birds are moving in on the target. We'll know if they get him within five minutes, maybe less. Stand by until we see how that goes, then I'll let you know."

Jesse stepped closer to the screen and stared a long moment, taking it in. "They'll never find it," he whispered.

Hawley moved to his side. "No, we've had a visual sighting. Our guys are already waiting for him—he didn't realize we had alert jets up in England—and they are in position to intercept the jet. The Ares pilot doesn't seem to know he's got interceptors waiting for him, and it looks like he has slowed down. Trying to save fuel, I guess. Our England birds have a very good intercept angle. We actually have a good chance."

Jesse studied the screen. "Where's the target?" he asked.

Hawley pointed to an empty spot south of the border of England, and Jesse converted the relative scale in his mind to estimate the distances and times it would take to run the intercepts. He ran his finger across the screen between the chasing fighters and the empty spot over the ocean.

"The alert birds out of Lakenheath are Eagles?" he asked.

Hawley nodded.

"They'll be in range of their AMRAAMs in a couple seconds, sir, but that won't do much good, not unless the Ares is bleeding so much radar energy that they get enough of a radar return to guide the missiles to the target, and we both know that's extremely unlikely. But if they can get within six or seven miles, they could use their Sidewinders, sir. I think that's our best shot. Whoever is flying the Ares isn't going to know how to use it, not to its complete advantage. He won't know the azimuths and vectors which expose him to IR bleed off, he won't know how to use the laser for self-defense or effectively maneuver the jet. He won't know how to minimize his radar or IR exposure. Now, he's got to be a better than average pilot, I think we'd all give him that, but he won't know the Ares, not the way that I do. I could tell the Eagle how to intercept it. And it's possible. If they all shoot at once, if they work very closely together, they can bring this dude down—"

Hawley cut him off. "I'm not going to shoot it," he said.

Jesse shook his head as if he didn't hear. "Sir?"

"I'm not going to shoot it," Hawley repeated.

"Are you're kidding me, sir?"

"We've got enough fighters out there. They've already boxed him in. I think we can force it to land."

Jesse stood in shocked silence. "No," he shot back. "Think about it, General. That thing is way too dangerous, way too destabilizing, to let it get away. If you have a chance to shoot it, you've *got* to take it down."

Hawley lifted his hand impatiently and gave Jesse a deadly look. "I've already discussed it with the president," he answered coldly. "He agrees with my plan. Now that we know where it is, now that we've got interceptors in range, we're going to use our birds to steer the Ares back here and force it to land. We've got more than eight billion dollars invested in that jet! We've got to do everything we can to save it."

"Sir, screw that aircraft. We've got another one sitting out there in the hangar. Once we get our full funding, we can build all you want. No, sir, you've got to destroy this thing, right now, while you can!"

Hawley took a step toward Jesse, shot a nervous look at the president, then lowered his voice. "Listen to me, Major," he hissed. "We don't know who stole our fighter, but like you just pointed out, we *do* know he's never flown the Ares before. He will be completely unfamiliar with the aircraft's weapon systems, how to employ the aircraft in any reasonable way. I doubt he can even fire the laser. He's got to be completely task-saturated just flying that thing, let alone trying to figure out how to use the avionics package or fire the gun. Meanwhile, as he's struggling to keep that jet in the air, we've got eight fighters converging on him, twelve if the French guys ever make it. I think that is enough of an advantage that we can force an inexperienced pilot to land."

Jesse stepped away, his arms rising in frustration. He started to say something, gritted his teeth, then turned his back on the general again. He had never spoken to General Hawley with anything but respect. He had never raised his voice to any general, but this was so stupid. No, this was insane! He took a deep breath and faced the general. "Sir, permission to speak freely?" he asked, his voice strained.

"You know you don't have to ask me that, Major James. I've always given you the freedom to be honest with me."

"Yes, sir. And now I have to tell you that I *respectfully* but urgently disagree with your decision. I have admired you, General Hawley, for many years now, and I have never questioned your judgment on anything. But this is a terrible risk you are taking. You must bring that jet down. If your guys have a shot, they have to take it."

Hawley shook his head. "The president and I have already decided. This is what we *both* want to do."

Jesse caught the meaning. *This is what the president wanted.* So that's how it was.

"Sir," he answered, "is it possible you are letting your commitment to the Ares program cloud your judgment right now? You have a chance to take care of this problem, but if you take a chance on saving that aircraft and you fail, then, overnight, the entire world becomes a much more dangerous place. Let's end this thing now."

Hawley stared angrily at the major, then saw the president walking toward them. "I want you to stand back," he hissed. "This isn't your decision. We've got a chance to bring back my aircraft and that's what I've chosen to do. I don't have the energy or the time to justify it to you, and the last thing I want is you second-guessing me in front of the president."

The two men stared at each other, both with their eyes on fire. The president stopped in front of General Hawley. "Robert . . . ," he said.

Jesse nodded respectfully to the president and took a step back.

"How long until our fighters are in range?"

"Two, maybe two and a half minutes, sir."

"Will we be able to watch it?"

"Not really, Mr. President. The air traffic controller's radar isn't set up for us to see much of what is going on, but we can set up a communications relay with the pilots so you can hear what they say."

"Do it," the president said, "I want to hear everything that's going on."

OUTSIDE AULNAY-SOUS-BOIS
SEINE-SAINT-DENIS
EIGHTEEN KILOMETERS NORTH OF LE BOURGET AIRPORT

The road was narrow and lined with tall, sapping pines and birch trees with dry leaves that were beginning to fall, not from the weather but the drought of a long summer without rain. The trees had been cut away from the road's edge only ten or twelve feet, and the blacktop was heavily rutted and poorly maintained, for it connected a couple of the poorest neighborhoods in the city. Inhabited mostly by Muslim refugees and North African immigrants, the neighborhoods and small towns on the northeast side of the city were decrepit and bleak, with signs of the riots and ethnic violence that took place in this part of the city. Traffic was sparse and slow. A cement canal followed on the right side of the road, but it was dry now except for sporadic pools of murky, moss-filled water sitting where the cement had sunk into the ground. Occasional breaks in the trees revealed quick glimpses of old buildings and houses, some with small gardens, on the other side of the canal.

At 5:02, a little more than half an hour after the Ares had taken off, a fiery explosion rocked the forest, sending a rolling fireball skyward and black smoke drifting through the trees.

The old Mercedes had been sitting on a gravel pull-off near a bend in the road. When the dynamite detonated, the Mercedes was rocked up on its front bumper. It almost rolled forward to its roof but fell back again, puncturing its rear tires and bending the rims. The explosives had been placed under the backseat, and the two rear doors were blown off their hinges, the trunk lid sent flying through the air, clearing the tops of the trees, while most of the roof was peeled back like the top of a tin can. The fuel in the gas tank exploded, adding its heat to the flames, and the tires started burning, billowing black smoke into the sky. Rolling tornadoes of fire shot through the broken windows, the deep orange inferno rolling in violent vortices that sucked the oxygen from the air.

Around the wreckage, scattered pieces of human remains began to fall here and there—part of a torso, the trouser belt still attached, a piece of scalp, a few fingers, the body pieces having exploded from the shattered car a millisecond before it burst into flames.

In the front seat, behind the wheel, most of a charred body remained, the stumps of the arms cooking to the plastic on the steering wheel. Pieces of another body, mostly legs, were scattered across the passenger seat. Parts of another body were flung around in the back.

Ten or twelve feet from the Mercedes, a small yellow SmartCar was parked. No one was inside it. At least not anymore.

TWELVE

HOWL 44 FLIGHT
OFF THE SOUTHERN ENGLISH COAST

It was the most frustrating thing the F-15 pilot had ever experienced in his life. He could see the fleeing aircraft right in front of his eyes, a dark silhouette against the washed-out horizon. He could make out the swept wings and twin tails and, occasionally, when the sun hit it just right, catch a flash of the setting sun glinting off the top of the wings. But there was nothing on his radar. Nothing at all.

He'd been trained to identify enemy fighters by nothing but a flash of their outline or a quick glimpse of their wings, and he was certain this was an aircraft he'd never seen before. But like a man staring at a ghost, he had to force himself to believe his own eyes.

Eighteen years of training and experience and gut-level reactions were hard to deny. Rely on your systems, he had always been taught. Your radar can't be fooled and you've got to believe what it says. Visual illusions are not uncommon, so don't be tricked by your eyes.

For eighteen years, whether in combat or training, he'd been trained to rely on the multimillion-dollar hardware tucked in the nose of his jet. Now the hardware assured him there was no fighter there. Nothing showed on his IR. There was no growl in his helmet telling him his radar was locked, no piper box on his HUD tracking a fighter through the sky, which meant he was going to have to do it the old-fashioned way.

So he concentrated on the fighter, terrified of losing sight of the target. It was no more than six, maybe seven miles ahead of him now, a few degrees off to the left and below, somewhere between twenty-five and twenty-eight thousand feet.

Punching the radio switch on his throttle, he talked to Air Traffic Control.

"Howl has a tally on the bandit."

"Roger. Negative radar confirmation," the American controller replied.

Negative radar confirmation. There would be no assistance or backup. It was up to the guys in the air.

The pilot switched over and talked to the other fighters in his formation on his secure radio. "Howl Three, you got a tally on the bandit?"

"Three's got a tally."

"Tactical split," he instructed.

Fighter four rolled up on his side and pulled, splitting away from the others. Howl Three immediately followed, climbing while turning away. Seconds later, fighters three and four were two thousand feet higher and abeam of their leader. They rolled out quickly, the number-four aircraft maintaining his position now off of number three.

"Bogey looks like . . . five miles," the flight leader said.

"Two's got a tally."

"Three tally."

"Four."

All of the fighters had the stolen fighter in sight.

There was a moment of silence, then the number-three aircraft said, "Lead, confirm we've got a bogey, not a bandit?"

Bogey. Unidentified aircraft.

Bandit. Hostile aircraft.

There was a crucial distinction and she wanted to know which it was.

"Howl Three, the target is a bandit," the formation leader corrected himself.

Another moment of silence, then the number-four pilot said, "What kind of aircraft is *that*?"

The flight leader shook his head. Staring at the stunning gray-black aircraft, he was wondering the same thing.

The bandit started moving ahead of them, growing smaller against the hazy sky. Before the F-15 pilots even realized it, they had fallen another mile behind.

Lead glanced at his fuel flow and airspeed. He was already going just about as fast as he could without using afterburner, yet the target kept moving out before him. "Howl, going burner," he announced over his radio. Shoving both throttles forward to their stops, he pushed through the detents into full afterburner, and three hundred pounds of jet fuel was burned instantly. His F-15 accelerated with a rush of raw power, twin tails of orange and blue flame spouting at the back of his jet, the force of the acceleration pushing him back in his seat as he watched the airspeed indicator through his HUD.

Point-nine-six Mach.

Point-nine-eight and accelerating.

A cloud began to develop over the top of his canopy, a fuzzy oval that formed when the humid air was superheated by the friction of the passing jet. The hazy cloud formed a broken donut around his cockpit and extended to the tips of his wings. Approaching the speed of sound, the cloud matured, forming a perfect ring around his cockpit that stayed with the aircraft until he pushed through the speed of sound, when it suddenly disappeared, blown back by the powerful sonic wave that washed over his jet.

Mach 1.2. Mach 1.5. Faster and faster he flew, but the target stayed out in front of him. He was still getting away!

Glancing back, the pilot checked his wingman's positions, assuring himself that the other fighters were exactly where they were supposed to be. Number three was a couple miles off his right. Number four was behind her. His own wingman, number two, had fallen back into a tactical trail. From this position, two had a large cone in which he could operate; anywhere from the four to the eight o'clock position as well as above, behind, or below the lead jet.

His fighter continued to accelerate and the leader checked his fuel flow. At full burner, the engines turned into enormous sucking machines, gulping down fuel at a frightening rate. He glanced ahead, estimating his closure on the target. The Eagles started gaining on the target. "Howl, out of blowers," he announced as he pulled his throttles back.

Without any radar information, he could only estimate how far away the target was, but the stolen fighter was growing larger on the lower edge of his canopy now. The sun was low, almost directly off his nose, so he couldn't use it to hide, but he still wanted to take every advantage he could. He kept the formation high, maneuvering to come in from the left, knowing most pilots were right-handed and tended to favor that side whenever they were searching the airspace behind them, anticipating an attack.

The bandit grew even larger in his windscreen. They were closing very quickly now. His own fighter was beginning to slow, the force of the sonic bow wave pushing him back. The black fighter was three miles in front of him and maybe five thousand feet below. He dipped his nose and armed his Sidewinder missiles, ready for the attack.

The bandit flew straight and level, unaware it was being trailed.

CECOC COMMAND CENTER
LE BOURGET AIRPORT

Jesse James watched the radar relay from Air Traffic Control. He could see that the controllers had cleared the airspace around the fighters, moving all other airliner and civilian air traffic out of the way to give the Eagles space to engage the target. He could also see that the formation had split, readying for the attack. The F-15s were heading almost due west now, across the empty air space south of England and accelerating to an unsustainable speed.

He moved forward and spoke quietly to Hawley. "If those dudes get in a chase, this thing is over. If they try to race him, we lose. The Eagle guys know that, right?"

Hawley shook his head. "I don't know if they do, but what choice do they have?"

"They need to bait him, to try and get him to turn around."

Hawley lifted his hand, the radio breaking through.

Jesse listened to the speakers mounted on the top corners of the plasma screen. "Howl has a tally on the bandit," he heard the Eagle pilot say.

"Roger. Negative radar confirmation," the American controller shot back.

The president glanced at General Hawley. "What does that mean?" he asked. Hawley explained. The president frowned. Jesse kept his eyes on the radar screen. The digital readout showed the Eagles were going faster than the speed of sound now, accelerating on a target that none of them could see.

A small crowd of military officers and security agents silently gathered behind the three men, all of them watching the ATC screen.

"Can you enhance the picture?" the president asked.

Hawley turned to a French lieutenant, who shook his head. "I'm sorry, Mr. President," he said.

Ten seconds passed. Jesse watched the fighters accelerate until they reached Mach 1.4. That was screaming for the Eagles, close to the limit of their practical speed, and he knew they would be burning massive amounts of fuel. It was also too fast to maneuver aggressively, even for the F-15, and worse, they would have to slow to launch their missiles or they would likely malfunction as they came off their rails.

But Mach 1.4 was a cakewalk for the F-38. Jesse knew that better than any other man in the room. The Ares wouldn't even be in afterburner to maintain that speed, and it could maneuver like a rabbit at anything below Mach 1.8.

They're doing it wrong, he screamed to himself as he watched the screen. *They need to slow down and conserve their fuel. This guy is itching for a fight. If he had wanted to run away, he would have been gone by now, he could have blown away from the Eagles at Mach 2 or more. But he's sticking around, trying to bait them into a furball. The Eagle drivers are following conventional rules of engagement, which are all doomed to fail. They needed to box him in, take his corners, give him no room to maneuver. They needed to take their shot now.*

"Come on, guys," he whispered, coaxing the fighters on. "Come on, launch your missiles. Do it now, while you can!"

Hawley heard Jesse whisper and tried to hide a grimace. President Abram glanced at General Hawley as if he expected some kind of explanation. The general said nothing, keeping his eyes on the screen.

The room was deathly silent. Every eye watched but no one breathed.

Go, Jesse prayed, his chest growing tight.

The F-15 pilot's voice broke the silence. "Control, Howl flight, is . . . looks like four miles from the target. I don't know what this guy is burning, but he's screaming along. We've got to do something before we use all our gas. We are ready to engage. Confirm we are cleared to fire!"

Jesse sucked a breath and watched Hawley. The president of the United States stared straight ahead. Hawley's eyes darted to the air force officer sitting at a desk next to him. The officer stared up at the general. Hawley nodded. The controller spoke into his mike. "Howl 44, this is the military liaison at Paris Control. Your instructions are to make all efforts to *intercept* the bandit. Fire warning shots if necessary, but *do not* bring it down. Repeat; you are to intercept the bandit and try to force it back to Le Bourget."

Jesse let out a long breath of air.

"Paris Control," the F-15 pilot answered, "confirm we do *not* fire on the target? We are to try and intercept it and force it to land?" It was pretty clear he thought that was going to be impossible.

Jesse smirked. As if he had any idea at all.

"Roger," the controller shot back. "Do not engage the target. Warning shots if necessary, but do *not* shoot it down. We believe the renegade pilot is unfamiliar with the aircraft's weapon systems and that you will be able to force it to land."

Hawley glanced back at Jesse, then leaned toward the president and whispered something that Jesse couldn't hear.

The F-15 pilot watched the target carefully, studying the blended design on the airframe, the canted wings, cutting angles of the fuselage, and angled rudders. It looked a little like the F-22. But it was larger. And faster. Baby, this thing could scream.

He dove on the aircraft, angling to come in on it from the south. He knew that, for now, he still had the element of surprise and had to move in quickly, getting into position to box the bandit in before the other pilot could know they were there.

He waggled his wings a couple times and his wingman pulled in, tightening up the spacing between them. He glanced to his right. Number three and four were in position, coming in from the bandit's right. The Eagles were two miles now and closing. Plenty close for heat-seeking missiles. Close enough for guns.

The bandit continued flying straight and level, seemingly unaware. The Eagle pilot moved his formation closer. He had one chance to box the target in and he had to get it right.

"Two take the left side," he said over his radio. "Three, keep on the right. Four, you go high at the six. I'll stay on his tail.

The fighters split off, moving into position. Two moved to the stolen fighter's left side but stayed back, waiting for the signal from lead. Three moved to the right side, number four moved above.

The lead pilot dropped his nose to get directly behind the fighter but stayed back two miles. Checking his formation a final time, he flipped his radio, turning the channel selector so he could broadcast over guard.

"Unknown rider, unknown rider," the pilot said. "This is Howl Four-four flight. Respond on guard."

The pilot waited for an answer. Anxious, number three moved up a thousand feet.

"Unknown rider," the F-15 pilot said again, "Unknown rider on the two-four-five radial, seven-nine DME off the Tieberg TACAN, this is Howl Four-four flight. Respond now on guard or signal with your wings."

The stolen fighter continued straight and level, heading west, out to sea.

"Unknown rider, this is the U.S. Air Force intercept fighters on your left and right wing. You are to follow our instructions."

The stolen fighter dropped its nose, then maneuvered wildly, his wings rocking as if he was fighting to maintain control, the fuselage rolling right and then left, the nose cocked awkwardly to the side.

"Howlers, *go!*" the pilot shouted over his formation frequency.

The F-15s at the side of the F-38 hit their burners and accelerated while angling toward the fleeing jet. The lead pilot pushed up his power and closed in as well. Above him, he caught a flash of dark gray as the number-four aircraft accelerated with him, staying above the fleeing fighter, giving it no space to maneuver.

The four fighters moved in on the Ares, coming to fifty feet off its wing so that it was boxed in. The Eagles stayed in a tight formation, the pilots staring through their cockpits at the fleeing aircraft. With the fighters in position, there was absolutely nowhere for the stolen fighter to go.

"Unknown rider, heading two-eight-five, now eighty-three miles southwest of the Tieberg TACAN," the interceptor pilot repeated, "this is U.S. Air Force interceptor flight Howl Four-four. We have you boxed in. There is nowhere for you to go. You must follow our instructions, or *we will* bring you down. Confirm on guard or with a dip of your left wing."

The pilot counted to ten. "Unknown rider—,"

The stolen aircraft dipped its nose for the sea. All of the fighters accelerated, passed through eighteen thousand feet, still descending, approaching Mach speed again.

"Unknown rider, *this is* your last chance to comply!" The pilot's voice was calm but deadly over the radio.

Nothing but silence. The pilot waited another five seconds, then switched radios. "Confirm, Howler is cleared to fire?" he demanded.

"Affirmative, Howler you are clear."

"Howlers, give me spacing *now,*" the pilot commanded the three aircraft on his wing. The other fighters broke away, leveling off one mile away from the fleeing jet. The lead pilot maneuvered to the left side of the target, selected one of his heat-seeking missiles, disarmed the seeker head, moved the nose of his jet ten degrees to the front of the fleeing fighter, and pressed the fire button on his stick.

The Sidewinder dropped from the guidance rail on the tip of his right wing, its engine firing at the same time, leaving a puff of white smoke. The missile accelerated very quickly, firing straight ahead, a billowing vapor trail behind it. Like an arrow it raced forward, slashing right in front of the jet.

With the seeker head disarmed, the missile had no guidance and flew blindly straight ahead. It passed eighty feet in front of the target, the vapor trail from its engine leaving a white, puffy trail. The target flew through the smoke from the missile's engine, the white vapor washing over its canopy. The missile continued straight ahead, ran out of fuel, and exploded in the air, a huge black and yellow fireball lighting up the late afternoon sky.

The F-15 pilot leaned anxiously forward. The target knew they were serious now.

He waited for some kind of response, either over the radio or from seeing a dip of the wings, the international signal that it was under distress. The aircraft continued to ignore them, flying almost due west. He glanced at his fuel readout. They were running out of gas, out of options, out of patience, out of time.

Getting no response, the pilot tried his radio for the last time. "Unknown rider, this is U.S. Air Force Howl Four-four. In ten seconds I will fire and *I will bring you down.*"

He waited. No response. Alright, that was fine. There were two ways to end this. Moving to the six o'clock position, he set himself up directly behind the target. He climbed forty feet or so, not wanting to fly through the fireball or exploding debris that was about to be scattered through the air, selected a heat-seeking missile, and took a deep breath.

It was an easy shot—good spacing, a little close, but not too bad, directly behind the target's red-hot engines. At the speed they were flying, there had to be lots of heat being generated up there. And even if the target had IR diffusers, or heat sumps, or icicles, or magic, or whatever friggin' thing they used to keep it from emitting an IR signature, he was so close now there was no way his missiles could miss. There had to be enough heat being generated just from the friction on the aircraft's skin that his missile could sniff the target.

Arming the seeker head, he pressed the red, covered button on his stick. The missile's engine fired and accelerated forward, racing toward the F-38's twin tail.

The F-15 pilot watched his missile carefully, instinctively bracing for the kill. He grabbed the stick like a vise and moved his left hand to grip the cockpit panel over the radar screen.

The heat-seeking missile raced forward, perfectly in line for the kill.

Three seconds to impact. The missile flew straight and true.

The stolen aircraft kept flying straight and level, completely unaware the missile was homing in on his tail.

The Eagle pilot instinctively braced for the impact, certain he had a good kill.

Then he saw something he had *never* seen before.

THIRTEEN

OVER THE NORTH ATLANTIC
SOUTHEAST OF THE ENGLISH COAST

The Sidewinder shot toward the stolen fighter, closing at an incredible speed while locking on to the hot gases that trailed from the jet. The heat diffusers and baffles at the top and the rear of the Ares did a marvelous job of diffusing the heat from the engines into the cold air, but there was only so much they could do. When a missile was launched at such a close range there was just too much heat to diffuse, and the seeker head was too sensitive not to track toward the jet.

The pilot watched the missile fly.

Less than a thousand feet from impact, the stolen fighter snapped suddenly. It did a complete aileron roll, continued spinning another ninety degrees, then *pushed,* the pilot subjecting himself to negative g's, incredibly painful, even dangerous, if held for any length of time. The F-15 pilot jammed himself forward in his seat. Had the renegade pilot lost control of his jet?

Its belly exposed to the missile, the F-38 aircraft seemed to slow, stabilized in the turn, then vibrated visibly.

Six hundred feet from impact, the Sidewinder blew apart. No fireball. No counter-missile. No visible beam of light. The missile just seemed to fall to pieces, instantly ripping itself to shreds.

The F-15 pilot blinked, his mouth hanging open inside his oxygen mask. For a moment he froze, his eyes wide.

A defective missile? It couldn't be! He cursed angrily to himself.

Moving his fingers across his weapons switches, he selected another missile, pressed the trigger, and fired again. The second Sidewinder dropped, ignited its engine, and accelerated toward the Ares. The stolen aircraft rolled again, showed its belly to the missile, and the missile blew apart.

The pilot stared in shock. Then panic and uncertainty drove him into instinctive mode.

Two more shots.

Two more missiles blown apart in the air.

The missile wreckage fell toward the dark sea, pieces of the white and blue fuselage scattering as they fell. Below him, the first rocket motor splashed into the cold water as the other pieces fluttered seaward, taking their time to fall.

The major swallowed painfully, his mouth bitter and dry.

"Howl . . . did you . . . ?" The pilot in the number-two aircraft started to say something, but his voice trailed off.

The pilot jammed his stick, pulling up and rolling right. He did a snap-barrel roll, moving away from the target and off to the side. "Two, take my position," he called halfway through the roll. As the horizon revolved across his cockpit, the pilot kept his head moving, looking downward through the canopy to keep the target in sight. Fingers on the stick, he moved the aircraft expertly, rolling out a hundred feet above and five hundred feet to the right of where he had been only two or three seconds before.

"Four's cleared to fire. Your choice of your cannons or guns."

The number-four fighter snapped into a tight bank, his aircraft screaming across the hazy sky. He rolled on top of his leader, completing a wide circle that ended wings level but two hundred feet underneath where he had been before. He pushed his throttles forward and accelerated from underneath his leader while moving in from behind. As he accelerated, aircraft number three tightened up her position, moving in on the stolen jet, and the last jet backed off to a half-mile trail.

The stolen fighter started to jerk wildly, but the Eagle stayed behind it, remaining in a position to fire.

Jamming his throttles into afterburner, the second aircraft closed the spacing on the target while maneuvering to the six o'clock and selected his cannon. Flipping the switch to arm his gun, he kept his eyes outside the cockpit, staring through the Head-Up Display. Instinctively, he searched for the steering piper, the white box on his HUD that would allow the computer to help him aim by automatically compensating for airspeeds, yaw, winds, drift, target velocity, and direction. It took him a second to remember that, without his radar locked on the target, the piper couldn't work.

So he aimed visually, doing the best that he could.

He was so close now, less than four hundred feet. The target had leveled off and was flying straight ahead, as if waiting to die. It would be an easy shot. Too easy. But after what he had just witnessed, his mouth was still dry. Could the target destroy him like it had destroyed the missiles that had been fired up its tail?

Moving his finger to the trigger, he checked his gun camera and adjusted his aim one more time.

"Interceptors, hold your weapons! Hold your weapons!" his radio suddenly crackled to life.

The pilot pressed lightly on the trigger, a quarter second from firing his gun.

"Hold your weapons!" the man on the radio shouted again. It was a deep voice, low and husky.

Reluctantly, unbelieving, disappointed, the pilot dropped his finger from the trigger and slid his hand down the stick.

"Howlers, confirm weapons hold," the formation leader cried over the radio.

"Two copies," the second pilot said, keeping his finger away from the trigger. Three and four replied the same way.

The formation leader moved his fighter closer to the target and pressed his microphone again. "Unknown rider, do you read?"

"I will comply," the pilot in the stolen fighter pilot replied in a voice so soft and muffled that it was barely understandable.

A moment of stunned silence, then the F-15 pilot said, "Unknown rider, turn left now, heading one-five-five. Maintain this altitude and slow down to five hundred knots. These are vectors back to Le Bourget Airport. We will escort you to the airport. We will set up for a straight-in approach and you will land. We will maintain our position behind you and on both of your wings at all times." As he spoke, two Eagles started moving into position fifty feet off the stolen fighter's wings. The lead pilot watched them, then continued his instructions to the pilot of the stolen jet. "Do not make any aggressive or hostile motions or we will bring you down. Confirm our instructions and start turning *now*."

The Ares started turning, the aircraft gently rolling up to thirty degrees. Heading southeast, it rolled out on heading, then started to slow. The Eagles decelerated with it, but the Ares seemed to float, as if its engines did not want to slow down.

"Confirm my instructions," the formation leader repeated as the fighters slowed.

"I will comply with your instructions," the pilot in the stolen fighter said again.

The Eagle pilot hesitated.

Something in his voice . . . he didn't know . . .

He thought a moment, then saw that his aircraft had slowed to cruise speed. "Unknown rider, five hundred knots now," he said. "Descend to ten thousand feet. We will coordinate for arrival with Air Traffic Control. You stay on this frequency and comply with our instructions precisely."

He waited for some kind of response. The microphone clicked twice in reply. Satisfied, he switched his radio over to his formation radio and talked to his pilots. "Two, stay in position behind him. Looks like he's scared of our guns, which is really good because he sure isn't afraid of our missiles. You absolutely have to stay with him, stay in range of your gun. Three and four, maintain position on his wings so we can corral this guy home. I'll stay on the perch and coordinate our approach into Bourget."

The other pilots answered quickly and the pilot switched another radio over to Air Traffic Control.

"Paris Control, Howl 44 flight."

"Go, Howl," the controller shot back.

"Howl 44 has intercepted the target and is escorting the bandit back to Le Bourget. We need emergency vehicles standing by and *lots* of security. We're planning on a straight-in approach from the west, so keep the runway clear."

"Howl, confirm you have the bandit under your control?"

"Roger that, Paris. We've got the bandit in a box."

A long moment of silence. "Sierra Hotel, guys. Sierra freaking Hotel." The controller almost laughed with relief.

The F-15 pilot continued. "Howl is estimating the runway in two-nine minutes. We'll bring the bandit down for a straight-in and force him to land. We'll stay in position on his wing in order to force him to the ground if necessary. Once he's down, the Eagles will circle back around and land on the other runway. This guy is a snake, I don't trust him, so we want to do this quick."

"Roger that, Howl. We'll be waiting for you." A moment's hesitation, then the controller added thankfully, "Great job there, Howlers. The president sends his personal thanks and regards."

The Eagle pilot hesitated, shook his head, and clicked his mike.

The president? President who? Who was he talking about?

He started to question but thought better, deciding to let it go.

CECOC COMMAND CENTER
LE BOURGET AIRPORT

The command center erupted in shouts and applause. Major General Hawley stared straight ahead as he listened to the radio exchange between the Eagle pilot and ATC. President Abram moved toward him and slapped him on the back. He smiled broadly, his face cracking with relief. "Good job, Robert, good job," he repeated.

Hawley shook his hand. "Thank you, sir," he said.

"Get that sucker back on the ground, we'll take the pilot out and shoot him, then get our stolen bird back in the hangar and get out of town before something else can go wrong."

"Yes, sir," Hawley answered, though his face remained taut.

Jesse stood without moving, a disbelieving look on his face.

A couple of 1984 vintage Eagles were escorting his F-38 back to base! The pilot gave up so easily? It didn't make any sense. "Tell them to kill it," he muttered desperately, "Tell them to kill it, kill it now, while they can!"

But no one paid him attention through the shouts and the cheers.

The president slapped Hawley on the back one more time, then walked away to talk to his chief of staff.

The general glanced at his watch. A little less than thirty-nine minutes since the aircraft had been stolen. Thirty-nine minutes of adrenaline, disappointment, rage, and fear. Thirty-nine minutes of feeling the earth shake at his feet, the longest and most agonizing thirty-nine minutes of his life. He was drained and exhausted. He felt like falling on the floor.

Jesse stepped toward him, putting his hand on his arm. The general nodded to the screen. "It's almost over," he said.

Jesse hesitated. "I don't think so."

Hawley shot him an angry glare, then shook his head in disgust, sick and tired of his defeatist attitude.

INSIDE THE ARES

The pilot stared through the dark visor that covered his eyes. The oxygen mask was jammed against his face and it forced a tight crease against both of his cheeks, trapping the sweat that formed on his neck and face. He wet his lips, tasting the salt, then swallowed, forcing his ears to pop again.

He glanced left and then right. The F-15s held a tight formation directly off both of his wings, staying five, maybe ten feet off to the side. Looking up through the tinted canopy, he saw the third F-15 directly overhead and he knew that, if he were to look over his shoulder, he would see the last of the fighters hanging back at his six.

Turning forward in his ejection seat, he saw that the aircraft were descending now and, far in the distance, the greens and yellows of the French countryside gave way to dark browns, tans, and blacks as the city began to slide into view. The airport was a little more than thirty miles now before him and he swallowed again.

There was still time. If he chose to, he could turn back. He didn't have to take the last step off the gangplank. He could still turn around.

He took a deep breath and held it, a moment of uncertainty smashing against the sides of his head. His vision seemed to tumble, the self-doubts growing like a monster climbing out of the dark pit of his mind.

No! Do not do this! You have another choice!

But he knew that he didn't. It was this or nothing else.

He had prepared himself for this moment, for he knew it would come, and he fought his way through it, casting his doubts aside.

No, he didn't have to do this. It was something he *wanted* to do! He had been planning for this moment for many years and he would not turn away just because he was scared.

Many times he had faced fear, and he had always fought through it.

So he gripped the control stick, cursed the demons, and kept on flying the jet.

FOURTEEN

MARMARIS VILLAGE
SOUTHWESTERN TURKISH COAST

The men could have met almost anywhere in the world. They were, after all, two senior officers of an independent nation-state and they had the right, as free men, to travel anyplace they might choose. The fact that they represented a nation whose people were certainly less than free, that most of their citizens could only dream of ever visiting anywhere but the local rat-infested market, and that, though leaders, most of the free world considered them hardly more than common criminals with the blood of their own people on their hands, none of this stopped them from traveling around.

Besides, they were on a roll. A serious roll. And they wanted to be together to watch things unfold.

It was an indication of their supreme confidence that the conspirators had chosen to meet in a Muslim country that had fairly open relations with the West. They knew their movements would be tracked to Turkey. They knew that, despite their top-notch security forces and secret travel arrangements, the CIA and DIA would certainly know they were there. But they didn't care. They were feeling positive. And rebellious. They were confident men.

The meeting took place in a private villa south of a small Turkish village at the crossroads of the Aegean Sea, a beautiful blue and pink stucco home that jutted out almost to the turquoise-blue water and white sands on the beach. To the south, the Mediterranean sparkled with diamonds from the setting sun. To the north and west, on the other side of a small mountain range, was the Aegean Sea. A little more clear, a little less warm, it was smooth as black marble under the perfectly calm air. A narrow mountain, barely three hundred meters high, separated the two sides of the tiny peninsula, its rocky slope and dry foothills dotted with scrub oaks and junipers along the west side. Like all the villages and small towns along the Turkish coast, Marmaris was an ancient fishing village, though it had recently seen much more prosperous times. Along its sparkling beaches, some of the most powerful men in the world had built private retreats, and its reputation as a playground for wealthy Arab and European families was becoming well known.

The private road to the villa was gated and heavily patrolled, yet the homeowner had added additional layers of security beyond what the builder had provided. The seventeen-acre estate was surrounded on three sides by a ten-foot brick wall hidden behind rows and rows of tall trees. Only the ocean side of the lavish villa was exposed, and unseen guard houses had been built along the rocky coastline. From their positions, the guard shacks could monitor both sides of the beach. Overlooking the villa, a series of buried, cement bunkers looked out on the private estate. Motion sensors and audio listening devices dotted the outer perimeter. Armed guards, always hidden, were never far away.

The two men sat on a marble balcony and gazed out on the Mediterranean Sea. The younger man was in his early forties, the other more than sixty, though he looked at least ten years older than that, the hard years of fighting having taken its toll. The older man, the leader, was round, with thin hair and dark eyes. The younger man was lean and chiseled, with a square jaw and mean eyes.

Though age had taken a toll on the older man's body, making him puffy and soft, the dark fire in his soul had only grown more powerful. Knowing he would die soon—there were some things that even *his* money couldn't buy—he was even more dedicated to completing his mission before old age made him too senile to make a difference anymore.

As the two men talked, one of their aides moved toward them, a single paper in hand. "Sir, this from our trawler in the North Sea," he said, handing over the report.

The leader hesitated, then took it. "When did this come in?" he demanded.

"Less than sixty seconds ago."

The fat man read the report, which was just a few lines, then handed it to the other man and smiled as he watched him read. "He got the aircraft," he muttered as the other man placed the report on the table between them.

The younger man nodded proudly. "Did you ever doubt that he would?"

"You know that I did. And my friend, so did you."

Both men stared as they thought, taking occasional sips of their wine. For a moment they dreamed together as the breeze blew in from the sea. "He's given up, returning with the American fighters back to Le Bourget," the older man said.

"Yes, that is the first step," the younger officer reminded his master carefully. "Still, we have a long way to travel yet before we can celebrate."

"A long road, yes, my friend, but one way or another we will know where this road leads before the sun sets tomorrow night."

The younger man, the mastermind of the plan, who had bet his future and his life on the outcome of the operation, continued to stare at the diamonds of light that dazzled on the blue water. "I am hopeful," he offered, keeping his optimism in check.

The older man nodded. He wore dark glasses, but underneath the tinted glass, he still squinted from the slanting rays of the sun. He preferred large rooms and dark chambers to sitting out here in the sun. Raising his hand, he shaded his eyes, the loose skin on his underarm hanging down in a flap.

"To tomorrow then," the leader said as he lifted his glass in a toast.

"To tomorrow," the other answered, taking a sip of his wine. Then he added with sarcasm, "As the glorious day progresses, may Allah, the One God, shower us with sweet praise and delight."

The leader looked at him, dumbfounded, then broke into a wide grin. Both men started laughing. It was simply too much.

Neither of them believed in Allah or Buddha or any other god. Power was the only God they worshiped and the only thing they loved.

But like any true believers, once they had a master, they worshiped it with all of their might.

FIFTEEN

CECOC COMMAND CENTER
LE BOURGET AIRPORT

Minutes after the F-15s started escorting the stolen aircraft back toward Le Bourget, the president's chief of staff moved silently to his side. "A private moment with you, sir," he said.

The president nodded, and the two made their way to the private conference room at the back of the command center. A dark, one-way glass looked out on the commotion, but the walls were solid, the glass thick, and it was quiet inside. The chief of staff sat on the corner of the table, facing the president, who stood at the window and stared out on the command center.

The American officers had pretty much commandeered the entire command post by now, and the U.S. uniforms outnumbered the French officers by at least two to one. In addition, more than a dozen men moved through the command post wearing dark suits and white shirts, Secret Service agents always on the prowl. With no place to stand where they could stay out of the way, and unwilling to leave the president alone, they stood guard at each door and throughout the command center. The senior Secret Service agent, the president's personal detail, had followed the president to the conference room, and he stood on guard now on the other side of the doorway, not more than two feet from the glass.

The chief of staff rubbed his hands across his face and said, "Sir, I don't need to state for you the problem we have here, but out of loyalty to your legacy, I need to say this. General Hawley is your friend, but he's made a real mess. Regardless of what happens this afternoon, we've got a public relations nightmare on our hands. This could be a tipping point, Mr. President, an event which may define your eight years in office as much as anything else you have done. Every president is defined, to one extent or another, by events they wish the public would entirely forget. Hostages in Tehran, Iran-Contra, interns and grand juries, the list goes on and on.

"Now, a few weeks ago we made a decision to make a spectacular show of revealing our newest war-fighting machine. You came all the way to Paris, invited most of the significant world leaders to sit at your side, the international press, every aviation executive and their dog. Then we sat there and watched as our secret superjet takes off, flies over our heads, breaks some windows and then *disappears!* Do you have *any* idea how this is going to play in the press? We will be the laughingstock. We already are! I think we have maybe just a few hours to get this fixed and get our story straight. And what you do over the next few minutes could make a huge difference in depicting how this thing plays out."

The president continued to stare through the dark glass. "Hawley's boys have intercepted the aircraft. He's sure they will bring it home now."

"I'll believe it when our fighter is back on the ground, sir. But even then, we still have a problem. Best case, we get our fighter back and only scorn and derision are heaped upon us for being unable to secure our own supersecret jet. We still must explain why it happened and where we failed. We'll still have to investigate and explain what the thieves were planning to do. Was our new superfighter stolen for political purposes? Money? International blackmail? Sabotage? Just to embarrass the U.S.? Worst case, we find out a terrorist organization stole the Ares and was planning to use it to attack the U.S."

The COS hesitated, letting the president think. "If that is what has happened, Mr. President, there will be blood to pay. It will be impossible to survive that, politically. Your pet project will be a monster that turned around and bit off its own master's head—"

The president angrily raised his hand to cut him off. "You don't have to paint the picture for me, Edgar, I can paint it myself."

The two men stood in painful silence.

The president and Edgar Ketchum went back many years, but their friendship was strained now and based far more on mutual dependence than any affection for the other. Back in the early days, before the president had any position or power that Ketchum could take advantage of, Ketchum had determined that Abram would be somebody, some day, and had hitched his wagon hard to his friend's rising star. Since those days, Ketchum had always been the president's right-hand man, the man with the hatchet, the evil chief of staff who watched his backside. It was a role Ketchum savored almost as much as the president appreciated having him there.

But Ketchum could be so cold and calculating it sometimes made the president's skin crawl. Still, Ketchum had saved his political life too many times for him to ignore. He was the snarling Doberman that guarded his door; frothing spit, eyeing strangers, he protected the jewels. And though Abram didn't like him, at the end of the day he was always glad he was there.

Ketchum drummed his fingers impatiently while the president thought. "Sir, do you have any idea how tight the security was around our fighters?" Ketchum finally asked. "We had armed guards, motion sensors, heat detectors, the whole bit. From the moment those two aircraft touched down here in Paris, they have been constantly guarded. Then tell me, sir, how a thief walks up to our aircraft and steals it right out from under our nose. Taking it during the air show was brilliant, absolutely brilliant, otherwise it would have never got off the ground, but still, before that, someone had to remove the real pilot and get inside the aircraft without anyone stopping him. Knowing that, Mr. President, you must realize that whoever stole the fighter couldn't have done it alone."

The president didn't answer as he stared through the glass.

Ketchum dropped a thick, red binder on the table. It fell against the wood with a *slap* and the president turned.

"General Hawley is sinking in debt. Did you know that, sir?" Ketchum asked. "He's got himself in a hole that will be hard to climb out of—the divorce, all the moves, a couple bad investments to help a few friends, it's all chipped away at his assets."

"What? What is this?" Abram demanded, an angry look on his face.

"And Major James, sir. A good kid. Smart. Ambitious. Real ambitious. I mean, look how far he's come, chief test pilot of the most secret and advanced fighter ever built. Pretty good, especially for such a young kid. He grew up in group homes in L.A., did you know that, sir? We used to call them foster homes—new name, same thing—he was bounced around here and there. His old man drank more beer than water. And his mother . . ." Ketchum opened the folder, flipped through it, and pulled out a photograph. "His mother is interesting as well." He dropped a picture of a beautiful dark-haired woman on the table. "She was an illegal immigrant who found herself expecting when she was just fifteen. At twenty-six, she took off, heading back to Mexico, where she's done pretty well for herself. Her new husband is a German businessman who retired young to the Mexican Riviera. Had a little trouble with the German authorities, it seems. Before he left Germany he made a lot of money. Manufacturing. Metals. And a small but growing aeronautical engineering firm that specializes in advanced avionics. Ketchum hesitated, then added, "All sorts of advanced technologies, including stealth."

The president grunted, incredulous again.

"I've got to tell you, sir, this is one interesting guy. Every time he takes a leave, he heads off to some wild, foreign country. He's gone backpacking through Tibet, the Yucatan Peninsula, Chechnya, if you can believe it, Russia and Greece—what kind of judgment is that, exposing himself in such dangerous locations? If he was to be captured by some lunatic local terrorist and they found out who he was, what kind of position would that leave him in? We have regulations and limits on travel like that, and yet he pushes every line. He's like some homeless bum who prefers to live out of a backpack when he's not in the air. And every out-of-the-way or dangerous assignment that comes along, this guy is raising his hand. He volunteered to be an army ground liaison in Iraq, just to see the ground war. Remember, he was an army Ranger, so he's used to eating snakes, but come on! And you should see a list of his friends, some real interesting characters, I promise you that. I don't know, sir, he's just a little too . . . bohemian to me. He simply has too interesting of a background not to call a little attention to himself."

The president took a step toward Ketchum, his face white with rage. "Are you saying Major James and General Hawley had something to do with the disappearance of this jet? Are you accusing, Mr. Ketchum, because, if you are, you've got to do a whole lot better *than that!*" The president's hands were balled in anger. He was absolutely nothing if not loyal to his friends.

Which was, of course, the problem. He was loyal. Far too trusting.

Two problems Ketchum didn't have.

The chief of staff moved toward the president and stood by the glass. He smelled of sweat and coffee and some kind of cream he used to soften the dry skin on his head. "All I'm saying, Mr. President, "is we don't know—"

"That's right!" the president jabbed a finger in his chest. "You don't know squat, Edgar, you don't know squat at all. And for you to come in here with your secret folders and files, the results of your always snooping around, and to make even a hint of an accusation, to even cast an aspersion, is patently offensive. And ridiculous! I won't support you on this!"

"Sir, I just think—"

"You just think what, Mr. Ketchum? This officer, Major James, he comes from a broken background, a stupid father, a mother who had enough and decided to head back home, but instead of recognizing the incredible force of will it took to overcome that, you intend to hold it against him! He grows up in the backstreets of L.A., overcomes all these obstacles, and you consider that a *bad thing!* Heavens, man, I know what it takes to make it as a pilot, and this guy not only makes it, but makes it to the top of the pile. But he likes to travel, do a little hiking, and you think that ties him to this!"

Ketchum's face was stoic and he held the president's eyes. He was on firm ground, he knew it, and he was not going to back down. "Sir," he continued, though his voice was softer now, "whoever stole our Ares *had to have inside help!* Someone had to train him on the aircraft, teach him some of the basics at least. And how did he get through security? No way, absolutely no way, an individual—especially an Arab—could have pulled this thing off by himself. I don't care how good a pilot he is, none of that matters if he can't get in the jet, and no way he gets through security without some inside help."

Ketchum paused a moment, letting the president think, then motioned to the red folder he had placed on his desk. "One hundred and fifty-six military personnel were assigned to come here to Paris to support the Ares demonstration. They include crew chiefs, two pilots, security specialists, maintenance officers, avionics specialists, mechanics, munitions officers. At least one of them had to help in this operation. You just don't go walking up to our aircraft and steal it out from under our noses without some kind of help. It is obvious. Now we need to find out who it was."

The president fumed. The Ares wasn't even back yet, and Ketchum was scrambling to find someone to blame.

Ketchum watched the president closely. "Let Hawley concentrate on retrieving the jet," he said. "But while he's doing that, it would be very, *very* helpful if we made some progress finding out how they pulled this thing off. We retrieve the jet, make some arrests, and this story doesn't develop any legs. *Yes, the aircraft was stolen, but we got it back already and arrests have been made.* We hold a single press conference, explain this situation, make this a one-day event. But if we appear hesitant or unsure, or worse, if we seem like we are reluctant to investigate our own people, then the press will take this thing and run with it and end up who-knows-where."

The president closed his eyes wearily, running his hands across his face. "So what are you suggesting?" he demanded.

"Let me ask a few questions, Mr. President. That's all I'm asking, sir. You concentrate your efforts on retrieving the aircraft. You work with General Hawley to bring that thing back. But let me start coordinating with the FBI, CIA, military intelligence—"

The president snorted at the red dossiers. "Looks like you've already done that." His voice was thick and sarcastic.

"No, sir, not at all. Everything I have there is information that was contained in the standard annual security review. It was easily available on our White House Security Net. It only took our staff a few minutes to gather this up. But it isn't enough, not by a long shot. We've got to start digging deeper and wider, talking to more people."

The president shook his head. "This is a military operation. Hawley will have jurisdiction. When it comes to the investigation, he will be in charge."

"Fine, sir. But there's no reason we can't run our own thing."

The president hesitated. He didn't like it.

Ketchum shook his head in frustration. It was *so* clear to him. "We've got a rot on the inside, Mr. President," he said in a sharp tone. "Someone, probably several people, helped to steal that aircraft. All I'm asking, sir, is that you let me start coordinating the investigation that will root them out. Let me go and find them, Mr. President, before they do any more harm."

The president nodded slowly. "Alright," he said. "I'll talk to our people, tell them you're running the show. But keep me advised of your actions. And let me know the instant you learn anything."

The chief of staff nodded. It was all he could ask.

He started to leave, but the president grabbed his arm. "And stay away from Hawley," he instructed, his voice hard as nails. "He's one of the finest men in this government and I vouch for him myself. Don't go poking into his bank accounts or his old girlfriends. There's nothing there, you understand me?"

Ketchum stared at the president and nodded. "Of course, sir," he said.

SIXTEEN

A French police officer was waiting for Ketchum when he came out of the private meeting with the president. "Mr. Ketchum?" he asked as he moved to his side.

Ketchum glanced at his uniform and name tag. *François Villon.* Ah yes, the great poet, a wonderful hero to the French. *How splendid,* he thought sarcastically.

He studied the man—older than sixty, flushed-faced, and round. *How is* anyone *supposed to be afraid of these guys?* he thought derisively.

Villon leaned forward and whispered in his ear, and Ketchum looked surprised. "Alright," he answered quickly, then slipped away from the president and followed as the French officer pushed his way through the crowded command post. Villon nodded to the guard at the door, walked quickly to the end of the hall, then up three flights of stairs. Ketchum hurried at his side, never quite catching up until the two men came to stop outside the French policman's office.

DIRECTEUR DE SÉCURITÉ
DÉPARTEMENT DES PROBLÈMES INTERNES

was written in black letters on the white metal door.

Ketchum studied the title on the door, suspecting it was a front for a secret, all-encompassing French security organization that had its fingers everywhere.

Villon swiped his ID card through a security reader, punched in a code, and pushed open the door. Ketchum was the first to walk in and he glanced quickly around. The office was cramped and poorly furnished with metal chairs, a plastic table, a small wooden desk, and a couple of phones. Court papers and investigative reports were piled everywhere. Two doors, one on the left and one on the right, led to his deputy's office and a small administrative center. Ketchum heard several voices on the other side of the doors.

The back wall was cluttered with awards and citations from a distinguished career, along with some newspaper clippings and photographs. One framed clipping stood out from the others. The headline, a front-page article from the British paper, the *Guardian,* read:

INTERNATIONAL RAID ON SAFE HOUSE
EIGHT SUSPECTED TERRORISTS DEAD

Villon was pictured kneeling beside a body. His eyes were cold and he was frowning. Whatever Villon had done before coming to work for Transportation Security, it was clearly a whole lot more than writing parking tickets at the *Palais de Chaillot,* Ketchum realized.

A picture of the investigator's family sat on the corner of his desk: a pretty wife, much younger than her husband, two blond children, a boy and a girl. *Not bad,* Ketchum thought, *not bad at all.*

He gave the captain a second look and for the first time since meeting him, began to relax. There was something in Villon's eyes, something hard and determined, that he immediately recognized. Like one snake crawling over another, he sensed this was a man he could trust. If he was right, and he was very good at this kind of thing, this was a man whom he could do business with, who could take care of problems without screwing around.

Good. He took a step back as he stared at the *Supervisor of Security, Internal Concerns* and scoffed to himself. No. He was certain now. Villon worked for the ultrasecret, knuckle-dragging, shoot-first organization that was rarely acknowledged outside the French security world.

He motioned around him. "This is your office?" he asked.

The Frenchman hesitated. "I have several," he replied. "One downtown. A couple others."

Bingo, Ketchum thought.

Villon pulled out a cigarette, offered the pack to Ketchum, who declined, then lit up a smoke. "We just received a security video from the hotel where your pilots were staying," the French officer began to explain as he moved around to his desk. "The images are typical security quality, five frames a second, black-and-white. You can make out the faces, but there are no . . . how do you like to say . . . no Kodak moments here." He tapped at the keyboard and moved his mouse, then turned his flat-screen monitor so that Ketchum could see.

Ketchum sat in front of the monitor and watched, sometimes leaning until his nose was no more than a foot from the screen. The overhead lights reflected off his glossy head and he sucked air through his nostrils, which whistled as he breathed. The French security officer sat down at his side, and Ketchum sniffed at the cigarette smell on his clothes and breath.

He watched the entire length of the security video, which was less than sixty seconds, then leaned back in his metal chair. "Again," he commanded. Villon clicked his mouse. The COS watched. "One more time," he said.

After watching three times, he turned to the Frenchman. "Can you send this down to a computer at the CECOC?" he asked.

The French officer nodded.

"Do it, please, *Monsieur,*" he said as he stood from his chair.

Five minutes later, General Hawley and Major James were huddled around a small monitor. Captain Villon and Mr. Ketchum stood behind them, ready to watch the security tape.

"We've don't have a lot of footage," Villon explained before it rolled. "All of the security cameras on the hotel's fourth floor where the pilot was staying were incapacitated, tazed with an electric probe that rendered them useless, it appears. As surveillance cameras get more common, we're seeing more and more of this kind of thing. They use an instrument—kind of like a cattle prod—that fries all the wiring inside the camera, a simple thing to do.

"They didn't, however, incapacitate the surveillance cameras in the stairwell. Forgot about them, I would guess, though they might have been mounted too high for them to reach. We only have one camera angle, but it's not too bad." He clicked on the keyboard and the digital file started to play.

Jesse watched, his face grim. Hawley stared at the monitor as well. The camera looked down from near the ceiling on the stairwell. The images were gray and jerky, but clear enough to see everything. The camera showed an empty stairwell, a young woman in a maid's uniform walking up, a few seconds of nothing, then the abductors on the stairs.

Jesse gasped as four men came into view.

Colonel Ray, United States Air Force, commander, ARES Test and Evaluation, was hustled down a dark and narrow flight of stairs, his hands hanging at his sides. Two men held him on each arm, and he appeared to be drugged. No resistance. No fight. He barely lifted his feet. Another man led the way, a small gun in his hand. All of the men wore dark glasses, white shirts, black pants, Western loafers. Two had short beards, but the leader was clean-shaven, with short hair.

The video went blank for two or three seconds, then came back again. Another security video from the next level on the stairs. Colonel Ray barely moving now. He was sinking fast. The two men at his side were holding him under his arms and he was dragging his feet.

Another two seconds of blackness, then the final flight of stairs. Ray appeared to be unconscious now, his head slumped down to his chin, his feet dragging behind him, his toes spread awkwardly to the side. The two men had to use both hands to hold him as they pulled him along.

The video was over.

The four men sat back. Jesse stared straight ahead, a dumbfounded look on his face.

"Adar Ushar is the man on the right side of your pilot," Villon started. "He's Syrian by birth. Has strong ties to Hamas. Spends most his time in Gaza and Iran, who finances his operations. The other man with your pilot is Hammid Al-Kalid. Jordanian. Spent three years working as an advisor to the insurgents in Iraq." The officer cleared his throat uncomfortably. "He lives here in Paris now. Been watching him for some time, though he's been pretty low on our priority list. The other men we don't know but we're trying very hard to find out."

Jesse started to speak, but his voice only croaked. The other men stared at him, waiting for the words to come out.

"This particular stairwell opens on a side street at the north side of the hotel," Villon explained when Jesse didn't say anything. "But we don't have any footage on the outside, for that surveillance camera was incapacitated as well."

Jesse lifted his hands, as if asking for silence, his face a white as the dead. Villon waited again, expecting him to say something, but when Jesse turned his back on the group he went on. "We've already digitized the photographs. Sometime in the next hour, ten thousand of these photographs will be circulated through all of our security agencies—the *Directeur Central de la Police Judiciaire, Directeur Central de la Sécurité Publique, Directeur Général de la Police Nationale.* We are coordinating with Interpol as well. Most importantly, however, the *Directeur de la Centrale du Contrôle de l'Immigration et de la Lutte contre l'Emploi des Clandestins* has taken personal responsibility . . ."

Jesse rubbed his eyes with his fists, then dropped his hands and turned back to the men. "I know him," he announced, his voice so thick and disbelieving it was hard to understand what he said.

"What?" Hawley pressed him.

"I know him!" Jesse cried, pointing to the video. "That other man on the screen."

The four men stared.

"Run it again," Jesse said.

The French police started the file.

The empty stairwell. The maid. The four men hustling down the stairs, the point man in the lead, his two goons behind him, Colonel Ray in their arms. "Stop! Stop right there!" Jesse cried, jabbing a finger at the screen. The Frenchman tapped the mouse. Jesse pointed at the first man. "Prince Abdul Mohammad bin Saud," he said.

"Who?" Ketchum asked in a disbelieving tone.

"Prince Abdul Mohammad bin Saud," Jesse repeated. "He's some kind of relation, a nephew or second cousin, to the king of Saudi Arabia. He's one of a dozen little princelings that run around the kingdom, jockeying for position, building their own mini-kingdoms, positioning themselves to be king."

Ketchum shook his head in disbelief. "Where did you meet him?" he demanded.

"Euro-NATO training in Texas. It's a program we set up to train foreign pilots. We train lots of Arabs, Jordanians, Saudis, Egyptians, Iraqis now, a few from Pakistan. The crown prince of Saudi Arabia has started to use it like his own private pilot school. If you're a member of the royal family, you're almost guaranteed to get a slot. Like a lot of the young princes, Abdul Mohammad bin Saud was admitted into the Royal Saudi Air Force and sent here for military pilot training. We flew together for almost four months."

Ketchum shook his head and stared. "Unbelievable," he muttered.

Such a coincidence, he thought in sarcastic disbelief.

"Gentlemen, this is most excellent," the French captain said, oblivious to Ketchum's stares. "We've got a name. An identity. You can get down to work."

"Get down to work. Are you kidding?" Jesse mocked. "This guy is a pilot, don't you get it! He's *up* there in *my* jet! And let me tell you something, gentlemen, this guy is as good as it gets. If anyone could steal the Ares and fly it, this is one guy who could. He's a truly gifted pilot. Could fly rings around most anyone. He's aggressive and ambitious. No, this guy is *mean*! He'd drop a nuke if he had one, I promise you that! He hates America and everything we stand for. He used to openly laugh about it. He hated our country and yet we still had to train him because the king asked us to. We trained an enemy of our country because the State Department insisted it was the proper thing to do! Calling it ironic isn't strong enough. He laughed about our stupidity every day."

The other men were quiet. Hawley slowly took a breath.

Jesse turned toward him, his eyes pleading now. He thought of the Ares. It was still out there, flying toward them, U.S. Eagles off each wing. "Please sir, you've got to tell those F-15 guys to take this guy out while they can."

Hawley shook his head. "But we've got him now."

"You don't have him, General Hawley! You know the Ares! No F-15 guy could ever really have him."

"Look!" Hawley answered. "We've got this guy completely surrounded. You say that he's good, and I don't doubt that, but he's sitting in an aircraft that he's *never flown before!* And it's not just another fighter, it's the most sophisticated weapon on earth. I don't believe, and the evidence supports me on this, Major James, that this guy, prince or not, knows how to use the weapon systems on that jet. He tried to steal the aircraft and make a dash for it, but we caught him. Simple as that. We got him caged now, surrounded, and they are on their way home. Why, then, should I order our guys to shoot him down? We've got a chance to save our aircraft. That's the priority now."

Jesse looked away, his fists clenched in rage.

This was more than stupid!

If Hawley was wrong, this was suicide!

SEVENTEEN

HIGHWAY A1
ELEVEN KILOMETERS NORTH OF LE BOURGET AIRPORT

The French driver saw the explosion as he came around a gentle bend in the road. Startled, he jerked his wheel to the right, straightened, then rolled to a stop as he watched. He felt the gut-thumping *booom* several seconds after seeing the first flash of light and fireball. Peering through his windscreen, he watched the rising fireball, large and rolling, boiling with heat and flame. Fire rolled into red heat and the smoke was black and thick as it climbed into the sky. He swore in wonder, put the car into gear, and moved cautiously toward the scene.

The Mercedes was completely engulfed in deep flame. The paint was gone, the windows shattered, every piece of plastic or rubber blown off or scorched into char. The smoke cast a long shadow as it lifted with the heat, the calm air allowing the billowing blackness to rise vertically toward the pale sky. Fascinated, the Frenchman stared for several seconds before he finally came to his senses and reached for his cell phone to call the police.

The French authorities, already on hair-trigger alert for the G-8 summit meeting, were quick to respond. Fire/rescue and an ambulance were quickly dispatched.

Twenty minutes later, the fire was out and the charred remains of the car sat on the side of the road, an obscene hunk of burned metal. The tires were charred to the rims and the only thing that remained of the interior seats were burned metal springs and steel frames. The plastic on the dashboard and the fabric headliners were gone, leaving hunks of melted plastic on the floor.

The blackened hulk of the Mercedes sat like a burned-out skeleton against the backdrop of green trees and grass that lined the side of the road.

Beneath it, the gravel was baked brown, and the oil in the road had boiled out and gathered in a pool of black ooze underneath the front wheel.

By the time that the forensic investigators arrived on the scene, the police had cordoned off the area with yellow tape and red cones.

The chief investigator was a surprisingly old woman with salt-and-pepper hair and round legs underneath a tight, blue police uniform that seemed uncharacteristically un-French. Half a dozen policemen ignored her as she started looking around. All business, she toed a straight line, and they were more than happy to leave her to her gruesome task.

Dozens of little red flags had already been placed across the ground, marking the body pieces that had been located so far. Torn hunks of charred flesh scattered in a circle around the burned car, and the French captain moved carefully, knowing the smallest piece of evidence might be hidden in the grass or the dirt. At the rear of the car, she looked up. The trees nearest the road had been scorched, the leaves brown and brittle from the heat of the flames, and she noted a few scattered pieces of metal imbedded in one of the lowest branches. Above the metal was a piece of leather—looked to be a shred of seat cover—with a piece of bloody skin still attached. She motioned to one of the uniformed policemen, who nodded and waved to the fire truck and started walking toward it. A ladder was pulled from the side of the truck and the uniformed officer climbed up to tag the evidence.

On the passenger side of the car, the investigator stopped and stooped over. The red flag at her feet was marked B-3: B for the second victim, the man in the front seat, passenger side of the car, and 3 for the third piece of body that had been located on the ground.

It was a man's finger from the first knuckle down. A ring was still attached to the finger, and she couldn't help but frown. Reaching into her jacket, she pulled out a set of latex gloves, pulled them on with a snap, opened a small bag, pulled out a set of metal tweezers and lifted the dead man's finger, holding it by a fold of torn skin. Caucasian, fingernail short and clean, flesh puffy, a little wrinkled: a middle-aged man. The ring held on to the flesh, and she rotated the finger to get a better look. It was a gold ring with a moderate-sized ruby and a couple of small diamonds on the side. Nothing elegant, and she frowned again as she read the writing etched around the outer rim of the ring.

CR
USAFA
1984

She studied it a moment, then motioned to an assistant and showed him the ring. He shook his head and hunched. He didn't know what it meant. Examining the piece of flesh, he touched it with the tip of his finger and she pulled it away.

"Interesting," he muttered curiously.

"What's that?" she asked.

He pointed to the exceptionally clean cut on the finger and the neatly trimmed piece of bone. "It's such a perfect separation. With the power of the explosion, I would have expected more tearing of the flesh and fractures or cracks in the bone."

She nodded at his ignorance. A perfectly understandable amateur mistake. "You make the mistake of assuming the finger was separated from the hand in the explosion," she explained. "That was not the case. The hand, fingers still attached, perhaps an entire arm, was pushed through the window at a velocity greater than the speed of sound. The finger was cut away from the hand by a flying shard as it passed through the glass."

The assistant nodded slowly. "So then we should be able to find the rest of the hand out here somewhere, sans a finger, I guess."

"Bet on it. The rest of that hand is out here, I'm sure."

The assistant nodded. He was new, she was the master, and once again he was awed.

So much to learn. So much yet to know.

The forensic investigator studied the finger again. "I think he's an American," she said.

The assistant leaned toward her. "Madame?" he asked.

She pointed to the ring. "Check the font. Big, bulky letters. I don't know, it just looks foreign to me."

Again he slowly nodded, then turned back to his work, cataloging the remains.

The woman held the piece of finger up to the dimming light, then returned it to the ground where she had picked it up. It would be placed into evidence along with everything else: the tattered torso, the skin on the leather seat cover that had landed in the tree, the hulk of burned-out metal, the entire crime scene.

As she stood, her assistant walked quickly back toward her, an anxious look on his face. "Let me see the ring," he said as he dropped to his knees. She bent down with him. Grabbing her tweezers, he lifted the finger again, turning it in the light, his face taut and grim. "U.S. Air Force Academy. Class of nineteen-eighty-four," he said.

She glanced at the ring and then nodded. "I suppose that's one of several thousand possible meanings," she suggested, a little perturbed she had not thought of it herself.

He shook his head again. "No, I am certain, Madame. We had a general alert less than an hour ago. You might not have seen it; it went to the field offices and checkpoints. There was an incident at the airport during the G-8 summit and the Paris Air Show. They are looking for an American pilot. They believe he might have been taken hostage—"

"They believe! They only believe?"

"It was very vague, Madame. They know that he is missing, but the message was circumspect and extremely vague. I paid it little attention, but now, when I look at this . . ."

She took the tweezers from him and stood as she stared. "*Oui, oui,*" she muttered softly. "You might be right, you might be right."

Glancing to the passenger side of the exploded vehicle, she studied the tattered remains of what was left inside. It was only parts and pieces of a body, the hips, part of two legs, not much else. And most of it was burned all the way to the bone. She pressed her lips. "This won't be easy," she said.

Still, her assistant was excited. "But he is U.S. military. They'll certainly have DNA samples available. All soldiers have to submit DNA for identification."

She nodded her head. "Yes, yes. Give a call down to Des Champs Elysées. Tell them to get in contact with the Americans and we'll see if you're right."

EIGHTEEN

CECOC COMMAND CENTER
LE BOURGET AIRPORT

The formation of fighters flew toward Bourget Airport. All of the arrangements had been made to receive them. Jesse sat alone at a table listening to the intense work going on in the CECOC. With nothing to do, he felt useless. To make matters worse, the conversations between him and Hawley had turned very tense, the general starting to freeze him out from what was going on.

That was fine. Get the aircraft back. That's all he cared about.

He heard the general's voice behind him and quickly stood up. "CIA and the guys from State have got some information on your old friend Prince bin Saud from our embassy in Riyadh," the general said. "Seems the prince was recently disciplined by his father, one of the eight Saudi princes vying to be the next king. He's pissed off a lot of people in the kingdom in a very bad way—his own father, his uncle, the Saudi king. Half of his cousins want to kill him. He's not very popular right now."

"Hmm," Jesse said, "a pretty respectable list of enemies."

Hawley nodded.

Jesse reached into his chest pocket and took out a stick of gum. "I am not surprised," he said as he tore it in two and put half a piece in his mouth. "Like I said, this is one disagreeable SOB."

"There's more," Hawley continued. "The embassy has confirmed—and someone had to beat this out of the Saudis, I'm sure—that the kingdom has listed the young pilot as AWOL. It's been almost four months since he has been seen. He was added to their watch list more than six weeks ago."

"His own people are after him?"

"Looks that way, Jes."

"They put them on their own watch list? They listed him as a threat?"

"Family breakups can be ugly."

Jesse cocked his head. "You know the Saudi watch list is a death list. Anyone on the watch list, if they're caught, are never heard from again. Royal family or not, this guy is as good as dead. He can never go back to the kingdom. And bin Saud is no fool."

Hawley nodded and let his eyes drop to the floor. "How did this guy get through our security? How could so much go so wrong? It just doesn't make any sense."

Jesse didn't say anything. Hawley didn't expect an answer; he was just berating himself.

The general ground his teeth, then looked up. "The French guy, what's his name?"

"Villon."

"Yeah. He and Ketchum have been meeting. Apparently they received a call at the communications center just a few minutes ago. Some police officers found something on a road north of here. A car bomb, it looks like. Haven't identified any bodies, but apparently they found parts of a finger with what they think is an Air Force Academy ring still attached."

Jesse nodded slowly. "The boss wore his all the time."

"Class of 'eighty-four."

Jesse nodded.

"These guys chose a real nasty way to get rid of him."

"Trying to make it impossible, or at least difficult, to identify the body, no doubt." Jesse's eyes drifted away, looking at nothing.

Hawley hesitated, a pained look on his face. "Someone's going to have to call his wife. I mean, we'll wait for confirmation on the body, but someone's got to call her."

Jesse folded his arms across his chest, his flight suit pulling tight around his waist. "Mortuary Affairs back in the States will send someone—you know, sir, the chaplain, the base commander—they'll gather up a few of her friends . . ."

"I know, I know, but I'm going to have to call her as well. I've got to let her know how it happened, tell her how I feel."

"It's a tough one," Jesse muttered.

Hawley clenched his teeth and looked away. "So many men, sacrificing so much . . ."

Jesse stared at him. Who was he talking about? The dead colonel or himself?

A liaison from French security moved quickly toward the general and spoke in his ear. Jesse couldn't hear what he told him, but he watched Hawley's face. The general turned back toward him. "The jets are getting close now," he said.

Jesse nodded to south. "Are you still going to go up to the airport tower to watch them land?"

"Yes. I've already called for a driver." The general hesitated. "The president wants to go up there as well."

Jesse shook his head, wishing the president would just stay where he was. There was no reason for him to be up there; it was dangerous and an imposition on those who were trying to work. But what the president wanted, the president got, and he didn't even consider suggesting the president stay in the command post.

The two men were quiet a moment. Jesse turned to the ATC screen, growing more agitated with each agonizing second that passed.

It wasn't right. It was too easy. This guy *wasn't* giving up! Not now. Not like this.

He watched the radar. The inbound formation of fighters was now depicted as a blue triangle on the screen. He shifted his weight, bouncing on the balls of his feet as he pictured his Ares tucked between the F-15s. He stared as long as he could stand it, then turned his back on the screen.

General Hawley moved past him and watched the ATC relay. He pulled on his chin in worry, then burped into his fist. "I'll meet the president at the tower," he then said. "Once the Ares has been forced to land, I want you to go down and secure it, get it back in the hangar, and put the security plan back in place."

Jesse didn't answer.

"U.S. security forces will take the pilot into custody. I told them I didn't want him hurt. Once we have him, we can take a few minutes to discuss how we present this episode to the press."

Again there was no answer. Hawley cocked his head, looking partway over his shoulder, waited for a "yes, sir," then turned around again.

He was startled, looking left and right, then took a couple steps toward the middle of the command post.

But Jesse wasn't there.

NINETEEN

LE BOURGET AIRPORT

Jesse ran the half kilometer to the flightline, turned right, and slowed to a very fast but less conspicuous walk. As he passed through the open door of the French hangar, he glanced down at his watch. Twelve minutes, maybe less, until the Ares showed up at the base. He glanced around anxiously, his eyes adjusting to the dim light. A group of Frog officers and airmen were talking under the wing of a French Mirage, but he didn't recognize any of them, and his heart sank like a rock. One of the French officers noticed his U.S. flight suit, nodded to the others, and they all turned to stare. Jesse nodded, his breath catching, then saw a bulky and bald-headed captain move toward the others from the back of the hanger. "Marcos Mathieu," he called out in relief.

The French pilot stopped and turned. Jesse called his name again, then started running toward him.

Recognizing him, the Frenchman flashed a look of surprise, glanced toward his fellow pilots, then moved toward him. "Man, what's up with your aircraft," he started in heavily accented English. "We've been locked down here, did you know that? Hearing all sorts of wild rumors, Jesse. What's going on, my friend?"

Jesse stopped in front of him and hesitated.

The French Mirage pilot studied his face, then nodded toward the open hangar door. "Quit a show," he offered. "That aeroplane, what do you call it, that Ares . . . an incredible aircraft. I was talking with my boys. None of us had any idea such a machine really existed. You dropped our pants on that one, I assure you—"

Jesse raised a hand to cut him off. "Marcos, I need a favor."

The pilot raised an eyebrow. "I don't suppose you're looking to gin up another poker game," he wondered dryly.

Jesse's eyes darted to the other pilots and maintenance workers standing under the wing of the jet, then turned back to his friend.

Captain Mathieu looked anything but French; the sleeves on his flight suit were scrunched up past his elbows. Dark, hairy arms. Shiny head. A too-long moustache. And he was big. A hairy Ukrainian, Jesse thought, not knowing that Marcos's mother, an imported worker from Kiev, would have been proud that he had recognized the ethnicity of her son.

"How long have we know each other, Marcos?" Jesse asked.

The French captain thought. "Four, five years, I guess. Since that joint-NATO exercise in Canada. I bailed you out when those four MiGs almost—"

"Yeah, I remember. Now listen to me, Marcos. This is what I need . . ."

HOWL 44 FLIGHT
SEVENTY-TWO MILES NORTHWEST OF LE BOURGET AIRPORT

The formation continued toward the airport. All civilian air traffic had already been cleared out of the airspace to allow a clear path for their arrival. Inside the Air Traffic Control Center, the controllers worked with each other to coordinate all the clearances for the emergency approach. Fire trucks and emergency vehicles had already been deployed, and security forces were now positioned in place. French-made assault vehicles along with U.S. armored security carriers waited at the side of every taxiway, turnoff, and runway. A set of FBI SWAT/hostage teams were waiting, ready to take the Ares pilot into custody.

LE BOURGET AIRPORT

"Tell me about your aircraft," Jesse said.

Marcos Mathieu proudly patted the side of his jet. Like all pilots, it was a metal thing of beauty, half mistress, half machine. "The Mirage is a fine aircraft," he began. "Mach one-point-four, a mix of air-to-air missiles and bombs. You can—"

"I know all that, Marcos, but that's not what I meant. What I really need to know . . ." Jesse's voice trailed off. The other pilots had gathered around him and he kept his words low. Glancing at his watch, he swallowed in desperation again. The minutes were ticking. No more time to spare. "Listen to me, Marcos." He leaned toward his friend. "Why weren't you scrambled earlier to go after our stolen jet?"

"For one thing, at the time, we were surrounded by a quarter of a million terrified and nearly deaf civilians," the French pilot replied. "Besides that, we didn't have alert duty, which was assigned to our squadron mates down south, as you certainly must know since I hear you have scrambled our boys to go after your jet.

"Disappointingly, we were assigned to the air show. You know the deal . . . we pull our jet out for the crowd and stand around it, sign a few autographs for kiddies, check out the babes, try to look good in our flight suits, put on a good face for the military recruiters . . ."

Jesse turned and stared at the jet. It was loaded with fuel; he could tell that from how low she sat on her struts. He glanced up at the wingtips, then bent to the undercarriage. The Mirage 2000 had nine hardpoints for weapons: five on the fuselage and two on each wing. He also knew that the dual-seat model carried two internally mounted thirty-millimeter guns. More importantly, the Mirage was already loaded with four MBDA Sky Flash air-to-air missiles.

Turning back to the other pilot, he said, "What would it take to get your jet in the air?"

Marcos had expected the question, even hoped the American would be so foolish as to ask. "An order from my air wing commander," he said.

"Any chance we could, you know, take a little ride?"

The hairy-armed pilot smiled. "A little ride? Or an intercept?"

Jesse glanced anxiously at the deep sky through the open hangar door. "We intercepted the stolen aircraft and they are on their way back."

The other pilot whistled, shaking his head. "Amazing. From what I saw, I thought that thing would be over China by now."

"It should have been. It could have been. But it's on its way back.

"Now it would help me, it would help *us,* if we could . . . you know, add one more friendly aircraft to the mix."

The French pilot shrugged. "It seems to me," he started to say.

"Listen Marcos, I love you baby, and I'd love to stand here and talk. But I *really* need to know now." He pulled out his cell phone. "Call your air boss," he said.

The French pilot shook his head. "No way, man. Can't go bothering the head ho-ho just for a joy ride, my friend. You got your stolen aircraft surrounded. It's on its way home. You don't need us, Jesse. What do I tell the old man?"

"Tell him this," Jesse answered as he leaned toward him. "Tell him that Ares is not going to land here, I am certain of that. Tell him his base and his people are about to come under attack. I'd bet my life on it if I have to. Go ahead. Call your commander. Tell him what I said."

HOWL 44 FLIGHT

SEVENTEEN MILES NORTHWEST OF LE BOURGET AIRPORT

The formation of five fighters had been cleared down to five thousand feet and told they were clear to maneuver, pilot's discretion, to land on any of the airport's runways they chose. The American F-15s stayed close to the Ares, an aircraft a few feet from each wing, the leader fifty feet behind and number four, twenty feet above.

The airport looked like a crisscross of white ribbons, but the main runway could be seen clearly once the aircraft were inside of ten miles. The air was clear, with a broken layer of clouds above them, a little smog over the city, and the winds blowing gently from out of the east.

The formation descended slowly, then leveled off at three thousand feet and began to slow down. Pushing up the power, the major nudged his fighter forward and off to the right side of the Ares, staying above the stolen aircraft as his wingman slid out to give him a little room. He stared into the cockpit. The Ares pilot wore a gray helmet much like his, with the oxygen mask secured across his face and the dark visor down. The cockpit—all glass displays and CRTs in front of a highly angled ejection seat—was spectacular: clean, simple ergonomics, logical displays, and touch-screen commands. The difference between his 1970s vintage cockpit and the newest-generation fighter was stark.

Dropping back, the pilot studied the Ares all the way to the tail. The fighter seemed to float when the Eagles wanted to sink and easily maintained its airspeed even at minimum power. Slipping under the aircraft, he studied the belly of the jet, noting the black protrusion at the nose, the glasslike, rotating nub. He remembered how the mysterious fighter had rolled, pushed against the turn, then made his four missiles disappear. A tiny shiver ran through him. It was a beautiful machine.

Beautiful like a viper: shiny, sleek, and mean.

The major slipped back into position at the rear of the formation, concentrating on flying his jet.

Because he didn't know how much speed the stolen fighter needed to maintain during its approach, he let the Ares pilot set the pace as it flew toward the runway.

At three miles and one thousand feet above the airport, the five fighters began to descend. The runway loomed before them, almost ten thousand feet long. The approach lights began to shine through the afternoon sun and the white runway markings became very clear. The perimeter fence that surrounded the airport passed under the nose of the major's F-15. The rabbit lights flashed, guiding the aircraft toward the runway, and the Visual Slope Indicators told him they were on a nearly perfect approach. He proudly watched his formation of Eagles, his pilots maintaining their positions off the Ares' wings. Five hundred feet and descending. The pilot began to drift back.

The two Eagles on each wing would fly with the F-38 all the way to the ground, staying in position until the aircraft actually touched down. Once it was on the runway, they would push their throttles forward and take to the air again, then circle around the airport and set up to land.

Three hundred feet and descending. His radio crackled to life. "Howl flight and unknown rider, you are at decision height now. Check gear down, cleared to land.

"Unknown rider, these instructions are for you: land on the main runway and come to a stop. Shut down your engines, raise your canopy, and remain in your aircraft with both hands visible on the canopy rail. Do not attempt to egress the aircraft. Any attempt to deviate from these instructions will be met with deadly force.

"Eagles, once the unknown rider is down you're cleared for the touch-and-go, then any runway you choose."

"Roger, gear down, cleared to land," the lead pilot answered back.

General Hawley and three military officers stood on the steel walkway that wrapped around the outside of the top of the airport control tower. Hawley looked around awkwardly, wishing that Jesse were there.

"Any word from Major James?" he shouted to one of his aides.

A young captain shook his head. "Nothing, sir. He isn't answering his cell phone.

Hawley swore in frustration, wondering where the Ares pilot could be, then turned and looked up, focusing again on the sky.

The president remained inside the control tower—the Secret Service wouldn't let him out on the bridge—but he watched the aircraft as they approached, staring through the dark glass, his eyes never leaving the formation of gray fighters.

The airport was quiet and a breeze blew, whistling through the dozens of antennas on the roof of the tower.

General Hawley felt the gentle wind blow through his hair. He was sweating but his face remained calm. A determined colonel leaned toward him. "It's not too late, sir," he said, "you could still take it down."

Hawley shook his head. "I don't want to hear it," he answered curtly.

"Sir, I think Jesse has a point . . . we could still take it down."

Hawley snapped his head fiercely, then took a step away.

The aircraft were just emerging through the haze and, through a small speaker above the catwalk, they heard the tower controller clear the formation to land.

Hawley kept his eyes on the fighters.

He thought of Jesse's warning and shuddered.

Was it possible he was wrong? He swallowed anxiously, a sudden surge of self-doubt flooding his mind.

Had it wrapped up *too* easily?
What had he overlooked?

MIRAGE 59
SOUTH OF LE BOURGET AIRPORT

The French Mirage 2000 circled at twenty-four thousand feet, hiding in and out of the clouds. All of its sensors were inactive, as Jesse insisted on not giving away their position, and the two pilots listened to the radio calls between the F-15s and the controllers at Air Traffic Control.

Jesse sat in the backseat of the twelve-year old aircraft (a youngster of a fighter in aircraft years) and strained to see over the shoulder of the French captain before him. The back of the ACES II ejection seat obstructed his view, and a thick pane of Plexiglas separated the front and rear cockpit. Hoses, pneumatic lines, and electrical wires ran up both sides of the glass, limiting his visibility even more. Marcos rolled to 120 degrees of bank and let the aircraft slip into the clear air below. Jesse gripped a canvas handhold on the upper side of the cockpit and pulled himself forward. "You got a tally!" he demanded, his voice low and tense. He wanted to take the stick and maneuver the aircraft so that he could see, but he kept his hands away. Marcos had been very specific as they had climbed into the aircraft. "Keep your hands off my airplane unless I tell you to! If I have a heart attack and slump over or if I happen to eject, then feel free to do whatever you want with my jet. Any other time, keep your grubby little hands away from my controls. If I need your help, I will ask you, but don't count on it, friend."

He had smiled as he said it, but Jesse knew he was serious. Pilots were a jealous bunch, and as protective of their aircraft as they were of their little girls.

"Got that?" Marcos had repeated, one foot resting on the ladder positioned on the side of the cockpit.

"Got it," Jesse had answered as they had scrambled into the jet.

As they dipped below the scattered layer of clouds, Jesse strained against his seat again, trying to locate the incoming fighters, Marcos lifted his hand and pointed. "Tally. Nine o'clock. Can you see them?"

"No joy."

Marcos jammed the right rudder pedal, canting the nose off to one side. The sideslip maneuver allowed Jesse to see through the side of his cockpit, and he instantly found the formation of fighters flying toward the base.

"Eagles and unknown rider," he then heard the Air Traffic Controller say, "descend to two thousand feet. Cleared for the visual. You may maneuver, pilot's discretion, to any runway you choose. Winds two-three-zero at eight, gust to twelve. Altimeter two-niner-niner-five. Stay on this frequency for Tower. Cleared to land."

"Copy all," the formation leader called back.

Jesse listened and thought, considering everything that had happened since the Ares had taken off. He considered the chase, the intercept, the return flight back to Le Bourget. He glanced at the digital clock on the panel. Less than an hour had passed.

The formation was northwest of the airfield, setting up for a straight-in visual approach to land. The French pilot let out the slip and began a gentle turn. "Looks like they got him," he said, noting the incredibly tight formation of American fighters that surrounded the stolen jet. "He's boxed in like a pair of my mother's new shoes. He isn't going anywhere, Jesse James. Much to my disappointment, I think we're wasting our time."

Thirty seconds later, Jesse nodded, his ill-fitting, borrowed French oxygen mask and helmet bobbling on his head. "Could be," was all he said.

Marcos turned the jet and flew to a point that would allow him to come in from the south, keeping out of the formation's flight path.

The two pilots watched the formation descend and slow down. The Ares dropped its gear, the F-15s followed suit. Slowing, the American fighters tucked even closer to the stolen jet.

"I'll hang out here," Marcos said to Jesse, his voice slightly muffled through his oxygen mask. "We'll watch how it goes, but it's looking like we're the wallflowers at the dance. And if we don't get any action, I'll be in a bad mood."

"Don't count yourself out too fast, Marcos. One never knows when some shy girl is going to get the courage to ask us for a dance."

The other pilot only nodded, clearly disappointed at the prospect of not getting in a fight.

"Let's tighten it up, can we, Marcos?" Jesse asked while resisting the temptation to take the controls. "Get a little closer to the Ares. Just a mile or two."

The French pilot hesitated. "You know my instructions. We're to stay out of the way unless something goes desperately wrong. If we screw this up and make the Ares pilot panic, they'll boil us for lunch."

"Just a couple miles for me, Marcos. If not two miles, give me one. If not that, then I'm asking for a couple thousand feet."

The pilot hesitated, then moved both throttles forward just an inch. Jesse felt the aircraft accelerate and leaned back in his seat.

The Mirage approached the airport slowly, coming in from the south, ninety degrees from where the F-15s and the Ares were setting up to land. Moving to look over the front seat again, Jesse strained to keep an eye on the fighters, which were four miles up ahead. They slowed. They descended. Less than five hundred feet above the runway.

He sat back and wondered.

Had the general been right? Was the Ares giving up?

HOWL 44

The F-15 pilot mentally shot through his landing checklist for the third or fourth time: gear, flaps, speed, angle of attack, weapons secure . . .

Two hundred feet now and descending. The approach lights at the end of the runway passed under his wings, then the perimeter road at the end of the hammerhead, then the dark asphalt overrun that extended from the end of runway cement.

A hundred feet. His aircraft wobbled slightly as it flew into ground effect. There was barely enough room on the runway for all three fighters to land, and the F-15 pilots on the stolen fighter's wing closed in even tighter as they slowed to touchdown speed.

The end of the runway passed under the nose of his aircraft. The major tightened up on the Ares, giving it nowhere to go.

It was trapped. It was over. The stolen aircraft *had* to set down.

For the first time since taking off, the F-15 pilot began to relax. Releasing his grip on the control stick, he took a deep breath.

The Ares touched down with a puff of white smoke from its tires. It held its nose up, using the underside of its wings like a sail to help slow it down, then lowered the nose to the runway and began to roll out.

The Ares was halfway down the runway and slowing. Dozens of security and emergency trucks lined both sides of the runway, their lights flashing, and they started accelerating alongside the aircraft as it rolled by.

With the Ares on the ground, the F-15s hit their afterburners. Pulling up their noses, they lifted into the air and sucked up their gear. The leader had stayed above and behind the formation and he hung back, allowing the other F-15s to climb. Accelerating very quickly—they had burned a good part of their fuel—the F-15s raced to 250 knots and climbed to 1,000 feet. Last in line, the major snapped the lever to suck up his gear and accelerated too, following the other fighters into the sky.

He took another breath, feeling the firm pressure of his ejection seat against his back.

It was over. The Ares was back on the ground.

Then he saw the Ares accelerating below him.

And he knew he was dead.

Hawley watched as the fighters flew a standard approach, slowing, decelerating, descending. At three miles, they dropped their gear. Continuing their descent, they lined up on the runway, passed over the threshold, and touched down. The Ares held nose-high a few seconds, then lowered its front gear to the ground.

He bit his lip, his shoulders slumping.

His baby was home.

"Gotcha!" he muttered under his breath.

As the F-38 slowed, the F-15s pushed up their power. In seconds, all four Eagles accelerated in front of the stolen aircraft and lifted back into the air, the sound of their engines shattering the quiet afternoon. Emergency vehicles and security vans fell in behind the stolen fighter. The Eagles passed the tower and climbed to one thousand feet, soft blue flames shooting from the backs of their engines.

Then Hawley heard another sound.

And he almost felt sick.

The powerful roar of the Ares engines accelerating pushed him back against the rail.

In full afterburner, the Ares gathered speed so quickly it seemed to leap into the sky. With two thousand feet of runway still before it, it pulled its nose into the air, sucked up its gear, and retracted its flaps.

The Ares was chasing the four Eagles now, a quarter mile behind them. Hawley almost screamed as he watched, his stomach churning in acid. The Ares turned its nose on the closest fighter. There was no missile, no flash of light, nothing to indicate the attack, but as he watched, his mouth open, the Eagle exploded in flames, the fuel inside its belly igniting in a yellow and red fireball. The Ares turned again while still accelerating. Two more F-15s disappeared. Banking on its left wing, the black bulb under the Ares rotated and fired again.

In less than five seconds it was over. The four Eagles were gone.

Hawley stared, his face drained, his lips so pale they almost looked blue. He leaned over the railing, his hands gripping the steel as if he might fall. He stared in rage, a deadly fire in his eyes, black, hot, and ready to kill. Glancing over his shoulder, he shot a look through the dark glass of the control tower to see the president look ahead in a dumbfounded stare. His security agents moved around him, but there wasn't a thing they could do. The general felt another surge of sickness and he swallowed down a wad of bile.

The four fireballs were beginning to expand as they climbed in the breeze, the burning fuel creating black balls of smoke as the scattered pieces of wreckage began to tumble and spin through the air.

The air vibrated with the chest-thumping power as the pilot in the Ares pushed his throttles into full afterburner. Then it turned while accelerating and lowered its nose toward the ground.

The general took a step back. "No, no . . . ," he started praying.

He knew what the pilot was doing. "Close the doors!" he started screaming.

"Close the doors!" He waved frantically toward a hangar, but it was already too late.

Circling over the airport, barely a hundred feet above the ground, its enormous engines shattering the smoky air, the stolen fighter did a 180-degree turn and lined up on the hanger where the second Ares was housed. Hawley stared. The hangar doors were open, the second prototype completely exposed. "No, no, no," he breathed again, his voice coming in gasps.

He saw the fighter's belly door open and the single bomb fall. He watched it track toward the hanger, then—as if time had come to a stop—he watched the five-hundred-pound bomb hit the runway, skip across the hard cement, the firing pin still arming as it bounced, pass through the open door of the hanger, and explode in dark flames.

He stood there, dumbfounded, his heart slamming in his ears, then lowered his head and closed his eyes, his shoulders slumping in defeat. The sound of the Ares' engines pounded his ears as the fighter climbed to the west. He lifted his eyes to watch as it begin to fade into the haze.

Turning, he stared at the smoke rising around the airport where the Eagles had been, then at the hangar that had been protecting his Ares. An enormous fire flickered through the open door and black smoke began to rise in the wind as the orange flames filled the air.

The sirens started wailing but Hawley didn't hear them. The smoke was growing thick now, but he didn't see.

The Areses were gone. It was over. One stolen, one destroyed.

Four F-15s shot down in the battle. Four good men dead.

He stared at the black balls of smoke and listened to a sound, a slow moan, then realized the sound was coming from his own chest. He moaned again and then swallowed as he lowered his head.

Then he heard another sound, the deep, chesty rumble of a jet engine behind him. He turned, his knees weak, catching his first glimpse of the Mirage as it flew over his head. It was low now, but climbing, its afterburners glowing red as it accelerated through the sky. The power of the engines shattered the air and thumped against his chest, and he gripped the rail one more time.

The fighter flew directly over the airfield, then turned ten degrees to the west. It lined up on the fleeing Ares and closed the distance between them, afterburner engines spouting a golden fire of red.

MIRAGE 59

"Go and get him!" Jesse screamed into his oxygen mask.

Marcos had already shoved both of his throttles into full afterburner. The fighter, still heavy with weapons and nearly a full load of fuel, accelerated quickly but not nearly quickly enough. The Ares was moving away from them and, even though it was not in afterburner, was already flying faster than the French fighter could go. Jesse reached down and touched the dual throttles, making certain they were up against their stops, then leaned forward to watch the fleeing jet.

The Mirage climbed as it accelerated, and it only took a few seconds before the aircraft was passing through the broken overcast. Above, the sky was bright blue, the tops of the clouds a dazzling white. The sun was low now, and it cast deep shadows across the eastern sides of the mountainous clouds—shadows the fleeing fighter was using to hide.

"Where is he?" Jesse demanded, losing sight of the Ares.

"I don't know . . . I can't see him. I'm going to bring up my radar."

"*No!*" Jesse screamed. "You can't do that. Right now he doesn't know we're back here, least I don't think he does, but the instant you flash him with your radar he will know we are here. Do that, and he runs. Or he comes back and kills us. We don't want either one."

Jesse watched Marcos's back as he shook his head in frustration, then scanned left and right. "We're is he . . . where is he?" He moved his eyes across the horizon, blocking out chunks of airspace to search, then moving on to the next piece of sky. Then he saw it, a gray shadow forty degrees to his left. From this distance, it was tiny, hardly larger than a speck of dust in the air. "Tally," he called. "Ten o'clock. Climbing. Five or six miles. Moving quickly." He nudged the stick. "Go and get her," he said.

Marcos threw the fighter up on its left wing while talking to the air controllers in French. The Mirage was still accelerating, but the Ares had slowed down so the distance between them began to close visibly. "Guns or missiles?" the French pilot asked.

"Guns!" Jesse shot back. "I'm telling you, Marcos, the instant you bring up your radar to lock your missiles, this whole thing is done. You don't realize what that aircraft is capable off. So keep going. Get in closer.

There was a moment of silence between them. "I can't use my radar to create an aiming piper?" the French pilot asked, referring to the radar-assisted aiming-and-firing mechanism built into his cannon.

"Afraid not, partner. This one's up to you. But you've got a set of eyeballs. Just aim at him and fire."

"I've never done that, Jesse."

The American shook his head in disbelief. "You've never simulated radar-out! You've never manually fired your gun?"

"Oh yeah . . . I mean, yes, I have in simulator. But never for real. Never when it counted."

"It counts now, Marcos. It counts a whole lot."

The pilot in the front cockpit shrugged his shoulders and gently stirred the stick. "Let me get in firing range, then I'll bring up the radar for the final firing solution. Give me an aiming piper for a few seconds is all that I ask."

"No, Marcos! Do that, and you kill us. Come on, *you can do this,* man!"

The Ares was growing larger in the front of the cockpit. Three miles. Two miles. Marcos unlocked his cannon and put his finger on the trigger in the center of his stick. One point eight. One point six. The two aircraft were closing fast. The Ares continued straight ahead. It was still climbing but had slowed as it headed for the upper atmosphere.

One point five miles. Getting closer.

"Get inside two thousand feet," Jesse instructed the French pilot. "He's going to keep climbing, so don't get low on him. The Ares is engineered to maneuver in the thin air above forty-five thousand feet, so if you let him beat us up there, we won't ever catch him, my friend. So keep it up." He reached down and pulled back on the stick, pulling the nose of the jet above the running Ares. "Keep us up above him or we might as well turn around and go home." He felt Marcos on the controls, but the French pilot didn't complain about him momentarily flying the jet. The altimeter on the Head-Up Display counted through forty-eight thousand feet. Then fifty thousand. Fifty-two.

Jesse sucked a long breath of dry air through his oxygen mask, his chest tight. He knew they were getting near the upper limits of the Mirage's operational capability. Above fifty thousand the Mirage, like any other fighter, became a bobbing cork on the sea. Weak airflow over the control surfaces. Spinning compressors working double-time to compress enough air to burn. Engine compressor stalls, even flameouts were not uncommon up at this altitude, not to mention the fact that it took an ever increasing angle of attack just to keep the jet in the air.

The Ares was the only aircraft that loved it up here.

"Keep your speed up until we're inside a mile," Jesse desperately instructed, "then we can slow down. He doesn't know we're back here, so there's no reason to outrun him. And you've got to stay above him until we are in optimum gun range. Fall below or too far behind him and baby, we're done."

The French pilot nodded. "You think I can—"

The Ares suddenly rolled up on one wing and pulled. The circle of his flight path was incredibly tight. Jesse saw the forward slats and movable wing surfaces as they deflected to pull the Ares into a batlike turn. "Watch it!" he shouted into his oxygen mask. "He's coming around. He must have seen us . . . he's got us in his—"

Marcos rolled the Mirage up in a tight right-hand turn, attempting to follow the Ares, but it was too late. Too late and not nearly enough energy to maneuver about. The Mirage pulled through the turn, but it hardly reached a total of four g's; it just didn't have the horsepower or wing design to maneuver at such altitude.

The Ares racked up and flew toward them, the two fighters passing each other, both of them on their wingtips, holding almost exactly ninety degrees of bank. It was canopy to canopy, less than three hundred feet apart. Jesse looked through the top of his cockpit at the passing Ares as the two aircraft circled each other, both of them rolled up on their wingtips in a daisy chain.

Canopy to canopy, he saw the other pilot. The gray helmet. The dark visor. The green flight suit. The inside of the cockpit of the incredible Ares. He saw the enemy pilot looking at him as he craned his neck.

Two pilots. Face to face.

The start of a fight to the death.

They flashed by each other, no more than a few hundred feet apart, close enough that Jesse could see the other pilot lift a defiant fist.

"Pull it around, Marcos!" Jesse screamed into his oxygen mask. Grunting, he strained against the onslaught of the g's, then felt a sudden tingle of fear and adrenaline that pumped like a drug in his veins. "Don't let him get his belly to us."

The Ares rolled . . . the turn was tight. It rolled . . . it leveled off . . . it was . . . rolling . . . in . . . behind . . .

"Don't let him get behind us. Don't let him get his belly up . . . don't let him—"

The cockpit around him seemed to disintegrate in midair. There was fire and heat, then flying pieces of metal, broken glass, exploding plastic, and the sudden cold, bitter air. And there was wind. Oh, the wind. It pulled the breath from his lungs. It was as if a huge vacuum had been fitted over his mouth and sucked the oxygen right out of his chest. There was pain. He was blinded. A powerful throbbing ran down the center of his spine. There was cold air, then no air, then an incredibly painful push against the bottom of his ejection seat.

Flames from the rocket motor. Acceleration through the wreckage. Tumbling and spinning. A minus-fifty-two-degree blast of cold. He felt his cheeks pin back in the slipstream. He felt his eyes freezing closed.

Then there was silence. An apex in trajectory. A momentary feeling of perfect weightlessness as he hung at the top of the parabola.

Then passing wind. Bitter cold.

Then silence and darkness.

The pilot fell to the earth.

Jesse tumbled through the atmosphere, falling through fifty, then forty thousand feet. He accelerated as he fell at more than 140 miles an hour. Unconscious, his legs pinned back, his arms flailing painfully at his sides, he fell and tumbled and rolled toward the ground. As he fell, the air grew warmer, but his mind remained blank.

The sensors in the parachute apparatus counted through the atmosphere. Knowing a pilot would die of exposure and hypothermia if the parachute opened above eighteen thousand feet, the sensors kept the chute inside his pack until the proper altitude.

Passing through 17,500 feet, the sensors sent a fire signal to the battery-operated extraction mechanism. The drogue chute opened, caught, then pulled the main chute from the pack that was part of his ejection seat. The pilot's body *snapped* like a whip, his head still drooping, as the orange and brown chute filled the air.

Seconds later, Jesse became aware of a violent buzz in his head. He heard a sound, he felt the wind and a bone-level, deadly cold. His hands and fingers were nearly frozen, his mind a dark dream. He couldn't open his eyes. He couldn't think. He was barely aware.

He was underwater. Deep in the water. Far too deep to swim up. He was so far from the surface he couldn't even see the sunlight.

He couldn't breathe. He was dying.

But he started to swim. He pulled. He strained. He fought for the surface again.

The water grew warm and brighter. He saw the light from the sun. The surface was just above him. He started to breathe.

Still dark. He tried to force his eyes open but his lashes had frozen to his skin. He shook his head to clear it and felt a sudden pain in his neck.

He brushed his face, cleared his eyes, looked around, and saw another chute. He braced himself, completed his post-ejection checklist (canopy, drag lines, seat kit, life preserver units), then waited as the ground came rushing up.

He knew a survival beacon in his seat kit had already powered up. Looking to his left, he could see the runways at Le Bourget. The rescue helicopters would be launched in two or three minutes or less.

A thousand feet above the ground, Jesse began to maneuver between a set of high-power lines (the most dangerous aspect of his ejection sequence, he thought), then steered his square parachute toward an empty gutter along a narrow road.

He landed with a huff, his feet and legs together, then rolled from his ankles to his knees, to his hips, to his side, to absorb the shock of the descent.

He was on the ground for less than ten minutes before the helicopters picked him up. Marcos was already in the chopper. He glared coldly at Jesse as he climbed into the back of the noisy machine.

TWENTY

The president of the United States pushed his way through his security agents and moved out onto the catwalk that surrounded the top of the glass control tower. General Hawley turned toward him, his face resolute, a martyr facing the firing squad as they lifted their guns. The military officers with General Hawley took a step back as the president walked by, the smell of smoke and burning fuel drifting toward them as the sound of wailing sirens drifted back and forth in the wind.

The president looked calm, even peaceful, almost unnaturally so. He was in another place now, focused and intent. A man on a mission, he knew what he had to do.

Hawley braced himself, his back ramrod straight. He stared ahead, keeping his eyes focused on the empty space just above the president's head. He fully expected to be relieved of command, to be thrown out with the garbage at the end of the day, the focal point of the news report explaining how the unveiling of the Ares had turned out so wrong.

The president brushed by the other military advisors, paying them no more attention than he would have a fly. The president of the United States didn't deal with junior officers, not during times such as these. On a good day, when things were right, the president might have nodded to them, said good morning or asked how they were, but he wasn't going to take the time to acknowledge them with the greatest crisis of his presidency unfolding before his eyes.

The president came to a stop in front of General Hawley and looked him straight in the eye. "Robert," he started, his voice soft but cold as glacier ice, "you know me. I know you. We've known each other many years." The president's entire demeanor was so calm the other officers had strain to hear what he said. "I am a reasonable man, Robert, I try not to overreact and I try to be fair. But a man doesn't get to be the leader of the most powerful nation ever to grace this green earth by being understanding and sympathetic. There is no such thing as *nice* when you are president of the United States. If he is, he is crushed. There are too many obligations, too many lives depending on everything that I do.

"So listen to me, Robert, for this is the last thing I will say. This is your problem. You will fix it. And you will fix it today. You're going to figure out who stole my aircraft and you're going to kill him, understand? No more 'let's try and save it.' I want this guy dead and that aircraft destroyed before it can do us more harm. You have the CIA, FBI, military intelligence, NASA, NSA, the entire military—anything you ask for, I'll drop it in your lap—but you'd better produce for me, Hawley, or I will have your head."

The president paused, his eyes glaring, his lips rimmed with dry spit. "Do you understand what I'm saying?"

Hawley nodded.

"I want a briefing by eight. That's less than three hours from now. By that time I want you to tell me how you're going to find our aircraft and then bring it down."

Again Hawley nodded.

The president took a deep breath and tilted his head to one side. His voice was soft now; there was no menace or anger, only disappointment in his tone. "You're not my first choice to do this, you know that. You're not my national security advisor or even chairman of the Joint Chiefs of Staff. But my NSA and Chairman Shevky are back in Washington. You are here. They are not. And even if that were not true, I would still be relying on you, for you are the only one who truly understands the Ares and how we can bring it down. Now, since the fates have thrown us together, let's see if you can get this thing right."

"*Sir,*" Hawley answered curtly, his humiliation complete.

The president studied his pale face. "Things haven't gone very well so far, General Hawley. The Ares has been stolen, the second prototype destroyed. We lost four good pilots, four good aircraft, shot down before our eyes. The decision was mine, but I listened to you, General, and I regret that I did. The press will go crazy. Someone's got to stand up and take the bullet and that is fine, I will stand. But no one is going to hide behind me. You will stand by me, too."

Hawley didn't answer, keeping his eyes on the blank space above the president's head. The president watched him a moment, then moved toward the door. "I am counting on you, General," he said. "You must not disappoint our nation again. You've got to take care of this problem before my presidency is destroyed."

Hawley cringed.

This wasn't about politics or the president or the presidency anymore. This was about their survival.

And the general had failed.

Flying in the helicopter back to Le Bourget, Jesse crouched, his shoulders bent, his head resting on his arms stretched between his knees. The rescue specialists in the chopper had tried to get him to lie down, but he had refused, insisting on sitting in the canvas seat by the door. As the chopper flew, he relived the unbelievably short combat sequence in his mind: the turn, the approaching fighters, each of them racked up on their wings, a daisy wheel as they circled, a dog chasing its tail. Around they chased, two pilots staring at each other through the tops of their canopies. The Ares falling in behind them. No missiles. No tracers. His aircraft exploding all around him, breaking up in the air.

He sat up and stretched against the dull pain in his neck. Staring out the window, the sequence played again and again in his mind.

The president disappeared through the access door to the tower, pushed through the chaos of the controllers who were struggling to coordinate fire and rescue efforts, and disappeared, following his Secret Service agents down the single flight of stairs. Passing through the security doors, he walked to the elevator that would take him to the ground floor.

Hawley stared in a stupor, his face white as death. He was a proud man, too proud, but he had spent his entire adult life dedicated to only one purpose: serving his country and her people with all of his heart and soul.

And he had failed. Regardless of the outcome now, he had failed. He might mitigate the damage, but the damage was done.

He'd given up everything for his country: his family, his children, a life of money and ease. He could have been a bigshot CEO. He could have spent more time with his family. He could have saved his marriage, his kids, had a dog, taken long walks, watched his Yankees on TV. Yet he had sacrificed it all. Thirty-three years of dedicated service had been flushed down the drain. In the end, when it was over, this day would be the only thing anyone ever remembered of him.

He stared at the emptiness, a vacant look on his face, and slowly turned, as if it pained him, and moved toward the door.

The rescue helicopter began to descend toward the runway.

In the crowded cabin, surrounded by aluminum patient litters and medical supplies, Jesse was talking to the medic and shaking his head. "I'm fine," he insisted. "I do not need to be taken to the hospital. Let me get out at Base Ops. I've got things to do."

The medic bit his lip, then nodded slowly.

Jesse stretched and exhaled. Except for some painful bruises along his thigh and a couple of friction burns along his neck where the parachute lines had snapped, he felt okay. Perhaps not great—embarrassed, sore, angry, and frightened—but he wasn't going to keel over, and the last thing he needed was for some French doctor to prod him and then tell him what he already knew.

The chopper touched down at Base Operations and Jesse jumped out. Turning, he slapped the Mirage pilot on the shoulder. "We did the best we could," he shouted above the whine of the engines and the rotating blades.

The French pilot hunched his shoulders. Jesse forced a smile, then ran toward the building, listening to the sound of the chopper as it lifted away.

Ten minutes later, a working group was hastily assembling in the CECOC. Hawley stood before them and looked out on the crowded room, his eyes dark, almost lifeless, as if the fire was now gone.

The CIA branch chief from the embassy and the European director of the FBI were sitting on the front row. Behind them were various military officers including the vice commander of United States Air Forces, Europe (USAFE), representatives from Interpol, and the chief of the Pan-Arab Terrorists Evaluation Group. Around the side and back walls were members of the local police, French intelligence, the NATO security director, and EU military affairs—anyone and everyone who had any background in international security, terrorism, aviation, military operations, or crime. Most had deployed to Paris some weeks before to work the security details for the international gathering of G-8 nations, but a few had been pulled from other duties and shoved in the room.

Hawley moved his eyes across the group and cleared his throat. "Ladies and gentlemen," he started, his voice dull and slow. "You know the situation. I have no new information, therefore I will be brief."

Eleven men and four women began to take notes as he spoke.

"We have only two objectives, and I want them both to be clear." He raised a single finger. "First, we must find the Ares and destroy it, regardless the cost.

"Second," another finger came up, "we must take appropriate measures to protect our homelands until the Ares is destroyed. The Ares is very dangerous, as all of you now surely know. It has the range and capability to penetrate virtually any nation's airspace, completely undetected, including the airspace of the United States. It has the capability to inflict enormous damage, as I'm sure there is no doubt in your minds. Therefore, until we bring it down, we must develop a set of recommendations to our national leaders as to how they can best protect themselves and their people from attack."

Jesse listened from the back of the room. There was something in Hawley's voice, something in the choice of his words and inflection that made his hair stand on end. He leaned against the back wall, his senses wired and on edge.

"I know what some of you are thinking," the general continued. "And yes, there must follow an investigation as to how our security was breached and how the aircraft was lost. Something very serious broke down here, and it must be addressed. Who was involved, how they did it, all of that must eventually be known. But right now, our only priority is destroying the Ares. We will identify those who failed us—" his voice momentarily caught "—but none of that matters right now."

He pointed to a young colonel standing off to his side. "Colonel Savage is deputy director, Operations, USAFE. He will coordinate the efforts of all U.S., NATO, and foreign military units to destroy the Ares." Turning to a lean, black man on his right, he introduced him as well. "Mr. Bennett is the deputy director, national security staff. He will be coordinating our homeland security response. Of course, all of these men will be working with their superiors back in Washington, D.C., including directors at the Pentagon and the White House. But for your purposes these men are the voices and ears of the national security staff in D.C., and all your initial efforts should be coordinated through them."

There it was again. Jesse straightened.

The general seemed to look at him, then nodded as if reading his mind. "Major James," he said, and Jesse quickly raised his hand, "is the senior test pilot on the Ares, been with the program for years, logged more time in the Ares than any other pilot on earth. He knows the aircraft's limits—which are few—and the aircraft's capabilities—which are many—better than anyone under my command. His expertise is invaluable and may prove to save the day. Take advantage of what he can tell you, but always keep this in mind: The Ares isn't like anything you've ever dealt with before. It will be like trying to shoot a demon right out of the sky. It won't be easy, we all know that, but we've got to figure out a way to do it and you don't have much time."

The general paused. The room was quiet. "Important questions?" he asked.

A French Air Force officer raised his hand. "Will your president be leaving Paris soon?" he asked, obviously hopeful that he would.

"No," Hawley shot back. "It would be far too dangerous right now. With the Ares sitting out there, the president's 747 would be a primary target if he were to take off. Our Secret Service is adamant that our president remain on the ground until the Ares is brought down."

The aviation officer hesitated. "But if the president's aircraft might be a target, then other civilian aircraft might be targets as well?"

Hawley nodded impatiently. Wasn't that obvious? "Anyone and anything's a potential target. It will be up to each country to determine how they choose to respond."

The room was silent a moment. "Is it true we are going to relocate the command center to the U.S. Embassy?" the deputy NSA asked.

"Yes," Hawley answered. "The presidential caravan has already left. You will get your staffs working, then relocate to the U.S. Embassy as well. It will be more secure at the embassy. In addition, we'll have more direct access to secure communications, tactical information, military data feeds, our staff back in D.C., among other things."

Hawley paused and looked at his watch. "Further questions?" he asked. No one said anything. "Alright then," he concluded, "the president wants his initial briefing at twenty-hundred hours. I know that's not much time, but it is what it is. Come prepared with your recommendations. Prebrief as a group at nineteen-forty. Now let's get to work."

Hawley motioned to Jesse, and he pushed through the breaking crowd to the front of the room. "Be in front of the CECOC in three minutes," the general said. "You can ride to the embassy in my car."

"Yes, sir," Jesse answered. "I'll find your driver and be waiting."

"It will be a few minutes."

Hawley grabbed his shoulder and started to say something, but then changed his mind. Jesse nodded and left, moving quickly for the hall.

The room was empty now, and General Hawley stood alone, a crushing darkness around him. The world at his feet seemed to shake and he reached out to steady himself, but only grasped at thin air.

He looked ahead. He saw the darkness. He looked behind. He saw defeat. Around him there was chaos.

And it all was his fault.

In his very worst nightmares, he couldn't have imagined a worse scenario than he was facing right now.

Every ounce of energy he had ever mustered, every thought, every desire, every sacrifice and motion had been bent toward this day.

Every good thing he had ever worked on lay in a heap on the floor.

Was there any hope left inside him? He didn't know.

He stood there, breathing deeply, his mind racing with dread. Then slowly, as he thought, the darkness seemed to lift. The storm blew, then passed around him. He grew calm. His mind grew peaceful. All the confusion seemed to fade.

Ten minutes later, Jesse was pacing on the sidewalk in front of the CECOC. The U.S. Embassy was a thirty-minute drive away, but with the police escort that was waiting they could be there in twenty. Still, time was of the essence and Jesse was anxious to go.

Glancing at his watch, he started pacing again. Where was General Hawley? He cursed impatiently.

A young French sergeant pushed through the metal doors of the CECOC and raced toward him. His face was grim, his eyes wide. "Major James?" he asked.

Jesse nodded quickly.

"Come with me," the sergeant said.

French security agents had found Major General Robert H. Hawley inside a small bathroom in the main hallway leading to the underground command center, his military issue nine-millimeter handgun still in his hand. The sound of the gunshot had rung up and down the halls, and it had only taken a few seconds for security to respond.

He had fallen against the tiled wall behind the door. His briefcase was open, positioned carefully at his feet. The hole in his head was substantial, with blood, brains, and goo scattered everywhere.

The note was very simple. "I'm sorry," was all it said.

Jesse was escorted into the bathroom, where he fell on his knees beside his dead friend. He saw the shattered skull, the slumping body, the lifeless hands, and pale lips. He saw the pool of blood and fishy matter that had sloughed off the wall. He stood in shock and fury, then shook his head, his shoulders heaving, his mind swimming in despair. He lifted the bloody head—it seemed so heavy—then touched his fingers to his eyelids and gently forced them shut.

Then the animal began to rage inside him.

There was no reason for this!

Standing, he slammed his fist, cracking it hard against the wall. It bloodied and he swore, then stalked out the door.

The resolve was hard inside him.

He almost ran down the hall.

TWENTY-TWO

UNITED STATES EMBASSY
PARIS, FRANCE

The chief of staff got the call from the command center on his personal phone. He listened a moment, his face turning gray. He was surprised but not shaken, disappointed but not sad. More than anything he was angry that the dead man would have done this to him. Just when he needed him, the general checked out. What a coward! What a spineless and craven thing to do.

Still, the president would be crushed when he heard the news. Ketchum knew he had to tell Abram as quickly as he could.

Saving the presidency was all that mattered, not the bodies that they left along the trail. They could mourn over the bodies when things were under control.

Forcing his voice to choke up, he went to find the president, who was talking with the ambassador of France.

The president turned around, feeling Ketchum's gentle pull on his arm. He excused himself from the ambassador, something he was very happy to do.

"I'm very sorry, Mr. President, but I have something most unpleasant to tell you," Ketchum said.

The president waited.

"General Hawley is dead."

The president took a step back, his eyes wide. "What! How?" His voice choked with shock.

"Looks like suicide, Mr. President."

The president turned a sickly pale. "Please God, no . . . ," he stammered.

Ketchum placed his hand on his shoulder. "Sir, I'm sorry, I know the general was a close and long-time friend. I know this is a shock to you, but right now, sir, I've got to remind you that we—"

Abram brought his hand to his ear. "Quiet," he hissed. He felt his stomach shake and his knees go weak. Ketchum reached out to brace him, but he pushed him away.

He almost groaned as a blackness seemed to fall over him, a suffocating blanket that sucked the oxygen out of the air as his own words rolled around in his head.

You're not my first choice to do this.

I listened to you, general, and I regret that I did.

No one is going to hide behind me, general.

Let's take care of this problem before my presidency is destroyed.

And now the general was dead because of those words.

He felt the sickness rising, a sudden eruption from the very depths of his gut. "I need to . . . ," he stammered.

Ketchum took a step toward him, clearly concerned. "Are you alright, Mr. President?"

The president shook his head.

Ketchum pointed to the executive lounge. "Sir, do you need . . ."

The president moved to the private bathroom and slowly pushed back the door.

Ketchum watched him, knowing he would return soon enough. Yes, the president could be a sensitive and sometimes overly emotional man. Sometimes—at the very worst times—he could be driven by affection, or worse, hesitation and self-doubt. But when push came to shove—and the president had done a little shoving before—he was a strong man, a survivor who dearly liked being at the top of the pile. He'd been tried, he'd walked barefoot through hell, and there weren't many fires he hadn't been through before.

And he always came back. Ketchum knew the president would take a moment in the bathroom to collect himself, then come back, resolute and ready to roll over this nasty bump in the road.

While he watched the door to the executive lounge, the COS pulled out his phone, dialed the embassy switchboard, asked for a number, then demanded the communications specialist put the call through.

"Major James, this is Ketchum. Do you know who I am?"

A long silence followed. "Of course," Jesse answered, his voice steely and cold.

"I'm sorry to hear about General Hawley."

Another long pause. "I bet you are." Jesse swore.

Ketchum took an angry breath. "Listen to me, James," he said in a firm tone. "There's something you need to understand. I'm a one-trick pony; I protect the president and his legacy, I keep the whole thing on track. Yeah, I know it's not much, but I do it very well, and right now this presidency is starting to swirl down the drain. Someone's got to reach into the sewer and pull it out, do you understand what I mean? And the next few hours, the next few minutes, are the tipping point, I am sure.

"So you've got to step forward and pick up the pieces Hawley has thrown at your feet. It's ugly but we can't deal with that now. Hate me or love me, I could not care less. If you need someone to blame, blame me. All I care about is the presidency and making this right. We need your help. You will help us. Do I make myself clear?"

He could hear Jesse breathing. "Yes, sir," he said.

"Now listen to me, Major, you've got to step into General Hawley's shoes. I know you might not feel prepared, but you're the only man we have who understands the Ares technology and how we can bring it down. We are depending on you."

Another silence followed. "I know," Jesse said.

"I need you here at the embassy. I'll send you a car."

"Don't send a driver," Jesse shot back. "I can get there by myself."

"No. Take my driver."

"I've got a couple things to do first."

Ketchum swore. "The president expects a briefing at eight—"

"I know that," Jesse interrupted.

"Then shut up and do what I tell you—"

His cell phone went dead.

Ketchum stared at it, disbelieving.

The snot-nosed little jerk had actually hung up on him. The president's chief of staff! Could he be such a fool?

He flipped the phone shut, his hands shaking in anger, then swore violently.

This was an insult that would be impossible to ignore.

He snapped a finger to an aide. "James is on his way over here. I want to know the instant that he arrives. Keep me in the loop if anything develops. I'm going to Le Bourget."

TWENTY-THREE

Jesse punched the red button on his cell phone to end the call. He stared ahead a moment. Part of him wondered why he had done it, and part of him wished that he had done more.

He was standing in Captain Villon's office. Villon was seated on the other side of his desk. "You okay?" the Frenchman asked, studying the look on his face.

"Fine," Jesse answered quickly.

The French officer waited, giving Jesse time to think. Outside, the corridors had grown quiet, and the rooms on the other side of the inspector's doors had grown silent as well. With the president of the United States having relocated to the command post at the U.S. Embassy, and with the Ares gone, apparently not to return, the sense of emergency had died noticeably. This was a U.S. problem now; the French had done all that they could, and they were more than happy to extract themselves from the mess.

"What do you want me to do with your general?" Villon asked.

Jesse cocked his head. "You're kidding?" he said.

"Kidding about what?"

"No, I'm sorry. I just . . . it's just that you're asking the wrong person. I don't know squat about that kind of thing. There are a dozen FBI and Secret Service agents running around here. You've got to ask one of them."

Villon nodded silently, a little surprised. No way would the French military have ceded authority for an investigation to civilian authorities.

Jesse stood in the center of the room, feeling wrung out and weary to the center of his bones. He was sore from the ejection and his back muscles hurt. He was hungry and lost and feeling alone. Staring at the floor, he muttered, "I don't know what to do." Though he was talking to himself, he said it loud enough that the other man could hear.

Villon pressed his lips and hunched his shoulders. "I would help if I could."

Jesse looked up, embarrassed.

"This is, however, a strictly U.S. affair," the policeman went on. "More importantly, it's a military operation now, certainly not my area of expertise. I have neither authority nor proficiency in this area, Major James, and I don't know how I can be of any help."

Jesse hunched his shoulders. There was something about the French officer that engendered his trust, and he had nowhere else to turn. "My president is exerting enormous pressure right now," he explained. "He wants to know who stole our aircraft. How are we supposed to counter him? What is he planning to do? Is he going to use the Ares to attack the U.S.? Another nation? Do we need to warn Israel? Other allies? He's demanding answers to these questions, and I don't even know where to begin."

Villon nodded silently but didn't say anything.

Jesse shook his head and swore in frustration. "We can't bring the Ares down until we find it, and there's no way to find it until we know what he's going to do."

Villon looked irritated. It seemed so obvious! He stood up, moved around his desk, and leaned a beefy buttock against the corner. "If I could, Major, it's not that difficult." Taking out a thin cigarette, he stuffed it in his mouth.

Jesse hunched his shoulders and waited.

"Someone helped him." Villon spoke slowly, as if explaining to a child. "Maybe several people even, and some of them *had* to come from your air force team. I was out to the hangar yesterday; I saw the security surrounding your new craft. I couldn't have gotten within a hundred feet of your fighters, and I hold an aeroport security badge. There is no way the Saudi prince got to your aircraft without substantial help. You have at least one traitor among you, if not several more. Find those persons. Interrogate them. Get them on the blocks and they'll talk, I am sure."

Jesse stared, then nodded slightly.

"Find the greedy ones and break them. Do that and you'll have the answers for your president."

The fire had been put out, but the hangar where the Ares had been housed was still smoky and drenched with standing pools of greasy water and oil. The bomb had skipped through the open door before the timer had clicked, detonating the bomb ten or twelve feet in the air. Craggy pockmarks ripped across the cement floor, and holes had been cut through the metal walls where the scorching pieces of shrapnel had punched their way through. Six inches under the cement, an underground fuel line, one of dozens that crisscrossed the aircraft parking ramp, had been ripped up and punctured, spewing high-pressure fuel everywhere. The broken fuel line fed the fire, gushing thousands of pounds of volatile JP-8 around the hangar before the emergency cutoff valve had closed.

Inside the hangar, the air was acidic, tart and smoky with residue from the fire and the fire-suppressant foam the firefighters had used. A security tape had been stretched across the enormous metal door, restricting access, so Ketchum pulled out his secure-area clearance badge and clipped it on the lapel of his jacket before he ducked under the yellow tape and stepped carefully across the oily hangar floor. He wasn't alone in the hangar; half a dozen agents were milling here and there. FBI. French military investigators. Others he didn't know and couldn't guess. Near the back of the hangar three uniformed air force security guards with M-16s stared at him as he walked across the wet floor.

He walked quickly to the second Ares. A dozen maintenance workers surrounded the fighter, inspecting the damage. The senior maintenance officer walked toward him, an apprehensive look on his face.

"How is she?" Ketchum demanded.

"Who are you?" the captain asked him.

Ketchum's face tightened. How could the captain not even know who he was? He flashed his White House badge and the captain seemed to straighten. "You work in the White House?"

Ketchum nodded curtly, realizing there might be an advantage in not revealing his identity (something he was usually more than anxious to do). The kid might be more honest if he didn't know who he was dealing with.

"How badly is this aircraft damaged?" Ketchum repeated.

The captain ignored his question. "What happened out there, sir?" he asked. "Our own Ares comes and blings us!"

Ketchum grew irritated and glanced quickly at his watch. "Don't know, Captain. We're trying really hard to find out."

"Let me tell you something," the captain said. "There's too much crap floating around here, you know what I mean? Too many guys poking around in my house." He nodded over his shoulder at the government agents. "Those guys have been pulling us aside one by one, asking all kinds of questions. It's as clear as the sun they're looking for someone to nail. But let me tell you something, there might be a problem here, but it is *not* in my house. It's not with my guys or my unit. We had nothing to do with the theft of the Ares."

"I'm sure," Ketchum answered. But the truth was, he wasn't. There was a stink in the unit and it could be coming from anywhere. He nodded to his aircraft. "Now tell me about this Ares."

The captain shook his head. "It isn't good," he answered. "It isn't good at all."

TWENTY-FOUR

UNITED STATES EMBASSY
PARIS, FRANCE

Jesse left the CECOC. In the hallway, he passed half a dozen U.S. agents who were milling around. Picking out the nearest FBI man by his suit coat and tie, he walked toward him. The agent was talking to another agent, an older guy with short hair and an unlit cigarette in his mouth. Jesse flashed his security badge as he approached them and introduced himself.

"Agent Costas," the smoker answered. "Air Force Office of Special Investigations." Dressed in sloppy Dockers and a golf shirt, he offered no rank or first name. OSI operated in their own world and didn't give out such things. Costas nodded to the suit guy. "Robert Donahue, FBI," he introduced.

Jesse reached out and shook hands.

"Hear you're the man now?" Costas said.

Jesse nodded reluctantly. "Until they get their crap together and find someone who knows what they're doing."

The two men were silent. "You talked to Sergeant Espy yet?" Jesse asked.

The OSI guy was silent.

"The crew chief on the Ares," Jesse prodded. "You know, the guy who is responsible to launch the aircraft, refuel it, maintenance and—"

"I know what a crew chief does," Costas replied testily.

Jesse nodded. "I'm sure that you do."

The agent didn't answer.

"Have you seen him?" Jesse asked again. "He's the key to this, you surely understand that, the most important witness in this investigation. Do you have him? I want to talk to him and I need to see him now."

"So do we," Costas said.

Jesse frowned. "I was hoping you wouldn't say that."

"He helped launch the Ares for the air show, but no one has seen him since then. The hangar was secure for the engine start and taxi. No one but the crew chief and pilot were allowed around the aircraft until the hangar doors were rolled back, but no one has seen him since the Ares started taxiing toward the crowd."

Jesse looked away, the news striking him like a slap on the face. "You've looked—"

"We looked everywhere," Costas interrupted. "We've gone to his hotel, the squadron, mission planning, maintenance operations. We've got a dozen agents looking for him, a couple dozen French policemen as well. We don't know where he is. All we know is that he isn't here."

Jesse's jaw tightened. "Not a good sign, I suppose."

"Kind of suspicious," the FBI agent answered tartly. "But not as suspicious as this." He lifted a computer printout he'd been holding in his hand.

"What you got?"

The FBI agent unfolded the printout. "Turns out Sergeant Espy is a pretty wealthy guy."

"Really?" Jesse answered, his voice sarcastic and tight.

"At least he is since . . . what, four o' five yesterday afternoon. That was about the time that two and a half million dollars were deposited in his personal account in Nevada. But the money didn't stay there long. It was immediately transferred to another bank, this time in Antigua, then moved on again. We lost track of it now, but if this guy is good, or if he had some help, something which appears to be virtually certain now, then we might never find it."

"No kidding," Jesse muttered.

"Not bad, eh?" the agent mocked. "You lose your Ares in one spectacular, international bang! The pilot gets exploded in a car bomb. The crew chief can't be found. Now we find out he's a real saver, putting away a pretty decent chunk of money, all on a sergeant's pay."

"Seems kind of unlikely, doesn't it?" Jesse huffed.

"Like training a lion to give a tongue bath—kind of hard to be surprised at the disappointing result."

Jesse moved away from the others and concentrated. He had known Sergeant Espy for three or four years. He thought he was a good man, straight-up as anyone he'd ever known. Sure, Espy spent a night or two on the Vegas strip on the weekends, but all of them did. He used to drop by his office to talk politics, sometimes the Yankees or fishing, and seemed to be a decent guy.

Jesse swore and shook his head. He'd been suckered, that was obvious. The guy had taken him for a fool. For a cool two point five, he'd sold out everything they held dear.

He turned back to the others. "We've got to find him!" he demanded.

"No kidding?" Costas said.

"You don't understand," Jesse answered. "There are some things you don't know." He quickly told the agents about Prince bin Saud and his disappearance from Arabia. The FBI agent turned pale, his hands shaking as he listened.

"The Ares has been taken by a maniac who has the skills to use it," Jesse concluded. "We've got to find out what he's going to do, and Sergeant Espy is the key. The airports and train stations, you've got to get your people out there. It's only been a couple hours. How far could he go?"

Costas sucked his cigarette, then pulled it from his mouth. "This is Europe, Major James. You're two hours away from any of a half-dozen major European cities. Truth is, he could be anywhere. Open borders, open travel. He could have taken a taxi to Warsaw for a couple grand. He could have hired a private plane to Barcelona, even Saint Petersburg. If he wants to disappear, with a couple million bucks to finance him, believe me, he could. It could take us a year or two to find him, if we ever do."

They have the Ares, do you understand that? They're going to use it, and we don't know when or where. Our only link to that aircraft is Sergeant Espy. Now please, you've got to find him."

The two agents were quiet.

"Get him!" Jesse said.

The FBI agent raised his hand. "Look, Major James, it's just not that easy," he said. "How long have we been looking for the al Qaeda leaders holed up in their caves in Afghanistan? How long have we been looking for Faisal in Iraq? We've been looking for the guys who bombed the *Cole* for half my career. We know they're somewhere here in Europe, but that's as close as we seem to be able to get. I could give you a hundred examples to make this simple point: if someone has money and the right friends, and this guy appears to have both, I wouldn't count on Sergeant Espy showing up anytime soon."

"But that means—"

"You've got to find another option to track your aircraft down."

TWENTY-FIVE

Jesse walked out of the CECOC building in a daze and stood in the evening light. It had all come so fast, so unexpectedly. Over the past couple of hours there had simply been too much information to process it all without feeling stunned. He couldn't focus any longer and he felt dizzy, almost nauseous, as he walked across the cement.

The horrible sequence kept rolling around in his head. The Ares flying down the runway. The four F-15s exploding in flames. The Ares turning and lining up on the hangar. The single bomb skipping across the cement. The explosions, the smoke, the rolling fire.

The devastated look on General Hawley's face.

He shuddered, ducking his head as he walked.

The sun had dipped below the horizon and darkness was settling quickly. The southern sky was a hazy gray from the mix of twilight and the rising lights of the city, and the air was turning cool, a gentle breeze blowing on his back.

He had left another uniform in a personal bag in the trunk of his car and, after the ejection, he smelled like sweat and smoke. His car was parked in a small lot on the south side of the building. He glanced at his watch, thought he had time to change before the briefing, and started walking toward the access gate in the fence that separated the administrative buildings and small terminal from the parking lot and public road. Two guards manned the gate now (the day before there had only been one). He had to show his security badge to them both before they would allow him to exit. He watched as they noted his name and the time in their log, then turned left to the parking lot and his rental car.

Walking across a wide stretch of dry grass that separated the sidewalk from the parking lot, he tried to recall where he'd parked. He'd been so preoccupied, he couldn't remember, and he had to stop and think.

Feeling stupid, he scanned the acres of cars, searching up and down one row, then moved forward a dozen cars. Yes, there it was. He jogged toward his rental near the end of the third row of cars.

The security lights in the parking area were dim and widely spaced, and the shadows around the vehicles were deep and black. He heard a car turn down his row, following him from behind, but he didn't turn around. The car moved slowly, the headlights illuminating his back and casting his shadow before him as it crossed a speed bump. The car slowly passed, then pulled into an empty spot at the end of the row.

He watched it for a moment, then, moving toward the Fiat, he caught a shadow and movement out of the corner of his eye. A car door slammed behind him, the sound filling the dark, empty night. He looked over his shoulder as he walked, but no one was there. Slowing, he studied the car that had pulled into the parking space at the end of the row—a dark blue Pontiac, one of the few American cars in the lot. He stopped, his heart racing now, then started walking slowly toward it. The windows were so deeply tinted, and the ambient light so low, that it was impossible to see if anyone was inside. He stared at the Pontiac, then pulled out his cell phone, tapped in the number to the CECOC, and waited. A woman's voice answered on the third ring.

"This is Major James," he told her quickly. "I need to speak with OSI Agent Costas, who is investigating—"

"This line is not secure," the woman interrupted before he could say any more.

"Yes, okay, get Mr. Costas on the line."

"And this is who, once again, sir?"

"Major James. U.S. Air Force. I'm with—"

"Yes, sir, Major James, I'll get Mr. Costas for you now."

Jesse stepped to his right, coming to a stop between two cars. The blue Pontiac was thirty feet from him, parked against the curb at the very end of the row. He heard sudden movement, then angry voices. He was just starting to move toward it when Costas came on the phone.

"What you got, James?" Costas asked.

"Have you guys searched the parking lot?"

"The parking lot? Where?"

"Here, on the south side of hangar."

"Searched it for what, James?"

"I'm looking at a car that I'm pretty sure was his."

"A blue Pontiac, right?"

"Yep, that's it."

"We've been through every parking lot on the airfield. The car isn't here."

"I know it wasn't there before, Mr. Costas, because it barely pulled in. Now I'm staring at a blue Pontiac that I would swear was his."

Costas hesitated, suddenly not so sure. Jesse heard the rustle of paper. "Give me the license number," he said.

Jesse moved closer so that he could see while still holding the cell phone to his ear. "I think there might be someone inside," he started saying. "Wait a minute."

He dropped the phone to his side and stepped carefully. The car shifted on its wheels. Movement again from inside. He lifted the phone to his ear again. "You still there?" he whispered.

"What's going on, James? Are you—"

The car suddenly roared to life, the engine revving until it screamed. The automatic transmission was thrown into reverse while the engine was screeching, and the tires burned against the blacktop. The car jerked toward him, accelerating wildly, the tail spinning left and then right, barely under control. Jesse jumped to the side, dropping the phone as he scrambled between the rows of cars to his right. Stumbling, he fell and rolled, his legs propelling him forward to get out of the way. The Pontiac's wheels screeched as it came to a stop. The passenger's door was less than three feet from him, but Jesse was still rolling, his face tucked between arms. The driver revved his engine again, dropped the transmission into forward, and screeched his tires before Jesse could turn around. The Pontiac swerved violently as it raced forward, braked crazily to make the turn down a narrow row of cars, then swerved and sped away, screeching out of the parking lot. Pulling across four lanes of traffic, it accelerated down the access road that led to the main airport highway, merged, and slowed to blend in with the crowded lanes of cars.

Jesse stared, his heart slamming in his chest. The driver had tried to hit him! He swore in a rage, then pushed himself up, straining to keep his eyes on the fleeing car. He searched desperately around his feet, then picked up his cell phone. The color screen was cracked and the right hinge was broken, leaving the top of the phone clinging awkwardly to the base. He placed it to his ear, but the call had been lost. He punched the redial button but it didn't go through.

Panicked, he turned and started running for the CECOC building, the broken phone in his hand, then stopped, realizing he didn't have enough time to get help.

He stood on his toes, straining to see down the road where the Pontiac had disappeared, then scrambled on top of the nearest car, clawing up the windshield as he climbed to the roof.

He saw the Pontiac take the nearest corner and vanish into the dark.

Jumping down, he turned for his car, pulling the keys from his pocket as he ran. The door was unlocked, and he jammed the key in the ignition and started the engine. Dropping the manual transmission into gear, he screeched his own tires, pulling out of the parking lot.

Less than thirty seconds had passed since he had rolled on the ground.

The traffic on the road was steady, but he didn't slow down as he crossed the lanes. Holding his horn in one continuous blast, he raced onto the road, gunning the little Fiat for all it was worth. He didn't even look behind him when he heard the screech of tires, but half a dozen different horns started blaring at him as he raced onto the road.

Jamming through all five gears, he revved his engine up to six thousand rpm before shifting and popping the clutch violently. He kept the throttle down and started weaving through traffic, jamming his horn as he came to the turn in the road where the Pontiac had disappeared. Hitting his brakes, he took the turn, then looked ahead down the road, his heart jumping to his throat.

A stoplight. An intersection. Less than two hundred feet away.

Which way did the Pontiac go? Left? Right? Straight ahead?

He gritted his teeth, then took his best guess. The traffic around the speeding Pontiac had not seemed to slow. Could they have hit a green light? It must have been—please let it have been—a green light when the Pontiac had approached the intersection past the first turn in the road.

Gulping air, he prayed and accelerated straight ahead.

Approaching the intersection, the light turned from yellow to red! Fifty feet from the intersection, he started jamming his horn, slammed his brakes, then pressed the gas pedal again. Screaming through the intersection, he maneuvered behind the first group of cars, jamming his steering wheel right and then left. More screeching tires sounded from behind him, then another set of angry horns.

Stomping on the gas pedal, he sped away from the intersection as he shifted through his gears.

He glanced at his speedometer: 137 kph. Almost 85 miles an hour. Way more than double the speed limit on the industrial road. He swallowed hard, reached across his shoulder, and buckled his belt. He was approaching the cluster of traffic ahead of him, the group of cars that had made it through the previous traffic light, and he kept the accelerator on the floor to keep gaining on them as he hit 140, then 150 kilometers on the speedometer. The Fiat was beginning to top out, the engine whining like a beater, the steering wheel vibrating dangerously in his hand. Blasting his horn, he hit the brakes, slowed to 100, and began weaving through the traffic again.

Reaching to the seat beside him, he picked up his broken cell phone, punched the redial button, and put the phone to his ear. He thought he heard it ringing, but he wasn't sure, and a piece of broken glass from the color screen fell against his cheek. He heard a voice, weak and barely understandable, and started talking. "This is Major James," he cried. "I'm driving south on . . . I don't know, a road that runs toward the main airport road. I'm chasing a dark blue Pontiac that I think is being driven by—"

The car in the right lane pulled suddenly toward him, cutting him off. He swore, then yelled, then dropped the phone and gripped the wheel, pulling it to the side while hitting his brakes. The Fiat swerved violently, almost spinning out of control, and he fought to keep from oversteering and running off the road. Time seemed to stop as the landscape and traffic passed by like a dream. He bumped the cement barrier that separated the oncoming traffic, lurched to the right, almost rolled, spun the wheel to the left to keep the tires on the asphalt, then fishtailed and spun back into his lane again.

The phone had fallen onto the floor and slid between his feet.

He started reaching for it when the Pontiac came into view only four cars ahead. He pressed the gas pedal and forgot about the phone.

Steering into the left lane, he cut off a black Mercedes, then turned back to the right. The Pontiac was now only two cars ahead. He would be alongside it in seconds. He kept the gas pedal on the floor.

Then the question finally hit him.

When he caught up with the car, what was he going to do?

The driver in the Pontiac must have seen him, for it suddenly accelerated and cut into his lane. Jesse swerved and slammed his brakes. The Pontiac sped away—it was a much more powerful car—then swerved back into the right lane. Another intersection was coming up where the industrial access road merged with the main highway. Traffic was heavy in every direction, with cars backed up behind the stoplight at least ten or twelve deep, and Jesse watched in horror as the Pontiac swerved violently across two lanes of traffic, the driver trying desperately to make the ninety-degree turn.

The Pontiac's rear wheels started swerving as they lost their grip on the road. The tail veered to the left, fishtailed once, then spun around to the right. The driver lost control, jumped the curb, hit the brakes, plowed through a deep hedge, then slammed into a metal power pole.

Traffic screeched and stopped behind it, the cars bunching up at awkward angles across every lane. Jesse jammed his brakes, pulling violently to his right, then steered across the traffic and onto the shoulder of the road, coming to a stop at the hedge. Jumping out of the Fiat, he ran forward. Hesitating at the first car he came to, he pulled the door open. A terrified teenager stared up at him. Jesse flashed his air force security badge—it didn't mean anything, he knew that, but it was all he had—and screamed at the kid. "911," he cried. The French teenager stammered in bewilderment.

"Do you speak English?" Jesse demanded, his French completely escaping him now.

"Yes, yes," the kid nodded.

"Got a cell phone?"

The kid hesitated, then lifted his hand. Jesse saw a silver phone, the antennae protruding between his fingers.

"Call emergency," Jesse told him. "Tell them to send an ambulance. And police. Lots of security! Got that?"

The kid nodded again.

Ahead of him, an older man was just getting out of his car. Jesse ran toward him and flashed the badge. "Keep everyone back. There is danger. I don't know who's in that car, but they might be armed."

The man stared at him, not understanding. *"Dangereux! Retournez-vous!"* Jesse shouted. "Dangerous. Stay back!"

The man backed up, moving away from his car.

Jesse turned toward the broken Pontiac. It had crashed head-on into the metal power pole, hitting in the center of the grill. Steam escaped from the front of the engine, and one of the back tires, suspended over a narrow ditch, was still spinning, wobbling on a bent rim. The metal power pole bent over the car, almost touching the roof, and half a dozen broken power lines were dancing on the ground, sparks and arcing lights of electricity bouncing them two or three feet in the air. The air crackled from the sparks and there was an acidic, burning smell. As Jesse moved down the embankment, the ground grew spongy and wet, and he felt a sudden tingling building through the soles of his boots. The hair on his neck started standing up and he came to a stop.

Looking down, he saw that shallow pools of standing water had filled the sunken holes at the bottom of the ditch. The electrical wires danced around and through them.

One wrong step and it was over. One wrong bounce from the wires and he was dead.

He gritted his teeth and swallowed.

Taking a careful step, he felt the tingle again.

The engine sizzled as the water in the radiator sprayed over the searing-hot engine block. Then he smelled fumes and saw the gasoline beginning to pool under the back of the car.

He stood there, dumbfounded. What else? Poison serpents in the grass? How else might he be killed?

He stared at the arcing wires and sniffed the stink of the fuel as he ran toward the car, then hesitated again, ten feet from the driver's side.

A crowd was starting to assemble at the top of the embankment, but none of them made any effort toward him, too afraid to move. Jesse heard the wail of distant sirens as he turned back to the smashed car. Up the hill, twenty feet from the wet ground where he stood, another power line danced through the dry leaves and brush. The grass under the arcing power lines started smoking, then burst into flames. The fire quickly spread, the grass and knee-high brush providing plenty of fuel. Jesse listened to the crackle of the flames and felt the growing heat at his back. The fire spread with the wind, but then slowed as it reached the green grass on the downside of the embankment where the ground was wet and soft enough to leave footprints from his boots.

Ignoring the tingle in his feet, he moved forward again.

All of the Pontiac's windows had been shattered, and he approached it quickly now, moving in from the driver's side.

There was no sound. There was no movement. Three feet from the vehicle, he leaned down and looked in.

A man was in the seat, his head slumped to his chest. The seat belt hung unused from the door frame and Jesse could see a basketball-sized imprint in the windshield that must have come from his head. His skull was bleeding and, stepping forward, he could see compound breaks in his femur from where it had impacted the steering wheel.

Blood. So much blood! How did it splatter everywhere?

Gulping, he took a cautious step toward the car, reached in, and carefully pulled the man back, leaning his head against the top of the seat. The front of his face was crushed, but still Jesse gasped. Sergeant Espy's lifeless eyes stared straight ahead, his mouth hanging open in a bloody, toothless frown. Jesse felt the neck for a heartbeat, though he knew from the massive head injury that the Ares crew chief was certainly dead.

No heartbeat. He let the dead man's head fall to his chin.

Dropping to his knees, he looked across the car to the passenger side and gasped once again.

The only thing that had saved her was the seat belt that hung across the front of her body. She was slumped to the right, her head resting on the side of the door frame, her arms hanging loosely at her side.

He stared at the beautiful face, too shocked to move. Petrie Baha pushed herself back, moaned, and then opened her eyes.

"Adrien," she whispered. Coughing deeply, she winced.

"Petrie!" Jesse muttered.

"Adrien," she repeated, then closed her eyes again.

There was a sudden *crackle* behind him from the fire. The flames were spreading more quickly now. "Get back!" a woman screamed from the embankment, holding her hands to her mouth. The fuel that floated on top of the standing water suddenly burst into flames.

"*Get away! Get away!*" the woman screamed again, her high-pitched voice like scratching fingernails in Jesse's ears. The others in the crowd seemed content to observe the show.

Jesse felt the burning heat and lifted his hands to protect his eyes. Glancing to the back of the auto, he saw the leaking gas tank was half suspended, half detached from the undercarriage of the car. The flames were almost upon it. In seconds it would blow.

A horrible panic swept through him and he gritted his teeth. The instinct was nearly overpowering. *Run!* his mind screamed. His feet started moving uncontrollably, propelling him away from the car, but he forced himself back, holding his hands to his face to protect his eyes from the smoke.

Rolling across the smashed-up hood of the car, he moved to the passenger door and pulled. It was jammed. He knew it would be. Clearing away the shards of broken glass that protruded from the window, he unlatched the seat belt, grabbed Petrie by her shoulders, and pulled her gently through, holding her head to keep her neck level with her spine. Clutching her like a child, he carried her up the embankment until they were clear of the fire.

INSIDE THE ARES
OVER THE NORTHERN ATLANTIC

The Ares pilot fought against a sudden wave of fatigue. He wasn't sleepy. This was much different, and worse; he was gut-wrenchingly weary from his head to his toes. Every bone, every joint seemed to ache with fatigue, every muscle seemed to fight him as if he were heavy and fat. His mouth was dry, his throat tight, his eyelids heavy weights.

And he was in pain. Real pain. Pain in his back, which had been wrenched in battle a long time ago. Pain from his left hand, which throbbed as he held the throttles in his grip. Pain in his head. In his knees.

He felt a hundred years old.

The problem was, of course, that the flight was too long. Too much time to think, too much time alone. That was something he had hated for years. The deep sadness and melancholy was never far away. He needed the voices of others, even strangers, to keep the shadows at bay.

Time for reflection was never a good thing.

Yet here he was, alone in the aircraft, more than ten miles above the earth. Not a soul in the world had any idea where he was. It was growing dim. Deathly quiet.

And he felt so alone.

He stared ahead as he thought. From this altitude he could clearly see the curvature of the earth. Behind him, the evening stars were just beginning to show, but the western sky was not dark yet as he chased the sun.

Sitting in the ejection seat, he felt the power of the incredible jet. The simplest touch of his fingers caused his engines to surge, the slightest pressure on the control stick rolled his wings on their edge. But he paid it no attention. With the Automatic Flight Control System engaged, the computer was in complete control. Airspeed, altitude, navigation, threat sensors, heading, system checks, every critical function of flight was controlled by the computers, leaving him hardly more than a passenger as long as he allowed the computers to fly.

So the silence overwhelmed him and his mind drifted back.

Three years before. A thousands miles to the east.

He stood alone in a glass-enclosed walkway at the airport. It was a dual-use commercial/military facility, but the walkway where he waited was on the civilian side of the runway. He stood by himself, though members of his staff—not a man among them he considered a friend—waited forty feet to his right.

The small commercial airliner, white and gleaming with only a trace of blue around the windows and along the tail, taxied parallel to the concourse, following the yellow taxi lines, then turned abruptly ninety degrees to the left. Slowing through the turn, the aircraft approached the terminal at almost walking speed.

The man watched through the glass in mournful silence as the aircraft moved directly toward him. He saw the two pilots in the cockpit working through their post-landing checks. Glancing down, he saw the yellow hold line. Heavy braking. The aircraft compressing the front nose strut as it slowed. Chocks at the wheels. The gate extended to the front door. The left engine shut down, then the right, then the wingtip lights blinked off.

Three minutes passed. The pilot waited, staring at the tarmac, his face strained and pale. The luggage carrier pulled up next to the aircraft and the belly doors were pulled up.

He sucked a slow breath and held it, gripping the chrome rail that ran along the inside of the glass.

A small ramp was placed next to the aircraft. Two men in dirty work clothes appeared from the bottom door of the concourse to help remove the cargo from the jet.

The pilot watched, all the while gripping the chrome bar so tightly his bony knuckles turned white. He held the same breath, growing dizzy.

The nose of the blue coffin emerged and he felt his knees slump. The men maneuvered it onto the ramp and it slid downward toward the waiting luggage platform.

The pilot almost fainted, overcome with deep grief. His eyes stung, his chin trembled, but he pushed the passion back, keeping the wet snake of emotion deep inside its black hole. He would not cry. Not here and not now. Maybe later. Maybe never. The man didn't know.

As he watched, the casket was moved from the aircraft and loaded onto the waiting cargo platform. Glancing up, he could see through the oval windows to the passengers who were watching from inside. As a sign of respect for the dead, they had been asked to wait inside the cabin until the casket could be loaded and taken away. So the passengers watched, their faces impassive sheets of flesh pressed against the oval windows, as the only good thing in his life, a piece of luggage now, was strapped to the carrier and rolled out of sight.

The pilot considered the memory, then drifted back another twenty years.

Home. With his father. They were facing each other, the tension between them tight as stretched wire.

His father, a powerful man who controlled everything around him with an iron-fisted grip, had just slapped his son up the side of his head. The pilot, then a sixteen-year-old bundle of rage and fury, was humiliated and ready to fight his old man. "You want to hit me, Father? Come on, I will fight you. Is that what you want?"

His father had stepped back, a look of contempt on his face. He hesitated, then stared, then broke into a sarcastic sneer. Then he smiled, almost laughing as he gently patted his son on the cheek. "You're big enough to take me," he had laughed, taking measure of his son. "You're strong enough. Maybe fast enough." But then he had leaned toward him.

Even now, the pilot could feel his father's hot breath on his face. "You have all of the talents of a fighter except for one thing, my son. You're not tough enough. You're not mean enough. Not to take *me,* young man. I'm a snake and you know that. And that is one thing you're not."

The old man patted his head, pinched his cheek, then turned away from his son.

The two memories filled his dark mind.

The casket on the tarmac. The fight with his father. The sting in his eyes as he learned to fight back the tears.

He was *not* tough enough. He was *not* mean enough. His father had been right.

But the casket on the tarmac had changed all of that. He was a different man now. He was a snake like his dad.

He was tough now.

And a fighter.

And this was the last fight of his life.

TWENTY-SIX

CRISIS COMMAND CENTER
UNITED STATES EMBASSY, PARIS

Ninety minutes after the accident on the airport highway, United States Air Force Major James stood on the elevated platform at the front of the elaborately appointed embassy Situation Room. The lights had been dimmed enough for the projection screen and television monitors along the back wall to be clearly seen, but a small spotlight built into the ceiling shined down on him. Standing in the spotlight, he looked out on the crowd. There were some twenty people in the room, including the highest ranking officers and representatives that the intelligence, law enforcement, embassy, NATO, EU, military, and antiterrorist organizations the Continent had to offer. The entire U.S. national security staff had also gathered in the White House Situation Room back in Washington, D.C., and were linked to the embassy through a secure satellite video conference connection.

Jesse shifted his weight from one foot to the other, acutely aware that everyone in the group was staring at him. With not a single friendly face among them, not a person he knew, he felt hopelessly outnumbered as he tried to stare through the light.

His heart slammed like a hammer, pounding from his chest to his ears. His stomach was tied in knots and he felt like his knees couldn't bend. He had faced death in combat almost two hundred times, he'd been shot down and torn up, but he'd never faced anything that made him as nervous as this.

The president was sitting at the back of a U-shaped table that bent around the entire room. Jesse was standing on the podium between the two points on the U. An empty chair was reserved at the president's side for Mr. Ketchum, who had excused himself and was not in the room. The meeting had been going on for ten minutes, most of it with Jesse in the spotlight on the elevated stand.

"You're kidding," the president said after Jesse had explained.

Jesse swallowed, the tiny microphone attached to the collar on his flight suit amplifying the sound. "No, sir," he answered simply, trying to adhere to the only piece of advice anyone had given him before he briefed the president. *Keep it short. Don't say a single word more than you absolutely have to!*

Jesse watched as Mr. Ketchum slipped into the room and sat down at the president's side. The president nodded to Ketchum, then leaned forward on the table. "Tell me again, Major James. This information was found in the car?"

"Yes sir. After Sergeant Espy's vehicle crashed, the survivor was taken to the airport infirmary. Espy was pronounced dead at the scene and taken to the mortuary. By that time U.S. security agents had arrived. We did an initial search of the automobile and found this, sir."

"Where? How did you find it?"

"In the trunk, Mr. President. The latch on the trunk had broken open from the impact and the metal briefcase was found inside."

"Was it locked?"

"Yes sir, it was."

"Then how did you open it? Did you find the key?"

"One of the agents opened the briefcase, sir."

"How did he do that?"

Jesse swallowed again. "Mr. Costas shot the lock with his gun."

The president hesitated. "Okay, so you found the briefcase, opened it, and this is what you found inside?"

Jesse nodded to the large screen behind him. The documents inside the briefcase had been scanned into the computer and reproduced on the screen. There was an aviation map and a flight plan with notes, fuel loads, estimated times of arrivals, frequencies, possible fighter intercept points, winds, altitudes, civilian jet routes—everything needed for a successful combat sortie. A dark circle had been drawn around Le Bourget Airport. A black line picked up on the edge of the circle, headed northwest over the North Sea, then arced down the Canadian Coast to the northern tip of Maine. There the line stopped, but three dashed lines picked up, depicting three slightly different headings. The dashed lines ended at three red triangles drawn over Boston, New York City, and Washington, D.C.

Jesse half faced the screen, never turning his back on the U.S. president, then lifted a laser light and pointed as he talked. "The flight planning adheres to typical U.S. military standards and procedures. It's fairly simple, Mr. President. You have the launch point," he flashed the light on Paris, "the route of flight," he moved the laser northwest, across the Atlantic, then south to the northern coast of Maine. "These red lines are the threat rings from U.S. air defense locations, air defense fighter units, projected naval assets, missile sites, et cetera—all of which are highly classified and yet, interestingly, they have been accurately depicted here. The final point before the targets is what we call the initial point, or IP, which is this black circle, sir. From there, the routes move toward the three distinct targets." Jesse finished, dropping the laser to his side.

The president studied the aviation charts and flight plan. "Is it realistic?" he demanded.

Jesse hesitated. He kept his face passive, but something deep inside him wanted to scream. A sharp uneasiness seemed to cut him. *It just didn't seem right.* He didn't know why, but something was out of place and it rolled his gut into a ball. Still, the uncertainty was too vague for him to articulate, and so he answered the president, "Yes, sir, it is realistic. Whoever developed this flight plan pretty much thought of everything. As you can see, the selected flight levels and routes are designed to avoid all civilian air traffic. He's cruising across the pond at almost sixty-seven thousand feet and greater than Mach speed. The Ares is the only aircraft that can do that, of course. So, yes sir, in my opinion this is an authentic strike plan."

The president shook his head. He moved his eyes around the table as if expecting someone to say something, but everyone seemed to stare at the screen, unwilling to meet his eyes. "So this guy, this Prince bin Saud, he has the capability to strike our country," the president finally said.

"No doubt about it."

"He's going to strike one of those cities?"

"Most likely all of them, sir."

The president fell back in his chair, his eyes burning with rage and fear. The room took on a deadly silence, and no one even moved. Jesse stood erect, his stomach churning. The president leaned toward the satellite microphone in the center of the table before him. "You copy that?" he asked his national security advisor back at the White House in D.C.

"Yes sir," the NSA replied, his voice all business and cold.

"Comments to this point then?" Abram asked.

Five seconds of silence followed. "Major James," an unknown voice then said. One of the split screens on the back wall shifted to show the face of General Shevky, the chairman of the Joint Chiefs of Staff, who was sitting directly to the NSA's right in the Situation Room in D.C. The computer-operated video camera automatically turned and focused on him, following the sound of his voice. "I understand you were the senior test pilot on the Ares program?" the general asked.

"Technically, sir, as the chief of our branch, Colonel Ray was the most—"

"Yes, yes, I understand that. But I also understand that Colonel Ray is dead. And even at that, you are still the most experienced pilot when it comes to the Ares?"

"That is true, sir."

"How long have you been with the program?"

"Almost five years. I was the pilot on the maiden flight of the prototype."

"You have more time in the Ares than any other pilot, is that true?"

"Yes, sir, that is correct."

"Alright. Now the only reason I bring this out is I want to establish your credentials, because, frankly Major James, the advice you are about to give us will carry enormous weight."

Jesse didn't answer. The overhead light glared down on him.

"Tell us then, Major, and keep it simple; we've got lots of nonaviation people in the room and we all want to understand. What is the maximum range of the Ares? Bottom line—can it strike the U.S. from Europe without being refueled?"

Jesse had gone through the numbers a dozen times in his head. Stalling, he took a quick swallow of water from a plastic cup he had placed on the floor near the podium, then turned to the general's image on the screen. "Sir, you are going to hate my answer, but the truth is, it depends. On a normal combat sortie, yes, the Ares could fly from Europe unrefueled and strike the U.S. But there are further considerations we have to take into account. How much fuel did the pilot burn while he was being intercepted, escorted back to the Paris airport, and then launch his attack? That was a significant amount of time, and it would have cut into his gas. However, the Saudi pilot appeared to be absolutely committed to attacking the second Ares regardless of how much fuel it drained.

"Once that was accomplished, he still has to cross the pond to attack the States. Again, the Ares is designed for superaltitude, supercruise—I'm sorry, what that means is the Ares is designed to fly very high and very fast, much higher than any other aircraft and much faster than the speed of sound. Getting above sixty thousand feet allows for extremely efficient fuel settings, even at supercruise. And with the three targets along the east coast . . . it seems to me . . ."

"I need an answer," Shevky pushed him.

Jesse thought a final moment. "Sir, the bottom line is, the Ares is capable of striking the East Coast without being refueled, but under only one condition."

"And that is?"

"A one-way flight, sir. The pilot doesn't have enough fuel to strike the U.S., then make it anywhere that would be safe to land. But if he is willing to hit the targets and crash, then he has plenty of gas to strike without landing to refuel."

Again, the room was silent. To his right, someone in the darkness leaned forward and swore bitterly.

Jesse waited. *Not a word more than you have to!* kept rolling around in his head.

The chairman's face shifted on the television screen as he brought his hands together and folded them on the table. "You're telling us the Ares has the international range and fuel to strike the East Coast without landing to refuel."

"If the pilot is willing to crash before he lands, yes it does. But unless the pilot has arranged for a secret landing base somewhere very close, southern Canada perhaps, that is the only way it could be done. Even then, it will take a very good pilot, someone who understands how to get the very most from his aircraft. But, in this case, I think we have to assume this pilot is capable of that."

"Guarantee that's his plan," the president sneered. "Good heavens, gentlemen, it isn't like we haven't seen that before. Martyrs and paradise. The glory of Allah. Seventy-two lovely virgins waiting on the other side. This guy is on a one-way mission. We don't have long to prepare."

Judging from the grunts around the dim room, most of the others agreed.

"Which means he will be in a position to attack his targets in what . . . how long now?" the president asked.

Jesse looked at his watch. "About two hours, sir."

Another deadly silence descended over the room. "We've got to order an immediate evacuation of the target cities!" the NSA said. "We've got to get those people out of there."

"We can't do that!" the vice president shouted from the Situation Room in D.C. "You've seen what happens when we try to evacuate. It takes hours, even days to evacuate a major city like that. We could kill more people ordering an evacuation—"

"But we have to do something."

Other voices started talking. "We have to . . ."

"We can't . . ."

"Have we even thought about . . ."

The voices grew louder until Jesse couldn't understand what anyone was saying anymore. Ketchum raised his hand to stop them, but it didn't have any effect. More panicked voices and anger.

The room grew warmer and Jesse started to sweat.

He stood now, unnoticed on the stand, then forced himself to take a breath and swallow, knowing they were missing several critical points. "Mr. President," he started saying. No one listened to him. "Mr. President," he repeated, his voice sounding through the speakers built into the ceiling of the room.

The president lifted a hand for silence and the room fell quiet again.

"If I could," Jesse said, "I don't think I made myself clear."

The president shook his head. "We prefer clarity, Major James," he answered curtly. "Would you like to try again?"

Jesse took a step to the side, moving from underneath the spotlight so he could see the president without the glare in his eye. "First, sir, the Ares is an incredible aircraft, but it is far less lethal if it is used in the light. The only way to attack it and shoot it is to find it visually, which requires daylight, of course. Right now, it's midafternoon in D.C., which would mean Prince bin Saud would be attacking in the light. I don't think that would happen, not unless he was willing to significantly decrease his chances of success.

"Second, he has no weapons, at least as far as we know. Yes, the aircraft was obviously loaded with a couple conventional bombs for the attack here in Paris, and yes, he always has the laser, but powerful as that is, I think he has something else in mind. Think about it, Mr. President, do any of us really think the prince and his people went to all the trouble of stealing this aircraft just to attack the U.S. with a couple conventional bombs? That seems extremely unlikely. I think they have a much bigger, much more devastating plan in mind."

The president lifted both hands, his elbows remaining on the table. "Are you saying you think the prince is going to land somewhere and upload some kind of other weapon?"

"It seems very likely, sir. I simply can't imagine they would go to this trouble unless they had a much more lethal plan.

"And finally, sir—and this is pure speculation on my part—but I know Prince bin Saud. I think I know him very well. He is the last person in the world who would volunteer for a suicide mission. He doesn't fit the criteria of an Islamic fascist in any way. He's not religious. He hates authority. He can't stand being told what to do. More, he craves wealth and power. He loathes his father, there's no doubt, but he loves his father's money even more. He wants the thrill of glory and he wants it in *this* world.

"Taken together, I believe we can assume that Prince bin Saud stole the Ares with much greater intentions than dropping a couple conventional weapons and crashing into the sea. "No, I don't believe that at this moment the prince is flying toward the U.S. I think he's landed somewhere to refuel and load up some nonconventional bombs—nuclear, biological—we need to prepare for the worst. He will hold until later tonight, tomorrow night at the latest, and then he will strike."

Ten minutes later, after taking final inputs from the men around the table, the president asked for a private moment with the leaders of his national security staff. All of the others were escorted out of the embassy situation room, leaving the president and his men alone.

The meeting was short, the president getting straight to the point. "Alright, what are your recommendations?" he demanded of his staff.

"Noble Eagle," the NSA answered immediately.

The president looked into the eyes of the few men with him in the room. "No hesitation?" he asked them.

They all nodded their heads.

"You are unanimous back there in D.C.?" he pressed.

The satellite link hummed a few seconds as they took a final poll. "We are unanimous, Mr. President. Noble Eagle is our best option at this point."

The president huffed, wishing he had never quit smoking, desperately wanting to shove a cigarette in his mouth. "Alright, then. But I want *every* air asset we own up there in the sky. Until we locate and shoot down the Ares, if it's got wings and a missile, I want it looking for the Ares. Do you understand me, people? I want Noble Eagle to build a veritable wall."

"Understand, sir," the chairman of the Joint Chiefs shot back.

"Do we ground all civilian air traffic?" the NSA then asked.

"All international traffic. Everything along the East Coast."

"Mr. President, I just want to be clear. We are to halt or divert all international flights as well as all domestic traffic along the eastern coast?"

The president nodded, then hesitated. "Check that," he corrected himself. "I want to clear it all, the entire U.S."

"Sir, we could probably get by with just the East Coast right now."

"No. Clear all the air space across the U.S. If we see something out there, I don't want to wonder if it's one of our guys or him."

The satellite phone picked up a scratching sound as the NSA scribbled on his notepad.

"Alright then . . . the big one . . . the one we're all dreading to even talk about." The president faltered. "Do we evacuate the target cities?"

The NSA lifted his head from his notes, his face filling the video screen. "Sir, I've been going over the Noble Eagle plan with your staff back here in D.C. This scenario has been war-gamed and practiced a thousand times before, not against a threat like the Ares, but that doesn't change our overall game plan that much. Noble Eagle considers every option, with a matrix of time frames and options planned out to an excruciating degree. Knowing that, I would recommend we follow the protocols outlined in the Noble Eagle for right now, sir."

The president bit his lip, wishing for a cigarette again. "So we hold off on evacuation orders?"

"Sir, you know how difficult such a thing would be. The three largest and most congested cities along the East Coast. Fifteen million people. It's impossible to estimate the chaos and panic. It is my opinion, sir, that such an act is premature at this point. Let's implement Noble Eagle and trust it to do what it was designed to do. Noble Eagle will locate and destroy the Ares, I am confident of that, sir."

The president turned to the image of the chairman of the Joint Chiefs, a former Marine fighter pilot and air group commander, recipient of more flying medals than any one man ought to wear. He studied him carefully.

"General Shevky?" he pressed.

The general nodded slowly. "We *will* find the Ares, sir. We *will* bring it down."

The president hesitated.

If Shevky was so certain, why did his eyes flicker so?

And why did the president have such a cold knot in his gut?

He stared at each of his advisors. "A final comment," he added. "I've known the patriarch of the House of Saud for many years now. The king is two men, and neither of them are real. He shows one face to the free world, another to his Arab brothers, and I don't like either one. I don't trust him. He's a slimy snake. So if we find out he's behind this, I want to go after him. For five generations, they've been exporting and preaching nothing but hate of the West. Now it may be true that he can't control his own family—heaven knows I can't control my own son—but if we discover that he's involved, I want him to pay a heavy price."

The chief of staff watched the president carefully as he spoke. The animosity between Abram and the king of the House of Saud went back many years.

The president looked at his advisors. "Anything else?" he asked. No one spoke. "Then let's do it!" he said.

The president watched his staff gather their notepads, then made a final point. "I mean it," he said. "I want every air defense asset we own up there protecting our skies. We have to succeed in this, gentlemen, or we will go to our graves with nothing but remorse in our hearts."

As the room emptied, Ketchum pulled the president aside. Gripping him by the arm, he leaned toward his ear. "We've got an issue with Major James," he said in a whisper.

The president pulled back from Ketchum's dry breath. "Not now," he shot back.

Ketchum held on his elbow. "Sir, this really is something you need to know."

The president grunted. "Surely, Mr. Ketchum, whatever you have, it can wait?"

"Sir . . ."

The president relented, shaking his head. "Alright, what is it? And please make it brief. I've got a few things on my plate."

"Understand, sir." Ketchum relaxed his grip on the president's arm. "We've identified the survivor of the car wreck."

"Good."

"She's a known agent here in Paris, sir. Works for Hezbollah, among other Islamic terrorist organizations. Her father is a very influential and powerful man. She uses his cover and contacts to gather information, which she passes back to her contacts in Gaza."

"Okay, that is great, but there are no surprises there."

"Then does it surprise you, Mr. President, to learn that this woman, Petrie Baha, had a meeting with Major James earlier this afternoon? And would it surprise you, Mr. President, to learn that after that meeting, about the time the Ares disappeared, Jesse called Miss Baha on her private cell phone? Does any of that surprise you, sir, because it surprises me."

TWENTY-SEVEN

Jesse had been told to wait outside the command center and so he did, standing uncomfortably by himself in the hall. Some of the embassy employees and security staff nodded as they passed, but none stopped to talk. He saw the deputy U.S. ambassador to France standing in a doorway at the end of the hall and a few other faces he recognized from the meeting, but none of them seemed willing to do anything more than glance in his direction. He was radioactive, he could see that; anyone associated with the Ares had a stink that wouldn't clear until the jet was brought down and someone was sitting in jail.

He wished he had time to eat. Time to go to the bathroom. Time to sit in a corner and sort this thing out.

A red light was illuminated above the command center doorway.

CLASSIFIED BRIEFING IN PROGRESS

flashed in block letters. A miniature camera was hidden behind a bulletproof dome on the ceiling to monitor access to the locked door and, above his head, a series of speakers broadcast white noise into the corridor, making it impossible to electronically eavesdrop on the meeting inside.

The meeting with the president of the United States and his senior national security staff lasted less than five minutes. The red light went out, the door clicked, a camera hummed as it moved on its pivots, and the metal door swung back.

Edgar Ketchum was the first man to exit the room. He walked directly to Jesse, took him by the arm, and moved him down the hallway. Another man followed, someone Jesse didn't know. Two doors down, Ketchum pushed Jesse into a small, windowless office where he was surprised to see OSI Special Agent Costas waiting. The other man followed, and Ketchum shut the door. Costas moved toward Ketchum, nodded, then stood with his back to the wall.

Jesse turned around, confused. Arrogance and hostility was almost oozing from Ketchum's skin. The president's chief of staff moved around a small coffee table, sat on the leather couch, placed one foot on the floor, and crossed the other over his knee. Jesse turned to the third man—muscular, perfect hair, tailored suit—then glanced over to Costas, whose moustache was so thin he could see the sweat on his lip.

He turned back to Ketchum. "Sir?" he asked.

Ketchum reached in his suit pocket, pulled out a dark cigar, sniffed its length, bit the tip, wetted the end with his tongue, then pulled out a small matchbox and lit the cigar. "Ever heard of Navarrenx?" he asked Jesse.

The pilot shook his head.

Ketchum pulled on the smoke, then exhaled a thin line through his lips. "Navarrenxes are the best cigars in the world, outside of Cubans, of course. They grow the tobacco for them here in France, of all places. They say it's the temperature but I'm convinced it's the soil. Whatever it is, the outcome is very, very good." He pulled another drag.

Jesse's chest tightened as if waiting for a punch. His instincts were screaming, his hair on end.

"You know," Ketchum laughed, "the night before Kennedy announced the Cuban embargo, he had his press secretary get him two thousand Cuban cigars. One of the benefits of the presidency, I suppose." He watched Jesse carefully, then pulled a tiny piece of tobacco off his lip. "Are you a smoker, Major James?"

Jesse shook his head.

"Wow." Ketchum pressed his lips together. "I find that almost hard to believe. I mean, there you are, growing up in one of the nastiest communities in the nation. Crime. Drugs. Prostitution. And that's only in the kindergartens; it gets much worse after that. Yet there you are, so pure, like a virgin . . . are you a virgin, Major James? Oh, I'm sorry, not my business, though I'm sure that you are. And with your incredibly . . . unfortunate childhood, the fact that you have risen to such a position, I don't know, I just find it—" he nodded to the suit guy—"How would you describe it, Emit?"

The third man shook his head in mock amazement. "Remarkable," he replied.

Jesse turned toward him. "Have we met?" he asked coldly.

"No," Emit answered, not extending his hand.

Jesse met his cold eyes, then turned back to Ketchum, his face growing red with anger. "Have you got something you want to say to me?" he said.

Ketchum ignored him, sucking another puff of thick smoke from his cigar. "These really are very good." He smiled. "And I consider myself a bit of an aficionado, you know." He pulled the cigar from his mouth and eyed it appreciatively. "Every part of this cigar, the filler, the binder and wrapper, all are a different type of tobacco. Did you know that? Yet to make a good stogie, they have to come from the same farm. The French claim these are all rolled by virgins, but I think that's an exaggeration, don't you?"

Jesse waited, not the least bit interested in discussing Edgar's cigar.

"You know, Jesse, it's a very interesting coincidence," Ketchum finally offered. "Out of all of the men in the world who might be sitting up there in our jet, don't you find it curious that you know Prince Abdul Mohammad bin Saud? The fact that you two flew together, I mean how unlikely is that!"

He paused and lifted his eyes to Jesse, who was shaking with anger now.

"What do you want?" he demanded.

"I want the truth from you, Jesse. That's all that I ask."

"You've got that, you know that."

"The truth," Ketchum repeated.

Jesse stood over him.

Ketchum shoved the cigar in his mouth and stood up. "Major James, tell me something. What's the best way to track the fighter? How are we going to find it? What's the best thing to do?"

Jesse hesitated. Did Ketchum really expect an answer? Did he really think that he knew?

"Let me give you a hint," Ketchum started when Jesse didn't say anything. "What about our satellites?"

Jesse's expression didn't change. "It's a possibility."

"And why is that?"

"The tops of the wings . . ."

"That's right, Major James. The top of the wings bounce back significant waves of radar energy. If a satellite is in the right position, and looking straight down, it is possible they will get a flash of energy off the wings."

Jesse shrugged his shoulders. "I thought of that," he said.

"You've thought of that! Isn't that interesting? Yet you didn't mention it in the briefing. Which makes me wonder why."

Jesse didn't hesitate. "Some technologists think our satellites may be able to track the fighter. Many others don't."

"But what if they could, Major James? What could we do then?" Ketchum demanded.

Jesse thought a moment. "Once we have a location on the fighter, we could concentrate on the airfields in the region where it might land to refuel. If we can catch it on the ground, we can destroy it. That would be the only way."

"That's right!" Ketchum shouted. "*That* is our best chance to destroy it, isn't it, *Major James*. We move our satellites to monitor its intended route of flight, track it to the refueling runway, then destroy it on the ground, while we have a chance. It's the best plan we have, the best opportunity for success. Isn't that right, Major James?"

Jesse was unconvinced. "You may be right. As I said, some of our satellite specialists think it will work. But I've worked with the Ares. I don't believe them."

"You don't think it will work. Well that is interesting, because there is at least one officer who thinks it will."

"Who is that?"

"General Shevky."

"He told you that," Jesse answered quietly.

"Yes . . . yes he did. And he seems to be a pretty capable man."

Jesse nodded, his eyes hard. "I'm sure that he is."

"Now tell me again, Major. Why didn't you suggest this plan when we were in our previous meeting?"

"I have already told you. I don't think it will work. It will waste time and resources that we don't have right now."

"Really! You don't think so! Well then, I'm sure you must be right. After all, you're the expert on the Ares." He turned to the other men. "I guess we have to trust him, don't we, men."

Jesse bit his lip, his face flushing. "Our KH-11 and KH-15s *won't* be able to track the stolen fighter. We've done some initial testing. It is not going to work. Hook me up on a SatPhone to General Shevky and I will tell him that right now."

Ketchum shook his head. He didn't buy it. His dark eyes narrowed. "Hmm . . . so curious. So interesting."

Ketchum watched him carefully, then motioned to the suit man. "This is Special Agent Roger Emit. Mr. Emit is the head of the FBI field office here in Paris. He has been rather busy, as you can imagine, but he has found something interesting that we thought you might be able to help us with."

Jesse turned toward him but didn't say anything.

"Perhaps the reason you didn't mention the possibility of tracking the stolen Ares with our satellites is because of this," Emit suggested, dropping an 8 by 10 black and white photograph on the table.

Jesse stared at it and fell back, his knees weak as water. "How did you get those?" he stammered. "Who is she? What is going on?"

Emit took a step toward him. "You were the one talking to her. Why don't you tell me?"

Jesse stammered. "Her name is Petrie . . . Petrie something."

"Baha. Yes, that is one of her names, but she has many others. This is a girl who likes to get around. But you know that, don't you, Jesse. You know all about this girl."

Jesse took a menacing step toward him. "I don't know anything about her!"

"I see," Emit answered. "You didn't know then, I suppose, that Miss Baha has been working for Hezbollah for the last three or four years. You didn't know, I'm sure, that she's been passing information to a number of terrorist organizations, using her father's contacts and background to gain access."

"What I know about Petrie Baha could be written on the back of a matchbook!" Jesse snapped. "I met her once. Got that? One friggin' time! I spent fifteen, maybe twenty minutes with her, and that is it. I've never talked to her, never had contact with her, never seen her but one time in my life. You got that, *Mr. Emit*? I don't know what you're trying to say here, but you had better be careful, my friend."

Emit's neck tightened up. "Let me be clear, Major James, if I could. I will draw my own conclusions. And I am not your friend."

Jesse stared at him, meeting the glare in his eyes. Ketchum watched them closely, then stepped between the two men. "Mr. Costas," he said, "have you anything to add?"

Costas nodded, pulling a small business card from his chest pocket. "You have the right to remain silent," he started.

Jesse turned toward him. "You're kidding!" he stammered.

"You have the right to an attorney . . ."

Jesse took a step back and swore.

TWENTY-EIGHT

"You're arresting me?" Jesse sputtered, his eyes wide in disbelief.

"No," Ketchum answered, "we just want to ask you a couple questions is all, and before we did that, we thought it prudent to remind you of your rights. We don't want to give you any excuses later on."

"You think I was involved in the disappearance of the Ares!"

Emit pulled out a tiny recorder, punched a button, and placed it on the table. "Tell us about the girl," he said again.

"You consider me a suspect!" Jesse's voice choked with anger.

"Would you like to get a lawyer?"

"I don't need a lawyer. I haven't done anything wrong!"

The room fell silent. "You think I helped the Saudi prince steal my own aircraft. You think I helped him!" Jesse was whispering now.

"We don't know what to think," Ketchum answered simply. It was the most honest thing he had said to this point.

"The girl," Emit pressed.

"The girl . . . I *don't* know her, I already told you that."

Emit shook his head. Ketchum swore.

Jesse lifted his hands, turned away, then took a deep breath. "Alright," he said, turning back to the men. "I'll tell you everything I know about Petrie." His voice was softer now. "She's beautiful." He shot a look at Ketchum. "You'd have to be dead not to have noticed that." He smirked and turned back to Emit. "She's better at English than she pretends to be. She drinks tea. She seems nice. And that's it. The whole package. Everything that I know. Now I want you to tell me, am I under arrest?"

The three men glanced at each other. The silence was heavy again.

"Do I need a lawyer?" Jesse demanded.

"Tell you what," Emit answered, "let's take this one easy step a time. Let me ask a few questions, you think about the answer if you have to, then we'll take it from there."

"No, I don't think so. Not with the way this is going so far."

Emit opened the manila folder and glanced at his notes.

Jesse shook his head and stayed quiet, staring at the white walls. "Can't you see what is going on?" he almost shouted, the reality hitting him like a fist to the chest. "Can't you see? Are you stupid? You need me. They knew that! They knew I was the only chance that you had of ever finding the Ares. But they also knew if they could implicate me in this deal, it would make it that much more difficult, even impossible for me to help bring him down." His voice fell away to a whisper. "Brilliant," he muttered, almost talking to himself. "Brilliant and simple. One chance meeting in a café. So easy, but enough to cast me in a very suspicious light.

"But let me tell you something," Jesse finished, his voice rising now. "I didn't *do* anything. I'm not a part of this deal. And I'm not scared, because you'd have to prove it and *there is nothing there!* So go ahead and arrest me if you want to. But if you lose me, you've got nothing, and you lose the Ares as well."

The three men only stared at each other. An overhead fan kicked on, blowing cool air through the vents. Costas brushed his moustache and stared at Jesse, then turned to the FBI man. Emit nodded to Ketchum, a tiny move of his head.

"Tell me!" Jesse demanded.

"No," Ketchum answered slowly, "you are not under arrest. We'll keep digging, and I promise you, Major James, we will find out what's going on."

Jesse took a step toward him, his eyes hard as nails. "Yeah," he said, then started to leave.

"Stay close," Ketchum called to him. "We'll have more questions for you."

"I'll be here." Jesse sneered as he walked from the room.

Five minutes later, Ketchum met with the president again.

"What does Special Agent Emit think?" the president asked.

Ketchum hesitated, reluctant. "He thinks that we're barking up the wrong tree. If Jesse was involved with the Ares, she is the last person on the continent he would have agreed to meet with. No way he would call her, especially on a cell phone we can trace back to him."

The president watched him, noting the look in his eyes. "What do you think?" he pressed.

Ketchum tugged angrily on his chin. "I don't know."

The president nodded. The hesitation told him everything. "Yes you do,

Edgar. If you had any doubt in your mind, you'd have him sitting in a cell-block in the basement with someone pounding on his head."

"Probably," Ketcham said. "But I have to tell you, sir, in one sense this isn't good news. We've still got to find out who helped Prince Saud and nail his hide to the wall. And if we can't find the right person, then maybe Jesse will have to do."

TWENTY-NINE

The president had a final meeting with his national security staff. "What about the satellites?" he demanded.

The director of the National Reconnaissance Organization hesitated. "Sir, I'm afraid I don't have good news."

The president huffed, then waited for the explanation.

"Sir, our best satellites are not deployed to monitor our eastern coast," the NRO director continued. "It's going to take us a little time to move them, but, sir, I'm afraid that even when we do, it might not be any help. We've been looking into the data, going back over the little bit of information we know about the radar-reflective characteristics of the Ares, and the bottom line is we are beginning to doubt our KH satellites will be able to detect it anyway. They just aren't designed for this type of thing, sir, looking for stealth aircraft from space. And yes, we might get lucky, but we aren't counting on it anymore."

"Alright," the president answered, deep disappointment in his voice. He thought a long moment, then turned to the image on the screen of the chairmen of the Joint Chiefs of Staff. "Is Noble Eagle ready, then?" he asked him.

"Yes, sir, we are."

"It looks like we have all of our eggs in your basket."

"We are ready, sir."

On September 10, 2001, Air Defense Command was a dying entity, a fifty-year-old dinosaur from the cold war that was sucking its last breath, its oxygen bottle on empty, the generals waiting with their hands on the plug.

Twenty-four hours later, it was suddenly resurrected; a new mission, a new urgency, a new purpose in life.

By eleven o'clock in the morning on September 11, every air traffic controller around the nation was staring at completely blank radar screens. It was like the power had gone out or their machines had malfunctioned, for their screens were nothing but clouds and birds and blue sky.

A little more than two hours before, at 8:46 a.m. ET, the first hijacked aircraft had impacted the North Tower. Seventeen minutes later, the South Tower was hit. Other reports of suspected hijackings started bleeding in. When a third hijacked aircraft impacted the Pentagon, and with another turning off course and heading for D.C., all civilian traffic was commanded to land. Fighter aircraft were sent up to intercept them and shoot them down if they did not immediately comply. Thousands of aircraft were diverted to the nearest airports, leaving nothing but empty skies from L.A. to Boston.

The men and women at Air Defense Command knew, perhaps more than anyone else, that the world had just changed. No more looking for Russian aircraft skirting down the eastern coast. No more sitting for days, even weeks, with nothing to do but launch an occasional interceptor to chase a lost Beach Bonanza that had wandered off course.

A new threat had been hatched, more ugly, more menacing than anything seen before.

Operation Noble Eagle was born to counter the threat. Teaming with all of the federal agencies under the umbrella of Homeland Security, Department of Defense, Coast Guard, and the Canadian military, Noble Eagle integrated an incredible web of control centers and defense sectors throughout the United States whose mission was to protect the nation's borders by watching her skies.

The change in the day-to-day pace of operations was immediate. Within minutes of the 9/11 attacks, fighter aircraft under NORAD command were scrambled to fly Combat Air Patrol (CAP) missions over key U.S. cities. They kept up a crushing pace, flying almost 20,000 sorties in the first six months, 34,000 sorties within the first couple of years. Compared with the grand total of 147 sorties flown in 2000, the rate of sortie generation was an entirely different world. And not only had the tempo accelerated to an exhausting degree, the complexity of the missions had become overwhelming as well. Their new purpose was to plan, fund, organize, equip, and operate the entire air defense zone into one integrated force that was capable of locating, tracking, identifying, and neutralizing airborne threats to the United States. Everything from hang gliders and crop dusters to jumbo aircraft had to be tracked, and not just along the borders, but throughout the entire interior of the country as well. For the pilots, it seemed their mission had entered some kind of weird twilight zone where they were far more likely to intercept a civilian airliner with hundreds of innocent people onboard than a conventional fighter or bomber that they could happily shoot down.

National Guard fighter units were the tip of this haggard spear. The Combined Air Operations Center (CAOC) at Tyndall acted as a battlefield command center to coordinate the three subordinate air sectors around the country. Tyndall controlled the Southeast Air Defense Sector; Rome, New York, had the Northeast; and McChord AFB in Washington had responsibility for the West.

In the dark rooms at Tyndall, the battle would be coordinated. Over the cold waters of the north Atlantic, the war would be fought.

SWITCHBACK 27
FLIGHT OF TWO F-16 FALCONS
120 MILES OFF THE EASTERN COAST OF MAINE

The pilot of the lead aircraft looked out the left side of his cockpit, then to the right. He sucked a deep breath, the sterile air of his cockpit drying the inside of his mouth. His oxygen mask hung loosely from the left side of his flight helmet and he cocked his head down to speak into the secure radio to his wingman, who was flying a little more than five hundred feet behind.

"An awesome sight, ain't it, Killer?"

The radio crackled lightly. "True, that," his wingman replied.

The flight leader scanned the airspace around him, lifting his head to look straight up at the clouds and darkening sky overhead, then off to his left side again. There must have been three dozen fighter aircraft, and that was just off one side. His radar was tracking almost thirty in front of him, but he knew there were many more. Many more.

All to intercept a single aircraft! He shook his head in disgust. If the entire Russian Air Force, with the North Koreans and Chinese thrown in as well, had threatened to take out D.C., he could understand such a response. But all of this for one fighter?

The F-16 pilot was certain it was complete overkill. He had never seen so many military aircraft packed into so much small space. Most of them were fighters or interceptors of one kind or another, but there were also tankers to refuel them and AWACS to coordinate their flight paths. Amazingly, there were no civilian airliners among them, for they had all been turned away from U.S. airspace or forced to land. For a while he had listened to the chaos on the radio as the air traffic controllers had tried to coordinate all of the civilian flight plans—hundreds of aircraft, some of them getting low on fuel after a transoceanic flight, lining up for emergency landings in Canada or Newfoundland. Those that had the fuel were commanded to turn around, sent back to Europe, the Middle East, wherever they had come from. He had listened to the chaotic radio conversations for a few minutes, then finally turned the VHF radio off. Too much confusion. Too much noise. How did they keep it all straight?

The bottom line—and the only thing that really mattered now—was that the airspace had been cleared of all civilian jets. Anything out there not squawking a military code was to be considered hostile, which was just fine with him.

Keep the rules simple, and they were more likely to succeed.

In his head, he counted through the various formations of fighters around him: F-16s hugging the shoreline, four F-22s thirty miles off his right—they were just splitting up, going out to two-and-two—a flight of navy F-18 Hornets in a CAP a little more than eighty miles farther to the northeast. Beyond that, more navy fighters, a long way out there, over the cold northern seas. Let them have it. The F-16 pilot shivered, thinking of the cold water and carrier landings the navy guys would have to deal with that night. The world's best pilots landed on carriers in the dark, that was true, but the world's smartest pilots joined the air force so they didn't have to.

Above the pilot, and a little more than one hundred miles to his left, flying just inside the coast of Maine, was the E-3 Sentry Airborne Warning and Control System (AWACS) aircraft that was controlling most of the air force fighters, including his formation of F-16s. Between him and the AWACS, the pilot had counted at least fifteen other fighter formations, more than thirty aircraft in all. Below him, down at fifteen thousand feet, a Coast Guard C-37A Gulfstream V command-and-control jet had set up to loiter where it could coordinate the search efforts of the sea vessels and aircraft that were flying below ten thousand feet. It was the first time he had seen stacking of fighters like that. But this was a different battle. No radar, no IR sensors. They had to find the target by sight. So they had packed every inch of airspace with anything that could fly, to the point that running into each other was becoming as likely as landing safely at the end of the flight.

The pilot knew the military had scrambled fighter units from as far away as Florida, Wisconsin, St. Louis, and Illinois, as well as every active duty, reserve, National Guard, and navy unit up and down the East Coast. And more were waiting to launch when the first wave had to land.

He considered the instructions they had received on how they could bring the stolen fighter down. The good news, they were told, was that they had the target's anticipated route of flight, and so they knew, more or less, where he was going to be. The bad news—they didn't know when. Might be today. Might be tomorrow. So here they were, waiting for him to show up.

The pilot almost laughed. Heaven help the poor bugger who flew into this nest of pissed-off fighter pilots begging to shoot something down.

He shook his head once again, then glanced at the computer-generated flight plan he had strapped to his leg along with the notes he had scribbled on the margins of the folded page:

> FIST- Fighter Integrating Strategic Technologies. *("typical BS Pentagon acronym," he had scribbled next to FIST).*
>
> Indictable to radar and IR sensors.
>
> Mach 2.5 speed. Supercruise. Superstealth. *("believe it when I see it")*
>
> Munitions: capable of conventional and nuclear bombs.
>
> Self defense; a SSHCL-105B solid-state heat-capacity laser. *("What is this??")*

He swore as he glanced at his notes. Yeah, he'd heard rumors, all the military pilots had, but he had no idea it was real, no idea the aircraft had actually been through a flight test, and certainly no idea it was this powerful. But the Pentagon briefer had been very clear. *"The laser will reach out and kill you from two hundred miles,"* he had said. *"You won't see the Ares, you won't get a sniff on your radar; one second you might be there, and the next second you'll be gone. So be careful, ladies, and don't get too comfortable. The rules of engagement have changed. It is a different battle now."*

Which was the entire reason, of course, that the Ares had been built.

Problem was, they had intended an American would be flying the newest killing machine.

Still, the pilot wasn't worried. In fact, it excited him to the bone. So some raghead had stolen their fighter, which was a bitch of a machine. No problem. For one thing, he was sitting in the F-16, one of the greatest air-to-air fighters in the world. The Falcons were small but agile, short-legged but fast, making them one of the baddest dogs on the street.

Stealth. Lasers. Whatever.

So the Ares was fast and maneuverable. The faster they flew, the more fun they were to blow from the sky. The higher they flew, the more the pilot's remains could be scattered in the wind. Supercruise, superstealth, SSHCL-105 piece of crap. The pilot wasn't intimidated. He was sure of himself, for when push came to shove, when it came down to who died and who lived, when it came to air-to-air combat, it *always* came down to pilot skills. And a good pilot, a trained pilot, could *always* find a way to hit the enemy, find his weakness, and exploit it for the kill.

As he searched the sky, he couldn't help but lift his head and thank the flying gods for the light and the clear, cloudless skies.

He needed the light to find it, and he wanted to find it today. Supercruise and fancy lasers meant nothing to him. The stolen fighter was being flown by some jihadist who had more time steering camels than a flying machine.

So they had to locate the stolen fighter visually before they could bring it down. No big deal, not today. And once they found it, they would kill it, there was no doubt in his mind.

INSIDE THE ARES
TWO HUNDRED FORTY MILES TO THE NORTHEAST

The pilot, happy to be busy now, adjusted himself in the ejection seat, leaning slightly forward. The ACES IV seat reclined almost seventeen degrees in order to help his body absorb more of the pressure during high-g maneuvers, but it also forced him to lean slightly forward to put his fingers on the touch-screen displays.

Staring at his screen, the pilot was impressed. No, he was more than that. He was astonished at the wall of fighters that spread out before him. Even in the Ares, it would have been very difficult, perhaps impossible, to slip past them all.

Of course, he couldn't use his own aircraft's radar to detect and track the enemy fighters. Like turning on a flashlight in a dark room, using his radar would have illuminated the fighters around him, but it would have also shown every one of them where he was. But that didn't matter. He had something better, anyway.

Scribbled on his flight plan were the encryption data codes.

Now the American AWACS and interceptors weren't just sharing information with each other, they were sharing it with him.

After gaining access to the sophisticated encryption data links onboard the AWACS—something the Ares was designed to do if the pilot had the codes—he was able to mimic the AWACS's radar screens within his own cockpit. As a result, he saw all of the fighters that had congregated off his nose. A sidebar on his avionics displays kept a running total, giving information on each fighter's location, distance, speed, and altitude. It even showed him what weapons they were carrying, how many missiles and rounds for their guns, as well as their fuel remaining and the estimated time before they had to hit one of the air-refueling tankers or head back for gas.

After taking appraisal of the fighters, he knew he only had a few moments to act. Already he was critically low on fuel; no time to get into a furball just because he wanted to. Still, he had to send a message. He had to let them know (if they didn't know already) that he was a serious pilot who understood the machine in his hands.

Flying through the partly cloudy sky, he took the time to sum up his aircraft once again.

Mission systems software was key to the Ares' ability to sift and present incredible amounts of information in such a way as to make it obvious to the pilot what the logical action should be, a process that greatly enhanced the quality of the pilot's decision making. Centered around the OODA Loop (Observe, Orient, Decide, Act), the fourth-generation synthetic aperture radar (SAR) included such features as ground mapping and inverse SAR for ship classification, cued and passive search, beyond-visual-range tracking, and multitargeting capability. The system was so fast, it was able to move from target to target in a millionth of a second or less.

Multitarget capable! The pilot almost scoffed to himself. This thing was more than multitarget; it could track the mosquitoes in a swamp if he asked it to.

Flying southwest, he glanced through the cockpit Plexiglas at the sky, instinctively noting the position of the setting sun. Then he looked across his cockpit. Like the Joint Strike Fighter, the Ares featured a huge multifunction display, an 8-by-20-inch screen that contained every piece of information he could ever need to either fly or attack. All of the functions could be activated either by touching the screen or through hands-on-throttle-and-stick (HOTAS) commands. The Ares also featured a helmet-mounted display system (HMDS), which replaced the traditional head-up display and a communications, navigation, and identification (CNI) system that provided every imaginable function: VHF/UHF voice, HaveQuick I/II, Saturn (HQ IIA), satcom T/R, Identify Friend or Foe transponder and interrogator, navigation and landing systems (ILS/MLS/MLS/Tacan), tactical data information link, 3-D audio, and TACFIRE.

The pilot almost purred as he flew the machine. The aircraft responded crisply to his commands, but it did much more than that. It was so forward looking, it almost did the thinking for him.

His job was so easy, he actually wished for more stress, a little more of the uncertainty and thrill that used to make flying so much fun.

He studied the tactical display, counting the U.S. forces before him. So many targets. So much opportunity. This was more than a target-rich environment, this was the mother lode.

Checking his fuel display a final time, he selected a flight of two F-16s, the closest group of fighters that were climbing up to a tanker to air refuel.

SWITCHBACK 27

The setting sun was low now, two fists above the gentle waves of the sea. It would be a beautiful night, clear, hardly a cloud in the sky, calm winds, lots of starlight. The Falcon pilot loved flying on nights like that.

Three miles ahead of him, he saw the air-to-air tanker, an enormous KC-10. Huge. Fat-winged. Three engines. His fuel station in the sky.

"Switchback, call tally on the tanker."

"Tally, lead," his wingman replied.

"Husky," the pilot spoke to the AWACS controller, "Switchback is going over to tanker frequency now."

"Roger, Switchback Two-seven, talk to you after you get your gas."

Back to his wingman. "Switchback Two-seven, go preset ten."

Two clicks of the mike.

Reaching down, the flight leader switched his tactical radio to the air refueling frequency. "Exon Three-one, Switchback Two-seven with you, tally at three miles."

"Roger, Two-seven," the copilot in the enormous KC-10 replied.

With communications established between them, the F-16 formation leader pushed up his single throttle to close in on the tanker. Maintaining an altitude five hundred feet below it but accelerating quickly, he closed the distance from three miles to three thousand feet. As he did, his wingman pulled up to his right side. The flight leader would go in first, maintain his position directly under the tanker's enormous tail, while the boom operator in the aft end of the tanker flew the refueling boom into the receptacle behind his cockpit. He would take on four thousand pounds of fuel, then back out and let his wingman get gas.

Once he had stabilized in position five hundred feet below and one thousand feet behind the KC-10, the Falcon pilot waited for the tanker belly lights to come on, his signal that he was clear to move in to refuel. As he waited, he glanced through his cockpit once more, checking his systems a final time, then flipped the switch to open his refueling door. Twenty seconds passed. The fighter pilot grew impatient, anxious to get back on patrol. Every second, every mile that he sat behind the tanker was one more second, one more mile in which the stolen fighter could slip through. His knee started bouncing nervously off the cockpit floor. Still no belly lights from the tanker. "Exon?" he asked.

"Stand by," the tanker pilot told him. "We've got a little something . . ."

Even in the growing dark, there was only the slightest ray of light, just a hint of straight vapor as the cool air was heated from the passing beam. It was over in an instant, no more time than it took for the pilot to blink. The ray of faint light, fuzzy, almost warm, a light blue strand that seemed to be no larger than the width of his finger, impacted the belly of the giant tanker like a spark in the night. The laser hit the tanker twenty feet behind the cockpit and on the right side, striking at a twenty-degree angle that burned almost from the nose to the tail. Forty thousand degrees of energy melted through the aluminum skin and frame, which then tore away from the aircraft, peeled back by the powerful slipstream of the 350 mph wind.

The tanker had more than 87,000 pounds of JP-8 jet fuel sloshing around in its tanks.

All 87,000 pounds of fuel ignited instantly, exploding the jet. The inferno was a single fireball blasting outward at five times the speed of sound. Huge chunks of metal and aluminum scattered through the air, spreading in every direction and sending a slice of metal to impact the glass cockpit of the F-16 with enough force to cut almost entirely through the jet. At the precise instant when the piece of metal cut the pilot in two, the laser fired again, impacting the nose of his jet. The beam hit at a bad angle, missing his fuel tanks, but cutting the nose of his aircraft away from the jet, severing control lines and electrical boxes while creating dysfunctional aerodynamic forces sufficient to rip the fighter apart. There was no explosion, no fire, no great ball of flame; the F-16 simply broke into pieces and scattered as the wreckage began to fall from the sky. Two seconds later, the laser hit the second F-16, striking through the right side of the cockpit. It cut through the metal boxes and wires of the avionics compartment, then the underwing fuel tank, exploding the aircraft into flames.

Over the next eighty seconds, seven other fighters were also shot down.

Chaos and confusion broke across the sky.

The pilots saw the explosions. They saw their brothers die. And they finally understood, in that instant and for the first time, how quickly and unexpectedly they could die, too.

On a broken line that spread from northeast to southwest for some fifty miles, the sky was dotted with wicked fireballs.

The radios exploded, everyone talking at the same time, their voices rising, the quarter-second delay on the secure radios deferring each word until the pilots, AWACS officers, and ground controllers were simply talking over themselves. The reports were short and panicked and almost indecipherable. The confusion grew as the fireballs illuminated the sky in various stages of birth or death, some still building, their hot cores rolling upward in flaming fire, some dying now—the destroyed tanker and the first two F-16s—their fireballs cooling as the burning fuel dissipated and the wreckage fell.

"Switchback Two-seven, Switchback Two-seven, do you read?" the AWACS controller repeated again and again.

"Husky Four-three, Husky Four-three," another controller said.

"Mother Eagle Four-four flight. I've got visual hits at my nine and one o'clock. Looks like we've had . . . what . . . we've got nothing on our sensors. Check that! Three fireballs . . . four now. The sky is lighting up . . . Where's the bandit? Help us out here!"

"Mother, this is Giantkiller, the Air Defense Identification Zone controller in Maine. We've got a total of nine confirmed hits now. I say again, we've got—"

"Husky Four-three, do you read me?"

"One at a time, gentlemen."

"Mother, I've got a target, twenty-miles . . ."

"All aircraft, hold your chatter!"

"Husky, this is Saber on two-five-six-point-nine . . ."

"Mayday, Mayday, Mayday."

"Clear the radios for the Mayday!"

"I've got a target here . . ."

"Who's calling out a target?"

"Hog five-five confirm a target?"

"Negative. That was not me."

"Who's calling out the Mayday?"

It was too much; the sheer number of aircraft in the area, the sheer number of pilots shoved into such a tiny piece of airspace, the surprise and the fear, the sense of urgency, and the uncertainty guaranteed that chaos would follow as the explosions filled the sky. All of the pilots, adrenaline and rage surging through their veins, sat on the razor's edge, anxious and ready to move.

The low sunshine shone through the scattered cloud breaks and reflected off the swelling ocean. Across the sky, the lingering fireballs began to fade, leaving shadows of dark mushrooms illuminated by the slanting light.

Then a hundred aircraft slipped into battle gear.

Yet no one ever saw the Ares as it turned and slipped back toward the northeast, accelerating quickly through the night.

PIGEON AUXILIARY EMERGENCY LANDING FIELD
NINETY-SIX KILOMETERS WEST OF GANDER,
NEWFOUNDLAND

It was a tiny airfield, hidden in a remote valley due west of Gander. Built only as an emergency landing field for air freighters and single-engine, piston-driven fighters en route to Europe during WWII, even at its heyday the airfield was little more than a narrow runway, a few scabby wooden hangars, and a small Quonset building for the few men stationed there. Through the years it had been abandoned, rebuilt, then abandoned again. The runway was only five thousand feet long, pocked with rut holes the size of bushel baskets and overgrown with brush that had worked its way through the cracks in the cement. Rolling hills dotted the north and the western horizons while to the south and east, mucky swamps, frozen eight months of the year, extended to the flatlands that led to the sea.

The crew had moved in only two nights before. Always under the cover of darkness, twenty men worked feverishly, repairing the holes in the runway with quick-setting cement, cutting back the brush, and shaving the frost heaves where the asphalt had buckled from two generations of freezing rain. Even before setting to work on the runway, they put up camouflage netting to hide their equipment and posted guards on the winding road that led to the field. A little more than five kilometers to the south, the main highway (if it could be called that) was little more than a narrow two-lane road connecting two lonely ranch towns that most of the people even in the Newfoundland province had never heard of.

It took the men two nights of back-breaking labor to complete their work on the runway, and even then they were barely ready when the aircraft approached.

It was a gutsy move. No, it was a lot more than that. It was a stupid move, or would have been for any pilot not of exceptional skill.

There were no runway lights except for a couple of heavy trucks shining their headlights on the landing threshold. The runway was exceptionally narrow, rough, and broken, with no approach aids or instrument landing systems, no arresting cables, no published landing instructions to warn of any rising terrain, none of the normal navigation aids or guidance systems a pilot would use to bring in and land a supersonic aircraft.

Inside the cockpit, the pilot was sweating like a pig, huge drops of perspiration running down the sides of his ribs. The aircraft's avionics, with its radar and computers, was capable of building its own approach procedure, but the pilot didn't use them, preferring to use his night vision goggles instead.

Without the aid of the goggles, it would have been like flying into a black hole at the end of a very dark universe, but the goggles and the moon, which was white and bright now, turned the night into day, though still a one-dimensional dreamscape of dark shadows and greens. He lined up visually, peering through his goggles, while continually glancing underneath them to check his flying instruments. Approaching what he thought was the runway, he pulled back the power and let the aircraft descend. Fifteen hundred feet, two hundred knots. This baby wanted to float. He pulled farther back on the throttles and felt the aircraft finally sink. Eight hundred feet above the runway, the lights from the trucks came into view and he adjusted his aim, peering through the darkness while moving his throttles again. The angle of attack was a killer. He was coming in like a rocket, and he adjusted the angle of the nose, feeling like he was dropping straight down. But he knew he had to hit the first piece of asphalt on the runway if he had any hope of stopping before he ran out of cement, and he kept the approach angle dangerously steep, fearful, but knowing he didn't have any choice. Five hundred feet, three hundred feet, one seventy knots and still slowing. Way too fast, way too fast! He pulled both of his throttles to idle and waited for the aircraft to sink. Still too high. Still too fast! He pulled the nose up, started dropping, pushed in power . . . about right now, but slow . . . too dark to estimate the closure. It was like trying to hit a black baseball in the middle of the night. The runway suddenly grew much larger, the narrow field of vision through his goggles so disorienting it made his stomach churn. He jammed in power, adjusting his angle, still a little too high.

He hit the runway like a bag of dropped bricks. The aircraft bounced once, floated a hundred feet, then settled to the rough runway again. His teeth jammed against the front of his jaw, his back jarred, and he sucked a quick breath as he slammed on his brake, feeling the aircraft shudder from the force of the hydraulic pressure on the rotating disks. Despite the frantic work of the previous two nights, the runway felt like a dirt road in the mountains, and he was bounced left and right, the entire aircraft shuddering from the force of the landing and the rough cement.

The Ares quickly slowed. It was not heavy; it had no weapons and not much gas. With a little more than a thousand feet remaining, he had it under control.

A single man with two red-tipped flashlights was waiting for him at the end of the runway. He taxied toward him very quickly, complying with the light signals to follow him. The man jumped into the back of a beat-up Toyota pickup, which started moving, the man standing in the bed, holding his flashlights for the pilot to see.

A run-down hangar sat on the south end of the runway. Many years before it had been used to house the sand trucks and snowplows that were necessary to keep the runway open from October to May. It had been many years since a truck had been inside the large building, but the doors were built on steel rollers, and they had been pushed open for him now. Following the man with the flashlight, the pilot pointed the Ares toward the old maintenance building, shut his left engine down, rolled inside, then pulled the right engine to "off."

The doors rolled quickly shut behind him, their rusty rollers squeaking in the night.

The pilot raised his canopy, took off his helmet, and wiped the sweat from his brow.

His master was waiting. The two men beamed at each other in the darkness. Then they started to laugh.

UNITED STATES EMBASSY COMPLEX
PARIS, FRANCE

Major James paced outside the embassy office door. A group of civilian personnel walked by and eyed him suspiciously, but he ignored them, completely lost in his thoughts.

He paced a few more minutes, then gathered his courage and tapped on the office door.

"Come!" he heard Ketchum's voice boom through the thick wood.

Jesse entered. The chief of staff was on the phone, cursing at someone in an irritated tone. He looked up but continued the conversation as if Jesse wasn't there. Jesse remained by the door, staring at the floor. Thirty seconds later, Ketchum hung up. Jesse walked forward and stood directly in front of his desk. "Sir," he started quickly, "there's something I need to tell you."

Ketchum glanced down at the reams of papers spread across his desk. Jesse got the message. *Alright. Make it quick.*

"What is it?" Ketchum demanded.

Jesse took a breath. "I don't think the Saudi Prince bin Saud stole our aircraft," he said.

Ketchum cocked his head. "You're kidding me, right?"

"No sir. I don't think it was him."

"And why is that?" Ketchum asked him in a sarcastic tone.

Jesse hesitated. "When I was in the French Mirage I saw the other pilot at a very close range."

"And . . . ," Ketchum prodded, already losing patience with him.

Jesse took another breath and then told him.

Ketchum listened carefully, then leaned back and swore.

THIRTY

PIGEON AUXILIARY EMERGENCY LANDING FIELD
NINETY-SIX KILOMETERS WEST OF GANDER,
NEWFOUNDLAND

The pilot wanted to keep an eye on his baby as it was serviced and refueled.

Before the refueling could begin, he walked around the Ares, checking all of the access panels, the engine bays, the landing gear, and tires. He pulled on the exhaust vents, then positioned a small ladder so that it would not touch the skin of the aircraft, took off his boots, pulled on a pair of clean socks, and climbed onto the left wing. There he inspected the top of the aircraft, paying particular attention to the heat vents and RAM.

It took him almost twenty minutes to complete his post flight inspection, then, satisfied, he walked back to his master again. Standing back, he watched as the highly trained technicians, the very best the general had to offer, surrounded the aircraft and set to work. Huge Ford 350 pickup trucks, with two-hundred-gallon plastic fuel tanks mounted in their beds, were pulled into position on the right side of the fighter. An electric pump was inserted into the first tank while a black hose was run up to the overwing access point.

The foreign officer waited, his dark eyes piercing the dim light in the creaking hangar. "So . . . ?" he slowly asked.

The pilot turned to the aircraft. "She looks alright," he said. "Needs some oil for the engines, and after landing on that prairie trail you call a runway, I would change the main tires if I could. But other than that, she looks to be in good flying shape."

The master was short, with lanky arms and slender shoulders that could have passed for a girl. Dark hair. A smooth face. Eyes like burning coal.

Though the pilot towered over him by six inches, it was clear the other man was in charge. (The one who paid the bills gave all the orders; it was the same around the world.) The foreigner pulled out an unfiltered cigarette, which he stuck between his teeth but didn't light, sucking on the shredded tobacco instead. Noticing the pilot was still wearing his flight gloves, he nodded. "You need something for that?"

The pilot pressed his lips, far too proud to admit it even if he did. "I've been taking things," he answered.

The foreigner hesitated, expressing his displeasure by his silence. "Even when you are flying?" he finally said.

The pilot grunted in disdain. "Would you like to try it?" he answered curtly. "It would have you drowning in whiskey and valium, I guarantee you, my friend. So don't criticize me if I popped a few pills while in the air with your jet."

The master only nodded. Like all military generals, regardless of the army, he wore silver stars on his shoulders, and they reflected the overhead lights as he moved. "You did well," he said simply, pretending to make amends. "We are happy with your performance so far."

The pilot didn't answer. He frankly didn't care. They could have been happy or furious; he wasn't doing this to please them, and both parties understood that all along. The hard truth was, if he could figure out a way to accomplish the mission without them, that would have been fine with him.

The pilot shook his head. No, he wasn't doing this to please them. He wasn't doing it for the money, the infamy, or power.

His reasons were much more personal. Much more subtle. And much closer to home.

Family. And friends.

How often in a man's life did it come down to that?

He watched as the ground crew started refueling the plane. "Be careful! Don't touch the skin of the aircraft!" he cried.

But no one paid him attention, not understanding what he said.

He motioned to the general, who called out to his men in their own tongue. They stopped working and nodded, then proceeded much more carefully. The master watched them a long moment, then, satisfied, motioned to the hangar doors. "Go. Get some sleep," he instructed. "You must be exhausted."

The pilot didn't move. "I want to stay until we are finished."

The two men didn't trust each other; that was perfectly clear.

The master grunted, waited a moment, then walked away. Shouting his instructions, he hurried his men. A little more than an hour later, it was finished; the aircraft was ready to fly once again.

The pilot glanced down at his watch. "Let me sleep until noon," he instructed. "Don't bother me before then. Keep a man on the radio and satellite. When I wake up, I want to know what is going on. We'll check their reaction, their planning, and how they have prepared their military to respond."

The older man muttered in deep excitement that almost bordered on joy.

The pilot turned to stare at his plane. It was beautiful, oh so beautiful, such a marvelous machine. He walked toward it, touched the nose, patting it lightly, then turned. "Where is my tent?" he asked.

UNITED STATES EMBASSY
PARIS, FRANCE

The president of the United States sat at the head of the table, his hands wrapped around a mug of lukewarm coffee. A steward moved silently forward and replaced it with a fresh cup. Plates of warm pastries and toast, along with French jellies and fruits, had been spread about the center of the table, but they were the only fresh things in the room. Everyone around the table looked haggard, even exhausted—loose ties, rolled-up sleeves, crumpled dresses, sweat-stained armpits. The room smelled like coffee and sweat, and the president sniffed.

Many of his staff had tried to get a few minutes' sleep, but most had been unsuccessful. The president had been able to nap here and there, grabbing ten minutes, a half hour, knowing he would not get any real sleep for the next couple of days.

Sipping at his coffee, he felt it burn, the acid irritating the emptiness that had settled in his stomach.

He thought back on his presidency. It felt like a lifetime, not the few years it had been. He honestly couldn't remember what it felt like not to feel the crushing pressure; every hour, every minute, every second, it was there. He hadn't slept a full night in more than seven years, hadn't gone to the bathroom or taken a shower without someone standing on the other side of the door. He hadn't really relaxed since that gray afternoon in early January when he had placed his hand on the family Bible and stared into the eyes of the Supreme Court's chief justice.

Glancing at his watch, he checked the time, then stared at the lights that reflected off the dark coffee in his mug. *If I had known what I know now,* he thought, *If I'd had any idea, would I have made the same decisions? Would I have worked all of my life, sacrificed everything, fought and scratched like a cat, just to get to this point?*

He considered a long moment, then turned back to his men. The anger burned inside him—it had been burning there for years—and it drove him now, chasing the hesitation away. Instead, he drummed his fingers impatiently while listening to the chairman of the Chiefs of Staff who was sitting in the command post back at the White House. "So you think the Ares has turned around now? He will not strike his targets tonight?" the president quickly asked.

"It appears that way, Mr. President. He had to be extremely low on fuel to even do what he did. He was testing us, dipping his toe in the water, getting a little experience in the jet, but he must have turned around now and landed somewhere to refuel."

The president stared at the satellite receiver. "How many aircraft did we lose, then?"

President Abram heard him move some papers across the table, and he pictured the scene taking place back in D.C., his national security staff staring at each other, passing notes back and forth, flipping through their red binders, trying to keep their heads low. "Mr. President, we don't know for certain," Shevky finally answered. "At least ten fighters and two air refuelers, but there might be a couple more. We're trying to make contact with a sortie of Falcons out of Maine."

"A dozen aircraft! Just like that! *Poof*, and they're gone!"

"Yes, sir," the general reluctantly said.

"We saw nothing on our radars? No visual sightings? No infrared readings at all?"

"No, Mr. President."

Sitting to his right, Edgar Ketchum rested his hands on the table and turned toward him. "Sir, we knew it would be this way. The Ares is completely undetectable by any of our ordinary sensors—"

Abram cut him off with a slice of his hand. He had learned, thank you very much, what the Ares was capable of. His mind flashed back a few hours to what he had witnessed while standing on the airport tower, his four F-15s exploding in flames, then glanced at the hastily written report the military had data-linked to the embassy, describing the destruction of their fighters and tankers off the eastern coast of Maine.

No, he didn't need any more lectures on the extreme capabilities of the Ares.

He sat back, a previous experience flashing unexpectedly through his mind: several years before, Walter Reed Army Medical Facility. Meeting with some soldiers who had been wounded in Iraq. One of the marines, his foot severed just below the ankle, had lifted his hand and held onto the president's arm.

"How you doing?" Abram had asked him.

"Better than some of my buddies, sir."

Abram cleared his throat. "I understand," he had answered slowly. "Each death hurts us all."

The marine officer pushed against his pillow. "I want to get back to my unit, sir."

"It might be a while, Captain."

The marine nodded angrily toward his missing foot. "They can do a prosthesis, Mr. President. Get me cranked up in a couple months. I'll be ready to go but I'll need a medical waiver before they will let me go back. Please, sir, tell the marine commandant to sign it. I want to get back with my men."

The president looked into the young marine's eyes. He saw the duty and devotion. But there was something more. A dull, angry light that seemed to rage from his eyes. Leaning toward him, he saw the burning fury there.

This wasn't about duty. This guy wanted revenge!

And that's how he felt now. It wasn't right, it wasn't holy. But he didn't care anymore. Some guy was out there, in his aircraft, threatening the United States. He'd seen enough. He'd lost enough. It was time to fight back.

The marines called it "amped."

And he was amped up tonight.

"Get the king on the line," he demanded, setting down his coffee mug.

Edgar Ketchum leaned toward him. "The king of Saudi Arabia is up in Mecca."

"I don't care where he is. Get him on the telephone now."

It took less than three minutes for the communications specialist at the embassy to reach the royal communications center in Riyadh and be patched through to the king of Saudi Arabia at his personal palace on the outskirts of the Holy City.

The president was handed the receiver—he hated speaking through a speakerphone—and his staff gathered around the table, listening through the teleconference speakers.

The president was so direct that his staff sucked in a collective breath of dismay. No formalities, no introductions, no "How's the twenty-three wives and kids?" The president was far too weary and discouraged to care about diplomacy anymore.

"You know about our stolen fighter," he started the instant the Saudi king came to the phone.

"I've been told some," the king answered carefully, his English halting but clear.

"And you know, I am certain, who is sitting in the pilot seat of *my* aircraft?"

The king huffed. It seemed he really didn't care.

"You have a nephew . . ."

"I have many nephews. I cannot know them all."

"This one you know, King Fahd. Abdul Mohammad bin Saud has—"

The king huffed again. "Abdul Mohammad bin Saud is not of my loins."

"Of course he is, Your Royal Highness. My intelligence people tell me he is very well known."

The king seemed to scoff. "You might ask yourself, Mr. President, is this the first time your intelligence might be wrong?"

"Prince bin Saud may be a renegade, but he is your family," he said. "And even if you are truly unaware of his actions—something I am only reluctantly willing to presume for the moment—there have to be people around you who know what is going on. This is far too large an operation not to have some level of official support. I have already lost good men and good aircraft to your renegade. Now he threatens our borders. He has the ability to hit us and hurt us in ways that I simply will not endure, and we will not stand idly by. Whether he has the support of your government or is acting alone, it doesn't matter; our response will be the same. There will be no UN resolutions, no briefings with the press, no phone calls to warn you, no belated ultimatums or threats. We will act, King Fahd, and it will be devastating and direct. So I'm telling you, your Royal Highness, for the good of us all, if you have any influence to stop this, you *must* act on it now."

The king of Saudi Arabia protested, but the president knew from the tone of his voice that he understood. He listened for as long as he could stand it, then ended the conversation and disconnected the line. "Get me the king of Jordan," he then said to his staff. "And Syria and Iran. I want to talk to them all. I'm going to deliver them the same message. We are not the only ones who are in danger now."

WHITE HOUSE SITUATION ROOM
WASHINGTON, D.C.

The group of national security advisors stared at each other after disconnecting the satellite phone. The conversation with the leaders of the Arab and Persian nations had been far more direct than they would have preferred. There was not a coward among them, and they were warriors all, but they were also conditioned to use diplomacy and finesse to the utmost degree.

Their president had just chosen a far different approach. So they stared at each other, a hot stuffiness in the room.

For almost a minute, no one spoke until the chairman stood up and directed an unexpected question to the Air Force chief of staff. "Let's say the Ares gets through our defensive line of fighters," he said, "something, based on what we've seen up to this point, we certainly have to presume. If he gets in position to strike our cities, could we FlashPack him?" he asked.

The four-star general thought, aware of the silence in the room. "The weapon has not completed its field testing," he finally answered.

"FlashPack? What is FlashPack?" the chief of the army asked.

The chairman turned toward him. "It's a new weapon. Another laser. Designed to protect very high-value targets, it will temporarily blind anyone who is looking at it when the laser is fired. Right now it's mounted underneath a KC-135 test aircraft out at Kirtland Air Force Base. Though it hasn't finished final testing, so far it looks pretty good."

The chairman turned his attention back to the air force officer. "We could use it, couldn't we?" he pressed. "It would be a last-chance weapon. We don't know for certain if it will work, and a few minutes isn't much time, but it might be enough."

The air force officer took a long moment before he nodded. He was reluctant; that was clear.

"And it blinds him for what—a lifetime, a couple hours, a year?"

"Less than ten minutes, sir," the air force officer said. "Though sometimes there are burn spots that may last a few minutes more than that."

"Where is the prototype right now?" the chairman demanded.

"At the testing range in Tonopah, Nevada. For very obvious reasons we've had to do the testing in the most remote location in the U.S."

"Could we get it here in time?"

The chief of the air force leaned toward his own aide, a full-bird colonel with what seemed like half a million badges on his chest. "We can do it," the colonel answered for his boss. "It's only a matter of a couple hours' flight time once we get it in the air."

The chairman of the Joint Chiefs nodded urgently. "Do it," he said. I want the option of using the FlashPack if everything else we have up there fails."

THIRTY-ONE

PIGEON AUXILIARY EMERGENCY LANDING FIELD
NINETY-SIX KILOMETERS WEST OF GANDER,
NEWFOUNDLAND

The pilot dreamed again.

In his dream, he saw the prisoner's face. So close. So familiar. So much like his own.

The captive knelt, his head bowed, shoulders slumping, his bare stomach heaving with each pained breath. The four assassins stood behind him, holding Russian AK-47 rifles slung at their sides. Two of the men wore dark masks with holes cut for their eyes, but the other two were bare-faced, though their bushy beards and dark glasses made it difficult to identify who they were.

Moving to the prisoner, the lead assassin grabbed him by the hair and jerked, pulling his head toward his back. The prisoner strained, showing every tendon, muscle, and blood vein in his neck. The assassin jerked again, crunching the vertebrae, and the prisoner opened his eyes and screamed, the muted cry nothing more than a gurgle through the terrible strain in his neck. The assassin looked into the prisoner's eyes for a very long time, then finally nodded, releasing his hold on his head. The prisoner fell forward, gasping for air, then placed his hands to his face once again.

He didn't plead for mercy; he knew it wouldn't do any good. He didn't plead for justice; there was no justice with these men. He didn't pray, he didn't cry, he didn't say anything. Knowing he was a dead man, he had decided how he was going to die. He would suffer in silence. He would pass with as much dignity as he could retain.

The assassin grumbled, disappointed in his silence, then took a step back and nodded to the man at his right. The second man was hooded and so the sound of his voice was slightly muffled as it passed through the cotton mask. He lifted a parchment and started to read:

> Having been found an Enemy to the kingdom of God on this earth, having betrayed the Will and Wishes of those Leaders who have been selected by Allah to rule over this Land, you are hereby condemned to suffer the death of the Infidels who fight against God.
>
> With the Blood of your guilt we wash ourselves clean.
>
> May Allah, praise His Holy Name, show no mercy to you in the world yet to come.

The reader dropped the parchment and bowed his head. Two of the assassins stepped forward, grabbed the prisoner by his arms, jerked them mercilessly behind his back, then put their knees on his spine and leaned forward, forcing his face to the cold cement. The third man, the leader, moved forward and grabbed the prisoner by the hair, pulling his neck back again. The lead assassin waited a moment. His face was peaceful, almost passive. Nothing but a goat to be slaughtered. There was no shame in this task.

Reaching under the fold of his black uniform, he extracted a long, dull knife with jagged teeth. Stepping forward, he started hacking. He did not cut, but he sawed with the serrated knife, and it took a full thirty seconds before he had finished the job.

The pilot jerked up with a start, stifling a scream of terror by jamming his fist in his mouth. His eyes were wide open in horror, but they still did not see.

It was so dark. And so quiet, he could hear the sound of the blood in his ears.

He looked around at the darkness, still in terror, his eyes wide, his shoulders sweating, his thick hair matted on his brow. He gasped a couple times, trying to assure himself that it wasn't real.

But nightmare or real, the impact of the dream was the same. His heart pounded like a hammer, his palms were sweaty, and his chest heaved with each breath that he took.

For a long time he didn't move, then he finally rolled his feet to the floor. The Newfoundland night was cold and crisp, the wind still. Staring through the darkness, he sat on the edge of his cot. Glancing at the illuminated dial, he checked the time on his watch. Less than an hour's worth of sleep. With what he had to do the next day, he needed much more than that.

He lay down on the cot again, hoping dreamless sleep still might come.

THIRTY-TWO

UNITED STATES EMBASSY COMMAND CENTER
PARIS, FRANCE

Ketchum led the way out of the room, the president close behind. As he pushed through the door, he was alarmed to see Jesse standing in the hallway, obviously waiting for them.

The pilot stood against the wall, staring down at the floor. His hair was tousled, the lanky bangs hanging in front of his eyes, and he looked tired. Ketchum glanced around nervously, not knowing whether he should be anxious or concerned, then shook his head angrily. It made him furious that Jesse, a mere major, a gnat on the sidewalk to be crushed if he chose, should have the guts to presume he could stalk in the hallway and talk to *the president!* What was he thinking? Where was his sense of protocol, his sense of proportion and importance in the world?

Ketchum tried to ignore him, not meeting his eyes as he held the door for the president, then started walking down the hall, but Jesse moved forward, almost blocking his way. Ketchum stopped and nodded angrily. Jesse met his eyes, then looked over his shoulder to the president, who was standing behind him. "Mr. President, sir, could I have just a moment of your time," the pilot said.

Ketchum started walking, pushing Jesse with his shoulder as he passed. "No, son, you may not," he answered sharply.

The officer held his shoulders tight, and Ketchum was forced to step to the left as he passed. He felt the blood rising and his face flushing red. Who was this kid? Did he really think he could lurk here in the hall and demand even a moment of the president's time?

"Sir," Jesse pressed as he held his ground.

Ketchum swore. "Listen, *Major* James—"

The president stepped forward, placing his hands on Ketchum's shoulder. "It's alright, Edgar," he said. "I've wanted to have a word with him anyway." The president studied the younger man as they stood face to face.

Ketchum watched from the side. The two men were the same size, the same build. In fact, looking at them, Ketchum sucked in a quick breath. They almost looked like a father and his son—same square shoulders, same dark complexion, same burn of ambition in their eyes.

Jesse took a short step toward the president. "Sir, I need you to know something," he began, his voice respectful and low. "I didn't have anything to do with the disappearance of the Ares. Whatever you are hearing, you have to know, Mr. President, that it is not true. I have been loyal to my country. I have been loyal to you. I have been loyal to General Hawley. I have never once even considered being anything else."

The president stared at him, his face remaining passive, the perfect poker player. "You go by Jesse, don't you, son?" he asked him.

Jesse nodded his head.

"Jesse, you realize my position, I'm sure. I have advisors, and I have to trust their judgment as the investigation goes forward. I can't interfere with their work. And there is far too much at stake here not to chase down every lead."

Jesse cleared his throat, his nervousness showing. "I understand that, sir. Were I in your position, I would do the same thing. And I'm not suggesting, Mr. President, that you do anything else. But I want you to know—man to man, face to face—that I was not involved in any way with the theft of our jet, if you will allow me to assist you, I will do everything in my power to help make this right."

The president hesitated, still looking into his eyes. "I appreciate that," he answered.

Jesse didn't say any more.

"Is that all?" the president asked.

Jesse hesitated.

"Is that all?" Abram pressed.

"Sir . . ." Jesse wavered, his eyes darting to the side. Then he finally answered, "Yes sir, that is all. Thank you for taking the time to hear me out, Mr. President."

The president glanced at Ketchum, patted Jesse's shoulder, then walked away.

Jesse stood in the hallway, watching the president and Ketchum go, and cursed himself. Why didn't he have the courage to tell him? Abram might have listened.

He slowly shook his head.

The truth was, there was something else on his mind. Something about the flight plan they had found in the trunk of the car. His doubts were vague but constant and powerful. They lingered at the back of his mind, never leaving him alone.

Were they making a mistake?

Was the flight plan even real?

He concentrated, his mind racing, then took half a dozen quick steps down the hall. "Mr. Ketchum," he called out.

The president kept on walking, but Edgar Ketchum turned around.

"I'm going to the hospital," Jesse told him. "Something . . . I don't know. I want to talk to her now."

THIRTY-THREE

HÔPITAL D'INSTRUCTION DES ARMÉES PERCY
FRENCH MILITARY HOSPITAL
CLAMART, FRANCE

It was only a medium-sized hospital, with 430 beds and a staff of 1,200, including 110 attending physicians, but it had developed a reputation for top-notch work, and the security it provided was second to none. Having attended to many distinguished if controversial patients (Yasser Arafat, members of the Royal Saudi family, the king of Jordon, the Israeli PM, to name just a few) the hospital understood the need for discretion and patient privacy.

The hospital was also the predescribed facility the United States government had contracted with to provide forensic autopsies that might be required for any U.S. citizens who died in France.

The sergeant's body arrived in the hospital in an unmarked, silver van. The corpse had not been sealed inside a black body bag but instead had been placed on a gurney and covered with an evidence sheet, the sterile, single-use, white piece of cloth that was more commonly used overseas.

The forensic pathologist, a French army colonel, was waiting. White-haired and slim, he had a grandfatherly look that created a visual paradox as to why he would be interested in such grizzly work. He wore a military uniform, camouflage fatigues, and black boots. The pathology badge on his right chest was etched with the symbol of an ancient crown that dated back to medieval times, when coroners were called "crowners" because of their obligation to visit the families of the newly dead to ensure the king got his fair share of their estate.

The colonel escorted the Ares crew chief's body into the examination room, where three autopsy tables, large chrome and aluminum structures mounted against the wall, were ready for use. It was a quiet night; so far this was the only body that had been brought in. Normally, he would have waited to start his work until morning, but his commander had made it very clear that he would finish this autopsy and report to him absolutely as soon as he could.

So the pathologist put on his scrub suit and gown, two pairs of gloves, then pulled on protective coverings for his shoes. While he dressed, an assistant moved the body to be X-rayed, not removing the sterile sheet or the clothes before directing the energy beam through the corpse. The body was then disrobed, examined, photographed, the wounds chronicled and noted for the autopsy report. Then, after being cleaned, weighed, and measured, it was placed face up on the autopsy table. A rubber block was placed under the shoulders, forcing the chest to protrude while the arms and neck fell back.

The doctor pulled a large plastic shield over his face, marked his work with a colored marker, reached for a large scalpel, and started cutting a huge *T*-shaped incision across the front of the chest, shoulder to shoulder, then down to the pelvic bone.

Skin was folded back, the rib cage separated, then the organs separated from the muscle and bone and extracted from the chest. Tiny slices of the major organs were cut for the toxicology tests. The contents of the stomach were examined, then the bladder and the spine. Everything from the esophagus to the pelvic bone was carefully scrutinized.

Two hours later, the body cavity empty, the pathologist was ready to look at the head and neck. The blunt trauma to the head was the obvious cause of death; the crushed skull and damaged vertebrae made that pretty clear, but still he proceeded very carefully, not prejudging the result.

He cut across the brow, making an incision from ear to ear, split the cut, and peeled back the scalp. Using a vibrating saw, he cut through the skull, exposing the brain underneath, then extracted a sample of liquid from the spinal cord at the base. Staring at the clear liquid, he held it up to the light, sensing that something was wrong.

The faintest bit of cloudiness tinted the fluid in the glass. He stared at the syringe, rolling it, then held it again to the light. The feeling in his stomach was as uncertain as the trace in the glass, hardly more than a vapor or tint of faded color, but he had learned to trust his gut as much as he trusted anything. Another doctor would have probably dismissed it, but he wanted to know.

He started working very carefully, examining the brain. Five minutes later, he pressed a call button on the wallboard near the head of table to summon an aide. He needed some help, a second pair of eyes—and a witness—in case his gut feeling proved right.

Was he acting on suspicion? Absolutely. But that's what made him a master of the secrets of the dead. And as a military doctor who specialized in detecting the most terrifying of diseases, he had been trained to look for certain things that other doctors might miss.

A young aide entered the room, her smock already bloody from her previous job. The doctor nodded toward her. "I want stool and serum samples from the colon," he said. "And triple tissue samples from the intestinal wall." He wiped his hands on his smock. "And be careful with that," he instructed as she reached for the scalpel on the table. "Biosafety Level Two procedures. I want the samples refrigerated but not frozen. And call Colonel D'orsay. Tell him to get down here to the lab."

THIRTY-FOUR

HÔPITAL D'INSTRUCTION DES ARMÉES PERCY

On the second floor, and almost directly above the basement morgue where the body of the dead U.S. Air Force sergeant was being cut open and emptied for study, the E-wing of the hospital jutted to the north, opposite the public parking lot. A series of double doors, both of them requiring digital passkeys to open, controlled access to the entire wing. Beside the second set of doors, a guard stood behind a small reception center. There being no need, and certainly no desire, to call attention to the fact that this was the hospital's VIP wing, the guard was dressed in blue scrubs with a light jacket to conceal the compact weapon holstered at the small of his back, allowing him to blend perfectly with the nurses and doctors around him.

Four doors down the hallway, directly across from the circular nurse's station, two guards from the French Special Investigation Office stood watch over a private room with no nameplate on the door.

Inside the room, Petrie Baha lay on her hospital bed. The room was semidark, with only the dim security light near the doorway and a yellow nightlight mounted on the wall at the head of her bed casting any light. It was also uncluttered and quiet—no concerned family members sitting at the foot of the bed, no flowers, no gifts, no friends waiting in the hall. Though her parents had been notified, so far they had not appeared.

Petrie rested her head on the pillow, her dark hair combed back, bare arms atop the sheets. An IV dripped slowly into the back of her left hand, but she knew she didn't need the medicine or the hydrate or whatever it was they had dripping into her body. She had a nerve-wracking headache and her back hurt, but she wasn't seriously injured. She could walk. She could think. She could get up and run if they would let her. She would have run all night if the guards would only let her slip out of the room.

She stretched her legs and felt a sudden shudder again.

No, she wasn't injured.

But she was terrified.

Her eyes always moved, darting between the windows and the door. The hallway outside was not carpeted, and she tensed with every set of footsteps that moved up or down the hall. A nurse, so far the same one, came into her room every fifteen minutes or so, but she didn't say much, which was okay with her.

Outside, the wind had picked up, blowing in a band of low clouds that completely obscured the bright moon and sucked up the lights of the city. A cold mist began to fall, creating lonely halos around the lampposts. It was very late now, the sidewalks deserted, the parking lots nearly empty. Over time, the mist turned to rain, and a sudden gust began to rattle the leaves on the old birch trees outside her window.

Petrie listened to the rustle of the leaves and stared through the dark. She felt her heart beating and wondered how long she had to live.

She heard heavy footsteps that stopped outside her hospital door and her mind raced, praying it wasn't her father or any of his men. She heard a male voice, low and determined, and her chest grew tight, knowing the hospital couldn't protect her from her father or the anger of his masters.

She heard the latch click and saw the nurse push the door back to let him pass through. He stepped into the dim light and she froze, too shocked and surprised to react.

He moved into the room with a determined walk and stopped at the side of her bed.

She looked up, her face flushed. She was confused now, surprised, concerned about his presence, but no longer scared. She turned toward him, brushing back a strand of dark hair. "Hi there, Jesse," she said in a mouse of a voice.

He looked at her a moment, taking in the bed and IV, then stared quietly through the black pane of glass. Outside, the wind continued blowing, pushing a dead leaf against the rain-soaked window and pasting it there.

She watched him intently. As he turned his head away, she seemed to shrivel again.

A wave of weakness crashed over her, a sudden sense of mortality that cut her to the bone, and she felt a nearly uncontrollable desire to reach out for his hand. If she could have, she would have fallen into his arms, buried her head in his shoulders, and wept like a child. She would have tried desperately hard to explain. She would have asked his forgiveness and told him the truth, but she had no choice. She was nothing but a puppet, controlled by someone else. She wanted to lean against his neck and cry a lifetime of tears, for her sister, and for herself. She wanted to beg him to take her away.

But she couldn't, of course, and so she held it all in. He was a stranger, after all. Why should he even care? It wouldn't matter anyway. Her father would find her and kill her.

Jesse stood over her bed in his air force flight suit. He had clipped his security badge to the zipper on his forearm, and a special E-wing pass hung from a silver chain around his neck. His hair was tousled and he looked tired, and though he seemed to be angry, something about his manner made her wonder if the emotion was sincere.

"Hi, Miss Baha," he finally said.

She pushed herself up in the bed. The gown was thin and so short that it exposed one leg from her midthigh down, and she quickly wrapped the thin cotton blanket around herself, pulling it around her shoulders and holding it tight.

She studied him, but his face was a mask that she couldn't stare through.

Jesse watched her carefully. Inside, his gut scrunched. He didn't know what to think. Seeing the green eyes and perfect cheekbones, he felt completely dazed and confused. Could she really be what they told him? Could he have been such a fool? Would she be able to fool him again?

Petrie's eyes darted again to the window as it rattled and she sank back into her pillow. She trembled under the blankets, pulling them close. It seemed as if she dared not look at him, and as she turned away, he finally saw it and took a step back. How did he miss it? The gut-wrenching fear that tensed her dark face? The quiet desperation that dulled the light in her eyes? Yet he recognized it now, for he'd seen the same look before, the same expression of desperation and subjection to grief, the same surrender to forces that were greater than her will.

As if it had come to an end. Now there was no way to turn back.

General Hawley had the same look.

Jesse studied Petrie's eyes.

Seeing her slumping frame under the covers, he wondered whether this girl was not what he thought. There was tough history here. Tough stories to tell.

He pulled over a chrome stool and positioned it beside her bed. "Are you okay?" he finally asked her.

She nodded, still not looking at him.

He huffed, almost smiling. "You almost got me."

She slowly turned her head. "What?"

The dance of their eyes continued, and this time he looked away. *Do not look at her eyes,* he thought. *Do not allow yourself to be drawn in!*

He forced a grim look. "You almost got me," he repeated.

Again, she looked confused.

"With the car!" he explained, trying to sound impatient now.

"I don't know what you mean," she answered simply.

Don't believe her, you fool! Don't look in her eyes or she'll convince you that she is telling the truth!

He shook his head, truly frustrated. "Come on, Petrie. There's no reason to play games. We are way past that now."

She kept her eyes on him. "I understand," was all she said.

Jesse nodded toward the door. "There are, or course, FBI agents stationed in the hall. They came with me, they are waiting, but I wanted to talk to you first. Our government is working out the details with the French to take you into custody; you know what to expect more than I do, I suppose. Someone doesn't, you know . . . do the work that you do without having thought through the repercussions. The only reason I am able to speak with you now is because we are . . . what, almost friends."

Petrie shook her head sadly. "Oh, Jesse, how I wish that was true."

He spun a quarter turn on the chrome stool. She was good. No, she was a lot more than that. She was so good, she was perfect. No wonder he'd been fooled. Any man would have been taken in by her lies.

He swung again on the stool.

How many others had she used?

He shook his head, angry at his ignorance. He was playing with a rattlesnake, but he wouldn't let her strike again.

Grunting, he stood and moved to the foot of the bed. "The guy at the café, ol' Guido with the muscles? I don't suppose you had anything to do with that?" he asked her sarcastically.

Petrie shook her head, disgusted at the thought of the muscle-bound man. "He's an old friend from way back; it seems another life ago. Every time I see him, it leads to trouble. But I promise you, Jesse, his showing up at the café was a coincidence. He's a jealous fool, an empty t-shirt, but he had nothing to do with this."

Jesse pressed his lips. "We could be friends, Petrie, I suppose, but of course, as a matter of courtesy, most friends try to avoid running the other one down."

She pushed her hair back again and tucked the blanket by her legs. "Jesse," she asked him, "what are you getting at? I really don't understand."

"You and Sergeant Espy almost killed me, Petrie. He almost hit me with the car."

"You were there?"

Jesse only stared.

"I have no idea. He was driving so crazy. He was drunk, I don't know . . . maybe drugs. He was completely out of control. I didn't see you, I was just hanging on . . . I had no idea you were anywhere around until you showed up after the crash!"

"You didn't see me in the parking lot?"

"The parking lot? Where?"

Jesse shook his head. "You lie too well, Petrie. It must take years of practice to be this convincing."

A single tear fell across her dark cheek, and, embarrassed, she angrily brushed it away.

"I swear to you, Jesse, I don't know what you are talking about. I didn't know you were there, anywhere, I didn't know it was you chasing us in the car. I thought it was—" She stopped. "I thought it was someone else," she finally said.

Jesse watched her closely. "Did you think it was Adrien?" he asked.

Petrie stiffened but didn't answer.

"Who is Adrien?" Jesse asked again. "The nurses tell me you have asked for him constantly."

Petrie shook her head. A long moment of silence followed. Jesse waited, almost hopeful. "You cannot help me," Petrie finally said. "And since you can't help me there is no reason to explain."

Jesse bit his lip. Was it even worth trying again? "Petrie, neither of us has much time. Soon the FBI will have their agreement with your government and they will come in and take you into custody. Once that is done, I doubt they will let me talk to you again. So, please, for the moment at least, can we not pretend?"

Petrie turned to face him, looking deeply into his eyes, her voice as weak as a child. "I would really like that, Jesse."

And *that* was the truth. More than anything in the world, she wanted to be honest with him.

Shivering under the covers, she turned to the window again.

Petrie Baha had lived anything but a storybook life. The younger of two children, both daughters, she had moved around the world as was necessary for her father to maintain his schemes.

For going on twenty years, her father, Mohammad Akbaf Baha, had been one of the primary fundraisers for various terror regimes. To date, he had been responsible for collecting and distributing to a secret arm of the Saudi government more than 105 million dollars, a few hundred thousand more or less, all of it illegal, and all of it funneled to various terrorist organizations throughout the Middle East. He was a hard man, a committed Islamist who treated his own wife and his daughters not quite as well as he treated his dog, a man who had dedicated his life to the utter and complete destruction of Israel (the sooner and the more violently, the better) as well as their pimp, the Great Satan, who dominated the world, filling the hearts of every new generation with more filth and lies.

Petrie's older sister's life had ended tragically if not bitterly when, at the tender age of seventeen, she had come to her father, crying with devastating disappointment and fear. Having been raped by her uncle, a man who was three times her age, she was expecting now and had no idea what she ought to do.

The scene was seared like a brand in Petrie's mind. She was just fifteen, but she knew exactly what was going on. She remembered her mother wailing in terror in the corner of the room. She remembered the screams of anguish as she begged her husband to think before he did anything. She remembered her older sister standing before her father, her eyes cast to the floor, her shoulders shuddering with each breath that she drew. She remembered watching her mother slink back, hands on her wet face, too terrified to watch or listen anymore.

But her father, the gentlemen, never so much as raised his voice. He simply listened, nodded with understanding, then stood up, walked to his desk and picked up the phone.

The travel arrangements were made. Next morning, father and his daughter were on their way to Saudi Arabia.

Her father was only gone for two days.

Her older sister never came back.

But Petrie knew. She heard her mother crying. And she heard the hissing voices from the bedroom down the hall.

Petrie imagined the scene: the quiet drive into the barren desert, her father's determined eyes. Such things were technically illegal in the kingdom but still understood, for all he was doing was protecting the patriarchal name. Their family's honor retaken, he drove back from the desert alone.

Her mother never recovered, for whatever was left of her shallow soul at that point had been completely shattered when her husband returned from the kingdom alone.

Three weeks after her father's trip to the kingdom, two days after her sixteenth birthday, Petrie found the letter her father had written to his brother lying on top of his desk. With trembling hands she had picked it up, looked around in fear, then read the words he had written, asking to be reimbursed for the cost of his travel to Saudi Arabia.

And that was it, the only punishment the rapist would ever face.

Such were the lessons Petrie had learned through the years.

Initially, her father had been extremely disappointed that his wife had not presented him with sons, but as time passed, and as his remaining daughter had grown into beauty, he had begun to realize what an asset such a beautiful child could be. The fact that Petrie's mother's French citizenship—unhindered passports, drivers' licenses, the full faith and privilege of the government of

France—was automatically transferred to Petrie presented even more of an asset that he could take advantage of.

So it was that, soon after her older sister had been taken to the Saudi desert, he put Petrie to work. Over time she had become his primary courier, passing messages to his men, secret bundles of cash, documents from his masters in Persia, instructions on covert operations, letters between leaders of the various organizations he helped fund.

At first Petrie didn't question what he was making her do, but as she grew older and more sophisticated, she realized just how dangerous every task that he gave her might be.

But it never even occurred to her that she might tell him no. She never had a choice, and she knew that. He was her father, and she had been raised in a faith that didn't allow her to question in any way. Yes, he allowed her certain privileges that many other fathers didn't allow; she could drive, go to school, read, or be in the city alone. She had friends. She could travel. But there was the constant threat of what her father could do, and not just to her but to her mother, who was helpless as a child now. As much as she hated her father, she loved her mother even more, and after the death of her sister, she knew just how far he would go.

Staring out the hospital window at the darkness, Petrie felt another shudder of fear, knowing her father would never forgive her for what she had done.

In the basement of the hospital, the examining physician, the French army colonel, had completed the autopsy and was just moving to his desk. His hands were still moist from the disinfectant scrubbing, and he had changed into clean clothes. He rubbed lotion onto the back of his hands (the constant washing tended to keep his skin dry), then turned to the side wing on his desk, pulled the wireless keyboard a few inches closer, and punched at the keys. After a quick search, he started to read from the United States government's Centers for Disease Control and Prevention Web site.

> WHAT IS BOTULISM?
>
> Botulism is a rare but serious paralytic illness caused by a nerve toxin that is produced by the bacterium *Clostridium botulinum.* All forms of botulism can be fatal and are considered medical emergencies. Foodborne botulism can be especially dangerous.
>
> WHAT ARE THE SYMPTOMS OF BOTULISM?
>
> The classic symptoms of botulism include double vision, blurred vision, drooping eyelids, slurred speech, difficulty swallowing, dry mouth, and muscle weakness. In foodborne botulism, symptoms can occur as early as six hours after eating a contaminated food.

HOW IS BOTULISM DIAGNOSED?

The most direct way to confirm the diagnosis is to demonstrate the botulinum toxin in the patient's serum or stool by injecting serum or stool into mice and looking for signs of botulism . . .

The doctor quit reading and stared at his notes. He thumped his hands nervously across the top of his desk, sat back, stared at the ceiling, then picked up the telephone to his supervisor, a one-star general who commanded the hospital.

He described his findings, his voice professional but strained. He'd done a thousand autopsies, from murder to accidents and suicides and everything in between, but he had never seen anything quite like this and it clearly had him on edge.

After explaining the situation, he waited for the general's reply.

"You are certain?" the commander asked skeptically.

"Negative, sir," the pathologist answered back. "We have injected the samples into the mice, but you know it can take up to four days before we have the conclusive results."

"Is there any way to accelerate the tests?"

"We might start getting a detectable reaction within a few hours, sir, but the results would only be preliminary."

"I want someone staring at those mice until you know something," the general demanded. "I'm getting heat from this case and it's starting to burn. I've got everyone calling; the Americans, the Secret Security police, military intelligence. That dead guy on your table is linked to the stolen U.S. fighter. I want you to keep on this colonel and get me some results."

"Yes sir," the doctor answered after a frustrated pause.

"I'll call you in two hours." The general hung up the phone.

THIRTY-FIVE

OFF THE EASTERN COAST OF MAINE

For hours the U.S. interceptors searched the night sky, desperately looking for any sign of the stolen Ares. The night passed in silence, then shortly after four-thirty in the morning, the radios again burst to life.

"I've got a tally on the target!" the flight leader of an F-15 formation suddenly cried.

Somewhere far in the distance, almost to the northern lights that shimmered on the horizon, lightning flashed, causing a quick pop of static as the F-15 pilot went on. "I had a target on my radar but it is gone now. But he was there, I got a flash before the bandit slipped away. Must be the Ares."

"State your location for those not data-linked to your aircraft!"

"Bull's-eye, one hundred-fifteen DME, four-niner radial."

The AWACS controller was cool as chilled lemon, his voice calm but clear. "Copy that, everybody. Now state the location of the bandit! We've got nothing here."

"He slipped off my radar, but last known hack was Bull's-eye one-eighty DME, sixty . . . sixty something radial . . . I don't know, I've got nothing now. You tell me!"

"Eagle One-one, Mother's got nothing on our radar. Nothing on our IR or other sensors. Are you certain?"

"Yes, man, we saw it. My wingman got it too. The Ares is out there and he's coming. Definitely west-bound, heading toward the border."

"Okay, Eagle. All aircraft stand by. That is just outside my effective radar coverage, I'm going to have to bring up the ground controller here. Giantkiller, you copy. That's your sector, buddy. Give us some news."

"Giantkiller's with you. Eagle, Raptor, Sailor, Hawk, and Homer flights, I want you to come up my freq two-four-four-point-six. Eagle, turn right heading zero-eight-four. All other fighters, stand by."

Giantkiller was located on a small spit of land on the northernmost tip of Maine. Designed to monitor and control international airline traffic flying between the continents, it also acted as the sometimes controller for a small military block of airspace used for air-to-air exercises. The controller wasn't proficient in controlling military aircraft, but he had done it once or twice before and was not completely overwhelmed.

One by one, the five fighter formations switched their radios over to the new frequency, and the ground controller went to work. Issuing complicated but concise orders, he moved half a dozen aircraft toward the section of airspace where the stolen fighter must have been.

The aircraft converged, spokes on a wheel flying toward the same point in the sky. As they flew, they armed their weapons.

Thirty seconds later, they were ready for the kill.

LANCER 17
ONE HUNDRED FORTY-SEVEN MILES NORTH-NORTHEAST OF MAINE

The twin-engine Air Force F-117 stealth fighter flew through the night.

Inside the aircraft, the pilot was nearly overwhelmed. The smoke was toxic and thick, and it burned as if acid had been poured into his eyes. His oxygen mask was snapped tight around his face, the regulator flipped up to "emergency," forcing 100 percent oxygen into his chest, but still he struggled to breathe, his lungs having been singed by the heat and the smoke. Reaching down, the pilot selected "RAM" on his panel. His ears popped and his eyes seemed to suck against their sockets as the emergency door aside his cockpit opened, forcing cold, clear air into the cockpit, washing the acid smoke away while depressurizing the cabin to match the altitude of 28,000 feet. The smoke-filled air cleared, and the pilot could see his instruments and flight panel for the first time since the fire had ignited in his cockpit almost a full minute before.

The air force pilot shook his head and wiped his Nomex flight glove across his eyes, pushing aside the tears of irritation that had been streaming down his face. His ankles burned, and he could still feel the heat from the fire that smoldered somewhere in front of him. Looking down, he watched as the smoke continued to drift from the instrument panel to his left. Moving his feet, he felt them stick, the soles of his boots having almost melted to goo. He swore and swallowed hard. The pain was just beginning to register. His legs would soon blister. The pain was intense.

Not a good flight. Not a good night. Time to get this jet on the ground.

He had already turned back toward the emergency field outside Bangor,

Maine, but it was still a long way away. How far away, he didn't know for certain, for his entire avionics panel had been burned to a crisp.

No navigational aides. No instruments.

No radios . . .

The stealth fighter flew through the dark sky, invisible to air traffic control and not talking to anyone.

He was a couple engines and a seat and not a whole lot of anything else.

Searching the night sky, he turned farther west, using the North Star as his guide. Far, far in the distance, he could barely see the shimmer of the water where the cold waves crashed onto the beach, the tops foaming and white underneath the glimmering stars. On his left, he saw a flash and wondered what it was, but not for long; his entire attention was focused on his own smoking jet.

Moving a switch on his UHF radio, he flipped over to "guard." "Giantkiller, Giantkiller, this is Lancer One-seven on guard."

Nothing. No static. Not even the subtlest change in the sound from the radio earpieces built into his helmet. He tried again. "Giantkiller, this is Lancer on guard . . ."

He could tell by the sameness of the sound that his radio was dead.

He tried VHF and the HF. His entire communications panel was gone, burned through, crisp as toasties, the wires burned to brittle copper from the fire at his feet.

The pilot swore and swallowed again, forcing down the acid bile.

The afternoon before, fat, dumb, and very happy, he had been en route to Langley Air Force Base in Virginia to do a private air show for some visiting dignitaries from Bangladesh or India, or somewhere. Soon after, he'd been diverted and sent up north to assist in the search for the stolen Ares. An air-to-ground fighter, the F-117 had no air-to-air missiles or guns. (It should have been called a bomber—which is exactly what it was—but *fighter* sounded so much more sexy than *bomber,* as the generals who named it clearly knew.)

Even though the F-117 didn't have any guns or missiles, it had a great radar and target sensors, and so it had been sent up north to help out if it could. If nothing else, it was another set of eyeballs in the sky, another radar, another pilot, and the United States was putting everything it could muster in the air.

Problem was, while en route from his base in New Mexico to Langley, the pilot had been resetting circuit breakers the entire flight. When on the ground at Langley, the pilot had worked with some maintenance troops to find the problem, but they had been unable to pin it down. "Maybe you ought to stay here," one of the MX guys had offered.

No way the pilot was going to miss out on this show, no way he was going to sit this out because a couple wires had been crossed, causing a few circuit breakers to pop. "Forget it," he demanded as he climbed in the jet. "It's no big thing. I can handle it. Let's get this jet in the air."

Now, an intensely opposite desire had suddenly kicked into gear. "Come on, baby, let's get this jet on the ground," he coaxed.

Below his knees, a handful of sparks sputtered as they fell to the cockpit floor. He felt the heat building up and swore again into his mask.

"Mayday, Mayday," he broadcast for the fifth or sixth time.

Nothing. Not a hiss. Not an answer. His radios and transponder were completely dead.

Flying west, he aimed for the coast, estimated the distance to the emergency landing field, and began to descend.

The two F-15s flew at top speed, their wing roots transonic, creating clear puffs of vapor that washed over the back of the cockpit. They were screaming—.96 on their Mach indictors—and they had just slowed down.

"Whacha got, whacha got?" the flight leader called again as he flew blindly ahead.

"Continue your vector," Giantkiller replied.

"Tally on the target?"

"No joy. Continue heading. We're working with some navy assets just below you. I've got them on another frequency. Stand by. Give me time."

PIGEON AUXILIARY EMERGENCY LANDING FIELD
NINETY-SIX KILOMETERS WEST OF GANDER,
NEWFOUNDLAND

The pilot was shaken awake. "Come with me, sir," he was told.

He turned wearily on his bed.

"Come, sir," the aide insisted. "You will want to hear this."

The pilot threw on a coat and ran with the aide to the hangar where the other men were listening to the relay from their ship along the East Coast.

The Ares pilot listened to the chatter over the radios, wondering who the AWACS controllers could be talking about. They had a tally on the target and were vectoring fighters to engage?

No. He didn't think so. Unless they were somewhere above him and aiming for his bed.

It took him a couple of seconds to figure it out.

They had the wrong guy. The American fighters were tracking one of their own.

He shook his head and laughed.

Some dumb U.S. pilot was about to get shot down.

OFF THE EASTERN COAST OF MAINE

The USS *Lassen* had more radars and surface-to-surface, surface-to-air sensors than any one ship ought to have. The Aegis Combat System included the AN/SPY-1D phased array radar; the MK 41 Vertical Launching System (which could fire up to ninety standard surface-to-air, Tomahawk surface-to-surface, and VLA antisubmarine rockets); the AN/SQQ-89 Antisubmarine Warfare System; and a bow-mounted AN/SQS-53C sonar as well as the AN/SQR-19 towed array. *Lassen* also had eight Harpoon antiship missile launchers and six MK 32 torpedo tubes, as well as two MK 15 Phalanx Close-In Weapon Systems and a five-inch, rapid-firing deck gun. At full combat capability, the Aegis system was capable of directing twenty missiles at one time, making it the best sea-based, war-fighting system in the world.

The sensors and guns literally cluttered the entire deck.

With the ability to act as a key contributor to an aircraft-carrier battle group or as part of surface action group (SAG), the *Lassen* was able to control and direct U.S. interceptors up to five hundred miles from the ship. For this reason, it had a twofold mission: to protect friendly forces by destroying enemy missiles and aircraft (as well as submarines and surface ships) and to kill the enemy using its long range antiship-and-land attack missiles and guns.

When the Navy commissioned its first Aegis cruiser, the USS *Ticonderoga,* it changed the shape of naval warfare for the next century. The *Lassen* was another member of this war class, deadly and dependable. With a crew of 350 of the best young sailors the navy had to offer, the *Lassen* was a proud but extremely expensive battleship.

But the investment had proven worth it. There wasn't a threat on the ocean or in the sky the American destroyer couldn't see.

At least that was true up to now.

Could it track the Ares? No one knew.

But from close range, and from below, looking up at the wings, the *Lassen* could certainly track the older and much slower F-117.

"*Lassen,* do you have . . . confirm you have a track on the bogey."

"Affirm, Giantkiller," the controller inside the ship's combat center shot back. "Bogey is one-seven radial off our ship, thirty-eight miles. Westbound.

Descending. It's not taking any evasive maneuvers. Looks like it's relying on its stealth."

"Copy that," the ground controller said. Turning to another frequency, he commanded the navy and air force interceptors, "All aircraft within ADIZ sector Walker, ident at this time. Repeat, all aircraft within Walker, check your Modes Two and Four and then ident."

One by one, each of the fighter formations within the area hit their transponder buttons, illuminating both their ATC-assigned codes as well as the classified combat Identity Friend-or-Foe codes within their systems. The ground controller turned toward his supervisor, who was checking them off one by one.

"That's everyone," the supervisor determined.

The controller checked his screen, cross-checked the thin slips of paper slotted beside his radar, and nodded.

"What about the F-117?" the super asked.

The controller pointed toward a sector farther east. "The AWACS guys have got him. They sent him further east, thinking his radar might be one of their most effective tools in looking for the Ares."

The supervisor grunted, knowing that was wrong. The F-117 was almost thirty years old now. Yes, it was an incredible machine, but so was the '76 GTO he had owned in high school, and the NightHawk was almost as old. It was not the father but the grandfather of the Ares, and it would have never found the stolen fighter, he was sure.

"Everything but the kitchen sink . . . ," he slowly muttered to himself.

The controller shot him a quick look. "Yeah, everything but the sink is up there right now."

The super grunted. "You've still got nothing on your radar?"

The controller motioned with his chin toward his screen. "Nothing but what you see there."

"But the *Lassen* claims to have him?"

"You heard it, sir."

The controller thought again. "Confirm this. I want it on tape. Everyone else is accounted for? We're not going after one of our guys?"

Again the controller nodded, this time toward the slips of paper beside his screen. "Everyone that's out there has squawked the proper ident."

"Then that's got to be the Ares," the super concluded. His blood was boiling now. This was his chance to be a hero, to blast the stolen fighter from the sky.

The controller sat in silence, waiting for his boss to make the call.

The seconds passed in silence, and then the supervisor said, "Get the interceptors to back out a bit. Keep them close enough to get in the fight if we need them but let the USS *Lassen* take the first shot."

"Roger that," the controller answered.

"Tell the *Lassen* the bogey is now a bandit. Tell them to go and get it. They're the best chance of getting the Ares that we have."

The American F-15 pilot saw a flash on his radar screen. And it was close. Really close. He turned in his seat, jamming his neck to look past his shoulder as he stared through the dark.

He saw a flash. A couple miles. A black shadow of a fighter against the moon and the sky. He could see the wing and taillights. Red and White. Standard military lighting. He even saw the illumination from the cockpit, the fighter was that close.

He recognized the silhouette. He'd seen it many times before.

An F-177 NightHawk was flying off his wing.

Did Giantkiller have him? Did the ground controllers even know he was there? He hadn't heard the NightHawk pilot checking in on the radios, but he might have been on another frequency, or he might have missed the call. The NightHawk pilot might be talking to the AWACS. It was crazy stupid up here right now . . .

Still, he had to wonder. Did they know he was there?

The F-117 pilot kept his eyes half closed against the smoke that still filtered into the cockpit. His throat and eyes burned, and though he didn't know it, his face was smeared with black, the filthy smoke coating every inch of bare skin.

He concentrated on his flying, but once every couple of minutes his mind would flash to his kid. No way he wasn't going to be there for her. No way he crashed this jet.

Worst case, he'd pull the handles and eject out of this mess. Yeah, he'd spend a cold night bobbing on the ocean, but someone would find him in the morning and take him home to his kid.

The coastline was coming closer now and he studied the terrain, comparing it to the small map he had strapped to his leg. Without his navigation equipment, he'd have to do it the old-fashioned way, but that was okay, he was pretty good at that, too. He spent a lot of weekends in his own Cessna 172, and his eyeball navigation was better than most. He looked north, identified the larger set of lights as Fredericton in Nova Scotia, then turned forty degrees to the south. He checked his descent and airspeed, noted his fuel flow and fuel remaining (a force of habit; without midair refueling, the F-117 had notoriously short combat legs) then, just for grins, tried his radio once again. "Giantkiller, this is Lancer One-seven on guard. Say again, this is Lancer One-seven on guard. I've lost my radios and navigation. Heading now, two-four five. Descending through twenty-three thousand feet. This is a call in the blind. Lance One-seven is penetrating the ADIZ."

He released the transmit button and listened, but heard no reply.

The controller center inside the *Lassen* was dimly lit. Recessed bulbs in the ceiling created intermittent circles of lights, and the various computer and radar screens cast green and bluish hues across the floor. The room wasn't crowded, there was plenty of space to work, and the men and women spoke in low voices as they brought the ship up to combat status, readying their missiles to fire.

An all-hands had already been issued. The missiles had been armed, the control keys and codes inserted. All they were waiting for was the final word to fire.

"How's your track?" the captain demanded.

The weapons officer replied, "It's not good, but it's doable. It's clearly a stealth, but its underbelly is reflecting enough for us to keep an acceptable track and course."

"Say target status?"

"Bandit descending now through twenty-one thousand feet. It turned forty degrees to the south, but is on a constant track now. Constant airspeed. Southwest heading."

The CO scowled. He didn't know anything about the stolen fighter, but something didn't feel right. It should have been higher. It should have been faster. It should have maneuvered to keep from exposing itself. He stared at the radar . . . something was familiar to him . . . something *too* familiar.

He slowly shook his head.

"*Lassen,* this is Giantkiller. The bogey is our bandit. Say again, the bogey you are tracking is our target. You are the number-one option. Your discretion as to the best means to engage and destroy. You are cleared hot to fire. Confirm, *Lassen,* you are cleared to engage."

"Copy that," the communications officer answered, "we are cleared to engage."

"Go and get him, buddy," the ground controller couldn't help but add.

"Distance and bearing to target?" the CO demanded for the last time.

"Target zero-five-zero, fifteen miles. He'll pass overhead and almost right off our nose."

The commander took a breath. It was a nearly perfect attack position. Like shooting ducks in a bathtub.

So why did his gut crunch?

He swallowed once, then turned away. "Do it," was his command.

Seven seconds later, the *Lassen*'s deck was illuminated with a ghostly white-hot light. The missile seemed to catapult from the launch tube, then almost hang in the air before the thrust took control, sending it into the night. The surface-to-air missile turned slightly north as it accelerated upward, the small engine exhaust port spouting a constant stream of flame.

The F-117 pilot never saw it coming. Never knew it was there. He was concentrating on his navigation and his flying and the smoldering fire at his feet. He was concentrating on everything but the possibility that some U.S. missiles might be coming for him. *He was the good guy.* What did he have to fear?

Somewhere above the *Lassen,* another fireball illuminated the sky.

The enormous missile hit the F-117's underbelly dead-on, then exploded with a fury that blew the little fighter into bits.

"Got him, got him, got him!" Giantkiller shouted over the radio. "Way to go, *Lassen.*"

There was moment of silence as the Eagle pilot turned his face so that he could speak into his mask. "Check that, Giantkiller," he said in a husky voice. "Check that really close. I think we have just shot down your own guy. There was a NightHawk up here."

CENTRAL OFFICE OF SECRET SPECIAL SERVICE
BOULEVARD ST-GERMAIN
CENTRAL PARIS

François Villon sat alone in his office. The only light in the room was a small Tiffany lamp on the corner of his desk that cast a green-tinted shadow across the papers spread out before him.

He glanced at the wall clock. He should have been home. He needed a few hours' sleep. But he couldn't until he had sorted this out.

He considered the small couch on the other side of his desk, knowing it was likely he would end up there for the night. Not the first time that had happened. He hated every night on the couch. His wife stared at him from a photograph on the corner of his desk, and he mumbled something to her, then pulled another lungful of sweet smoke.

Feet on his desk, he leaned back; the old leather chair, a family heirloom, creaked under his significant weight. He smoked passively, enjoying each draw, the cigar smoke forming in a visible haze against the ceiling. His eyes, half glazed, were staring upward, and he looked half asleep, though his mind was churning as the clock ticked away.

His phone rang and he started, the sound penetrating the quiet of the night. He turned in his chair, feet still on the desk, until he saw it was his personal line. Then his cell phone started ringing and he swung his feet to the floor. He checked the caller ID on his desk phone, lifted his cell, checked the number, saw the phone call was coming from the same government office, silenced the ringer on the cell, and picked up the desk phone.

"Villon," he answered quickly. "Do you have any idea what time it is?"

He listened to the gruff voice on the other end of the line, the cigar drooping from the corner of his mouth. "Who knows this?" he demanded.

His mind raced at the sound of the name. Adrien! He'd never heard of him before! If he worked for the agency, he must be one of the deepest moles. "Who is this agent she calls Adrien?" he demanded.

He listenened, then jerked to attention, the sound of the name enough to bring him out of his chair. "You're kidding . . . ," he stammered, his voice respectful now. "The vice chairman—"

The caller cut him off and he listened again, turning pale. "Are you certain?" he finally muttered.

The answer came through the receiver in a growl. "Of course I am certain! Now where is the girl?"

"I don't know. She was taken to the hospital, but . . ."

"l'Hôpital d'instruction des armées Percy?"

Villon thought a quick moment, "Yes, yes, of course!"

"Then you'd better move on this, Villon! Her father will do anything to silence her. And don't try to remind me that she's his daughter because we both know he won't care. We've got to figure out a way to help her or she's a dead girl now."

THIRTY-SIX

Jesse stood at the foot of Petrie's bed. He watched her intently as she stared, obviously lost in her thoughts.

Their last words hung in the air.

So, please, for the moment at least, can we not pretend?

I would really like that, Jesse.

But was she really ready to be honest with him?

He thumped his fingers against the chrome footboard, then glanced down at his watch. It was almost one in the morning. He realized he was starved. He needed a shower and some sleep, but more than anything he needed something to eat. "Are you hungry?" he asked.

"Are you kidding? You mean we could actually . . . you could get me out of this room?"

"I'm sure that I could."

She sat up enthusiastically. He nodded to the IV, but it was too late; she had already reached for the tape on the back of her hand. Pulling with her nail, she peeled the white bandage back, exposed the flexible needle, and slipped it out from the vein.

"Can you do that?" he wondered, his eyes wide.

"If I'm dehydrated, I'm perfectly capable of drinking a glass of water," she said.

"Are you sure? I mean . . ."

She swung her feet to the edge of the bed, flashing ankles and calves. "Please, Mr. James," she pointed to the back of the door. Jesse turned to see a white bathrobe hanging there. The VIP wing of the hospital, he remembered, as he grabbed the thick robe and brought it back to her. Holding the cotton blanket around her chest, she turned her back to him as he placed the robe over her shoulders. The blanket dropped and she wrapped the oversized belt around her waist. The bathrobe, square-shouldered and high-necked, was thick enough to keep even the most feeble patient warm, and it seemed to Jesse that it drowned her in bolts of terrycloth.

She pulled her hair over the collar. "Let's go," she said.

Leading the way, Jesse opened the door. Two FBI agents were waiting in the hall.

"We're going to get something to eat," Jesse said.

They glanced at each other. "I don't think so," the senior agent said.

Jesse reached back toward Petrie, pulling her through the doorway. "There's a cafeteria on the main floor. We'll be down there."

One of the agents stepped forward. "You can't—"

Jesse squared his shoulders. "I can't do what?" he demanded. "Remember, Agent Horton, I'm not under investigation here!"

The agent held his ground. "We have our instructions."

"Follow your instructions, that is okay with me. But right now I'm hungry and I'm going downstairs to get something to eat."

"She can't leave this room."

Jesse put his arm around Petrie and pulled her to his side. "That is not correct, Agent Horton, I've read the orders, too. She can't leave the *hospital grounds*, but she is not confined to her room. She is free to move around, to have treatment, to meet with her doctors, and yes, she is free to go and get something to eat."

"We will have to—"

"I understand. Come along. I'll order something for you too."

He pointed Petrie toward the hallway doors and they started walking. Looking over his shoulder, he nodded to the agents, and they shook their heads angrily.

The assassin was waiting in a two-door Peugeot on a narrow side street that ran to the back of the hospital grounds. He'd been forced to play the role of the distraught uncle to get her room number from the telephone receptionist, then a few more panicked questions to discover that it was on the second floor, but with this information in hand, he was ready to begin. Sitting behind the wheel, he held a laptop computer against his chest. A USB cord ran from the back of the silver computer to the laser instrument in his hand, and an antinoise headset rested over his ears.

Pointing the laser beam at the hospital, he moved it to the first window and listened carefully. Though he kept a watch out for traffic moving along the narrow road, his eyes were generally unfocused as he concentrated on the sounds that emitted through his headset. The sounds were sometimes scratchy, but he had enough experience with the laser to identify most of what he heard.

The invisible laser hit the thin glass of the first window and bounced back tiny variations in the signal, picking up any sounds on the other side of the glass.

He listened through the first window, identifying the sounds: a respirator hissing, a constant ticking on the wall, someone breathing very deeply, then a loud and masculine cough. No, this wasn't it. The next room was quiet—had to be unoccupied. He moved the laser to the third window and listened: two nurses talking, an older woman making a rude and bitter reply. He cringed at the sound of the bedpan, an ugly reminder that wealth and power meant nothing when it came to the indignities of having to have someone to take care of your most basic needs.

He snorted, disgusted, then moved another window down.

At first there was only silence, then he heard a nurse speak. He concentrated on the patient's voice. She answered in French, but yes . . . there it was, the accent he had been looking for.

Bingo! He had her. He glanced down at his watch.

Wedging his laser instrument against the car door, he fine-tuned the range and settled back to listen. He knew he couldn't get into her room, at least not right now, but he was not overly concerned; it was a hospital, after all, not a jail or the central intelligence complex, and he would have his chance. If nothing else he would pop her when the Americans came to take her away. They would have to walk from the building to their car, and she would be completely exposed. It would be more dangerous for him then, but he had the right weapon, and it could certainly be done.

For the next hour it was much the same thing. Every fifteen minutes the female nurse would enter the room, turn on the lights, and ask her how she felt. It seemed pretty clear she had been instructed to not let the patient get any sleep. The nurse would adjust a piece of equipment—an IV stand perhaps—circle the bed, then promise to return very soon. On the third visit she called the patient Petrie, the final confirmation he had been waiting for.

He sat back, deciding how best to proceed, keeping the laser focused on the window, picking up every tiny movement or vibration from inside. He heard the door being pushed open again. An unknown man and the nurse talked for a moment—he checked to ensure his computer was recording—then the man and the target spoke in English. He had to struggle to keep up, as his English was not nearly as good as his Russian or his French. The conversation was halting and unspecific: talk of pretending, talk of friends, a long moment of silence, then talk of getting something to eat.

His heart slammed in his chest. Could they really make such a stupid mistake? Would they really allow her to leave the only part of the hospital where she would be safe?

Listening again, he realized that was exactly what they were going to do. Clearly they didn't know yet who her father was.

He slapped his computer shut and pulled the headset from his head. The cafeteria was on the main floor, just inside the front doors.

He smiled to himself.

He reached into the hidden seam under the left side of his seat, pulled out the Glock handgun, checked the clip, and opened his door. Leaving the keys in the ignition, he got out of the car, screwing the silencer onto the weapon as he walked.

The rain had stopped, leaving puddles of leaf-filled water across the uneven cement. The sky was dark, and he shivered, pulling up the collar of his jacket. He kept his head down, though his eyes constantly moved. The parking lot was almost empty and there wasn't a soul to be seen.

He followed the sidewalk as it wound its way around to the front of the hospital. The main doors were brightly lit, with floodlights illuminating a French flag and the revolving door.

Shoving the handgun deep into his jacket pocket, he thought of the pictures they had shown him and reviewed their instructions in his mind. His client had been very specific, even adamant, about how she was to be killed. Point blank. From behind. One shot in the back of the head, execution style. Why they wouldn't accept a pop in the forehead, through the ear, a couple shots in the heart, he didn't know, but since the Mongol-eyed foreigner was paying the bills, he would follow his instructions to a *T*. For the money they were paying he would have done a lot more. He would have worn a clown suit and stood on his head in the corner before he shot her if they had asked him to.

As he moved toward the main doors of the hospital, he thought of the photographs again. She would be very easy to identify. There weren't many women who looked as good as she did.

The military forensic pathologist sat alone in his office. He leaned back, enjoying the silence around him. He knew it had been storming outside, for he had just returned from a quick smoke break on the patio, but the basement of the hospital was as quiet as . . . well, as quiet as a morgue. He smiled at his humor, good enough for the dead, then rubbed wearily at his eyes, ready for a few hours' sleep.

In the deep silence of the basement he stared at the initial test results, feeling completely satisfied.

He had been right. One hundred percent on the money.

The mice were so infected with bacteria, they would be dead within minutes, their tiny lungs already swimming in fluid and disease.

Which meant that, yes, the American Air Force sergeant had died of massive head trauma as a result of impact with the windscreen during the course of the automobile crash, but none of that mattered; he would have died anyway. At the time of the crash, he had maybe a few hours left to live. At the time of the impact with the light pole, his body was already a veritable sewer of toxins that had already started the process of shutting down his major organs. Beginning with his brain, neurological systems, and lungs, he would have checked out piece by piece, each organ waving white flags of pus in surrender as the toxins shut them down.

The doctor was certain the sergeant would have been experiencing the initial symptoms of the toxins at the time of the crash: poor muscle coordination, blurred vision, drooping eyelids, slurred speech, and delayed thought. It was a wonder, the doctor noted, how in that advanced state of toxicity the patient could have maintained control of the automobile at all.

He stared at the lab readings, noting the highly accelerated toxin count in the mice. Whoever had poisoned the sergeant had done a masterful job. There was enough *Clostridium botulinum* bacteria in his digestive tract to bring a bull elephant down.

The doctor checked his autopsy record, taking special care to note the estimated time the poisoned item had been ingested by the dead man.

Approximately 16:00 local.

Wasn't that about the same time the U.S. aircraft had been stolen?

He pressed his lips, satisfied.

He loved a good mystery as much as anyone.

THIRTY-SEVEN

UNITED STATES EMBASSY
PARIS, FRANCE

French Security Special Agent François Villon waited impatiently in the main lobby of the U.S. embassy. The building was much larger, he thought, than it needed to be, and ornate, an awkward mix of European style and typical American un-grace. He stood on the three-foot checkerboard tiles of the floor, surrounded by faux mosaics, a high-ceilinged concourse, security guards at every entrance, and several wide hallways jutting at forty-five-degree angles to his left and his right. The embassy lobby was completely empty but for the after-hours receptionist, and it was quiet, being past the middle of the night.

Huffing impatiently, he paced. He had many things to do now, and this visit was taking far too much of his time. The receptionist eyed him over her glasses, pretending to read from a manila folder in her hand.

He pulled a cell phone from his pocket, jabbed at the numbers, then held it to his ear. Walking toward a corner, he lowered his voice. "What is going on at the hospital?" he demanded.

"The surveillance teams are on their way."

"Get them in position. I'll be there absolutely as soon as I can."

He slapped the phone closed and went back to pacing, his short legs pumping his vast weight around. Two minutes later, he couldn't stand it any longer. He walked to the night receptionist and leaned his fist on her table. "Any word?" he demanded.

The middle-aged woman looked up slowly. "Sir," she answered curtly, "we are doing all we can to locate him, but you have to understand how busy they all have been."

"Yes, yes, I know that. But it is urgent, do you understand that? I must speak with him."

The sound of leather heels clicking on the tile echoed through the empty concourse, and Villon quickly turned. The American was descending the stairs. "Monsieur Ketchum," Villon said, walking across the empty space in between them. "I must talk to you."

The president's chief of staff frowned. "Mr. Villon, what could be so urgent that a phone call would not do?"

HÔPITAL D'INSTRUCTION DES ARMÉES PERCY
FRENCH MILITARY HOSPITAL
CLAMART, FRANCE

Jesse led the way down the hospital hall. He nodded to the guard at the reception desk but walked past him without saying anything. The guard started to move toward him, then glanced down the hall at the two FBI agents in tow. The senior agent motioned for him to sit down. "We got it," he muttered as they passed.

The cafeteria quit serving at 8:00 p.m. and was entirely deserted, but there were more than a dozen coin-operated machines along the back wall that offered sandwiches, hot soups, homemade bread, and a dozen choices of coffees. The floor was gray tile and along the far wall, a series of floor-to-ceiling windows looked out on the rain. The room had a dozen Formica tables surrounded by plastic chairs and was well lit with recessed neon lights.

Jesse looked around. The cafeteria seemed cavernous and empty with the bright lights and vacant chairs. He pointed to a table near the bank of dark windows. Petrie made her way past the empty chairs and sat down, her back to the door. The FBI guys followed them into the empty cafeteria, nodded awkwardly at Petrie, then sat at the table nearest the door.

Jesse walked toward the row of machines, pulled out a twenty-euro note, punched a couple of buttons, extracted the food items as they dropped, and tucked them under his arm. Two swiss-and-turkey sandwiches, a bag of vinegar chips, and a cardboard carrier with four hot coffees in hand, he turned away from the machines. Stopping by the suit guys, he dropped two coffees on their table, then walked back to Petrie and put the food down.

She looked at it, realizing she was famished, tore through the clear plastic wrapping, and took an uncertain bite. Jesse sat down, opened the chips, and sipped at his brew. Reaching to the center of the table, he grabbed some weak French hot sauce, opened his sandwich, dribbled the sauce, and closed it again.

They ate in silence a few minutes until Jesse looked up. "You know that I'm not a government investigator?" he said.

She paused and nodded.

"Anything you tell me, anything that would help us, I would pass along, you surely know that. But I'm not here to interrogate you, Petrie. I have no training in interrogation or criminal investigations. I just want . . . you know, I just want you to tell me why."

She placed her sandwich on the table but didn't say anything.

"You can't continue hiding behind your silence."

If you only knew, she thought bitterly.

She was nothing, she had nothing, she was spit in the wind. Having betrayed her own father, she was alone and abandoned and would soon be dead. But since she had nothing left to lose, the only thing she feared now was *not* having a chance to explain. So she leaned toward him, her green eyes growing soft. "I will tell you anything you ask me," she said in a low voice.

"Prince Abdul Mohammad bin Saud? How did he get into the aircraft?" he asked.

She cocked her head, looking blank. "I do not know what you mean."

"The Ares, Petrie, the stolen aircraft! How did the prince get through our security? What is he planning to do?"

She swallowed hard, looking innocent. "I have absolutely no idea what you are talking about."

He sat back, disgusted. "Come on, Petrie, please. We need your help! Can't you see that? We've got a stolen aircraft heading toward our nation, an aircraft which is capable of doing incredible damage. You are involved, you can't deny that, and we need your help."

The bright neon cast her face in a harsh light, and the empty cafeteria seemed to suck up her voice. "I have no idea what you are talking about. And believe me, please, I would tell you. I would help you if I could. All I have ever done, Jesse, is deliver messages for my father. I don't read them, I don't write them, I never know what's going on." She stopped and looked around as if she was trying to decide. "I also pass the information on to Adrien," she added weakly.

Jesse leaned toward her. "Who is this guy you call Adrien?"

She stared at him, then sat back, suddenly changing her mind.

Jesse leaned against the table, his anger building. Everything she told him didn't make any sense. His eyes burned with frustration. "Prince bin Saud," he repeated.

"I do not know him. I have never met him, never spoken to him, never—" She struggled for the words. "If you are talking about the Saudi royal family, then of course I know who he is, but that is all I know of him. And this Ares you talk about, I don't know what that is. A coming battle or war because of this thing? I really have no idea what you mean!"

Jesse studied her, then turned back to his sandwich. Was she lying? He didn't know and didn't trust his instincts enough to rely on his own judgment any longer. He didn't trust her . . . no, that wasn't the only problem. He didn't trust himself to evaluate what she said anymore.

He chewed a few times, poured a couple of chips onto his plate, ate them, then sipped at his coffee. "This afternoon in the café . . ."

"I was told to follow you and report back anything. That is all there was to it, I swear. But you seemed so . . . innocent. A little lonely. You did not seem like a threat. My father will be furious when he finds that I made contact with someone I was sent to keep an eye on, but there was no evil purpose in my approaching you, I promise you that."

"And being particularly ignorant to what we are dealing with here, I don't suppose you knew that you had the plan for an attack against the U.S. in the trunk of your car."

Petrie stopped eating. She stopped moving, stopped breathing, stopped every motion of life. She stared, her eyes fixed on the table, then painfully lifted her head. Her face was still blank, as if she had not yet processed what he said. "I . . . what?" she stammered in disbelief.

And in that instant, Jesse saw that she really didn't know. This wasn't a professional at work. This was a scared and lonely girl, a young woman who had been pulled into something she clearly didn't understand. He glanced across the empty room at the FBI guys, then leaned toward her. "You really don't know anything about this, do you, Miss Baha?"

She still barely breathed, her hands shaking on the table. "I've never hurt anyone in my life."

"You don't know about the Ares, the Saudi prince, Sergeant Espy, none of these things."

She closed her eyes. "I want to talk to Adrien." She was crying now. "He will explain everything."

"Who is this Adrien? I don't know what you mean."

"I don't know! I don't know who he is."

"Petrie, don't you see what this looks like?"

The sheer terror of his words, his accusations, were simply more than she could bear. He watched her try to swallow, thinking she might throw up on the floor. She tried to speak, but there was nothing but a tight sigh through her throat. "My father sent me to watch you, to report back where you were. Then I was sent to the airport to pick up a man and his car. That's all I know, Jesse, I promise."

Jesse watched her a long moment. "Petrie, there is a dead American in the basement downstairs. He was a traitor to our nation. But you don't know about that, do you?"

"I'm going to tell you everything I can tell," she began, her voice even now. "I'm going to start with my father. I'm going to tell you about my family, my sister, I'm going to tell you everything. You see, Mr. Jesse, I cannot hide anymore. I am at the end of my road now, and your people are the only ones who can protect me from what I have done to myself."

She took a breath and started talking, beginning when she was a little girl.

Across the table, the two FBI agents listened intently to the radio signal in their ears. The tiny transmitter, small as a pin, had been slipped into the collar on Jesse's flight suit. The chief of reconnaissance at the embassy had done a masterful job, slipping the needle-shaped transmitter through his collar with just a slap on his back. When the air force major had insisted on talking to Miss Baha, the opportunity seemed too valuable to miss. But the tiny transmitter's battery would only last a few hours, and the way she was talking, they wondered if that would be enough.

With both of them listening so intently to the conversation taking place on the other side of the cafeteria, neither agent noticed when the assassin walked into the room.

THIRTY-EIGHT

UNITED STATES EMBASSY
PARIS, FRANCE

Villon looked around the cavernous embassy reception area. "Sir, is there somewhere we could talk?" he asked.

Ketchum nodded, his bald head shining as he moved. "Come," he answered quickly, leading him into a small reception office off the main hall.

Ketchum quickly closed the door behind him. Villon glanced up at the corners of the ceiling, looking for the bugs he knew had to be there. "Your government is seeking permission to interview Miss Baha," he began.

"You got that straight, *Monsieur* Villon. Give us five minutes with her, and we'll nail her lies to the wall. She's a child, a mere plaything, in a very rough world. Give us five minutes with her and I promise my people will know everything."

Villon shook his head, fingering the buttons on his suit. "Your people will never talk to her," he said, his voice low but determined. "The United States government will never have access to Miss Baha. I'm sorry, but that is the simple truth, my friend."

Ketchum stood back, his eyes growing narrow with rage. His fuse, always short, was like a powder keg now. "Explain that!" he demanded.

"My government has sent me to tell you that Miss Baha is in our custody and will remain in our custody for the foreseeable future. She is a French citizen on French soil, and we will not release her to you. You will not speak with her directly. It will never happen, I'm afraid."

"Do not attempt, Mr. Villon, to stand in our way."

"I stand in front of nothing, Mr. Ketchum. But I have been sent here to tell you how it's going to be." He straightened his tie. "You see, Mr. Ketchum, there are other considerations, I have learned."

"Screw your considerations! I want to talk to that girl!"

Villon pressed his lips. "She is working for us now," he answered simply.

"Working for you. What? She does your laundry? She's your mistress? What are you talking about?"

"It means, *Monsieur* Ketchum, that Miss Baha has been double-crossing her own father for almost two years. She has been working for us, passing critical information along. Because of this, she knows things—proprietary information, we might say—that my government would prefer to keep within our own channels. Information we are not willing even to share with our friends."

"We have to talk to her!" Ketchum demanded. "She is the only link that we have."

Villon nodded, faking sympathy. "I understand. But Miss Baha is so deep, so undercover, there are maybe four men in our entire security operation who know who she is. For almost two years, she's been working with a person she calls Adrien, our very most senior counterintelligence agent. And from what I understand, she has done a marvelous job. She is a most remarkable woman, Mr. Ketchum, I can assure you of that. Through her efforts, we have gleaned invaluable information. Unfortunately, some of it is rather . . . sensitive, for we have a certain ah . . . Islamic problem of our own. Because of this, it might prove awkward if we were to release her to you. We will interrogate her regarding the disappearance of your aircraft and then pass any relevant information along, but we will not release her to your custody or let your people have direct access to her."

Ketchum clenched his fist and swore. "That is unacceptable!" he cried. "We need her information and *we need it right now!*"

"We will do the best we can, but that is all we can do. And may I remind you, Mr. Ketchum, the Ares is not our problem. The missing aircraft was your doing, and we have already complied with every request for assistance you have made. But we have our own issues, that we must deal with now."

Like ten million Arab immigrants ready to burn Paris to the ground, Ketchum thought, forcing himself to bite his tongue.

His eyes flashed, dual spots of dry spit forming on the corners of his mouth. "I want her," he demanded. "I'll send my own people down to get her. We'll storm the hospital if we have to—"

"Think about what I have just told you, Mr. Ketchum," Villon interrupted, his voice growing angry. "Don't you see? Miss Baha is in grave danger right now."

Ketchum stared straight ahead.

"Miss Baha's father will not be happy that she is in custody," Villon huffed. "It is a very delicate predicament, surely you must see that. We can't go sweeping in with security forces; what would that tell him? We can't treat her any differently than we would another patient or he surely would know. We must move carefully as we try to figure out a way to bring her in without exposing her work. If we blow this, Mr. Ketchum, we will have ruined her life. She will live under the constant threat of assassination for the rest of her days. And not from some stranger, but her own father, you see. So we've got to create a believable situation where her father will trust her. If we don't, he will kill her. Now are you wise enough to see that, or am I wasting my time?"

Ketchum froze, his eyes blank. "You must protect her," he said.

Villon only nodded. "We will do that, Monsieur." He stared at the wall for a moment before turning back to Ketchum. His gray eyes were troubled as he cleared his throat. "There is something else."

Ketchum watched him carefully, reading the stress that tightened his lips.

"Something what, Mr. Villon?"

"Something important, maybe critical about the girl. It complicates things. Something even we didn't know."

Villon talked. Ketchum listened. Then both men stared at each other and scowled.

HÔPITAL D'INSTRUCTION DES ARMÉES PERCY

Passing through the front door of the hospital, the assassin did a quick recon, walking down the main hall, checking the empty reception center, opening the stairwell doorway to see if anyone was there, even pulling on the door of the admittance office to make sure it was locked. The hallways were semi-dark. There was no sound anywhere. Finally, he went to the elevators, sent them both to the top floor (he only needed a few seconds but it would be much better for everyone if he was not interrupted in the middle of his work), then returned to the information block in the foyer, read the directory, and headed down the hallway toward the cafeteria. The bright lights bled through the glass squares in the doors, casting distorted cubes of light on the floor.

As he walked, the assassin noticed the security camera in the corner of the hallway, just above the cafeteria door, but he made no effort to avoid it. He wore thick spectacles (clear glass, no prescription), shoe inserts that added almost three inches to his height, hair extensions, and a fake moustache that was dyed to match the artificial color of his hair. The video would prove almost worthless in identifying who he was.

Pausing at the cafeteria door, he looked through the squares of glass. Across the room, he saw a man in a military flight suit facing him. The target, easily identified by her hair, sat across from him with her back to the door, but there was a problem: two men in sloppy suits. They were silent, both of them seeming satisfied to stare ahead while occasionally shooting knowing looks at each other. Americans? He was certain, the Wal-Mart suits giving them away easily.

Then he saw a tiny wire leading into the nearest man's ear and swore angrily.

Turning away from the glass, he stared down the hall. Cursing again, he thrust his hands deep into his pockets. What a mess! A much bigger bite than he wanted to chew! A total of four bodies. Very ugly. Very dangerous. In the hallway, he pulled out his cell phone. No way he made this decision on his own. He had to talk to the client before he escalated the job.

Petrie finished talking, laying her ugly history and family secrets on the table for Jesse to see.

She had told him everything—no—not everything. But everything she could.

Jesse stared at the young woman and forced a comforting smile. It was a remarkable story—sad, frankly depressing, and completely believable. He swallowed his coffee, which was very cold now, swirling the creamy mixture around in his mouth.

He'd been around long enough to know that everything she had told him was consistent with Islamic terror underground, which only made him more furious, knowing what she had been through.

"Your sister," he began. "Does your father ever talk about her?"

Petrie looked shocked. "Of course not," she answered. "You have to understand, she didn't disappoint my father, she betrayed him completely. Her name is forbidden, utterly unspeakable in our home. My father would beat me, or worse, were I to mention her name."

"And yet you have been willing to work for him."

"My father controls me, don't you see that? He controls every element of my life. I was just a little girl! And at first, I had no idea what he was asking me to do, then when I got older, as I started to understand, it was too late. And my mother can't help me, she's so weak and helpless, the only reason he keeps her around anymore is because he knows she is the key to keeping me. She lives her life as a hostage. Both of us do."

She paused and looked away. Did she dare tell him the rest? But Adrien had been so specific, so adamant, even at the threat of her life. *"Do not tell anyone about me! Trust no one! Not a soul! Regardless your instinct, you must keep it a secret or you endanger yourself!"*

So she fought the urge to tell the American who she was working for.

Jesse ate the last piece of drying sandwich. "And the car, at the airport?"

"My instructions were very simple. I was supposed to meet someone and take him to my father. An American, I was told. He was there, in the parking lot, like he was supposed to be, but when he got in, he scared me. I thought he was drunk. He acted crazy. And he was crying. Crying and mumbling like a terrified child. Then he took off, driving and cursing like he wanted . . ." she hesitated, searching for the word. *"Se donner la mort,"* she slipped into French.

Commit suicide, Jesse translated, then nodded thoughtfully. "And the café this afternoon?"

Petrie's face flushed, her eyes closing slightly, now a shy little girl. "I have already told you. I was sent to the café to report on your movements. I watched you for a moment and thought you were someone . . ." She turned and stared through the dark glass. "I thought you were someone I would like to know. The conversation was my initiative. It had nothing to do with my father, I swear."

Jesse shook his head, then pushed against his chair and closed his eyes, not wanting to look at her as he thought.

Outside the cafeteria, the assassin flipped his phone shut and swore once again. Sure, the client had doubled the price. And yes, he was willing to pay in cash and immediately, but he had demanded that he do the job now. The fact that he would have to kill two U.S. agents hadn't mattered a whit to him.

The assassin stared down the hall, peering at the patches of light on the floor, the client's words rolling round and round in his head.

Do this, Amourie, or you will be my next job. I know your best competitors. Can you run from them all?

He cursed bitterly, furious with himself.

He could have stayed away from the foreigner. How he wished that he had.

Finish this job or you die! It is that simple, Amourie.

He knew he had to have a jolt. Reaching into his front pocket, he took out a hit of Ecstasy and popped the little blue pill in his mouth. He chewed, his mouth puckering with spit, then felt the acidic burn as the heavy drug went down. He leaned against the wall and waited, knowing it wouldn't take very long. Then his nerves started to settle.

This would work now. Things were going to be fine.

Using his cell phone again, he called his companion who was waiting in the parking lot outside. "Get in here," he demanded when the older man answered his phone. "I need you. Bring your weapon. It will take both of us to do this right."

Something didn't fit. There was a piece of the puzzle that was the same shape, the same angles, but when he tried to insert it, a couple edges didn't fit.

He rubbed his eyes, very weary, then stared into space, trying once again to link the final pieces in place. Prince Abḍul Mohammad bin Saud was the mastermind, but he hadn't worked alone. Sergeant Espy—maybe others—had helped the thief and his men. Petrie's father was involved, funding and assisting the prince. While the Ares was being stolen, Petrie had been sent to the café to divert him if she had to (despite her protestations, he believed) and make certain that he didn't interfere.

Now they were going to use the aircraft to attack the United States.

But if it was that simple, why did the hair on his neck stand on end? While they were chasing a rabbit, was there a wolf chasing them?

After years of combat, some men developed a certain sixth sense, an ability to know when the real danger was coming, an unexplainable sense of brooding before the worst of it hit. Jesse had developed this instinct; all the good soldiers did. And his instincts were screaming, *Turn around! Look behind!*

He took another breath and held it, feeling the gut-deep fear.

Petrie placed her elbows on the table, then leaned toward him. "I feel it as well."

He shook his head and answered, "What are you talking about?"

She smiled at him sadly. "I can *feel* the same thing that I can see in your eyes."

Jesse didn't know how to answer, so he didn't say anything. Neither of them talked as the wind blew outside.

Petrie stared at her hands, deep in thought. "I have something to show you," she finally said. She reached into her pocket and pulled out a small picture. "I found this a couple nights ago," she began, holding the photograph in her hand. "It was on my father's dresser. I knew it was important when I saw it, though I'm not sure I know why. I was going to give it to—" She stopped suddenly. "I was going to give it to someone. One day you will understand."

Jesse stared at her curiously. "What is it?" he asked.

She hid the small photograph in her palm, then extended her hand. He reached out to take it, but she pulled it back suddenly. Hesitating, she placed it facedown on the table. "It seemed like such an odd thing for my father to have," she added awkwardly, as if trying to justify her theft.

"Yes," Jesse prodded.

Petrie cocked her head a final time, then moved the picture again, sliding it across the top of the table with the tip of her fingers to him.

Jesse picked up the photograph and turned it over in his palm.

It showed a young American soldier an instant from death. He knelt before his captives, his army uniform caked in dirt and blood. He stared in horror at the camera, his eyes wild in fear. Behind him, four hooded men stood. One of them held the U.S. soldier by the hair, the tip of the knife just penetrating the throat.

He moaned, a sack of bricks crashing down on his head. His face drained of color, his chest growing tight as a fist. "You got this from your father?" he cried, looking into Petrie's eyes.

Petrie slowly nodded, seeing his fear.

"Where did he get this?"

She shook her head.

"Oh no!" Jesse exhaled, falling back in his chair. He dropped the photograph on the table, his arms falling to his side. "No . . . no . . . no."

The assassin paused at the cafeteria window. The two FBI agents hadn't moved, though they huddled together now, deep in whispered conversation. The military guy was leaning back in his chair, staring up at the ceiling. He caught a profile of the girl, confirming it was her.

He felt a sudden presence behind him and quickly turned. The other assassin, a fifty-year-old man dressed in dark jeans, a black jacket, and a white shirt, glanced around anxiously, waiting his instructions. The leader quickly explained the layout as the other man peered through the glass partition in the door.

"You take the two agents at the table," the leader said. "I'll get the guy and the girl."

Jesse pushed back his chair. "I have to make a phone call," he said as he stood.

"Who are you calling?" Petrie asked him.

He lifted his hand, his cell phone already pressed to his ear. "Give me Mr. Ketchum," he demanded, then covered the phone. "Stay here," he hissed to Petrie as he walked toward the cafeteria doors.

"Mr. Ketchum," he started saying as he passed through the double swinging doors, "I have something I need to show you." Walking from the cafeteria, he passed two men who were standing on the other side of the doors. "Yes, I know you are busy, but this is something you really must see!"

The assassins let him pass.

Jesse paid them no attention as he talked on the phone.

The two assassins pushed the doors back and stepped into the bright room. The older assassin kept his head low as he walked toward the bank of cigarette machines.

The leader moved forward, his face blank, his eyes almost half closed. One of the FBI agents looked up at him, and he forced a dull smile, not too friendly—a man with other things on his mind. He kept moving until the agent turned back to his friend, then suddenly changed direction and walked toward Petrie.

She sat with her back to him and did not turn around.

Jesse forced himself to keep walking, not drawing attention to himself as he walked by the two men. He kept talking as he walked, then shot a quick look back at the doors.

He had seen the flash of metal underneath the second man's dark coat.

"Stand by," he told Ketchum, then quickly flipped the phone shut.

The older assassin turned and walked toward the FBI agents, coming to a stop just two feet from the back of the first agent's head.

"Excuse me," he said, just to calm his anxious nerves, "but could you tell me—?"

He fired through his jacket, knowing the exact position of the muzzle of his gun. There was no burst of gunfire through the silencer, only a dull, silent *thwaaat.* The hollow-point bullet entered through the agent's head, expanded as it hit the back of his skull, scrambled his brains into mash, and exited between his eyes, the bullet much larger now and flat, almost as wide as a penny, scattering blood and brain material all over his partner. By the time the second agent felt the warmth of the blood on his face, the assassin had pulled the handgun from his pocket and fired again, this time taking time to aim, one fist around the beveled grip, the second underneath his palm to brace his aim. *Thwaaat. Thwaaat.* Two shots, both of them at the head. The second agent jerked back, his hand frozen inside his jacket.

He shivered as he fell, the breath of life leaving him.

Turning, the assassin followed his boss toward Petrie, walking calmly across the well-lit tile floor.

Jesse instantly recognized the sound of a silenced gun. He instinctively crouched, then crept to the cafeteria doors and peered through the small window in time to see the second FBI agent fall. He shot a glance toward Petrie and fought the sudden urge to scream at her, *run!*

He fell behind the doors, his back against the wall, his mind racing with each pant of breath.

Two dead agents. Two assassins. Both of them armed.

He couldn't stop them! He didn't even have a gun!

He cursed in fear and anger, then peered through the narrow window again. Both of the men had their backs toward the door now and he made his move, slipping into the room. Moving past the dead FBI agents, he stepped lightly through the quickly spreading pool of blood, feeling the floor growing slippery under his boots.

Petrie faced the two assassins, her face white as death. She tried to scream but she only gurgled and then bowed her head.

Jesse's heartbeat tripled and his chest grew rock-tight. A powerful surge of adrenaline shot through him. He didn't think. He only acted, the primal brain now controlling everything that he did as hard years and combat training and bitter instinct took over.

Silently, his feet hardly touching the floor, he moved toward the lead assassin, coming up from behind.

The older man had let his guard down, letting the hand that held his weapon fall loosely to his side. He had already killed his targets. His boss would kill the girl now. All he had to do was watch.

Jesse reached up and jerked his neck. He felt the jaw clench and the bone twist, but the man was strong and the vertebrae didn't break. The assassin cried as he struggled, lifting his gun. *Thwaatt, thwaatt*—he fired two shots in panic. Two holes penetrated the ceiling, dropping chalky powder on the floor. The two men struggled for control of the gun, grunting and swearing as they fought. Jesse's boots, wet with fresh blood, slipped from underneath him and he almost fell. While the assassin aimed his Glock and moved his finger over the trigger, Jesse lurched for the gun, pressing the small lever that secured the metal clip. The ten-shot magazine fell out of the grip and onto the floor, leaving one round in the chamber. Jesse kicked out, his heavy boots hitting the other man in the knee. He heard the bone crack and the older man's knees collapsed. Screaming in pain, he aimed the gun as he fell.

Jesse jerked the barrel toward the falling man and pulled the trigger guard. The assassin's own finger pressed the trigger and the bullet impacted his chest, the one-inch hole penetrating his heart. His white lips moved slowly as he bled. Like a fish on the seashore, he flopped a couple of times, then lay still.

With the assassin's weapon now in his hand, Jesse rolled to a shooting position and aimed at the lead assassin. His eyes were wild and red, his reflexes slowed from the Ecstasy that was beginning to peak in his brain.

It wasn't supposed to be this way! All he had to do was hit the girl. His partner was supposed to take care of the rest! Yet there he was, on the floor now.

The assassin stood halfway between the American officer and the girl, his gun pointed at the officer, his left arm pointing at Petrie. She was crying, her eyes large as green saucers, her dark hair thrown back. "Don't move," the assassin told her, his eyes darting back and forth. She staggered, reaching to brace herself against the table. "*Stay there!*" he screamed.

Jesse rose slowly, keeping his gun pointed at the other man's head. The Glock felt heavy and awkward. It was a powerful weapon but short-barreled and hardly accurate. He needed to get a few feet closer to make sure of his hit.

He started inching toward the assassin and the other man stepped back. Petrie cried again and the assassin turned toward her. "Don't move!" he screamed.

"It's okay, Petrie," Jesse calmly told her. "Back toward the window slowly."

"Don't you move!" The assassin sneered.

Jesse took another step toward him, kept his hand steady and waited for the right moment, watching the other man's eyes.

"Jesse," Petrie called, her voice soft and terrified.

The assassin glanced at her and Jesse took his shot. But the gun didn't fire. He pressed again. Nothing happened. Then he remembered the bullet clip on the floor, seven feet away, a black piece of metal shining against the bare tile.

Jesse almost lunged toward it, but he held himself back, keeping his gun trained on the assassin.

The two men faced each other, both of them aiming their guns.

Yes, his gun was empty. But the assassin didn't know.

Jesse started inching in a wide circle around the other man.

The assassin glared at him.

"Don't move!" Jesse said. "Make a move toward her and I'll kill you. Take it easy. There's a way out of this so that we can both live!"

The assassin started a counter circle, moving opposite of Jesse, inching toward the cafeteria doors. "What are you doing?" he demanded.

Jesse kept moving in a circle. "Just walking to the woman, that is all. Now we've got to work together."

The circle was half complete now. The two men stood apart, aiming their guns at the other man's chest, each of them moving with excruciating caution to the side. "Hold tight," Jesse whispered. "I don't want to shoot you. You don't want to shoot me. But there's a way out of this. I'm going to walk toward the girl. You keep walking for the door. I'll let you go. We both are happy. We both get to live."

Jesse came to a stop behind the table, Petrie at his side.

The man felt his way, his eyes on Jesse, backing now toward the door.

"That's okay. You keep going," Jesse said, his voice calm but firm. "You keep backing up. I let you go. The police are coming. You only have a few seconds to get out of here."

The assassin moved another foot. Feeling the piece of metal, he glanced down and saw the pistol magazine. He hesitated, then looked up, his lips pulled into a sudden sneer. "You don't have any bullets, do you!" he whispered. He took a sudden step toward them and tilted his gun ten degrees to the right.

Petrie screamed out in fear.

Dropping to his knees, Jesse slammed the table over, forming a barricade between them. He grabbed Petrie and jerked her down, then pulled her shoulders over, cracking her head on the floor. She stared at him in sickening fear.

The assassin fired three rounds. Three fist-sized holes blew through the table, forming a nearly perfect triangle around the outline of her head. She screamed again, cried in French, holding her hands to her ears.

"*Run!*" Jesse screamed, pushing her toward the plate-glass window behind them. Then he stood and lifted the table, holding it up like a shield to aid her escape. She hesitated, then covered her face with her hands and threw herself through the window, a thousand pieces of shattered glass raining down on the floor. Adrenaline and rage surged through Jesse and he threw the table toward the assassin in a rush of raw power, then jumped through the broken window, landing on the wet grass as the table crashed onto the floor. He tucked his head toward his chest, rolling, then came to stop on his knees. Petrie scrambled right beside him.

"Go!" Jesse screamed as Petrie pushed herself to her feet.

But it was too late to run now.

The assassin appeared at the window, pointing his gun at them. Only eight feet away, his outline was illuminated by the bright lights inside.

The assassin raised his weapon, spread his feet, and aimed at Petrie's head. Jesse watched, his world slowing, his heart pounding like a drum in his ears. Without thinking, he lurched toward her and forced her back to the ground, then spread his arms and pressed his weight over her to keep her body down.

Petrie didn't move but lay flat, her face pressed into the wet grass. She didn't breathe or struggle. The two of them waited to die. *Good girl!* Jesse thought, seeing the peaceful look on her face. *You are brave.*"

Then he heard the gun fire.

Another gunshot.

Then it was over. Petrie screamed once again.

Jesse felt the first bullet, red hot and searing, grazing the side of his head. It zipped by his cheek, an angry buzz, then brushed through Petrie's hair before impacting the wet ground in a geyser of spraying mud and grass.

The second gunshot fired and he shook. It was not a silenced *thwaat* but a powerful roar that echoed through the inside of the cafeteria, bouncing off the bare walls.

Jesse didn't move for a moment, too shocked to react.

He was alive.

Then he slowly turned his head.

The assassin had fallen onto the wet grass. He still held his weapon, though his fingers had relaxed, allowing the beveled grip to slip forward from the palm of his hand. He lay facedown, his legs jutting awkwardly, his left arm tucked underneath him. The wet ground beneath his chest was quickly turning violent red.

Jesse turned to the broken window. François Villon was standing there. The French officer held a massive .357 revolver in both hands. He swung it between Jesse and the dead man, then jumped through the shattered window, landing with a huff on the wet ground.

Jesse rolled over, releasing Petrie as Villon moved to the assassin's side. Keeping his .357 pointed at the back of his head, he kicked the gun away from the assassin's fingers, then rolled him over with his boot. Bending quickly, he felt for a pulse, pushing two fingers against the soft flesh on his neck, but it was pretty clear the man he had just shot was dead. The investigator recognized the dull eyes staring blankly, the blood oozing from the nostrils. Holstering his gun, he moved toward Jesse, who pushed himself to his feet.

Two more men rushed to the broken window, their hospital security badges flashing in the dim light. Villon nodded toward them and shouted, giving his orders so quickly that Jesse could not understand what he said.

His legs weak as wet paper, Jesse looked around in a daze, then touched the burn on his cheek where the bullet had passed. He was bleeding, the trickle running down the side of his neck. He looked at the blood on his fingers, then turned toward Petrie, who was just pushing herself to her feet. "Are you hurt?" he demanded.

She slowly shook her head. "I don't . . . I don't think so," she answered, then turned to him. "What did you do?" she whispered, her eyes pleading and dark. "You lay your life on me, Jesse! Why would you do such a thing?"

He shook his head, embarrassed. It was a gut-instinct reaction; there'd been no time to think.

"How could you . . . why would you . . ." She stared at him in shock and amazement. "Oh no, you're wounded!" She put her hand to his face. "Please tell me you are—"

"I'm fine," he answered quickly. He touched his own hand to his cheek, then pulled back his bloody fingers. "Pretty close, though," he murmured slowly, feeling suddenly weak in the knees.

Petrie pressed her fingers to his face. "You need to see a doctor," she ordered.

Villon moved to their side. "Miss Baha," he asked, "have you been hurt? Are you injured?"

She glanced at him quickly. "I am fine, but this man has been hit."

Villon turned to Jesse and nodded. "Good to see you, Major."

"I can assure you, dear Inspector, the pleasure is disproportionately mine."

Villon nodded to Jesse's cheek. "Is that it?" he asked, examining the bloody scratch on his face.

Jesse flushed, even more embarrassed.

"I've seen much worse when my kids have been climbing trees."

"Trust me, Inspector, I won't be applying for any Purple Hearts."

Villon slapped Jesse on the shoulder. Turning to Petrie, he reached for her hand. "Come with me," he ordered.

"Who are you?" she cried.

Villon leaned toward her while holding her wrist. "Adrien sent me," he answered. She looked immediately relieved. "Now quickly, come with me. You are in danger. And we have little time."

He glanced toward Jesse again. "Good job, Major James. We are grateful. Now go put some dressing on that gun wound, and please, get some sleep. You look like a walking dead man, and that's being generous, my friend."

Jesse watched Villon pulling Petrie away. "Where are you taking her?" he demanded.

Villon stopped, still holding her wrist. "She'll be all right," he promised.

Petrie pulled away from Villon and reached out for Jesse's hand. "Thank you," she offered simply. Then she put her lips near his ear. "He can protect me. I *have* to go now."

Villon reached for her again, anxious to get her out of the open. Wailing sirens began to sound, seeming to fill the dark night. Behind them, at the window, half a dozen cops had already gathered, taking in the crime scene. Villon's men directed the officers, speaking quickly in French.

Petrie looked into Jesse's eyes. "My father," she offered, praying somehow that he might understand.

Jesse shook his head, then turned away. "I don't think you need to worry about your father," he answered slowly.

She cocked her head. He was wrong. With her secrets in the open, she had to worry very much. "There are things you don't know," she tried to explain, but Villon started pulling her away.

Taking Jesse by the hand, she whispered, "You know the man in the photograph, don't you, Jesse?"

He slowly nodded.

She let her lips touch his ear. "Then go. Do your work. We will see each other again."

"When?"

"I don't know. But I must go now. It is dangerous."

She ran toward Villon. Two other men emerged from the darkness, followed by an older woman, and Petrie ran into her embrace. It only took a few seconds to get her into a waiting van.

Jesse watched the military vehicle pull away, then reached into his pocket.

The picture had been crumpled, and was now smeared with blood. He wiped it off on his pant leg, then turned for his own car.

FORTY

MARMARIS VILLAGE
SOUTHWESTERN TURKISH COAST

The old man was being wakened. "Sir," his senior aide offered softly as he entered the bedroom and turned on the light. "Sir, we have a problem. There is a message for you."

The old man, fat and rumpled, the weave on his pillow having left a soft mark on his face, rolled over and groaned. A bit too much to drink the night before had made his motions labored and slow. But though he kept his eyes closed, his heart was racing now. "What is it?" he demanded.

The military officer moved to the foot of his bed. "They caught Baha's daughter," he answered.

The old man took a long breath. "She doesn't know anything," he offered cautiously, forcing himself to keep faith.

The military aide shook his head. "It seems, master, that our friend *Sayid* Baha may not have been as discreet as we hoped."

The old man glanced at the illuminated clock on his nightstand. The sun would soon be rising. He took a deep breath of cool air and rolled to the side of the bed. "Have you told General Xian—" he started.

"Yes. He is dressing, sir."

"And what is he thinking?"

"He demands that we launch the jet. We can't wait another moment. If the girl knows, if she talks . . ."

The old man scoffed. "What could she possibly tell them?"

The military officer turned his eyes away from the pouchy old man. "Don't underestimate the Americans," he whispered coldly. "They are not fools. If they identify the remains from the car bomb in time, this whole thing crashes down."

The old man slowly nodded. "How many hours of darkness do we have on the U.S. East Coast?"

Three . . . almost four if we get him in the air right now."

The fat man thought for less than ten seconds. "Do it," he said.

The military aide bowed and then departed. He had much work to do.

After giving the order to his agents working with the stolen Ares in Newfoundland, he started making preparations to evacuate his master. They would have to catch a private jet and fly east as quickly as they could. Things were just uncertain enough that they couldn't stay in Turkey anymore.

Time to go home and watch this thing from afar.

PIGEON AUXILIARY EMERGENCY LANDING FIELD
NINETY-SIX KILOMETERS WEST OF GANDER,
NEWFOUNDLAND

The pilot had only been asleep for a few hours when the foreign officer entered the tent, knelt by his cot, and shook him awake. "Get up," he told him. "We have to move."

The pilot rolled over, cursing unintelligibly. He was exhausted, and it took several seconds for him to open his eyes. He finally focused on the dark face and dark hair slicked back with thick oil. "What is it?" he muttered angrily.

The other man shook him again. "We have an issue."

The pilot rolled his feet to the floor and sat up, rubbing weary hands through his hair.

"They have the girl."

The pilot froze. "His daughter?"

"Yes. There was an accident. They took her into custody. We sent a man to kill her, but it looks like he failed."

The pilot shook his head, swearing in a bitter, angry voice. "Who screwed that up?" he said sarcastically.

The other man didn't answer. "Get dressed," he said.

The pilot was already standing.

"Time is critical now. Remember, mercenary, you don't have one target, you have two, and you must hit them both. Every hour now is precious. You'll have to fly tonight."

The pilot was reaching for his flight suit. "Is the aircraft ready?"

"It was ready an hour ago."

The pilot looked up from his dressing. "What about the interceptors?"

"It is as you said would happen. The Americans have positioned all their interceptors to protect the East Coast. They have set up a wall to protect the targets from the ocean but left their northern flank exposed."

The pilot smiled. "And the two weapons?" he demanded.

The other man moved toward him. "They are ready, *Sayid.*"

The pilot nodded. He knew their nuclear weapons were certainly not made to U.S. specifications, and so they leaked radiation like a poison wind through a sieve. "What kind of Geiger readings are you getting in the cockpit?" he demanded. "Will the aircraft provide me protection from the bleed-over?"

The other man stiffened, his eyes growing hard. It was far too late to turn back now, so what difference did it make? "I don't think you'd want to camp out in the cockpit for a week if that's what you're asking," he answered truthfully. "But for the short time you'll be in the aircraft you should be alright."

The pilot tightened his jaw. "Alright then, have your people pack me something to eat, lots of coffee and water but no Chai. Pour every drop of fuel that you can in that aircraft and have it ready."

He looked through the only window at the low, scuzzy clouds. "I've got to check out the weather, then I'll be ready to go."

Twenty minutes later, the pilot was standing underneath the Ares. Cold drops of freezing rain dripped around him from the leaky roof. The old hangar bled cold air and freezing rain, which was just turning to snow. The inside was dimly lit, both out of necessity and lack of capability, and the pilot held a powerful flashlight as he completed his preflight checks.

He walked around the aircraft, checking the engine bays, flight control surfaces, exhaust pipes, oil levels, and tires. Stooping under the open bomb bay, he flashed the bright beam above him. The foreign officer knelt beside him, impatient for the mercenary to get in the air. The pilot took his time staring upward at the bombs. This was the most critical check he would do on the entire aircraft, and he wasn't going to rush. He stared at the two warheads. Silver. Bullet-shaped. Clean lines. Steering fins. A small satellite receiver and computer to guide them as they fell. He imagined the bombardment of radiation that was leaking from the bombs and almost stepped back. The foreign markings had already been removed from the warheads, leaving no way to trace them, not in time anyway. He flashed the light on the weapon buckled on the right side of the bay. "That's it," he confirmed, "that is the good one?"

The other officer nodded. "Your computers will recognize it. It is wired into station two."

"Station two. Okay." He moved the beam of light to the other bomb. "Station four?"

"Yes, sir."

The pilot dropped the beam and flashed it into the other man's face. The foreign officer squinted but didn't look away. "You are *certain* you have it right?" he demanded.

"Absolutely certain."

"If you are wrong, I will kill you."

"You will do no such thing. But either way, it doesn't matter. We would never be so stupid as to make a mistake. We know that both of these are necessary to start the next war."

**UNITED STATES EMBASSY BUILDING,
PARIS, FRANCE**

Jesse walked into the command post at the U.S. embassy. "Where's Ketchum?" he demanded of the first man he saw.

One of the controllers nodded toward a back room. "He told us not to interrupt him," he explained.

Jesse ran to the door, knocked once, then pushed it open. Ketchum was asleep at his desk, his head on his arms. Hearing the door open, he looked up wearily.

"We've got a problem," Jesse said in a tired, angry voice.

Ketchum slowly rose. "Heard about your little adventure at the hospital," he said.

Jesse threw the bloody photograph on the table. "Look at that, Mr. Ketchum. Do you know who that is?"

Ketchum picked up the photograph of the beheading and stared. Jesse watched him closely, then said, "The car bomb this afternoon. Have we got DNA confirmation of the victim yet?"

"No, we haven't, Major. Now what's going on?"

"We need DNA confirmation, and we need it right now. Then we need to speak to the president. And believe me, Mr. Ketchum, we don't care if he doesn't want to be disturbed."

Five minutes later, President Abram was escorted into the room. Edgar Ketchum walked behind him while Jesse paced, his face tight, his flight suit wrinkled with sweat. He bolted to attention. "Sir!" he said.

The president nodded and sat down in the nearest chair. "What you got, Jesse?"

Jesse nodded to the wrinkled and blood-covered photograph the president was holding in his hand. "You've seen that, sir?" he asked him.

The president glanced again at the photograph: four hooded men, a single soldier, a cutting knife, vacant eyes. He shivered as he stared, then looked at Jesse. "You know him?"

"His name is Sergeant Ray."

President Abram shook. "Sergeant *Ray!*" His voice was strained and dry.

"His father is Colonel Ray, test pilot for the Ares."

The president thought a long moment, and Jesse watched the obvious questions and concerns crease his face. "You're talking about the man who was taken from the hotel yesterday morning? The man who was blown up in the car?"

"The same," Jesse answered. "Colonel Ray's son was taken hostage several years ago in Iraq. He was captured with his four-man team while on patrol in Kirkuk. The three other soldiers were killed in the firefight. Sergeant Ray was taken hostage, then killed the next day. He was beheaded with a long knife, the murder taped on video, then released to the press. Al Jazeera ran the video of the beheading for almost two days."

A cold, sullen silence seemed to permeate the room. The president stared. Ketchum swore. Jesse stood, his back straight.

"You are certain?" Ketchum asked him.

"Perfectly, sir. You can have the photograph analyzed, but I know it is him. That is Sergeant Kenneth Miles Ray, my former commander's son."

The president shuddered again.

"Which begs an awkward question," Jesse finished. "Is it only coincidence? I have a hard time thinking so."

The president didn't answer. "Can we do DNA analysis on the human remains in the car bomb?" Jesse asked.

Abram turned toward his chief of staff.

"I will check," Ketchum answered.

Jesse looked at Ketchum. "We need DNA on the remains, but we also need something else. There is a special unit within the CIA. They call it the Forensic Catalogue, I think. They have stored samples of DNA material from most of the world's government leaders, suspected spies, terrorist masters—do you know what I mean?"

"Of course," Ketchum answered quickly.

"Would they have samples that would allow us to compare DNA and identify Prince Abdul Mohammad bin Saud?"

Ketchum furrowed his brow. "Prince bin Saud. Are you crazy? Why do you need a DNA sample for him?"

Jesse took a quick step toward him, not explaining. "We will need one more DNA confirmation."

"Who?"

"Mohammad Akbaf Baha. He's an Iranian here in Paris. Petrie's father."

Ketchum nodded slowly, his mind racing, his face growing tight.

"How long will it take to complete the test?" Jesse asked.

Ketchum shook his head. "I don't know. It won't be easy. We don't even know if we've got hair or tissue samples we can use to compare. On the prince,

I'd say it's possible, although we've been building our sample depository for only five years. But having available tissue samples on this other guy, this Baha, it isn't likely. I'd say it's extremely unlikely, in fact."

"We can get some from his daughter."

Ketchum gritted his teeth. Of course, he should have thought. He shot a look at Jesse. "His daughter? Yes, that would work."

"Time, sir?" Jesse prodded. "How long do you think it will take to do the testing?"

"It can take months. Usually weeks. If we really push—and you know the French won't care—we might have results within a few days."

"A couple days! Are you kidding? We don't even have a couple hours."

Ketchum almost snarled. "I don't need lectures from you, major, on the proper sense of urgency that may be required."

"Sir, we don't have that much time," Jesse offered bluntly while holding Ketchum's stare.

"We'll do what we can," Ketchum shot back, "but like I said, you know the French. They would be more than happy to see this thing blow up in our faces. They're enjoying this fiasco and you know it. They are a roadblock, not an ally, and they have been for years. Unless . . ." Ketchum's voice trailed off. "Unless we find the right buttons." He fell silent.

President Abram instantly recognized the look. Ketchum was working his ugly magic. This is what he paid him for.

Thirty seconds of silence, and then Ketchum turned to Jesse. "The French Inspector? Villon? Have you got his number?"

Jesse pulled out his cell phone and dialed François Villon, Handed the phone to Ketchum, and took a step back. Ketchum gave a quick nod to the president, who walked out of the room.

"We need your help," Ketchum began when Villon came on the phone. "I need to know who does your dirty work. And don't tell me you can't help me. We both know what I mean."

The two men talked for only minutes. Jesse listened, sometimes grimacing, sometimes shaking his head.

HÔPITAL D'INSTRUCTION DES ARMÉES PERCY
FRENCH MILITARY HOSPITAL
CLAMART, FRANCE

A little more than two hours later, Jesse knocked, then walked into the French hospital commander's office without waiting for a reply. The one-star general, a hulky-framed officer with dark skin and long eyebrows, looked up from his work. "Yes?" he demanded.

Jesse assumed a military posture as the French doctor noted the gold leafs on his shoulders. "Sir," he started quickly, "your hospital has been asked to perform some DNA testing for my government."

The general hesitated, then nodded. "Who are you?" he commanded.

Jesse pulled out his ID and told the general. "Your staff will be performing the test?" he asked again.

"Yes," the general answered, "along with some members from another team."

"Sir, you'll forgive me, but I need to urge you, as one officer to another, to accelerate the testing as quickly as you can."

The French officer was neither impressed with Jesse's urgency nor inclined to extend the courtesy. "We are all very busy," he explained with disinterest, pointing to the stacks of paper on his desk. "You have priority, the people at my government have already made that clear."

"Then we will have results very soon?" Jesse prodded.

"You will have results when they are ready."

"And when might that be?"

"When we have completed all our tests."

"But you just indicated that you have been instructed to make this a priority."

"And I have."

"Then when will you have at least the initial results?"

"I told you already, when the tests are complete."

"But sir—"

"I have other *priorities,* Major. You are not the only crisis on my desk. His voice trailed off, acid and sarcastic. "You'll get your results when they are ready," he finished.

Jesse frowned in frustration. "And when will that be, sir?"

"Two days. Maybe three."

"We don't have that much time."

The French general pulled out a pack of cigarettes and stuck one in his mouth. "I'm sorry," he said.

Jesse stared at him in anger. "I don't know, sir, if you are."

"Think what you want. It doesn't matter. And I frankly don't care. Now if you'll excuse me, Major—" he glanced at his name tag "—James," he concluded, turning back to his desk.

"Sir, don't you know about our stolen fighter?"

The general kept his head down and picked up a medical folder to read.

Jesse took another step toward him. "There is nothing you can do?"

The general looked up. "You don't understand," he shouted back. "These tests are extremely sensitive and time-consuming. I've already requested additional help to augment our staff. Now, the people at your embassy can shout and complain or jump up and down if they want to, but I remind you, Major James, just as I have reminded them, this is not your country and that is not how we work. We will do our job, then inform you when we have completed the task. But your problems are not my problems and I will not allow you to put your dirty sheets on my bed. And I won't stand here and be bullied by some stinking American *major* with an ego as big as your States. I don't know how things operate back in your country, but over here we have procedures. We follow our policies. We don't go running here and there, always looking for the next fight. You will have your results in two days unless you anger me any further. Then it might be a week, who knows, maybe more. Now if you'll excuse me, Major James." He swung around in his chair.

Jesse watched him, disgusted. How could he not understand?

He stood without moving for a long moment. "Sir, is there nothing you could do then?"

The general kept his head down, waving a dismissive hand.

"Nothing, sir?"

"Good evening." The Frenchman general sneered.

"Do you realize, sir, that I am here at the direct request of my president?"

The general scowled. He clearly didn't care.

Jesse pulled out his cell phone, punched the redial button, and listened. "Mr. Villon," he said, "I have the general here before me. Would you please talk to him, sir?"

He extended the cell phone. "Mr. Villon for you, sir. I think you know who he is."

The general looked up, a surprised and angry look on his face. "François Villon," he whispered, his eyes turning to slits.

"Of course," Jesse answered. "He would like a word with you, sir."

Jesse listened from the corner as the general spoke to the French inspector on the phone.

"You can't do that!" the general stammered.

His face turned white with anger as he listened. Jesse turned away, uncomfortable at being in the room.

"Inspector Villon, you have to understand . . ."

A few stutters followed before the general's voice trailed off. "It will be done then," he muttered angrily, "but you remember that you owe me. I expect you to make this right."

The general flipped the phone closed and threw it on the desk.

Jesse walked across the office, took his cell phone, and left without saying any more, then walked toward the hospital's front door.

Villon had many friends. Very powerful friends.

FORTY-ONE

PIGEON AUXILIARY EMERGENCY LANDING FIELD
NINETY-SIX KILOMETERS WEST OF GANDER,
NEWFOUNDLAND

The pilot pressed back against the ejection seat, the dry air from the cooling systems blowing straight against his face. The night was dark as the heavy overcast and falling snow sucked up the light of the moon. The runway lay before him, but he couldn't see anything beyond the steeply canted nose of his aircraft. There were no lights on the deserted airport and everything before him was an empty black hole.

He held the brakes on the aircraft, the enormous engines on the Ares almost skipping the jet across the semifrozen cement, then checked his systems: takeoff positions on the leading-edge slats, trailing-edge flaps and horizontal stabilizer, engines, pressures, fuel, avionics . . . Not wanting to waste a single drop of fuel, he went through the pretakeoff checklist quickly, the CRT listing every item in order.

Finally, he was ready. He checked the local time, then punched the *initiate* button on his comm/nav computer, commanding the system to bring up his flight plan on his navigational display. His nav pointer immediately moved twenty-three degrees to the left, giving him the steering position to his first navigational point. He lifted his oxygen mask, snapped it over his face, then pushed up both throttles while still holding the brakes. The fighter's engines surged—he kept them out of afterburner power or he would have skidded forward—as he did a final engine check. Turning on his landing/takeoff light, he was immediately surrounded by a disorienting tunnel of blowing snow against an endless, dark sky. Peering through the falling snowflakes, he confirmed he was in the center of the cement runway, then took a breath.

Releasing his brakes, he felt the raw surge of power, the accelerating forces of his engines pushing him back against his seat.

The Ares was a heavy jet, bulky and awkward on the ground. Designed for long-range missions, it was crammed with thousands of gallons of fuel, not to mention the enormous engines, generators, laser components, computers, hydraulics—everything needed to keep the jet in the sky. Still, the aircraft almost lurched as it accelerated through the dark night. The snowflakes became a blur, then a dazzling line of white lines as the aircraft gathered speed through the falling snow.

The pilot watched his airspeed indicator through his helmet-mounted display, pulled gently back the stick when he hit 169 knots, felt the aircraft's nose and main gear leave the ground, snapped up his gear, then his flaps, then his leading edge slats. As the landing gear retracted into the belly of the jet, his takeoff light went out and the snow disappeared, leaving only blackness and dark sky. Turning all of his attention on the flight instruments inside the cockpit, he concentrated on climbing safely, then turned gently toward his first navigational point. Passing through five hundred feet, he pushed a button at the side of his cockpit and the automatic pilot kicked in. A tiny square of a light on the side panel informed him that the automatic flight control system (AFCS) was flying the jet, and he sat back, trying to force himself to relax.

Sitting in a four-wheel drive truck at the side of the runway, the foreign officer watched the Ares take off and disappear into the heavy overcast. He listened as the roar of the engines faded, then pulled out his satellite phone and dialed a number in Germany. The relay automatically forwarded his call through to a switchboard in Italy, then to Turkey.

"He's off," the officer announced when his commanding general came on the phone.

The fat man from the luxury villa in Turkey grunted. His own aircraft had just taken off from a private airfield in Turkey and he was flying almost due east now, away from the coming fight. At his location, the sky was still dark, though it would soon grow pink from the coming sunrise.

"Keep us appraised," was all he said before disconnecting the line.

Replacing the receiver into the arm rest, the old general nodded to his partner, then turned and leaned back in his executive seat and stared quietly through the oval window to his right.

He sighed deeply, melancholic, even anxious.

So close . . . so close. What would the coming day bring?

His was a patient race of people, simple and unwearily moving forward in the life that they lived. Six thousand years of culture had conditioned them to run the long race.

But after all the years of planning, after all they had done, after ten million dollars spent in stolen information, blackmail, torture, and bribes, there was nothing he could do now but wait and see if it worked.

ONE HUNDRED FORTY MILES NORTHEAST OF THE COAST OF MAINE

The fishing trawler moved slowly through the five-foot waves. The northwest wind gusted up to twenty-five knots, pushing the dark sea before it into never-ending mounds and valleys of froth. It was dark now, the moon high, the stars scattered across the nearly cloudless sky.

The small craft, thick-hulled, wide in the beam, rusty and barnacled, was registered to a small fishing company in northern Norway, but the crew were all foreigners—Taiwanese, Malaysians, Thais, a few Moroccans and Turks—the kind of men who were willing to work twenty-hour days in the cold and the wet, daring danger and loneliness to send a few dollars back home.

One hundred forty miles from the coast of Maine, south and east of the tip of Nova Scotia, the fishing boat slowed. The captain and a first mate were the only ones on the deck. The captain, a Turk, flipped open the cover on his cell phone. A thick, four-inch satellite antenna was plugged into the side of the phone, giving him worldwide access, even out in open sea. The small screen cast a bluish light across his face as he read the text message, then flipped the phone shut.

Nodding to his first mate, the seaman reached for a small chain and pulled, extending a four-foot metal arm over the side of their boat. A large, plastic-wrapped bundle hung from the end of the chain. Flipping a switch on the side of the hoist, the hook that held the plastic bundle retracted, dropping it into the dark sea.

The captain moved to the rusty rail and watched as the foaming water enveloped the bundle.

He checked his watch and nodded to his first mate. "Four hours on the fuse, check that," he said.

"Four hours, sir."

The captain pressed his lips, spit on the wet deck, then turned for his cabin to make his report. "Set a course to the east and give me fifteen knots."

The first mate grunted "Sir" and moved for the pilot house.

Fifty feet below the surface, the tightly wrapped bundle reached a point of neutral buoyancy and quit sinking. Inside, an electronic timer continued counting: three hours, fifty-two minutes to go.

Two hundred pounds of explosives, enough to send a mountainous geyser of water nearly five hundred feet in the sky, waited on the timer to explode. Packed around the explosives were half a dozen stolen pieces of military aviation materials—aircraft fuel tank baffles, pieces of foam from ejection seats, plastics, a four-foot piece of hydraulic hose—all of which, though soon to be torn apart by the explosion, would eventually float to the surface of the ocean again.

INSIDE THE ARES

The Ares pilot flew due west for just under one hundred miles, then turned forty degrees to the south, picking up the coastline and heading out to sea. He was high, sixty-six thousand feet, and he knew he needed to descend or no one would hear. A little more than twelve minutes after takeoff, approaching the eastern edge of the Nova Scotia coastline, the pilot pushed the nose over, letting the aircraft slice downward through the air. As the aircraft descended, he pulled the power back, then leveled off the rate of descent to half of what it had been. Seconds later, he realized he was accelerating far too quickly and he pulled the nose back even more to slow the rate of descent. Throttles at idle, the darkness of the ocean and the sky one continuous black hole around him, he passed through forty thousand feet, then moved his throttles forward and let the nose drop again. He felt the aircraft vibrate, an almost imperceptible shudder, as he passed through the enormous bow wave of pressure building off the front of his nose.

The sonic boom was horrendous, a powerful compression of thunder, which, because it was behind him, the pilot didn't hear.

After passing through the speed of sound, the pilot jerked the nose up and climbed. Less than a minute later, he was above sixty thousand feet again.

UNITED STATES EMBASSY COMMAND POST
PARIS, FRANCE

The president stood as he read, a thin pair of gold reading glasses (never seen in public and rarely photographed) hanging from the bridge of his nose. It was the first time he had seen the highly classified report, and he was a little surprised. Yes, he'd heard a few rumors, but he hadn't known the FlashPack had really come so far.

"Let me understand this," he said to his chief of staff. "Worst case, we can use this thing to . . . what do you call it . . . FlashPack him?"

The COS nodded. "General Skevky is confident it will work. Though the weapon hasn't completed the final phase of field testing, so far every milestone has been reached with resounding success."

The president thought. "So we can burn his eyes out," he wondered.

"Sir, you understand, we're not talking literally."

"Of course not. But if he gets through our defenses, as a last resort option, this might actually work?"

"We are counting on it, Mr. President."

"And the aircraft with the FlashPack could be in position?"

Ketchum glanced at his watch. "That depends on what we consider 'in position,' sir. To answer that question, we have to make a decision first: what are we going to protect, New York, Boston, or D.C.? On this issue, the entire national security staff is unanimous. They want to keep the aircraft with the FlashPack over D.C. If you concur with that judgment, Mr. President, then the FlashPack will continue on course toward the Capital. In this case, because it is a shorter flight from Nevada, the aircraft will be in position within thirty minutes or so."

The president placed the highly classified executive summary on the table. "Yes, D.C. has to be our priority. Any other decision would be a foolish—"

The back door to the private conference room burst open as the embassy communications director and the CIA station chief pushed into the room. "Mr. President," the comm director interrupted, "we've got a report from one of our naval task force commanders."

Abram turned to face him. "Go on," he said.

"The USS *Porter* has detected a sonic footprint. It was very high, but clearly detectable off the northeast coast of Maine."

The president hesitated. "Our Ares?" he asked.

"Yes sir," the communications director answered. "High. Flying fast. Heading for our East Coast."

INSIDE THE ARES

Forty thousand feet below him, the clouds formed a solid layer, smooth as a tabletop and white as a sheet. A billion stars and the half moon illuminated the top of the clouds, forming an eerie white landscape that seemed to stretch out forever until it merged with the dark horizon at the edge of space. A sheet of Northern Lights, pale blue and sharp green, shimmered in the north, and the cold air was calm, providing a very smooth ride.

The pilot had all of his passive sensors working, searching for the enemy fighters that were waiting for him beyond the range of what his eyes could see, but without being able to use his radar he was essentially blind. He had already attempted to data-link with an AWACS that was circling just to the west of the coast of Maine, but the airborne controllers had learned from their previous experience and had initiated all new code words to guard their sensor relays, making it impossible for him to "talk" to the data links that emitted from the aircraft. Being unable to link with the AWACS left him to operate in the dark, not knowing where the American fighters might be.

It was a significant disadvantage, not being able to use his radar to search the night sky. Still, he could picture the tactical situation before him, imagining the naval destroyers with their radars, all of them looking through the north sky, the AWACS airborne command centers controlling hundreds of interceptors, which had formed a wall of missiles and cannons that he would have to fly through.

There were too many fighters. He'd never get past them all.

But that was okay. He didn't have to.

He smiled under his mask, then banked his aircraft and turned suddenly west.

The Americans had taken the bait, believing the flight plan that had been planted in the trunk of the car. Hook, line, and sinker, right up to the gills, they had accepted that the Ares was going to attack down the coast, never even considering the possibility that it might be a fake. Now they had positioned interceptors north and east of Maine, out over the water, where they expected him to be.

The pilot smiled again. The whole thing had been his idea. He felt kind of proud.

Turning northwest, he set a course toward the Canadian border. It only took minutes until he was flying over the heavily wooded Canadian peninsula. Crossing Trois-Rivières, he looked down at the river that connected Ottawa and Quebec and continued flying west. Twenty minutes later, he touched a small icon on his central navigational screen and the aircraft banked up until she was flying almost due south. He took a drink from his water bottle, hacked, and spit on the floor, then settled back for the short flight to Washington, D.C.

His lights were out. He was invisible. He closed his eyes and wished for sleep.

THE WHITE HOUSE SITUATION ROOM
WASHINGTON, D.C.

The order to evacuate came from the president himself.

Speaking from the command post at the embassy in France, he commanded his staff. "Get out! We've detected a sonic footprint! This Ares is on its way."

"Sir?" the NSA began.

"We don't know what kind of weapons this guy is carrying! We don't know his intentions. And you can't wait there to see!"

The national security advisor hesitated, staring at the secure satellite phone. "Mr. President," he muttered. "Are you certain? You want us all—"

"Get out!" the president demanded. "Evacuate all the executive staff!"

No one seemed to move. "And the congressional leaders? The Supreme Court?"

"You know the drill for a Sandstorm. You only have a few minutes to get out of there."

ÉCÔLE SAFE HOUSE
AVENUE DE LA MOTTE-PICQUET
SOUTHWESTERN PARIS

By day, Paris is a nearly unending landscape of gray rock, tiled roofs, and stone. Unlike most U.S. cities, it has grown out and not up, and few buildings tower over the relatively flat cityscape. Standing atop the Montparnasse Tower, the most accessible outlook in the city, it is easy to locate the most significant landmarks. Chinatown in the Thirteenth Arrondissement has a cluster of high-rise buildings, but they fill only one block. Around the city, other structures stand out if not for their height, then for their mass: Notre Dame, the glass pryamid outside the Richelieu Wing of the Louvre, Luxembourg Gardens, Hotel de Ville (City Square), the Quartier Latin, are all massive and impressive landmarks, most of which are made of stone. The majority of the rooftops around the city are gray cement, though there are occasional dots of colored tile or steel. Above them all, butting the southern bank of the Seine River, the Eiffel Tower stands in the distance. On the other side, the imposing Tuileries Ferris Wheel twirls in the sky.

Below the buildings, on the streets, red storefronts, beige and pink sandstone flats, and graffiti-covered stone arches, some built by the Roman commanders who ruled at the time of Christ, fill the narrow streets with colors and light. Scores of small farms, heavily subsidized, form a green ring around the city, and hundreds of shops, also protected by government regulators, offer nearly every product or service on almost every block. With the wealthiest citizens living downtown (the poorest ones are crammed around the city's outer edges), Paris is an immensely livable and beautiful city. But like all major world cities, traffic is atrocious, the air is dirty, and the sidewalks, cafés, and bistros are always packed with a noisy, raucous crowd.

With eleven million people in the city, it was also the perfect place to hide.

The safe house was situated on the fourth floor of a two-hundred-year-old flat on a narrow side street that ended against a brick wall. The street-level storefront was occupied by a butcher, a small gift boutique, and a pay-toilet facility. A single set of steps ran behind a solid wood door to the second floor, with a second set of stairs running to the adjoining building, providing a second means of access (or escape). There were no windows on the third floor, all of them having been bricked over with a patchwork of scavenged bricks and mortar during the Second World War.

Petrie was in a small bedroom on the fourth floor. She didn't know it, but every room around her was occupied by officers of the *Département des Pro-*

jets Classés, the French secret service; the floor below her, all of the buildings around her, even the roof overhead. It would have taken an army to get through to her.

She sat on the edge of a high poster bed, a comforter wrapped around her weary shoulders. The woman looked at her, then moved quickly to her side.

"Do you know me?" she asked in a low voice.

Petrie watched her carefully. "You are Adrien?" she said.

The older woman nodded slowly. Fifty, dark black hair, brown skin, and piercing eyes, she was solemn and businesslike. Her job was extracting intelligence and information that would save her countrymen. Yes, she would baby-sit if she had to, but only reluctantly.

Petrie looked at her with skepticism. "I was expecting . . . I don't know . . ."

"A man, of course, darling. But it is what it is." The woman put her arms around Petrie and pulled the blanket tight. "I know you are very tired," she spoke softly now, though the undercurrent in her voice was still unfeeling and direct. "But we have to do something first before I can let you rest."

Petrie barely nodded.

"We need something from you, Petrie."

The young woman lifted her eyes.

"We need a DNA sample from your father. Something we can use to identify his . . ." She stopped, put her hands on Petrie's face and looked into her eyes. "I'm sorry, Petrie, but we must positively identify his remains. We have to find out for certain if he was assassinated in the car."

Petrie stared at her, dumbfounded, the words sinking slowly into her brain. *DNA from your father . . . identify his remains . . .*

She swallowed painfully, a single tear rolling slowly down her cheek.

Her father would kill her if he was still alive. He had already killed her sister. He was a monster, not a man. So why was this so painful? Why was it so hard to breathe? Why did she feel as if her soul was being wretched from her chest? She pulled back in anguish. "Please, I don't want to go there."

"Come. I will be with you. I won't ever leave your side."

INSIDE THE ARES

ONE HUNDRED EIGHTY MILES NORTH OF WASHINGTON, D.C.

The pilot looked outside his cockpit and tried to stretch. He was so tired and disoriented that his head felt light, and he flexed his back muscles to force some blood to his head. Shifting his feet, he felt the numbness in his thighs from sitting in the jet.

He had slipped the Ares in from the north without being detected, and now the capital of the United States lay before him, bright and beautiful. His prebomb checklist complete, he snapped the oxygen mask across his face and climbed another couple thousand feet, squeaking out every inch of spacing that he could between his aircraft and the missiles that were waiting up ahead.

With the nation's capital protected by a ring of antiaircraft missiles, he knew the best protection he had was to get up as high as he could. Taking advantage of the jet's sleek design, he nudged up to sixty-six thousand feet, careful to keep his engines out of afterburner both to save gas and to reduce his infrared signature.

Most of the citizens who lived in and around Washington, D.C., were unaware of the army missile batteries that surrounded their city. Set up to provide a last-chance ring of protection, the antiaircraft missiles were carefully hidden from view, both to protect them from a counterattack and to avoid rousing fear or suspicion from those who lived nearby.

Designed as a long-range, all-altitude, all-weather air-defense system, the Patriot missile system had a proven capability to counter tactical, ballistic, and cruise missiles. Equipped with a track-via-missile (TVM) guidance system that allowed midcourse correction right up to the terminal stage of flight and with ninety kilograms of high explosives packed in their warheads, the Patriots were also capable of bringing any aircraft down. Indeed, the only U.S. aircraft downed over Iraq or Kuwait had been accidentally shot down by the Patriot missiles. With a range of forty-three miles and a maximum altitude of more than seventy-eight thousand feet, the Patriot was guaranteed to bring stabs of fear to any pilot's heart.

The Ares pilot knew the Patriots around the capital had been upgraded with the Patriot Gem+, an improvement that included a new fuse as well as the insertion of a low-noise oscillator, significantly increasing the missile seeker's ability to detect, identify, and track low-radar, cross-section targets.

Low-radar, cross-section targets. Targets like the Ares.

Could the Patriot seekers find and track him? The pilot didn't know. They would eventually get a whiff, he was certain, but could they get enough of a radar signal to track him before it was too late?

He only needed a few minutes until his bomb was away.

A few minutes. A few seconds.

It all came down to that.

Below him, the soldiers inside the Patriot missile command-and-control units were on hair-trigger alert. They had their radar fine-tuned, concentrating on the short range, knowing they would never see the Ares until it was very close.

As the Ares penetrated the Positive Terminal Control Area twenty miles outside the borders of the city, one of the missile batteries got a sudden hit, a quick flash on their radar screen that lit up, then disappeared.

Seconds later, another hit, then a sudden chirp in their ears.

Unknown rider. Azimuth zero-one-four. Eighteen miles. Unknown altitude. Flying very fast.

The missile controllers turned to their commander with anxious eyes. No way they launched missiles over the city on an unidentified target without approval from him.

"Where is it?" the captain cried as he picked up the phone and was immediately connected to the command post at the Pentagon.

"Eighteen miles north-northeast of us, sir. Zero-four-one radial. High. Really high . . . looks like sixty-three thousand feet. And fast. Coming right at us, captain."

The battery commander repeated the information word-for-word into the phone.

"Heading now two-zero-one. He's heading for the Capitol or the White House."

The captain passed the information and then waited.

"Can you lock him up?" he demanded, holding the phone against his ear.

"The senior technician shook his head. "I don't know . . . we're not sure. We get a little energy in the low bandwidth, but I don't know if we can lock him . . . but, yes, yes, I think we can."

"Give me a number!"

"I'd say two chances in three."

"Yes, we can do it," the captain shouted into the phone. "Alright then." He listened, then turned to his men. "Go and get him! Send up everything that you have. Even if we can't hit him, we might scare him enough to keep away from his target."

Seconds later, the command post lit up as if the sun had suddenly lurched into the sky, the windows blazing with white-hot light as the enormous Patriot missiles started launching into the dark night.

Four miles to the north, another missile battery launched their missiles as well.

The Ares pilot watched the missiles launch and his heart jumped into his throat, as if someone had fired a bullet from a rifle after time had slowed down so much that he could watch it approach. Seeing the lines of fire coming at him, he rolled the aircraft up on one wing, held his course, and waited, all the time staring down. He had been through the exercise before, he knew what to do, and he was confident—not absolutely certain, but confident—that he would probably live. Still, the sight of the flaming light-pole-sized missiles, their enormous engines spouting white flame and blue smoke, made his gut tighten up so much the acid started to seep into his throat. He started counting as he waited, every second dragging on. Eight missiles, ten, then twelve. He quit counting after that.

The Patriot engines had a burn time of a little more than two minutes. But it would take them seventy seconds to climb to altitude, leaving little time to maneuver as they chased after the Ares. And the air was so thin above fifty thousand feet that the missiles would turn like a boat.

Still, they were so fast. And so many.

He swallowed, his throat pressing against his oxygen mask.

Rolling the aircraft upright, he pushed up his speed. The aircraft accelerated like a rocket, seeming to shoot through the sky. .98 Mach . . . .99 Mach . . . he blew through the speed of sound.

Accelerating, he fought the temptation to turn away from the missiles and put them off his right side. He knew that if he could reduce the relative closure between his aircraft and the missiles it would make the tracking calculations that much more difficult. Fighting the instinct to maneuver, he held his course, betting his life the stealth characteristics on his jet would be enough to keep him from getting hit.

Steady. Fast and steady. He counted the seconds and held his course.

He wasn't going to turn and run; that would be the worst thing he could do, for the aft radar cross-section of the Ares was the largest of any radar azimuth on the jet. And he wasn't going to turn and put the missiles off his right side, for that would screw up his bomb run and make him run out of time.

No, if he was going to do this he was going to do it right now.

And he only needed a few more seconds until he could release his bomb.

Accelerating through Mach 1.5, he rolled up and looked down at the missiles again. Some had already gone astray, wandering into the dark. As he watched, a couple more seemed to wobble, not knowing where to go before they self-detonated, filling the sky with a series of white and yellow explosive flames.

But five or six missiles kept on coming, a pack of rabid, hungry dogs.

Twenty seconds, maybe less to impact . . .

His heart raced. His hands sweat. His head beat like a drum.

Patience . . . he prayed for patience.

The missiles tracked, speeding toward him at incredible speed.

A few more seconds. He had to let them get into position.

He jammed his stick to the side and pulled back, throwing his jet into a severe high-g turn. The Ares maneuvered as his avionics began to lock the missiles up. The tracking CPU then moved the laser mirror while adjusting the surface to the millionth degree, then fired on the missiles in a series of millisecond bursts.

Six burns of light. Six exploded missiles.

And that was it.

The pilot didn't even smile as he rolled the aircraft up and turned back to course. He knew the United States had half a dozen fighter aircraft loitering somewhere over the city, and all of them were surely now speeding his way.

He looked at his time-to-target readout.

Just less than twenty seconds to go.

UNICORN SEVEN
UNDERGROUND MILITARY COMMAND POST
FOURTEEN MILES SOUTHWEST OF WASHINGTON, D.C.

The chairman of the Joint Chiefs of Staff listened to the relay from the army Patriot missile command. "Not one!" he cried in anguish. "Not a single missile got through!"

He listened a moment, then cried again. "Clear the airspace! Use the FlashPack on him *now!*"

INSIDE THE ARES
NORTH OF DOWNTOWN WASHINGTON, D.C.

The pilot hooked up the autopilot and commanded the APR-197 bombing avionics system to take control of the final bomb run. Relaxing, he rested his arms on his lap. Time-to-target display showed fifteen seconds to release. At eight seconds, his bomb bay doors would open, then a single nuclear weapon would begin its long, awful fall.

He lifted his eyes and looked through the thick Plexiglas that made up the cockpit around him. The city was a blaze of unending lights. He could clearly see the Mall and the White House, the shimmering LDS temple along the Beltway eight or nine miles to the north, and the blackness of the Potomac River that ran just a few miles on the other side of downtown. He could see the target and he squinted, looking at it for the last time.

Then he saw—no, he *sensed*—a flash of red-hot, piercing light. He felt the searing heat and the pain that seemed to scorch through his skull, his retinas burning as if he had opened his eyes to the sun. Then the backs of his eyeballs burst in pain and he screamed into his mask.

Then there was darkness.

For he was utterly blind.

The aircraft continued on course, the automatic flight control system controlling the jet. At thirteen seconds, while the pilot screamed and pressed his fist into his eyes, the computer automatically reduced power on both engines, slowing below the max allowable speed to open the bomb bay doors. At ten seconds, it made a final course correction and fed the terminal update to the warhead steering mechanism. Eight seconds from the release point, spoilers dropped from the belly of the jet, disturbing the flow of air under the aircraft to protect the bomb bay doors while they were in transit from the closed to the open/locked position. The bay doors split, held half a second, then rammed to full open.

The pilot heard the roar of the open bay doors and froze, still pressing his knuckles into the sockets of his eyes. The computer, just completing its final self-checks, didn't know and didn't care that the pilot was incapacitated and incapable of monitoring the final countdown. The bombing process proceeded without incident: a dull roar as the bomb bay doors ripped through the 730-mph wind, a slight buffet as the aircraft hit a pocket of cold air, the targeting and steering computer synchronizing with the GPS satellites overhead.

The pilot heard a bang, like a hammer slamming against solid steel, as the firing mechanism pushed the nuclear weapon away from its mounts. The aircraft bumped half a foot as the bomb fell away, then the bomb bay doors closed, their mechanical arms driven by powerful hydraulic pistons.

The warhead separated from the aircraft and started its long, cold fall.

The AFCS turned the aircraft northeast, away from the missiles and fighters that protected the city below.

The warhead fell toward the earth. Its nose tucked toward the target as it slipped through the dark night.

FORTY-TWO

The time-to-fall from sixty-three thousand feet was eighty-nine seconds.

The nuclear warhead accelerated as it fell, reaching terminal velocity a little less than twelve seconds after being released from the jet. A small antenna wrapped around a composite coil at the rear of the steering mechanism searched for, then found the signals from the GPS satellites hovering in space. Stealing their guidance from the U.S. transmitters, the steering computer compared the position of the falling warhead, the known coordinates of the target, the drift of the atmospheric winds, then combined this information to send tiny corrections to the small steering fins.

Some four years before, a postgraduate MIT student from Pakistan had visited the White House on a regularly scheduled public tour. At the perimeter security checkpoint, along with everyone else, he checked the GPS receiver in his backpack, which recorded the coordinates at the White House's eastern gate. A reasonable guess of the distance to the Oval Office was all that was required to surmise a set of coordinates for the presidential office suite. Days later, he posted the coordinates on the Internet, which were eventually downloaded more than half a million times from various locations around the world.

The coordinates weren't perfect, but it didn't matter all that much. The warhead falling through the dark sky didn't need to hit the target; a few feet, a few miles away, the desired result was pretty much guaranteed.

As the warhead fell, it cooled until the skin was ice-cold, but inside the warhead the avionics kept the critical components warm enough to complete their job.

Passing through twenty-two thousand feet, an internal altimeter sensed the proper change in ambient air pressure. A one-inch metal door flipped open on the side of the warhead, extending a tiny propeller into the passing air. Seconds later, the final safety pin pulled back, exposing the enriched uranium inside the nuclear core to the firing rods.

The warhead fell. The air became moist and humid from the Chesapeake Bay. The lights of the city began to reflect off the silver nosecone.

The steering fins continued to guide the weapon, moving so quickly they vibrated as they maneuvered toward the target, which was now directly underneath the bomb. The area of potential impact focused tighter and tighter as the weapon fell: the central downtown district, a mile square around the Mall, the White House to the north, then the West Wing.

A thousand feet. Final steering. Five hundred feet. Final arming. A hundred feet. The air, now warm and humid, rushed over the steering fins.

There was no sound but a soft whoosh as the warhead approached. Then the bomb penetrated the roof of the White House with a shattering sound before smashing through the ceiling and residential floor. It continued downward, crashing through the main level to the third floor in the underground complex, where it finally came to rest, a shattered hunk of steel, uranium, broken wires, crushed plastics, and splintered electrical components.

There the warhead fizzled amid the smoke and dust and the falling debris.

Then there was silence.

And that was it. Nothing more.

AVENUE WINSTON-CHURCHILL
COURS LA REINE
PARIS, FRANCE

Petrie sat in the backseat of the car, the older women beside her. Two agents moved toward the three-story home, their early morning shadows casting silent wisps of silhouette across the cobblestone. Farther down the street, Petrie was aware of at least two other cars that waited, but suspected there were more. Behind the private residence, a narrow, tree-lined alley separated the three-century-old buildings from the others along the next street. Half a dozen other agents watched the back of the meticulously maintained brick home.

A small radio crackled in the older woman's ear. The French agent listened, answered, "*Oui,*" then turned toward the girl. "Petrie, no one is in your home. Do you know where your mother might be?"

Petrie peered through the sedan's window toward the empty house. Five million euros, not counting the upgrades and restoration, but as lavish as it was, she had never thought of it as her home. It was a trophy for her father, a place to entertain and impress. "My father moved her out to the summer house more than a week ago," she answered softly as she stared at the house. "A couple of his men are staying with her."

The senior agent nodded, then spoke into the tiny transmitter attached to her lapel.

"Alright," she answered quickly, then turned back to the girl. "Let's go."

Petrie led the way. She opened the fence that surrounded the home and walked across the small yard. The old Victorian was dark and quiet, its windows empty eyes that seemed to stare back at her. A gust of wind blew across the rooftops and fell across her face, blowing dark strands of hair across her lips.

The woman stayed beside her, a firm grip on her arm.

Petrie approached the front door and took out a key. She inserted it into the door lock but didn't turn it. Moving to her side, she took out another key, then unlocked and pulled back a hidden panel built into the brick. A digital display blinked at her and she punched in the security code. Moving back to the lock, she turned the key and pushed the door open.

"Quickly," the woman prodded.

Moving into the house, Petrie held her hand out, holding the woman back. Turning to the nearest wall, she pulled open another hidden panel and punched in another code. The women watched her carefully, standing at her side.

Petrie shut the panel cover and moved up the stairs. At the top of the hallway, she turned left and entered the master suite, which took up most of the second floor. Above her, the floorboards on the third floor creaked as the old house settled against the north wind that was gathering strength outside. She paused and looked up at the creeping sound then moved through the master suite, past the elevated king-sized bed, perfectly made, past the enormous walk-in closet with more than four dozen dark suits and a wall of black shoes, past the Remington paintings and exquisite wooden cabinet.

Moving into the master bath, she stopped in front of the oval mirror and turned on the light. Opening a small drawer on her right, she pulled out a hair brush and extended it to her handler.

The French agent moved toward her, thin rubber gloves already covering her hands. "Are you certain this is your father's, not your mother's?" she prodded.

"My mother has her own bedroom and bathroom upstairs."

"Is there any reason to believe that someone else might have used this brush?"

Petrie hesitated, her face growing hard. "He does not bring his women here," she said. "My mother would not allow it. It was the only thing that she demanded, and he only reluctantly complied."

The French agent nodded, opened a plastic bag, extracted a thin comb, and pushed it through the brush. Holding the comb up to the light, she confirmed she had half a dozen strands of hair, then dropped the comb with the hair samples into the plastic bag, sealed it, wrapped it with red tape, and dropped it into a small purse. "Let's go," she said.

Petrie turned off the dresser light, then stood for a moment in the empty room, looking slowly around.

This would be the last time. One way or another, she would never come back to this house.

INSIDE THE ARES

The night was dark now, the moon having dropped toward the western horizon. The clouds were well below his aircraft, and what little moonlight there was glimmered off the scattered clouds.

A little than less than twelve miles above the White House, the Ares turned northeast. Moving silently away from the target, it slipped away undetected, flying toward the safety of the Canadian border.

Inside the cockpit, the pilot rubbed his eyes in a panic, his fists balled and tight.

He couldn't see. Not a thing yet.

And a blind man couldn't fly.

FORTY-THREE

ABOARD AIR FORCE ONE
ON THE TARMAC AT LE BOURGET AIRPORT
PARIS, FRANCE

The four massive engines were running and the aircraft was positioned at the southern edge of the airport tarmac, where it could take off with just a few seconds' notice if there was any need. The powerful engines created a muffled roar that, despite the insulation, vibrated through the aircraft's floors.

The presidential aircraft remained on the parking tarmac near the end of the runway. With everything going on with the Ares, it was an obvious security decision to keep the president's aircraft on the ground. Meanwhile, a sterile security area—a circle in which no one or nothing could enter or pass through—had been extended out to one thousand feet from the jet. Beyond that, a secondary security perimeter extended another thousand feet, with checkpoints guarded by military, civilian, and Secret Service officers.

On the other end of the tarmac, three enormous U.S. C-17 military transports waited, their engines running, their aircrews ready to go. The huge transports were stuffed with two identical presidential limousines, security vans, communications vehicles, mobile antiaircraft systems—everything that was necessary to provide the president with security and communications when traveling outside of D.C.

The 747-200B, tail number 29000, military designation VC-25A, was called Air Force One only when the president was on board. With the exception of the distinctive blue and white paint and presidential seal, the exterior of the aircraft looked like any other 747. It was a huge aircraft, almost six stories high, long as a city block, with four General Electric CF6-80C2B1 jet engines that produced a total of 240,000 pounds of thrust. Sitting at the edge of the tarmac, the aircraft was loaded with more than 400,000 pounds of fuel, giving it the capability to fly nonstop more than halfway around the world.

With a total weight of 833,000 pounds, it may have been the heaviest aircraft ever built.

Like other 747s, AF ONE had three levels, providing four thousand square feet of usable space. The lower floors were used for cargo, equipment, and food (thousands of meals were stored on the aircraft in case the president was ever caught in a situation where he was not able to land). The second floor was one huge executive office/hotel. The upper level was for the military and communications specialists and their equipment, providing the president with the means to communicate from virtually anywhere.

The walls of the presidential conference room were rounded, matching the shape of the aircraft's fuselage, and every space was meticulously planned, with various pieces of communications, security, and encryption equipment hidden behind wooden panels in the walls. The table was finely polished, the carpet dark blue, the seats small but comfortable. In the military command center on the upper floor of the aircraft, the Secret Service security team was still debating where the presidential aircraft should go. The president was insistent on getting back to the States (the entire presidential team certainly wanted to get out of France), but where to go and the route to get there was very much up in the air. Some were suggesting a military base in the southern United States, others pushing for Camp David, a few for the West Coast. All of them agreed, however, that the Capital was the last place they would go.

To the east, the sky had already turned from black to light blue as sunrise approached. The city, slow to waken, was still in the deep quiet of predawn, though the airport was a bustle of activity even then.

At 0642, after sleeping two hours in his private cabin in the nose of the aircraft, the president had been suddenly wakened by one of his staff. He dressed quickly, washed his face without shaving, pulled on a white shirt, dark slacks, and cotton blazer with no tie, and, four minutes after being wakened, rushed into the conference room.

His advisors were waiting. He saw the look in their eyes.

His staff stood as he entered, then settled back in their chairs. It only took a few minutes for them to explain.

The president stood at the head of the table, his mouth open, his eyes wide and unblinking, his lips almost frozen, a look of pure shock and incomprehension on his face.

He *couldn't* believe it.

They had actually attacked him with a *nuclear bomb!*

The room was deathly silent, every eye staring at the table, the floor, the walls, anything but him. The chief of staff stood next to the president and waited until the president turned toward him. "Tell me again!" he demanded.

The COS cleared his throat. "They dropped a single nuclear device, a satellite-guided weapon that penetrated the White House, coming to rest several floors beneath the main floor."

"But it didn't go off! *It didn't detonate!*"

"No, sir, it did not."

The president felt his knees wobble. He stared at the distance again, feeling an uncontrollable and suddenly renewed faith in a God. "I don't understand how it could not detonate!"

"We don't know, Mr. President. A team of nuclear weapon experts has already examined the weapon, but it is too early, sir, to develop an opinion of what might have gone wrong—or right, in this instance, at least from our point of view. However, they do know it is an enriched-uranium weapon. There's enough radioactive bleedoff in the White House to make it uninhabitable for years. But our people believe they can—"

"Can what?" The president shot him a deadly glare. "What do we do with a live nuclear weapon sitting in the middle of Washington, D.C.?"

The COS returned the president's cold glare. "First, sir, there is not going to be an explosion. The DOE weapons experts have already examined the remains of the weapon, and they assure us the weapon has been damaged to a point where it cannot detonate. They are taking steps to further neutralize it, just to make sure, and we have other teams standing by, experts in the mechanizations of such weapons. They all assure us, Mr. President, that they can neutralize the bomb."

The president turned away from Ketchum, his eyes on fire. "I want you to evacuate the city," he commanded.

"Sir, I really don't believe—"

The president turned to the SatPhone. "Where are you all calling from?" he demanded of his staff in D.C.

"Sir," the national security advisor answered, "we've already been evacuated to Haven, the national military command post in Western Virginia."

The president turned angrily back to Ketchum. "So the national security staff has been evacuated. But you don't want me to order a general evacuation of the city! Now how is that going to look, Mr. Ketchum, when the press and the people are made aware of that fact?"

"Sir, this is a different situation. Of course we would evacuate our critical staff. But if we evacuate the entire city, it will—"

"*Do it, Mr. Ketchum!*" the president almost screamed. "I don't know, you don't know, no one knows what is going to happen with that bomb! Until that weapon is completely disassembled, I will *not* take the chance. If that warhead were to explode and we didn't do anything about it, that would be the grossest miscalculation in the history of our nation. I won't let that happen. Not on my watch. No, I want the city evacuated and I want the order given *right now!*"

The president stared at the satellite phone. "Are you there, General Shevky?"

"Yes, sir, I am here."

"Are you there, Mr. Woodson?"

The director of Homeland Security answered, "Sir!"

"Then get to it, gentlemen. I want the city a ghost town until we are certain, understand?"

Grunts and yeses were heard. The president kept his eyes on the phone. "And General Shevky, I want a military response. Need I remind you, ladies and gentlemen, that we have been attacked with a nuclear bomb! It is *only* by the grace of God that our capital and a million people haven't been wiped off the earth." The president shuddered. "We will retaliate," he continued, his voice low and mean. "We will strike them like they tried to strike us. We will make this so painful to them that it will never happen again."

The conference room fell into silence, the hum of the engines the only sound in the air.

The chief of staff moved toward the president, his eyes burning bright. He started talking slowly, his voice deep and powerful. "I have spent my entire professional life protecting you, Mr. President—sometimes, if you'll allow me, even from yourself. Now you've got to listen to me before you make a colossal mistake. You can't use our nuclear weapons against them, sir. You can't go after their cities. How could we justify that? The laws of war require discrimination in how we respond. Yes, we have been attacked, but there is a critical sense of proportion we have to consider in looking at our options. Indeed, we are legally, morally, and politically required to react in a proportional manner to an enemy attack. You can't meet force for force in this instance, their evil intentions aside, for the fact remains, Mr. President, that their attack *didn't* work. If you go after their cities, if you command a nuclear strike, it will change the world forever and in the very worst way. You cannot—"

"I can defend my country!" the president cried.

"But sir, you can't order the destruction of their cities! Not when we have not suffered a single loss of life."

"We have always said, Mr. Ketchum, that if we were attacked by Islamic terrorists, we would retaliate in kind."

"Look, Mr. President, I understand we are dealing with a group of psychopaths here, cold, cowardly, sick, and evil men. But a nuclear strike is not the answer; it would only make things much worse. Some deranged prince came to hit us, but he screwed it up, sir. We can't demand tooth-for-tooth or we will see our civilization destroyed. The entire world would turn against us. And they would retaliate, maybe today, maybe tomorrow, maybe they won't hit us for a year. But if we destroy one of their cities, every Muslim in the world will cry out for revenge. There will be no stopping the coming war, Mr. President, and it will be a war to the end." The chief of staff was leaning forward now, his eyes burning and intent. He didn't blink. He was absolutely sure of his words. "Listen to me, sir. You can *not* use our nuclear weapons. It would be a catastrophic mistake."

The president took a step back, his face turning white. "What do I do? I have to answer this threat!" His voice was less certain now.

The chief of staff took another step toward him, placed his hand on his arm. "We have to take our time and talk about this. We have to think this thing through."

"No! No more talking. I want action now!"

"Sir—"

The president cut him off, turning away from his people to stare at the wall. He stood a full minute, his hands over his face. When he turned back to face them, his eyes had narrowed to slits. "Alright . . . alright," he lifted a hand. "We will measure our response. But we will not just sit on this. First, we've got to take care of the warhead, ensure that it cannot go off. I want updates every minute, and I want the city evacuated in case there is some kind of mistake. We simply can't risk it. There will be panic, I know that, but we must do what we can."

The president hesitated, collecting his final thoughts. "You are right, Mr. Ketchum," he continued, his hands thrust into his jacket pockets. "We must step away from a nuclear response. But we will not ignore their actions and we will not step away from this threat. None of them are our allies. Not a single nation in the Gulf. Some pretend to be friendly. They speak in such polite tones, then turn their heads and help fund al Qaeda, Wahabi indoctrination schools, the PLO, and Hamas. From Saudi to Syria and everything in between, they work behind our backs to kill us, conspiring in every way to bring us down.

"Now I want to go after them. Pick a group of targets, I don't really care, but pick something and destroy it, something that will hurt. Refineries. Government buildings. Terrorist training camps. Go after Gaza, Iran, Jordon, Syria, even the Saudi king. It doesn't matter what we hit now, so long as we hit. We are sending the entire stinking group a message, and I want it to be clear. No more hiding. No more double-talk. No more sitting on the fence. All of them are potential suspects, and we will hold their feet to the fire until we get some help. There will be no more smiling at us while hiding a knife under their robes. They all are coconspirators and we hold them all in disdain. If we have to, we will turn them all into homeless Bedouins again."

The president stared at the SatPhone, waiting for a reply. "You understand me, General Shevky?"

"Yes, sir," the general said.

"How long?" the president asked him.

"That depends on what you want, Mr. President. Do you want to start out with a whimper but end with a bang? Or do you want a massive, well-coordinated and overwhelming attack?"

"The latter," Abram answered without any hesitation.

"Then we need a little time, sir, to generate combat sorties, get rescue assets in the theater, coordinate between the different services, prioritize and assign the targets, get air-refueling tankers in position, deconflict the ingress/egress at routes—"

"How long," Abram interrupted, "to generate a crushing blow?"

"Eighteen hours to plan the initial sorties, then ten or twelve hours to get all the assets in place. We will want to launch at night, which takes us up to tomorrow after sunset. After that, another forty-eight to seventy-two hours of bombing to get the desired result."

"Do it," Abram commanded. "Do it right. Make it effective. And get started now!"

BANSHEE 12
OFF THE NORTHEASTERN COAST OF MAINE

The American F-22 air-to-air superiority fighter circled at fifteen thousand feet. Inside his cockpit, surrounded by glowing multifunction displays, the pilot kept his eyes focused out, knowing that even the ultrasophisticated and powerful radar system on the Raptor was incapable of detecting the stolen Ares. So he kept his eyes searching the night sky. Suddenly, to his right, he saw a fuzzy flash of light. He turned his head, then rolled the aircraft.

The black ocean had turned foamy, a bright circle of frothy white that glinted under the light of the stars and the moon.

His radio suddenly cracked. "Banshee, you've got something going on to your right," the AWACS controller said. "I've got some pretty good radar imaging showing a disturbance on the water. Looks like . . . yeah, something definitely hit the water. What have you got with your eyes?"

The Raptor pilot looked below him, keeping focused on the foam that was spreading across the open sea. "Something has impacted the water," he answered. "Better send a surface vessel and see what we got."

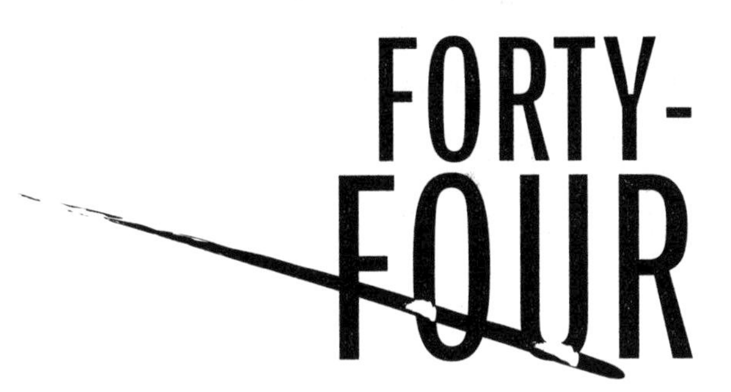

FORTY-FOUR

HÔPITAL D'INSTRUCTION DES ARMÉES PERCY
FRENCH MILITARY HOSPITAL
CLAMART, FRANCE

The forensic specialist was bitterly angry at having to work through the night, fatigue and low blood sugar making him nasty and irritable. He hadn't slept for going on twenty-four hours nor eaten since his late dinner almost six hours before, and his hands were now trembling from weariness and lack of sleep.

But the hospital commander, the one-star general, had been far more than adamant. "I want the results before tomorrow or I will have your head!"

The forensic pathologist had tried to argue, but the general had cut him off. "I don't care if you have to call in every genetic specialist in the city. I want results before midday or you will pay a dear price, Colonel Debri."

So here he was, his eyes bleary, with a long chore ahead.

He glanced at his watch, saw it was almost morning, then cursed once again and shoved a cigarette in his mouth.

After spending most of the night on the autopsy of the dead U.S. soldier, and after having proven to his superiors that the man had indeed been poisoned, he had then been tasked to run some DNA tests on the victims of a car bomb that had exploded on the outskirts of the city earlier in the day. He hadn't talked to the investigators—although it seemed a couple of them were intent on camping outside his door until he had finished his work—so he didn't realize yet that the two forensic investigations were related. To him, his work was just bodies and pieces of human remains, and he rarely saw the big picture.

Preparing for the DNA investigation had been a tedious task, scraping useful tissue and bone samples from the scattered remains. All of the human tissue that remained inside the vehicle had been burned beyond any degree of usefulness, but there were easily enough body pieces scattered around the bombed-out wreckage—the powerful explosion had scattered pieces of bone and skin and lungs and hair everywhere—and he only needed a couple of samples to finish his job.

Because time was of the essence, a team of DNA specialists, three microbiologists from the crime lab, along with a couple of professors from the university, were on their way to the hospital and would be there within a few minutes. What crisis had created such a rush, the doctor didn't know.

The doctor sat back and stared. This kind of work could take weeks, even months, to get acceptable results, and they had only given him hours to have an initial response.

He stared at the hair and nail samples that had been delivered to him in three sealed security bags sent over from an ultrasecret division within the Secret Security Service. Turning, he looked through the small window to the outer office where half a dozen French officers and policemen were waiting for his results.

There were Americans among the officers, though they had not spoken to him. But all of them were anxious. And some of them looked scared.

COMMAND AND CONTROL CENTER
UNITED STATES EMBASSY
PARIS, FRANCE

Major James had been invited to listen to the phone patch from the presidential command post aboard Air Force One. Other security and embassy staff members also gathered in the command post to listen to the president of the United States speak to the king of the House of Saud. At the head of the table, the U.S. ambassador sat in the executive chair, ruler once again of his kingdom now that the president had evacuated to Air Force One.

The conversation between the president and the king proved to be very direct:

"One of your pilots, a military officer, one of your nephews no less, has stolen our newest weapons system and used it to attack us with a nuclear bomb. No! Don't even try to deny it, we know it is true.

"The U.S. ambassador to the UN has already met with the Security Council. They have approved our resolution, calling for an immediate response.

"A military action will follow, deadly, precise, and complete. We have selected our targets and you are not alone. You aren't the only threat that we face now and our reach will be wide. Then, depending on the outcome of our investigations, we reserve the right to initiate a further response."

KING AZIZ ROYAL PALACE
MECCA, SAUDI ARABIA

Family, honor, tribe, and swords.

These were the only things that mattered in life. The only thing worth killing for, worth dying for, worth living for in the end. The code that they lived by hadn't changed in a thousand years, and the instinct to protect them was as deeply rooted in his DNA as the desire to live.

Now the king's enemies were plotting to violate them all. *His family. His honor. His tribe, and his sword.*

It couldn't be. He couldn't let them. There had to be something he could do . . .

The Saudi king stared out and thought, his mind racing.

The royal palace at Mecca, surrounded by a high stone and cement wall, was situated on the outskirts of the most Holy City, a city that non-Muslims are forbidden to enter, look upon, or even fly over. Considered one of the most important of the royal palaces (and there were hundreds) because of its location on the outskirts of the Holy City, the Mecca palace was used by the king and his closest family members during the Hajj, the yearly pilgrimage to Mecca where believing Muslims gather from all over the world to touch the Black Stone.

In addition to being one of the most beautiful and extravagant, the Mecca palace was also the most secret. No part of it has ever been opened to the public, photographs had never been allowed, and even distinguished Muslim visitors were rare.

Built at a cost of more than 1.1 billion dollars, it was a low, spreading structure that looked more like an enormous conference center than a palace, with its smooth granite walls, two-story windows, and grand, circular entryway. Surrounded by gushing waterfalls, artificial rivers, and pristine man-made lakes, the grounds were green and tree-covered, with exotic animals flown in from Africa and southern Asia to create a private, wild zoo. Marble and glassworks inside the palace created impossibly intricate reflections on the stone walls, all of them etched at angles to reflect the natural prisms of light. With glass walls and diamond-studded floors, the workmanship throughout the palace was perfect in every detail.

The king of the Royal House of Saud stood in his private office, his oldest son, son of his first wife, standing gloomily at his side. The king looked frail, almost sickly, as he stared at the wall.

"They're coming," he muttered slowly.

The prince shook his head. "How? When? Where will they strike?"

"I don't know," the king answered, a deadly look on his face.

The prince moved away from his father and stared through a tall window, looking east. From where he stood he could see the small rise in the desert that made up the central city.

The prince scowled, a bitter curse on his breath.

How dare they, the Americans, place this crime at their feet! How dare they make such deadly threats based on lies!

This was not his people's doing! They were innocent of this crime.

He turned back to his father. "What will you do?" he asked.

The king was silent a long moment. "I don't know."

For a long moment the two men were silent until the king finally moved to the window by his son. They stood together, looking out on the desert of Mina, the glint of the sun and the city, the heat waves coming off the enormous, black highway leading south.

The son turned and faced his father. "Do you really believe that our nephew, Prince Abdul Mohammad bin Saud, could have done such a thing?"

The king thought another long moment, staring out at the sun. "No," he finally answered. "He's an idiot, a fool who could shame his own mother, but he's not this evil."

The prince lifted his eyes to the window. "It may not matter," he muttered sadly.

"What do you mean?" The king's voice sounded old.

"I don't think the U.S. president really wants to know the truth. He's committed to this path no matter what he finds out. Abram is certain to attack us. It is already too late. The wind has started blowing and the storm is bearing down."

The king nodded slowly, his face tight and cheerless. "We cannot stop what Allah has preordained. It is impossible."

The prince thought. "But what will you do if they hit us and we are innocent of this crime?"

The king turned toward him, his eyes dark but bright. "Then we will unleash a fury such as has never been known. No American will be safe anywhere in the world. We are the Kingdom of Allah, Blessed Be Him, and we will not shame his name."

HÔPITAL D'INSTRUCTION DES ARMÉES PERCY
FRENCH MILITARY HOSPITAL
CLAMART, FRANCE

Hours after starting, the team of forensic microbiologists had the initial results of their tests.

The French military doctor stared at the initial report, shaking his head in surprise for the second time in two days.

The forensic investigator at the bomb site had reported that a total of three human remains had been located in the vehicle; two pair of legs and two hips in the front seat, a scattered set of human remains in the back. There had been three victims in the vehicle; her report was very clear. He had even called her to confirm, waking her at her home. "Yes," she had told him, "I am certain. There were three victims in the auto. Look at the photographs and you can easily see what I mean."

The forensic pathologist held the photographs in his hand. Yes, he agreed. There were only three people in the car.

Which begged another awkward question.

Why had his team identified four separate and distinctive DNA remains?

Three bodies. Four DNA samples.

It didn't make any sense.

PIGEON AUXILIARY EMERGENCY LANDING FIELD
NINETY-SIX KILOMETERS WEST OF GANDER,
NEWFOUNDLAND

The Ares landed just as the sun was rising over the barren horizon. The sky had cleared to an eye-piercing blue and the early morning light reflected off the frozen marsh water and snow. The airfield appeared to be deserted. None of the equipment or trucks from the night before could be seen, but a narrow trail had been plowed through the four inches of snow that had fallen in the night.

The fighter did a tactical approach, coming in extremely high, then spiraled down on the airfield. It flew over the runway once to make sure it was clear and broke hard to the left, using the force of the turn to help slow it down. As the aircraft slowed, the pilot dropped his gear, then rolled out parallel to the runway, heading in the opposite direction that he intended to land. His navigational computer told him the winds one thousand feet above the tiny runway were twenty-two knots out of the west, and he adjusted his flight path to compensate. Approaching the "perch"—the point in his approach when he would turn back to the runway—he dropped his slats and flaps, configured for landing, continued slowing, then rolled toward the runway again.

It wasn't easy, setting the heavy aircraft down on the short runway (the pilot was nearing exhaustion anyway), so the approach and landing were as ugly as anything he had ever flown; he was high, he was low, he was left, he was right. Then he dropped onto the runway with a tooth-jarring clang, pulled the throttles to idle, extended his speed brakes, then jumped on the wheel brakes.

He felt the antiskid systems vibrate as the aircraft slowed down, the computer keeping him from locking the brakes and skidding out of control.

He rolled out, turned at the end of the runway, and headed toward the old hangar he had holed up in before. The doors rolled open as he got closer and he shut his left engine down, then his right, coasting the last few feet to a stop.

The foreign agent smiled when he climbed out of the cockpit. The pilot dropped to the oily cement, sweaty and cold.

"Excellent," the officer exclaimed with excitement as the pilot climbed down.

The pilot pulled off his helmet and rubbed a hand across his eyes. The other man watched him, then took a fearful step back. The pilot's eyeballs were a bloody spider web of broken veins. He swore, his heart jumping, his mind racing in panic. "What happened?" he cried.

The pilot rubbed his eyes again, smearing the teardrops on his cheeks. "They lazed me," he muttered.

"They what?"

"They hit me with a laser!" the pilot almost screamed. "They call it the FlashPack, a combat laser designed to temporarily blind the enemy. It took almost ten minutes before I started regaining my sight. If it weren't for the autopilot, I would have certainly crashed. Even now, there are blind spots in everything that I see. I may never see the same again. They nearly ruined my sight!"

The pilot looked like a monster with his bloody, gruesome eyes.

"Is there anything I can get you?"

The pilot waved him off and tucked his helmet in the crook of his arm.

The foreign officer leaned toward him, his own slanting eyes glowing with apprehension. "You can see?" He sought assurance. "You can complete our next mission?"

"Of course I can."

"We are almost there, colonel. We are so close."

The pilot was silent as he rubbed at his eyes.

The officer nodded, almost bowing, then said, "In light of your sacrifice and effort, we have something for you." Reaching into his chest pocket, he pulled out a computer printout.

The colonel had to squint; his eyes were painfully sensitive to the light. Bending toward the paper and shielding it from the light with his hand, he read the printout, then swore. Wadding the paper, he threw it in the other man's face. "I don't want your blood money. I already told you that. What part don't you understand?"

"We just thought, sir, with the greatest and most dangerous part of the mission yet to come, that we ought to express our appreciation."

"You can't buy me! Don't you know that? Could I be any more clear?"

"We thought, sir—"

"Keep your filthy money. That is not why I'm here!"

The slant-eyed officer lowered his head and bowed. "I apologize," he muttered softly.

The pilot walked away. "Take your stinking money. Get it out of my account. Every penny. And never insult me with dirty money again."

The officer followed as the pilot walked away.

"I've got to get some rest now and I want to be left alone," the pilot told him. He'd had only two hours' sleep in more than thirty-six hours, and most of his waking time had been in the air.

The officer nodded, glancing down at his watch.

"Have the aircraft ready," the pilot finished. "The moment I wake up, I want to know what's going on. The U.S. will take twenty-four hours, maybe more, to get all their assets in place. Meanwhile, you've got to monitor their movements, everything that you can. They'll launch their first strikes sometime after dark tomorrow night, and it will be a massive hit. The strikes will go on for forty-eight to seventy-two hours, which gives us plenty of options to slip unnoticed into the fight. Unless something changes, I'll take off tomorrow afternoon."

The foreign officer smiled but didn't say anything.

The pilot started thinking, doing the math in his head, adjusting for the different time zones between their location and the target. With an afternoon launch, the Ares would be over Egypt sometime after midnight. From there it was a short flight across the Red Sea to the Saudi Arabian coast.

By then the U.S. attack forces would also be in the air. He would merge into their strike sorties, a wolf in sheep's clothes. Even if they detected him, no one would have any reason to question why he was there. He would be just another U.S. fighter among a hundred other jets.

At the Arabian coast, he would turn east . . . another six-minute flight to Mecca.

There he would drop the second bomb.

But this warhead wouldn't malfunction like the one he had dropped in D.C.

This one was real.

Another day was all he needed.

The Holy City would be gone.

After watching the pilot crawl into his tent, the foreign officer dialed up his satellite phone. "You were right. He didn't take the money," he said when the other man picked up. "Go ahead and move it out of his bank account."

He listened, then shook his head. "That's okay. It doesn't matter. He is not going to back out. And if he does, the Americans will trace the money into his account anyway, which will make one more thing that he will have to explain."

ABOARD AIR FORCE ONE
LE BOURGET AIRPORT

The president sat with his advisors around the table as they reviewed the final list of targets they were about to attack.

"We are almost ready then?" he asked.

"The air refueling tankers and fighters are ready. We've got B-1s and B-2s already en route. Destroyers with their missiles and naval assets are ready to launch. A few more hours to position rescue helicopters in the theater, then we are ready to go."

The president nodded. "How many sorties are you planning?"

"Some four hundred, sir. Seventy-two hours of bombing. You will be pleased with the results."

"I'm sure I will," Abram answered as he thumbed through the long target list.

HÔPITAL D'INSTRUCTION DES ARMÉES PERCY
FRENCH MILITARY HOSPITAL
CLAMART, FRANCE

The French military doctor stared at his phone, another unlit cigarette hanging out of his mouth. He had already talked to his commander, telling him the results of their tests, but there were two more people he had to call on his list.

He punched the intercom on his telephone and buzzed his senior aide. "The investigator who was here this morning? What was his name?"

"François Villon, Colonel."

"Yes, I need to talk to him. Get him immediately on the phone. And the American, the young pilot . . . I need to speak to him too."

AIR FORCE ONE
LE BOURGET AIRPORT

The short-haired naval captain was handed the report from the military command post at the Pentagon back in Washington, D.C. He read it twice, then walked up the narrow stairs to the top level of Air Force One, where the communications center was situated directly behind the cockpit and crew quarters. The center was cramped and cold, with a multitude of cooling vents to keep the electronics equipment from heating up. The naval officer stopped at the top of the stairs, flashed his access badge to the security officer, though he had passed by him no less than twenty times in the last two or three hours, moved to the communications supervisor, asked a couple of questions, smiled grimly, patted the younger officer on the back, then turned again for the stairs.

One level down, he stopped at the access doorway that led to the presidential suite, punched the code for access, then opened the door. "Mr. Ketchum, please?" he asked the civilian aide as he passed through the door.

Ketchum soon appeared. The military officer whispered in his ear.

Three minutes later, Ketchum walked into the president's private office, his face visibly lighter than it had been for at least twenty hours. The president was sitting in his chair, head down, a reading lamp illuminating the papers that were spread across his desk. "Sir," Ketchum started, "I think I have some good news."

President Abram looked up, his face nearly blank.

"Earlier in the evening, a military AWACS picked up indications of what they are calling a significant disturbance on the surface of the ocean somewhere off the coast of Maine. This was confirmed visually by a pilot in the area, and surface vessels were sent to search the area. They haven't found a lot so far, but they have picked up a few pieces of what appears to be the wreckage of a military jet: pieces of foam from an ejection seat cushion, a few rubber baffles used inside military fuel tanks, fiber insulation . . ."

The president moved toward him. "Are you saying it was the Ares?"

"We don't know for certain, Mr. President. It will take several days before we can do a proper postcrash analysis of the wreckage, but yes, it seems likely that the wreckage did come from the Ares."

The president shook his head. "No kidding," he muttered in pure disbelief.

Ketchum smiled in satisfaction. "There was absolutely no evidence of postimpact fire. No oil or fuel residue has been found on the surface. It seems, sir, the jet must have run out of fuel. The pilot stretched it too far and couldn't make it back home."

Abram shook his head again. He wanted to believe it. He *desperately* wanted to believe it. But the way things were going, he was reluctant to accept any good news.

He moved away from Ketchum, folded his arms, and stared at the floor. "But you believe it was the Ares?" he asked again.

"As I said, sir, we are not sure. But this much we know. A military fighter crashed into the sea. We have no reports of other missing airplanes, and we would be aware if one had gone missing by now. There are pieces of wreckage similar to the Ares at the crash site. That is what we have to this point.

"Now, was it the Ares? We don't know that. Very little of anything will float from that jet, but until we have gathered the wreckage and sent it to a lab for analysis we won't *know* for sure. But do we really *know* anything? All we can do is make assumptions based on the evidence. And the evidence is nearly overwhelming. The Ares has crashed into the sea."

The president stood without moving, gun-shy of accepting good news. Then he finally smiled. "Very good," he said.

Ketchum hesitated, rubbing his hands uncertainly. "Do we continue with our attacks against the targets in the Middle East?" he asked.

"Of course," Abram answered quickly. "We've been attacked. We will retaliate. This doesn't change anything."

"Yes, sir," Ketchum answered, then let himself out of the room.

U.S. BASES THROUGHOUT THE MIDDLE EAST AND NAVAL SHIPS ACROSS THE PERSIAN GULF

The sun began to set over the deserts and mountains of the Arabian Peninsula.

Time for the U.S. military to go.

Thirty minutes after sunset, the attacks started with a series of cruise missiles launched from a naval destroyer in the Persian Gulf. Soon after, other U.S. naval assets got in the fight, launching their missiles a few seconds apart. As the cruise missiles burned their way into the air, navy and Marine fighters were being catapulted from the deck of various carriers positioned throughout the Gulf. In Iraq, air force fighters also screamed from the runways and climbed to cruise altitude. A thousand miles to the south, in the middle of the Indian Ocean, huge B-1 and B-2 bombers had already taken off from Diego Garcia, a small military island that was controlled by the Brits.

Sixty minutes after sunset, 175 aircraft and missiles were in the air, heading to various targets throughout the Middle East and Persia.

FORTY-FIVE

AIR FORCE ONE
LE BOURGET AIRPORT
PARIS, FRANCE

Two thousand feet away from the aircraft, the dark blue van was stopped at the final checkpoint. The military driver stepped out of the van and a Secret Security officer took his place behind the wheel. After being cleared into the hot zone, the agent drove toward the aircraft on a predetermined route, slowly, carefully, following every protocol. Maneuvering the vehicle to the left side of the aircraft, he stopped near the tail. The rear access door was already open and a narrow set of stairs had been pushed into place.

She stepped from the van, wearing glasses and a white scarf pulled up to cover her face. Holding a colored folder, she grasped it tightly in both hands as the French officer, François Villon, emerged from the van. Keeping her head low, she rushed up the stairs, two men in dark suits holding onto her arms.

Villon stayed behind her, his heavy legs pounding each stair as he climbed.

Jesse was waiting at the top of the stairs. The foreigners stepped inside the aircraft as the van moved away, and Jesse shut the access door.

Stepping into the aircraft, Petrie's eyes opened wide. She stood a moment, staring, overcome by the dark suits, the luxury, the vibration from the engines rumbling under her feet, the security, the expectation, the *feel* of it all. "Is he really—"

"The president," Jesse interrupted.

"Yes. Is he really onboard this airplane?"

"Yes he is, Petrie. Now quick, come with me."

She hesitated, uncertain until Villon stepped forward and placed his hand on her shoulder. "It's alright," he assured her. "It is as we discussed."

She nodded to him weakly. Jesse reached out, took her hand, and pulled her toward the front of the jet.

The rear of the aircraft, designed for the press and other guests, was configured much like any other airliner except that all of the seats provided first-class leg room and foldable working tables. Moving forward, they passed a couple of galleys and the restrooms, the Secret Service conference room and their offices, then space for the presidential staff.

Stopping at a locked door in the hallway, Jesse knocked. Seconds later, Edgar Ketchum appeared. "Come on," he said. "President Abram is waiting. We don't have much time."

The three people started walking, then Ketchum turned suddenly, stopping in the center of the aisle. "Do you have any idea how extraordinary this is?" He whispered to emphasize his point.

Jesse held Ketchum's eyes, unsure of how to respond. The chief of staff leaned toward him. "The president of the United States has invited you to come in so he can hear what you have to say. He has never—*never once*—allowed staff-level personnel to sit in on his national security meetings, let alone be a part of the decision-making process. This is more than extraordinary, it's unheard of with this man. That's why he has assembled his national security staff, some of the brightest minds in the world, to wade through the BS and bring the filtered truth to him. Unfortunately, the situation now requires him to get right to the source. We have no time for analysis or abbreviations. He has to listen to you raw.

"But I have to warn you, and I say this as one who has climbed into your corner and wants you to succeed, you must be very careful in everything that you say. State your point, but keep focused, and never wander off base. You are a universe away from this man and the pressures he feels. So don't presume *anything*. He will eat you for lunch, then spit your bones on the floor if he feels you are pushing an agenda or not putting all the facts on the table.

"So be careful." He turned to Petrie. "Both of you."

The president listened to the military strike update from his security staff back in D.C. For the benefit of the group, the chairman of the Joint Chiefs ran down the list of the targets of the U.S. military operation that had just gotten under way. "The first wave launched at 20:30, local time, just after sunset," the chairman concluded. "They hit a total of thirty-one different targets with a combination of missiles, fighters, and bombers. Second, third, and fourth waves will follow. After that, we'll take a few hours, use our satellites, reconnaissance aircraft, and drones to evaluate the damage, then, based on what we see, we'll draw up frag orders for the next wave of attacks."

Abram listened, then turned to face another screen. "Madame Secretary, how goes it from your end?"

"Are you certain that you want to know, sir?" she replied.

The president almost scoffed. "I'm sure I don't, but let's hear it anyway."

Her voice was thick with indignation and it sounded almost nasal through the satellite phone. "It's about what you would expect," she started. "The French are furious, the Germans hostile, the Spanish threatening, the Belgians, Danes, and Italians indignant with rage. Anyone else in Europe is ready to nail our skins to the wall. The Brits and Poles are with us, barely, and maybe in the end a few more, but you know the drill; the UN will condemn us, the Russians and Chinese will cry. As always, we have to plan on moving through this episode by ourselves."

The president raised his chin from his palms. "And you explained to our friends that we have an unexploded nuclear ordnance sitting in the White House?" he asked.

"I explained the situation very clearly, Mr. President."

"You explained the Ares was stolen by a Saudi pilot with Iranian and Syrian conspirators? You explained this was an operation funded by Islamic groups headquartered here in France."

"They understand that, sir."

"Then screw 'em," he muttered. "I don't want to talk about them anymore. When this is over, we'll mend some fences if we have to, but until then, I won't waste another second bleating about these cowards we used to call friends."

The back door of the conference room opened quietly and Edgar Ketchum slipped into the stuffy office, moved to the president, and whispered quietly in his ear. The president listened, staring straight ahead, then nodded.

Ketchum turned around and left, pulling the door closed behind him.

"Anything else right now?" the president asked, looking into the faces of his staff through the video screens. No one seemed overly anxious to answer, and so he concluded, "Let's wrap this up then." He stood and placed his fist on the table. "I've got another matter that I need to see to."

"General Shevky, CIA, I need you to stay on line with me a few more minutes," the president said. "And get the FBI director. I'm told he needs to be a part of the next conversation as well." Abram started walking as he talked. "I'm going to my private office. We'll link the conference phone there."

Petrie Baha was escorted into the president's private office and guided to a leather chair where she sat anxiously, her knees together, both of her feet on the floor. Jesse stood beside her as Ketchum seated himself on the side of the conference table. The table also served as the dining table, and a white cloth with a few dishes and a coffeepot had been placed on the top. Ketchum nodded to the coffee, but both of them declined. Seconds later, a steward appeared from a door on the opposite side of the room, cleared the table, and quickly disappeared. Ketchum pressed a button in the armrest of his chair.

A square in the center of the table dropped two inches, then pulled back, driven by a quiet electrical motor mounted near the base. Another panel raised to take its place, this one configured with a secure satellite phone.

Ketchum reached across the table and punched in an access code on the hands-free button at the bottom of the phone. "Gentlemen, you still with us?"

General Shevky answered, "Yes, sir" for the group.

As if on cue, the president entered the room, followed by two members of his personal staff. Jesse jerked to attention as the president walked toward him to shake his hand. He greeted Petrie, taking a couple seconds to study her beautiful face, then sat at the head of the table. "What you got?" he demanded.

"Sir," Ketchum said, "we've identified the remains of the three bodies in the car bomb that exploded on the north side of the city."

The president nodded grimly. "The pilot . . . Colonel Ray. We need to send word to his family."

"Sir, I'm afraid this thing is suddenly much more complicated than that."

Abram stopped, staring at Ketchum's face as if he expected to read the situation from the look in his eyes. "What is it?" he asked.

Ketchum cleared his throat. "There were three people that were killed in the explosion, we are certain of that." He glanced uncomfortably toward Petrie, a quick but sympathetic look on his face. "Miss Baha's father has been positively identified as the driver of the car. Beside him, in the front seat, we have an unidentified victim."

Ketchum hesitated, glancing to Petrie.

She was aware of her father's death and she had braced herself for his words, still, a single tear fell down her face. Jesse watched her and wondered at the emotions that had to be boiling inside. Relief? Had to be some of that. But a daughter also couldn't lose her father without shedding a tear.

The president looked at her intently. "I am sorry," he offered softly. "I have been told, Miss Baha, what you have done for your country. We are in this fight together, your nation and mine, and all of us are grateful for the sacrifices you have made, the danger you have lived through, the loss of your father now."

Petrie met his eyes and held them. He nodded and smiled sadly, then turned back to his chief of staff.

Ketchum leaned toward him, a weary and uncertain look on his face.

The president caught the fearful expression and his gut tightened up. "And the last body," he prodded. "It had to be our pilot. Surely we can put this thing to rest?"

"Quite the opposite, Mr. President," Ketchum answered bitterly, avoiding the president's stare.

"Enough of this, Edgar! Who is the final body in the car bomb?"

"The Saudi prince Abdul Mohammad bin Saud," Ketchum answered in a voice of despair.

The president bit his upper lip with his teeth. "But the prince was in the Ares! He crashed into the ocean east of Maine!"

"No, sir. The prince is dead, that is true. But he died in a car bomb in France, not from crashing our jet into the sea."

The president sat back, his eyes showing pink rims underneath heavy lids. "That can't be!"

"It is, sir. There is absolutely no doubt."

"Then who was in my aircraft?"

The room was deathly silent.

So much awkward information to explain.

PIGEON AUXILIARY EMERGENCY LANDING FIELD
NINETY-SIX KILOMETERS WEST OF GANDER,
NEWFOUNDLAND

The foreign soldiers listened to the screams of terror as they echoed against the hangar wall and filled the lone and barren field.

They tried to ignore them, but it was unnerving and depressing to hear such cries of despair. After listening for an hour, they decided to act.

Walking from the hangar to the row of tents hidden under a clump of low trees, a young officer slipped into the double-layered tent. The flap was zipped tightly shut and a small kerosene burner sizzled and popped in the corner, even though the sun had warmed the outside air up to forty degrees.

The lieutenant pushed through the tent flap and moved toward the pilot just he screamed again. His eyes were wide open and his mouth was agape as if a stifled scream was struggling somewhere in his chest to come out.

The officer stared a moment at the terrified face. Pale. Tight as wire. The veins and tendons in his neck stretched against the thin skin. The pilot's lips were pulled back, exposing his teeth.

Moving slowly, he touched his shoulder. "Sir," he muttered softly.

The scream fought his way from his chest and pierced the quiet air.

"Sir . . . ," the officer repeated.

The pilot was lying on his back, his shoulders lifted off the bed. He clutched the mattress, his arms taut, his fingers scratching at the fabric.

"Sir," the aide repeated, gently shaking his shoulder. "It's alright. It's just a nightmare."

The colonel jolted up at his touch, his face waxy with sweat, his eyes wild and darting, looking for the unseen monster there. He stared at the young aide but didn't see him, then lay back and moaned.

In seconds he was sleeping again, his breathing heavy and slow.

FORTY-SIX

"Let me understand this," President Abram hissed. "You have three bodies in the wreckage. Two men in the front seat? Another man in the back?"

"Yes, Mr. President," Ketchum answered quickly. "We've identified Mr. Baha, the Saudi prince, and another Persian man."

"Yet you have identified a total of four DNA remains at the bomb site."

"Yes, sir, that is true. The three men in the car and the finger from the Ares pilot, Colonel Ray."

"But only his finger? Nothing else? No body pieces, no hair, no other identifiable DNA remains?"

"That is all, Mr. President."

The president stared gloomily and braced himself, expecting the worse.

Ketchum went on. "The forensic pathologists have determined that the finger was very carefully removed. A scalpel, perhaps even a cigar cutter; they don't know for certain, but they do know the finger was separated with a sharp instrument. More, sir, it has no explosives residue, nor has it been exposed to any source of heat such as would have been created from the car blowing up. Now, none of this will answer any of our questions, except that we now know the finger was clearly planted at the scene."

"But why . . . what are they . . . who *are* they and what were they trying to do?"

Ketchum anxiously thumped his hands across the top of the table. "Clearly, sir, he wanted us to think that he had been killed in the explosion."

"Who is *he,* Mr. Ketchum?"

Ketchum puckered his lips and then answered, "Colonel Ray."

The president shook his head in disbelief. "No, I don't believe it. It doesn't make any sense. Are you saying Ray was working with Baha and the Saudi prince, that he conspired to steal the aircraft and attack the United States? *With a nuclear weapon?* I don't believe that for an instant! I think you have all lost your minds."

Ketchum leaned toward him, a stern look on his face. "Believe it, Mr. President. There is no longer any doubt that Colonel Ray conspired to steal the aircraft and use it against the U.S. Miss Baha has seen copies of the documents, notes of meetings, heard them talking on the phone. Once we sat down and put it all together, it became very clear."

The president shot a glance at Petrie, his eyes burning with rage. "No offense to present company, but why am I to believe that that she is telling us the truth?"

Ketchum turned toward the satellite phone. "Gerald Gates, please, will you inform the president what you have discovered."

The satellite phone was silent as the FBI director cleared his throat. "Sir," he started gingerly, "as a standard procedure during this investigation, we have been monitoring the financial accounts of all of the parties involved. Earlier this morning, a very significant sum of money was electronically wired into Colonel Ray's personal account. The money only stayed there a few moments, then was transferred again."

"How much?" Abram asked.

The FBI director hesitated. "Twenty million dollars, sir."

The president exploded. "*Twenty million dollars!*"

The FBI director smacked his lips anxiously.

"So Colonel Ray stole our aircraft! He is piloting our jet!"

Ketchum turned to the president. "We are not certain, but we think so."

"*You'd better be certain before you bring this to me!*"

Ketchum pressed his lips into a tight crease. "Sir, this is what we know: Colonel Ray has been working for Petrie's father and the Saudi prince. The French have shown us transcripts, photographs, e-mail notes and accounts—" He glanced quickly to Petrie. "For almost three years this has been going on."

"The French knew about this and didn't tell us!"

"Like us, they have their reasons for their silence. We will address that with them, I assure you, when the opportunity presents itself."

The president cocked his head and fell silent, then laid his elbows on his armrests and brought his fingers to his lips.

"Your city was attacked with a nuclear bomb," Petrie began. "Yet I know for certain, *Monsieur* President, that neither my father nor the prince had access to any nuclear weapons. They had tried for years to get them, tens of millions of dollars they have spent, but they were not successful in gaining access to nuclear technology or materials, despite everything that they tried. This thing was not my father's doing. He had no part of that plan. I beg you to believe me, for I know that is true. And if that is true, *Monsieur* President, then this must be true as well. Colonel Ray has another partner. Someone else is working with him."

The president looked down on Petrie, his eyes growing soft with emotion. He didn't know her, but he wanted to believe her, and for some reason he did.

"Sir, I know it is difficult to consider the possibility that we have been betrayed," Ketchum pressed, "but think about it and you will see it is the only thing that makes any sense. How else could anyone, no less a Saudi prince, get into our aircraft and steal it right out from under our noses? That is the one thing we have never understood. It can only be answered if it was Colonel Ray."

"Then who killed Baha and Prince bin Saud?"

Petrie lifted her eyes to the president. "Your pilot killed my father," she said.

The president didn't answer, listening to her every word.

"My father had grown very fearful of your military officer," she continued. "He didn't trust his American contact any longer; that is clear in almost every communication he had. He was very suspicious. I have seen notes that he wrote to Prince bin Saud, expressing his dismay that they insisted on going through with the plan. Many times he tried to tell them their U.S. contact had secret motivations they did not understand."

It was too much for the president to endure patiently. Like water torture, it seemed to drag on and on. "Motivations!" he cried, "what are you talking about!"

Petrie lifted another picture and stood. She shot a glance toward Ketchum, as if asking permission to approach the president. Ketchum nodded and Petrie crossed the small office, holding out the photograph, which Abram snapped out of her hands.

The beheading of the American soldier. The masked men behind him. The dull, ugly knife.

Abram glanced down at the photograph. "I've seen this," he said.

Jesse explained the photograph. "Colonel Ray had a son, a Special Forces Army sergeant who was taken captive in Kirkuk . . ." He told the story quickly, then said, "Sir, Colonel Ray mourned his son every day since the day he was killed. He denied it, he tried to hide it, he said all the right things, but those of us who knew him and worked with him could see it was obvious in everything that he did. After his son was murdered, he was never the same. He became vengeful. Bitter and angry."

The room fell silent. The president stared and then cursed. "His son was beheaded. He hates all Arabs. He is dying for revenge. So he plots with Prince bin Saud to steal our aircraft *to attack the U.S.!* He crashes into the ocean and is dead now. I'm sorry gentlemen, but *it doesn't make any sense!*"

Jesse watched him, then leaned forward. "It makes perfect sense, Mr. President, if the Ares didn't crash and if Colonel Ray isn't dead."

Abram slapped the table. "I do not understand!"

"I promise you, Mr. President, Ray was *not* a suicidal man. Indeed, just the opposite, he was driven by rage; he had a mission, a holy purpose, and death was not a part of that plan. The last thing he wanted was to check out of this life, and I do not believe he crashed his jet into the sea."

Abram stared at him blankly.

"He isn't dead, Mr. President," Jesse repeated, "and the Ares hasn't crashed."

"But it has . . ."

"No it hasn't. It was part of the setup, another part of the plan."

"But why?" Abram muttered.

"He's going to start a war, Mr. President. He's going to avenge his dead son. The final fight to the death."

Edgar Ketchum and the president spoke to each other in quiet whispers. While they talked, Jesse slipped to the back of the room and pulled out his cell phone, but the signal was jammed, unable to penetrate the hardened electrical circuits that ran through every inch of the aircraft's walls. He stepped toward the window. Two bars. A week signal, but enough. He dialed the number and waited, keeping his head low. "Baby Doc," he whispered when the first chief of Ares Maintenance came on the line. "Can you hear me? This is Major James."

The maintenance officer swore. "Hey Major, where you calling from?"

"No time now. How's the second jet?"

Jesse heard the sound of maintenance work in the background: compressors, power tools, men's voices, the clang of a metal toolbox being opened. "I'm hearing lots of wild things out there, Jesse," the officer said to him. "A nuclear weapon in the White House! My brother works up in D.C. Can you tell me?"

"How's the jet? I need to know!"

The captain hesitated. "We've got most of our parts rounded up. Started installing the replacement engine. A few more days—"

"Not good enough. I need it now."

An irritated moment of silence. "Hey, that's cool, but this jet needs a lot of work. We've got burned-up engines. Broken panels, broken avionics boxes. It's going to take some time."

"When will it be ready?"

"If I push, and I mean push, I *might* have it ready by tomorrow night."

"That's not good enough, Baby D."

"What do you want me to do?"

"I want you to get that jet ready! Now I've got to go."

FORTY-SEVEN

Jesse clicked the phone shut, then moved to Petrie, who was standing along the back wall. The president and Mr. Ketchum remained huddled together on the other side of the table. The senior national security advisors in D.C. were still on the satellite line, but the conversation was primarily between President Abram and his chief of staff.

Without General Hawley, Ketchum was now the man that Abram trusted more than anyone else. And the decisions they were making were the most important of his life.

"Nothing you have told me fits together anymore," Abram said. "It started out so simple. Our aircraft was stolen. Prince bin Saud was the pilot. He attacked the U.S. Now you tell me that bin Saud is dead. Colonel Ray killed his friends, then used the stolen aircraft to attack his own country. I'm telling you, Edgar, it's a little hard to digest."

Ketchum hesitated. After nearly two days of crisis, which meant some fifty hours with only a few minutes of sleep, his mind had slowed down; the adrenaline was not enough to keep him powered up anymore. He sipped another black coffee, knowing it might boost him for a minute, but he would fall back into exhaustion as soon as the caffeine hit his kidneys. "It isn't simple, Mr. President, there is no doubt about that."

"Is Colonel Ray really capable of doing what Jesse is suggesting?"

"I think, sir, with an unexploded nuclear warhead sitting in the center of the White House, that it would be safe to assume he is capable of pretty much anything."

There was a sudden commotion on the SatPhone from the other end of the line. "Mr. President," the national security advisor broke in. "We've just been advised that the nuclear weapons team has completely dissembled the weapon. The nuclear core has been evacuated, that is, removed from the premises. It appears that D.C. is now safe."

The entire room seemed to let out a collective sigh of relief. The president turned away from Ketchum and brought his hands up to his eyes. He seemed to heave, then deflate as he pulled in and exhaled a long, tired breath. He stared at the floor a long moment, the words rolling around and around in his head. *The nuclear core has been evacuated. D.C. is now safe.*

Abram lifted his eyes. *Thank you.* His lips moved without saying the words.

The chief of staff only nodded. "Sir," he said, "we've got to make a few decisions."

The chief of staff lifted a piece of paper. "We have, at this moment, attacked no less than thirty-six different targets. Most of them have been destroyed. We have multitudes of aircraft for the next wave of attacks. Knowing what we know now, I think we have to bring them all back. We have to call off the attackers until we sort this out."

"Why?" Abram demanded. "Nothing changes the fact that for three years the Saudi prince conspired to steal our aircraft and attack us! I'd say, Mr. Ketchum, that is reason enough to continue the attacks."

"I disagree, Mr. President. It is not enough at all. We thought the Saudi prince was in the aircraft. Now we find out he is dead. And we don't know for certain the actual role that he played. At this moment, we don't know anything and, until we do, Mr. President, we need to pull back the attack."

The president turned to the SatPhone. "Do we have an agreement?" he asked.

The D.C. advisors were unanimous.

"Alright," he said. "Abort the mission, but stand ready if we decide to go up there again."

The SatPhone buzzed as the chairman of the Joint Chiefs quickly answered, "Sir."

It seemed as if the air had seeped out of an overfilled balloon. The room was silent a long moment, the advisors suddenly lost in their thoughts. Petrie folded her arms across her chest and looked away, her eyes soft, thinking. Jesse watched her closely, fighting the fear that still lingered inside.

The president took a long breath. "Alright then," he said, "what are we going to do now?"

Ketchum pressed his lips together. "Sir, we need to send someone to Saudi Arabia to explain what has happened to the king."

"Explain! I don't think so! And I will not go crawling to that man!"

"No one is asking you to go crawling, Mr. President. But considering that we have just mounted a significant aerial attack against his nation, it is critical that we defuse the situation before it grows even worse. We have to explain what has happened, the conclusions we came to, and how we came to them. We have to start mending fences. No, we have to do a lot more than mending fences. It will not be an easy task."

"He will not listen to me," Abram answered with bitterness. "There is too much bad blood between us. It goes back many years."

The group fell into silence.

"The king is in Mecca, and as we all know, non-Muslims are not allowed anywhere near the city," Abram added. "We've already recalled our ambassador, which leaves us without a single individual within the kingdom that we can turn to right now."

Again the room was silent. The clocks on the wall ticked away. Jesse cleared his throat.

"Sir, there is something I ought to tell you," a small voice announced from the back of the room.

Every eye turned to Petrie.

"I may be the only person in the entire world that the king would listen to right now."

"And why is that?" Abram asked her.

"Because . . ." She hesitated. "Because my father and the king were second brothers. Same father. Different mothers. My grandmother was a concubine. They never married, so we are not of the royal line, but I have known the king all my life. He and my father go back many years, years which my father dedicated to furthering the Wahabi cause, raising and funneling tens of millions of dollars into organizations that the king oversees or controls. I could explain the situation to him. I know as much about what has happened as anyone in this room. I will tell him you were acting in good faith based on the information you had. I think he might believe me." She stopped and then added, "We could hope."

Abram stared at her for a long moment. The other men sensed his thinking, and most of them felt too guilty to look at her anymore.

Abram's face turned soft and earnest. He had no authority to command or even ask her, but she was the only thing he had.

"Miss Baha, you have already done so much. I can't direct you, but I'm asking you, for you are the only hope we have. You are the *only* person the king will listen to, and it is critical that we explain this. He has been humiliated by our forces. *Even while in Mecca.* With these attacks, we have taken away his honor. I think we understand how important it is now to give it back!"

Petrie shook her head as she thought about her father. "You are not Arab. You are not Muslim. You do not understand what you have done to the king. Not the way I do."

She glanced around nervously. Her eyes were red, her lips tight. She knew more than anyone in the room, perhaps, how dangerous it would be to go. She knew the king, she knew his anger. She trembled, wondering if she had the courage to face him.

Finally she answered. "I will go to Mecca and talk to the king."

Abram glanced at Ketchum for confirmation, who hunched his shoulders. "If nothing else, Mr. President, it would buy us time," he said.

"Thank you," he said, placing his hand on her shoulder. Turning, he spoke into the telephone. "Get a military transport ready. I want her in the air."

Forty minutes later, a white Air Force C-21 executive transport lifted from the runway. Inside, Petrie Baha sat, terrified and wondering, in one of the front seats.

She looked at the digital clock on the front bulkhead, knowing she would be landing in Saudi Arabia shortly after the sun had set.

Jesse watched the C-21 taking off, the sleek jet lifting gracefully into the air. Then he pulled out his cell phone and called the Ares maintenance officer again. "How you doing?" he demanded when the officer got on the phone.

He listened a moment, then cut him off. "I'm coming over there," he said.

PIGEON AUXILIARY EMERGENCY LANDING FIELD
NINETY-SIX KILOMETERS WEST OF GANDER,
NEWFOUNDLAND

From time to time, the pilot moved in his tent. They could see the flap rustle and his shadow inside, but he hadn't emerged, and no one dared bother him until it was absolutely necessary.

But it was necessary now.

The two foreign officers stared at each other, both of them reluctant to take him the news. Finally, the senior officer approached the tent, announced his presence, unzipped the flap, and slipped inside.

The American pilot was sitting at a makeshift table in the corner. For a moment he ignored the other officer, concentrating on his writing, then finally lifted his head.

"The Americans have called back all of their forces," the foreign officer explained.

Colonel Ray stared at him, an incredulous look on his face. "Are you certain?" he finally muttered.

"Yes, sir, I am. The second wave had been launched, it was already in the air, but it has been called back now. They are completely standing down."

The American swore. "The girl. Baha's daughter . . ."

The other man only nodded.

Ray gently massaged the bandage over his left hand. It was seeping blood from where the scalpel had severed his finger, but just enough to turn the tip of the bandage scarlet red. The wound was healing, but it ached as the local anesthetic ointment wore off, the pain killer barely enough to take the edge off.

"I should have killed her," Ray muttered slowly. "I *could* have killed her. I had ample opportunity." His angry voice trailed off.

The foreign officer stooped; the tent was four inches shorter than his frame.

The pilot looked up from his folding chair. "I will launch now," he said. "There is no reason to wait any longer, not with the U.S. forces standing down. With the girl in their custody, who knows what she told them or what they will do."

Five minutes later, Ray emerged from his tent. The group of men were waiting by the hangar. One of them nodded to the others, who bowed at the waist, then turned to the broken wooden doors suspended on their rusty rollers. Leaning against the slivered wood, he began to push back the rolling doors.

The pilot pulled on his flight gloves as he walked toward the hangar, a dark green helmet bag thrown over his shoulder. The foreign officer nodded, but no words were exchanged as the pilot did a walk-around inspection of his jet. Finished, he placed his hand on the landing gear and closed his eyes. Lost in thought or prayer, no one knew which, he took a full minute to stand there, then he opened his eyes, pulled out his helmet, and slapped the landing gear on his jet. "You hang in there with me, baby," he muttered to aircraft, "and this will be our last flight."

A four-wheel-drive pickup was hooked up to the fighter with a long, steel metal tongue. With all four wheels spinning, it pushed the Ares back, then turned it, directing the jet blast away from the hangar for engine start. The run-up and pretakeoff checks only took a few minutes, then, without acknowledging the ground crews or the officers, the pilot pushed up the throttles, turned the nose, taxied to the runway, lined up without stopping, threw both throttles into full afterburner, and blew down the runway like a bat from a cave. The aircraft seemed to almost lurch into the afternoon sun, it accelerated so quickly. Gear up, flaps, slats retracted, the pilot climbed into the crystal-blue sky.

Turning away from the abandoned runway, the aircraft headed almost due east, making way for the cold waters of the North Atlantic.

Leveling off at fifty-seven thousand feet (a little too heavy to get much higher than that) the pilot completed his post-takeoff systems checks, ran a quick navigational update on the internal INS, then scrolled through the menus on the touch screen, calling up the distance and time-to-fly screen.

It was 5,027.4 miles to the target. He could go supersonic while he was over the ocean, which would be most of the time—altogether, little more than a six-hour flight.

Staring through the thick cockpit windows, the pilot began to picture Mecca in his mind: a glistening city in the desert, ultramodern buildings and ancient brick homes, pastels, minarets, spiraled buildings, enormous highways packed with very expensive cars, a startlingly clean city set a hundred miles away from the filth and wretchedness of civilization, an oasis in the desert surrounded by nothing but mountains of sand.

Dune upon dune of unspoiled, rolling sand. The waves spread in every direction, farther than the human eye could see.

He knew the sand would turn into glass from the heat. For miles around, the nuclear fireball would crystallize the desert, turning the dunes into a virtual sea of clear glass to glisten in the afternoon sun.

In the center of the white sea, nothing but a barren hole and gray ash, the ancient city of Mecca a black heap in the middle of a desert of glass.

He thought on that a moment, then sat back wearily.

His body was heavy. Every motion took such effort it seemed he couldn't even think. Then he smiled in relief, knowing what was going to come. The deep anger and the blackness were soon going to pass. Justice would bring relief from the rage in his heart.

He shook his head, then reached up and punched the AFCS, setting the speed to supercruise. He felt the aircraft wallow under his seat, the composite wings swaying gently in the thin atmosphere, then he closed his eyes and melded into the peaceful sway of the jet.

PIGEON AUXILIARY EMERGENCY LANDING FIELD
NINETY-SIX KILOMETERS WEST OF GANDER,
NEWFOUNDLAND

The roar of the aircraft receded quickly as it climbed into the clear sky. The senior officer then turned and nodded to his men. "Get it cleaned up!" he said.

The men went to work without instructions. They knew what to do.

Some of the equipment was buried in a trench they had dug at the back of the hangar, some was burned in a fire pit, some was packed up in the back of the trucks.

Four hours later, the men were gone, leaving the airfield completely deserted again.

AVON 16
C-21 MILITARY TRANSPORT
SEVENTEEN MILES WEST OF MECCA, SAUDI ARABIA

Petrie leaned forward in her seat, watching the glistening sands. The moon had not yet risen, the night was only minutes old, and the white and gray sand still reflected the dim evening light.

The airport was small, with only one runway, and as the military version of the cooperate jet turned to line up for final landing, she could see the white hangars and glass-enclosed ramps on the east side of the runway.

A military aide sat down next to Petrie and indicated for her to buckle her seat belt. Behind her, six men from the embassy anxiously watched the back of her head. After touchdown, they would be forced to remain inside the aircraft, and so they had spent the entire flight briefing her on every word she should say, coaching and prodding until she had the message down. The script was short and simple. "I have met with the president of the United States personally. The president regrets the situation and wishes to discuss it with you. He is honorable in his intentions. In the sacred name of Allah, I vouch for this man. He has sent me here to beg you to communicate with him."

INSIDE THE ARES
OVER THE CENTRAL MEDITERRANEAN SEA

Sicily was a couple of hundred miles off his nose. To his left, far in the distance, the pilot could barely make out the shadows of the coast of France and Italy, the water crashing against the black rocks, creating lines of white waves.

It had been an uneventful flight across the North Atlantic and so far the flight across the Med had been uneventful as well, but now the pilot was growing tense as he approached the central portion of the sea. Dangerous territory was up ahead: the Israelis, the Syrians, the Egyptians, Italians, Turks, American aircraft carriers, not to mention the U.S. bases in Northern Italy, the French and Jordanians—more natural enemies and more military might concentrated in this tiny piece of airspace than any other place in the world.

The pilot anxiously glanced over his head. The sun would soon set, but until it did, this was the most dangerous time for the Ares.

Twenty minutes earlier, his left fuel heater had started to freeze. Nothing critical—it was nearly impossible to fly such a sophisticated aircraft such a distance without some minor thing going wrong—but it had forced him to descend to the thicker altitude at forty-two thousand feet in order to ram more air through his heater. Although the fighter was still five or six thousand feet higher than any civilian traffic, and a scattered layer of clouds at thirty-three thousand feet helped to hide him, the pilot knew the angle of the sun could reflect off the aft portions of his wing and tail. The glint could be seen for miles, a bright calling card for those who knew where to look. So he was even more anxious as he flew across the central Med.

Far less than ideal conditions to be heading into combat, he knew. Much better to enter the combat zone at night, when it was impossible to be seen. But the timing of the mission didn't leave him any choice.

He kept his eyes looking out as he flew, waiting for the setting sun.

Fifteen minutes later, the pilot pitched the aircraft over and initiated another gentle descent. A line of billowing thunderstorms loomed before him, huge anvil-shaped monsters that reached up to almost sixty thousand feet, and he started to maneuver around them while letting the aircraft descend into the less turbulent air. He allowed himself enough distance to stay between the towering storms, knowing the forces of nature within them could rip his wings apart. Descending, he concentrated on maneuvering the jet. A few more miles up ahead and he would turn back on course and then climb back to cruise altitude. After that . . .

A flash of metal! He looked up, his eyes wide! Windows. Then lights. A blur of blue and yellow. He jammed the control stick and screamed.

The enormous airliner filled his windscreen as it flew in front of the Ares. It was climbing, he was descending, the two aircraft almost crashed. The 747's cockpit windows were so close that Ray could see the expressions on the pilot's faces. The captain was on the controls, his eyes wide, his mouth opened to a gaping O. The airliner captain immediately pushed down the nose of his jet, and the 747 began to descend. The copilot pointed, then ducked as the left wing of the Ares passed in front of his window. So close! Ray thought it would cut off the pilot's head.

He cried and jammed his flight-control stick to the left. The fighter rolled. The enormous 747's wing passed underneath him, then the rear cabin, then the tail. The Ares bounced in the turbulence of the passing jet, then almost rolled inverted as it passed through the vertices coming off the engines and tail. Ray fought the controls, leveled the aircraft, then licked his dry lips.

He sat up, his heart pounding like a hammer, every beat a violent throb from his chest to his ears.

He had almost died.

A few feet. *A few inches.*

It had been that close.

He felt his stomach rising and had to swallow it down.

The mission was almost aborted by the enormous passing jet.

He took a moment to breathe. Then, his hands shaking, he pushed up on his throttles and pulled back on the stick, forcing the jet into a steep climb. Minutes later, the thunderstorms behind him, his heart still beating like a hammer, he pushed back in his seat and tried to force himself to relax. Then he reached down to his radio and switched over to air traffic control. He knew the 747 captain would call in the near midair collision, and he wanted to hear what he said.

"*Yes, yes,*" he heard the civilian pilot cry, "*it was a fighter aircraft. Right off our nose! Dark gray. No lights on the wingtips! And it wasn't like any other fighter I have ever seen before.*"

"Alitalia Flight 172, are you certain?"

"Of course we are, you fool!"

"But I have nothing on my radar," the controller said again.

"I don't care if you've got nothing on your radar. We almost had it on our windshield and I'm telling you, that bloody jet was there!"

Ray listened, then shook his head, disgusted with himself.

With the 747 pilot on the radio, everyone would now know that he was here. His secrecy had been revealed!

But they wouldn't know his target. And they couldn't stop him anyway.

Still, he cursed at himself, then shoved both of his throttles to their stops.

Three more hours to the target.

He wanted it over now.

AIR FORCE ONE
LE BOURGET AIRPORT

The report of the near midair collision made its way up the chain. With events boiling around them, the controllers in the Med immediately recognized what it was.

Ketchum was working in his private office when he got the call. He listened to the explanation from the national security advisor in D.C., then turned to Jesse, who was standing on the other side of his small desk. "The Air Traffic Control Center in Naples has gotten a report of a near midair collision," he said.

Jesse took a step forward. "Over the Mediterranean!"

Ketchum swallowed, then continued. "South and west of Sicily. Flying east. An Alitalia 747 captain reported they almost ran into an unidentified fighter. He describes it as gray, large for a fighter, flying without any navigation lights . . ."

Jesse reached for the back of his chair and braced himself as Ketchum tapped a pencil on the table. "The fighter didn't show up on any military or civilian air traffic control radars."

The hammer hit the final nail on the head.

"That's him!" Jesse barked.

Ketchum didn't reply.

"The Ares didn't crash. It's *out there!*" Jesse cried, waving his hand to the south.

Ketchum snapped the pencil. "But the wreckage . . . the explosion . . . the Ares hit the water. It doesn't make any sense."

The two men were quiet for a long moment, both of them lost in thought. Ketchum considered the pictures he'd been shown of the wreckage in the ocean, pieces of aircraft tubing, a floating cushion. He had been so certain that the Ares had gone down. Now he felt off balance and unsure, as if he teetered on a cliff.

"What about the wreckage, Jesse?" he repeated.

"They *wanted* us to think that our Ares had been destroyed. What better way to get us to let down our guard? We think it crashed. We quit looking. The Ares is gone. We go home. It was a setup and we bought it. I don't know how they did it; it doesn't matter, but the Ares didn't crash!"

Ketchum moved his head in a barely perceptible up-and-down motion. Jesse was right. He'd been right all along. "Colonel Ray is out there," he said.

"Has to be him!"

"Where is he going, Jesse? What is that fool going to do?"

Jesse shook his head. He had no idea. He bowed his head in panic, his mind completely blank.

An idea started forming in the back of his mind, and he strained for the thought. Thinking out loud, he said, "What is the one target Colonel Ray could hit that would cause a world-changing effect? Not just a one-time big bang. No . . . he wants a lot more than that. He wants a once-in-a-millennium, a cosmic shift in the world. Something that will change the course of history . . ."

Jesse sat up suddenly. His cheeks started flushing, his two-day-old beard causing a shadow on his face. His eyes were dark but they burned as the thought began to jell. "Where is the king right now?"

"In Mecca," Ketchum answered.

"In Mecca . . . yes, in Mecca . . ."

Jesse suddenly stopped. "The *most* holy city," he muttered slowly. "Birthplace of Islam. Sanctuary of their prophet. Home of their God. Resting place of the Black Stone, the most sacred object on earth. . . ."

His mind started racing as the memory came flooding back.

Two years before. His squadron's mission planning room. Late in the evening. Everyone had gone home. He walked into the room and found Colonel Ray standing alone, staring at a large map on the wall. Jesse watched him, saying nothing. Several minutes passed until Colonel Ray hunched his shoulders. "Do you believe in God?" he asked Jesse without looking back.

Jesse thought a second. "Sometimes," he said.

"Well I don't. I think it's all a huge load of crap. My God. No, my God. Everyone has their own team. Everyone proclaims their faith, stakes out their territory, and claims to understand it all. They pretend there's something out there. As if someone really cares."

Another moment passed in silence until Jesse shrugged. "I don't know, boss, I think you might be a little harsh."

"No, I'm not. And I can prove it."

Jesse forced a smile. The air was stiff and uncomfortable. "How you going to do that?" he asked, trying to keep his voice light.

Ray tapped the map at Mecca. "If someone were to start here," he muttered, not really thinking of Jesse anymore. "Start here and it would spread. It could blow up the whole thing."

The colonel tapped the map again, then turned and walked away, leaving Jesse to stare.

"Oh please, no," Jesse muttered, his face growing pale. "Tell me he isn't going to Mecca . . ." He trembled as he told Ketchum the memory.

Ketchum shook his head. "Their holy city, their religion, it could all be destroyed."

They stared at each other, their mouths open.

"There is *no* equivalent target in the West," Jesse said. "Nothing we have here even comes close to the psychological and emotional attachment to Mecca. It is the center of their universe in every way—religion, power, history, economics, politics. Now consider what would happen if he hit it with a nuclear bomb!"

Terrified silence.

Ketchum lifted his head. "The final war between nations, between religions and cultures. War with a Muslim people who would never forgive the West. And how could you blame them? I mean, consider how this looks. They tried to hit the White House. We nuked Mecca. That is what they will think. We could deny it, but they won't believe us."

Jesse stood. "The last war," he answered slowly.

Ketchum stared at the floor.

Jesse thought of Petrie. She was in Mecca now. She only had a few hours left to live.

By now, the Ares would be at the eastern border of the Med.

"What can we do?" Ketchum muttered in complete despair. "We are as helpless as neutered sheep."

The two men stood in silence until Jesse said, "There is a way that I might get him."

"And how do you propose to do that?"

"It will be dangerous, but there's a small chance it might work."

Ketchum watched him closely. Could Jesse be thinking the same thing?

"Can you really do it?" he asked.

Jesse didn't answer as he turned for the door.

INSIDE THE ARES

Colonel Ray checked his combat systems—laser, power generators, the nuclear warhead in the belly of the Ares—everything was working normally. Then he sat back and listened to the satellite radios. Didn't the fools realize he would have all the frequencies?

Changing a channel, he listened as the military command post at Incirlik Air Force Base in Turkey began to scramble their jets.

Go ahead, he thought bitterly, *come and get me if you think you can. You can't touch me with your fighters. Haven't you learned that by now? I'm too high and too fast. If you get close enough, I will kill you, it's as simple as that. The Ares will tear you to pieces and scatter your remains across the sky.*

He smiled with anticipation, then sat back in his seat.

His fingers tingled, his mind focused and intent. He savored the thought of another battle. He was ready for it. They couldn't touch him. Not the Americans, the simple cowards who refused to avenge his dead son, not the Saudis who had killed him. He was unstoppable.

The nuclear bomb in D.C. had been designed to be a dud. The trigger mechanism had been completely removed. No one knew that, of course, except for him and his men. It was intended to force a reaction, and it had certainly worked.

But the bomb over Mecca was not a dud. The holy Muslim city was about to go up in nuclear fireball.

The nations of Islam would counterattack, but it would be suicide. The United States, even Europe, was simply too strong and determined to be taken by a bunch of mullahs who were only two generations removed from riding camels in the desert and eating dates from the trees. The West would fight with their hearts, for they would know that this time it was a fight to the death. Who would win? Why, the West would! The East might bite at their ankles but the West would crush their heads. The end result would be destruction for the entire Middle East.

And that was all he wanted.

Then he would have his revenge.

AIR FORCE ONE
LE BOURGET AIRPORT

Jesse dialed his new cell phone as he ran. The maintenance officer picked up on the second ring. "How's the other Ares?" Jesse demanded as he descended Air Force One's external stairs.

He hit the tarmac, his breath running short. "You're kidding me, Baby Doc," he said and then listened again.

"Okay, okay, it doesn't matter anymore," he said as he ran. "I'm heading over there. I will take what I can."

The president stared, then fell back in his chair. "Major James has gone to the Ares?" he repeated, his voice thick with surprise. "But why? I thought it wasn't flyable."

"Sir, the damage to the second Ares was significant, but apparently not fatal. It might be they have repaired it sufficiently to be flyable."

Abram shook his head, suspicious. He wouldn't send Jesse up in a coffin just to have him fall from the sky. "How badly was it damaged?" he demanded.

Ketchum wet his lips. "The most obvious damage was shrapnel cuts in the tail. In addition, exploding pieces of the bomb apparently trashed out the Radar Absorbing Material across the wings, severely degraded its stealth capabilities."

"What else?" Abram pressed.

Ketchum shuffled his weight. "The tires were heat damaged. No direct contact with fire, but the fire chief estimated it got up to a thousand degrees inside the hangar, which means there was heat and smoke damage to some of the less protected avionic boxes. But the primary damage was to the number-one engine. Multiple pieces of shrapnel cut through the engine casing all the way back to the combustion chamber and afterburner lines."

The president shook his head. "Okay, but have they fixed it?"

"Some of it. Not all of it. The bottom line—it may be flyable but it's a crippled jet."

KING KALID PRIVATE AIRPORT
MECCA, SAUDI ARABIA

The caravan of gray SUVs and black Mercedes screamed along the airport taxiway, almost a dozen vehicles in all. As the caravan moved, the American C-21 executive jet taxied to the hold line on the eastern side of the runway, set its brakes, turned off its lights, and, per the instructions from ground control, kept its two engines running.

A dozen security vehicles surrounded the military airplane and the soldiers got out, all of them armed, their American-made M-16 muzzles hanging down from their waist harnesses like oversized pistols that reached to their knees. The pilots remained in their seats, showing their hands, while the Saudi chief of the security forces glared at them hatefully across the hot tarmac.

Watching him, the pilots realized how dangerous their situation really was. Here they were, in *Saudi Arabia,* a nation the United States had just spent the better part of a day and half and a billion dollars attacking. Here they were, in *Injun* country, facilitating an unofficial mission to the Saudi king, a man who might just as soon shoot them and have it over with as listen to anything the girl had to say.

Minutes passed. The chief of security walked over and talked with the driver of the fourth car in the caravan.

"Metro 37, you are to open your passenger door and instruct the girl to immediately evacuate the aircraft," the pilots heard over the airport radio.

Immediately evacuate the aircraft! Something about that didn't sound right.

The aircraft commander turned over his shoulder and motioned to the airman in the back. "You copy that, Sergeant Diaz?"

The young airman nodded.

"Do not, under any circumstances, *do not* set foot on the tarmac!" the aircraft commander warned the sergeant again. "Though we aren't within Mecca's city limits, I don't want to screw around. You've got half a couple dozen pissed-off Saudis just itching for a fight. The last thing I want is to give them any reason to take their anger out on us."

The sergeant opened the aircraft door, careful to stay out of sight, then nodded to Petrie, who stepped back and she slipped through the small door and made her way down the narrow stairs. It was only three steps and she was on the ground.

A dark man in dark glasses motioned to her, and she moved toward him. He opened the rear door of the second Mercedes and she crawled inside.

The caravan accelerated forward, raced west toward the glass-enclosed terminal, and then quickly disappeared.

SENIOR OFFICER QUARTERS
CHINESE MILITARY HEADQUARTERS COMPLEX
DOWNTOWN BEIJING, PEOPLE'S REPUBLIC OF CHINA

The military officer was eating an early breakfast with his mistress and had given specific orders that he not be disturbed. He had been away from home for two weeks, his wife would soon return from her own trip to Taiwan, and that left him little time with the young women who sat across the table from him.

The two lovers, one a beautiful woman, the other a pudgy old man, ate and talked and laughed until the military aide slipped into the room. The Chinese general looked up and stared angrily as the aide moved toward him.

"The aircraft has been spotted—" the aide started to say.

"The Ares was spotted!" he demanded.

The aide leaned back on his heals and dropped his arms. "Yes, sir. There was a near midair collision. A civilian aircraft almost hit it over the Mediterranean Sea."

The general swore, folded his napkin, ignoring the girl, then followed the military aide from the room.

LE BOURGET AIRPORT

Jesse ran into the hangar where the second Ares was being repaired. The chief of maintenance looked toward him, his shoulders slumping.

"Is it ready?" he demanded as he ran toward the jet.

The captain shook his head. "Look, Jesse, I understand the situation, but it doesn't change the fact that this aircraft is simply not ready to go. It isn't even close. Now, you can threaten and curse and tell me that you don't really care, but it doesn't change the fact that this jet is not safe to take in the air."

"Have you replaced the damaged engine?"

"Yes, sir, we have. But you've got missing RAM panels—"

"That's it? A couple of the Radar Absorbing Material panels haven't been replaced?"

"Yes, they've been replaced, but the glue hasn't cured. They'll blow off on you, Jesse, before you hit fifty miles an hour. And we haven't had time to replace the Defensive System avionic boxes that were damaged."

"So I would be blind up there?"

"Completely blind, Jesse. You've got a radar, but no IR sensors or defensive sensors at all. Another aircraft could sneak up on your six and smack you with its missiles and you wouldn't even know it was there."

Jesse nodded. He knew what it felt like to have an aircraft break into pieces around him and to free-fall through the sky. "Even if I had all my sensors, it wouldn't help," he answered. "I'm going after the Ares, captain. Its stealth won't allow me to detect it anyway."

"But you'll be missing your own RAM surface panels. Without those panels, you lose all of the stealth capabilities on your jet. You won't see him. He'll see you. The worst of both worlds. It's suicide to go up there. What are you thinking, man?"

"I understand the situation. Now let's get that jet in the air."

"There's more, Jesse, lots more. The afterburner igniters on the new engine haven't been connected, which means no afterburner on that engine, which means you lose a quarter of your speed. We've got other boxes, other sensors—"

Jesse took an angry step toward him. *"Will that aircraft fly?"* His eyes squinted. "Will it get in the air?"

"Yes, it will fly, but that's about all it will do."

"Is the laser calibrated? Will I have an operating laser gun?"

"Yes, sir, you will."

"Then I'm not talking any longer. I want that jet now!"

The sound of screeching tires sounded from behind them and both men turned around. Three black SUVs screamed into the hangar, then came to a stop behind the jet.

Jesse nodded as President Abram and Mr. Ketchum climbed out of the backseat of the van. The captain turned ghost-white as the president started walking toward him.

Abram stopped before the captain, who straightened and nearly threw up on his shoes.

INSIDE THE ARES
APPROACHING THE EASTERN SICILIAN COAST

Ray was feeling bold. He was high. He was fast. And the experience with the missiles over D.C.—their inability to lock him, even when they knew exactly where he was—had given him loads of confidence. Even though he was approaching the Air Defense Identification Zone that protected the eastern portion of the Med, he didn't feel like hiding.

Quite the opposite. He was looking for a fight.

He knew the Italians would have scrambled their fighters. The American fighters at Aviano would have scrambled as well. The Saudis were ahead of him. They had some good jets.

But he didn't care. He wasn't going to hide anymore.

Reaching to the console on his right side, he brought up his radar, revealing his position while searching the darkening sky.

There they were. A flight of four fighters in close formation. He didn't know what kind of aircraft they were, likely F-15s out of Aviano, could be Italian Mirages; he wasn't certain.

Check that! Tomcats. A couple old U.S. Navy warbirds that had been sold to their NATO allies and were now flown by a single squadron out of Italy. He checked his radar one more time. Yeah, had to be.

Which meant they would be armed with the AIM-54 Phoenix CECCM/Sealed Missile. A very good missile, especially against high and fast targets. Thirteen feet long. Semiactive and active radar homing. Fast. In excess of three thousand miles an hour, 135 pounds of explosives in the warhead, range, 115 miles. The thing could reach out and hit you from a long way away.

He considered the capabilities of the Phoenix while he waited for his avionics to lock up the Tomcats, then sent the fighter's position to his laser. He ranged them with his radar. One-twenty miles. Thirty-nine thousand feet.

The Ares was in range of the Tomcat's missiles, but he knew the NATO Italian pilots wouldn't fire on him yet. They would wait to get closer, to get a better lock on him, for every mile they could get closer not only increased the accuracy of the missiles but also saved propellant so the missiles could maneuver on the target if it turned and ran.

No, the Italian pilots wouldn't fire until they were inside eighty miles.

His defensive system started growling. The enemy fighters were looking at him. The growl changed in pitch, and a warning light began to flash on his Helmet-Mounted Display. The fighters were ranging him with their radars, attempting to lock on to the source of the energy he was emitting from the radar in the nose of his aircraft. He watched as the group of fighters turned twenty degrees to the south, adjusting their course to intercept him. The rate of closure increased between them to almost 1,500 miles an hour. The NATO fighters knew they were being illuminated by radar energy from the Ares and they brought down their own radars in an attempt to make it more difficult for him to keep a bead on them.

Ray shook his head. It didn't matter. The F-14s were in open air, over the water, where there was no place to hide.

He continued to feed the updated coordinates to his gun, then commanded it into prefire mode. Microscopic variations on the surface of the mirrors went through millions of adjustments every second to compensate for range, humidity, air density, speed, ambient illumination—dozens of variables the laser had to compensate for in order to keep the laser focused on the target.

Scared now, aware that great danger was near, the F-14s split into flights of two and then individual flights of one. All four fighters changed altitude and maneuvered to make it more difficult for his radar to keep a solid lock on them.

His defensive system continued growling. All four F-14s had him locked up in their radar, their Phoenix missiles ready to fire.

Ninety-two miles and closing. Ten miles, on the outside, before the F-14s would fire.

Ten miles! Are you kidding? Ray scoffed. In ten miles, my pretty ladies, all of you will be dead.

A status light on his gun control panel turned from red, to yellow, to green. He rolled a crosshair over the top of the first fighter and fired his gun. A little noise as the generators kicked into high speed. A noticeable vibration as the mirrors moved and fired. But that was it. Nothing else. No light. No sudden flash. But somewhere out there in the distance, far beyond what he could see, he knew that his laser had destroyed the F-14.

Three targets left on his radar. He moved his crosshairs and fired. Then again. Then again.

And that was it. All of the fighters were gone.

He checked the range on the last fighter that he had just destroyed. Eighty-five miles from him. But with a *poof!* it was gone.

Skies cleared, he turned off his radar, making himself invisible again, then lovingly patted the side of the Ares. "Good girl," he told her. "You and me, babe. Ain't nothing that can touch us. I say, come on, bring it on!"

FIFTY

INSIDE THE ARES
FLYING DOWN THE EASTERN COAST OF THE RED SEA

Alexandria, Cairo, and then the Suez Canal were behind him. The Nile Delta and the Sinai, the dry block of rugged terrain that jutted like an arrowhead into the northern tip of the Red Sea, had passed behind him as well. It was dark now, and the clear desert air offered nearly unlimited visibility. To his right, far in the distance, he could see the Nile glimmering in the moonlight as it flowed north, clusters of lights illuminating the waterline on both sides of the shore. He could see the lighted pyramids, yellow and brown triangles that followed the fertile lowlands of the Nile. Slightly to his left and much farther in the distance, Medina glittered on the other side of the Hejaz Mountains, sparkling on the edge of the Saudi Desert like a fantasy city from some other world.

Ray was very high now, almost to sixty-six thousand feet, but he had slowed to .97 Mach so he wouldn't create a sonic boom. He was closing in on the target and the last thing he wanted was to reveal his exact location and route of flight. Sneak in and sneak out, that's all he was looking for now.

He checked his distance-to-target display. Less than three hundred miles to go. Eighteen minutes, twenty seconds to start his final bomb-release checklist. Twenty minutes, twenty seconds until he would drop the bomb.

He knew there was a beehive of fighters somewhere down below him to the south, to the north, certainly to the east. Having been detected by the 747, he knew the Americans would realize that he was going to attack. Now, where he was heading and what his target was, that they didn't know, but they were smart. The list of possible targets was relatively small, so they had to be close, somewhere below him, on his left and right. They would have concentrated their forces in the region to search for him.

And they had a lot of forces. Hundreds of missiles and jets.

But it was a lot of territory to cover. They would have to spread themselves thin. And the city he was going after was a target they would not have imagined before.

AIR FORCE ONE
LE BOURGET AIRPORT

The head of the Secret Service detail moved toward the president. "We are leaving," he whispered to him in a serious tone.

The president nodded, not surprised. With the Ares on the loose, it was time to get out of France.

The door to his private office was open, and he heard urgent voices and hurried footsteps in the narrow corridor outside. He felt his ears pop as the aft cabin doors were closed and locked, increasing the internal pressure in the jet. The aircraft was already beginning to vibrate as the pilot brought up his four engines. Looking out his oval window, the president noted the number of automobiles that still surrounded the jet. But the pilot didn't wait for them to clear before he started to move. Abram watched as the left wing crossed two security vans, the enormous wingtip passing directly over them.

Men and vehicles scrambled everywhere. Having made the decision to leave, they would wait for no man. A few members of the presidential security team were going to be left behind. Didn't matter. They couldn't wait. Bronco was getting off the ground.

Inside the cockpit atop the enormous aircraft, the 747 aircraft commander, an air force colonel, switched his radio transmitter to ground control. "Ground, Bronco and company on the south hammerhead, ready to taxi."

The ground controller hesitated. What was this? The American presidential entourage was suddenly ready to go! But there was no departure time or route of flight in the system! It would take some time to coordinate everything for the caravan of U.S. transport jets.

"Stand by," the ground controller replied.

"Negative," the colonel answered. "Bronco is on the go now."

The first aircraft off the runway was an American C-17, loaded with the two presidential limousines and security personnel. It took to the sky and climbed steeply away.

The C-17 was the first aircraft to take off for a reason, for hidden in the belly of the aircraft was a series of antennas, IR sensors, and highly sensitive snooping equipment. As the aircraft climbed away from the airport, the electronic sensors scanned the area immediately underneath the departure route, searching for any indications of a ground-to-air threat.

Air Force One was next in line for the runway, followed by three more military transports and an emergency backup executive jet.

Given the clear sign, Air Force One turned sharply from the taxiway onto the runway, stopped, held its brakes, spooled up its four enormous turbofan engines, scattered dust and debris two thousand feet behind it, then started rolling. Vapors of humidity spun off the wingtips as the nose lifted into the air. "Bronco, switch to departure on one-four-seven point niner," the tower controller said as the aircraft's wheels left the runway.

"Switching," the pilot answered.

"Bronco," the departure controller told the pilot after he had checked in, "cleared pilot's discretion to thirty-nine thousand. Cleared direct to Brest. Your own navigation after that."

"Roger, cleared to flight level three-nine zero, direct to Brest," the air force colonel shot back.

Inside the Departure Control building on the outskirts of Paris, the radar controller looked at the tiny slip of paper that contained Air Force One's flight plan. The flight plan only went as far as Brest, one of the mandatory reporting points on the southern tip of France. But that was it. Nothing else. No one knew where the aircraft was heading after that.

METRO 37
KING KALID PRIVATE AIRPORT
MECCA, SAUDI ARABIA

The satellite radios on the American aircraft suddenly burst to life. "Metro, Metro, this is Haven on emergency guard."

The two pilots turned and stared at each other. The copilot checked his transmit button, then answered, "Go, Haven."

"Metro, this is an emergency order from CENTCOM. Repeat, an emergency order from CENTCOM. You are to depart AOR now!"

CENTCOM. Central Command. The military command responsible for the entire Middle East. *Depart AOR*. Depart the area now!"

The two pilots were incredulous. "What are you talking about?" the copilot replied.

"Metro, confirm you have the message. Direct orders from CENTCOM. You are to depart the kingdom *now!*"

The aircraft commander shook his head and switched his radio to talk. "Haven, our passenger is not with us. She was taken away more than an hour ago in the king's caravan. We are still waiting for her. I say again, the passenger is *not* with us. We don't know where she is."

"It doesn't matter, Metro. You are directed to launch your aircraft. Leave her if you have to. You have to get out of there *now!*"

"Haven, we say again, our passenger—"

"Disregard the passenger, Metro. The Ares is inbound!"

KING AZIZ ROYAL PALACE
MECCA, SAUDI ARABIA

The king stared at his young niece. So beautiful. So endearing. She was a young woman now, but in his mind's eye and in his heart, she was still a little girl. And she had always had an ability to touch him unlike any other girl. Part of it was her beauty, part of it was the fact that he loved her father as much as he had ever loved a man.

Her eyes. They could be trusted. Her face. The face of Eve.

He shook his head and glared, his chest wrenching inside.

No. He had been fooled. This young woman was no Eve. She was a scorpion. A snake. A monster cloaked in beauty to hide the treachery inside. She had turned around and bit him. Now there was poison in his veins.

He considered the ancient proverb as he stared into her dark eyes. *You knew what I was before you slipped into my bed.*

"Your father," he asked her slowly, his voice low and powerful. "Your father is dead now?"

"Yes, my King. He was killed yesterday."

The king nodded slowly. This he already knew. And he knew who had killed him. He knew who this girl was and what she had done. He knew who she worked for and where her loyalties lay. He had agents. There were ears and eyes everywhere. The French government was like a sieve, leaking the most vital information for the smallest price.

She betrayed her own father!

He almost wept with pure shame.

What to do to set it right?

"Tell me again!" he demanded in a soft, deadly voice.

"My King," she started slowly, her head bowed toward the ground. She repeated what she had told him, changing nothing, and never lifting her eyes to him. "The American president—"

The royal king cut her off. "The American president is a liar! And you know that, my child!"

"No, my King, I swear to you on the grave of my father—"

"The father you killed!"

She looked up, her face dumbfounded, her eyes tearing in shock. "No, my King, I did not kill my father. The American pilot did."

"No!" the king screamed, "I will not hear it. The American president is a devil and you are his child. You are an angel sent to deceive me, and I will not listen anymore. We are finished. I am done with you, child."

Petrie stared, her mouth open, her eyes filled with dread. "Please, you *must* believe me. I have been sent here to tell you—"

The king stepped forward and slapped her hard across the face. He split her lip and she cried and lifted her hand to her mouth. Blood sprayed the floor. He slapped again, cuffing her cheek, then spit in her hair. "For your dead father," he whispered, then turned his back on her.

She didn't move. Total silence. She fought to keep her sobs in.

He would kill her now. There was a dagger on her heart.

She kept her head low and started crying.

"I am done with you, Petrie. Your name is anathema to me now. You betrayed your own father. *Family, honor, tribe, and sword.* You have betrayed them all, Petrie, and cannot live with this dishonor, but fear not, I will show mercy. It will be painless and quick."

Petrie stared at the floor, breathing deeply, fighting to keep from falling.

Then, without knocking, an aide pushed back the twelve-foot-high office door and ran into the room, his slippers flapping against the shiny marble floor. White-faced, he ran to the king and whispered in his ear.

The king stared at him, his old eyes burning bright. "No," he muttered softly. "No, no, that can't be."

The aide cleared his throat and assured him it was.

INSIDE THE ARES

Ray's gut crunched up, his nerves on edge, his mind racing. For a moment—just a moment—he considered what he was about to do.

A nuclear weapon would soon be falling over a city of a million innocents.

It would free-fall for a little more than a minute, then, four thousand feet above the ground, it would explode. There would be a flash of white light, a burst of radiation. A nuclear fireball, white, then yellow, then orange, then dull red, would boil as it rose in the sky. A blast of heat. Deadly fire. A wave of supersonic air crashing out. Another wave crashing back into the vacuum, less powerful than the first, but this time filled with debris—rock, pieces of cement, the remains of tattered buildings, splinters of wood from fallen trees, body pieces, the flesh of animals, shards of glass, nails, and pieces of broken cars—all of it flying through the air with more force than a monster hurricane. The heat would spread. The fires catch. The cloud of radiation would climb into the night sky and then rain down as the heat condensed the humidity in the upper atmosphere. A poison rain that would contaminate everything that it touched.

He was about to do this! He held the very keys of hell.

He was about to unleash the two most horrible forces in the world. The force of a nuclear weapon, so much power to kill. Then a greater force would follow. The forces of bitter hate and revenge. The forces of the human heart and all the blackness it contained.

His bomb would explode. A quarter of a million innocent Muslims would die.

And with that explosion, the world would be changed.

There would be no forgiveness. No mercy. No understanding.

All there would be is revenge.

The Great War was coming.

And *he* held the key.

The Arabian Peninsula was passing underneath him. Jeddah off his nose. Mecca five degrees off his right. Forty-five miles to the target. Little more than four minutes to go. He kept a straight course toward Jeddah. *If* the enemy aircraft were down there, and *if* they had seen him, he would make a last feint toward Jeddah to draw them off, then, at the last second, turn east, and line up on Mecca. The coordinates for the center of the city had already been fed into his flying machine.

The holy mosque. The Black Stone. It soon would be gone.

Two minutes and twenty seconds from the target. No enemy aircraft around. Twenty miles north of Jeddah now.

He turned east suddenly and lined up for Mecca.

Two minutes to the bomb-release point, he started the final countdown. Weapon armed. Internal gyros synched. Satellite guidance on. Target coordinates loaded and cross-checked. Internal batteries. Final aiming.

Sixty-two seconds to go.

Release point cross-checked and adjusted for air density, altitude, and atmospheric winds.

Fifty seconds. Final countdown.

He wiped sweat from his eyes.

Mecca dazzled right below him, the lights against the desert bright and beautiful.

Forty seconds.

He felt his heart race.

Was he *really* going to do it?

Thirty seconds. It was over. Every checklist and cross-check was complete. He sat back and activated the autopilot, commanding the computers to complete the final portion of the bomb run. Eight seconds before the release point, the computers would open the bomb bay doors, then automatically release the weapon inside the belly of the jet.

He gave his final consent to the computer for release, the last thing in the sequence that he had to do.

Then he heard it. A quiet chirp. Then a buzz.

The ALQ-142 defensive system sniffed another jet. Forty miles behind him. Closing quickly. At *sixty-eight thousand feet!*

Sixty-eight thousand feet!
It had to be the other Ares!

METRO 37
KING KALID PRIVATE AIRPORT
MECCA, SAUDI ARABIA

The two C-21 pilots stared at each other in anger. The aircraft commander was on the verge of panic, but still determined, his eyes fierce and bright.

The copilot glared back at him with the same gritty face. "We can't just leave her!" he cried. "This isn't her country. She is no more welcome here than we are—no . . . even less. They view her as a traitor. I don't care what those pukes back at Command Post are telling us, we can't leave her this way."

The aircraft commander shook. "The Ares is inbound to Mecca! A nuclear detonation is about to go off *right over our heads.* We have a few minutes and that's all to get in the air. Now get your feet off our wheel brakes and let's get out of here."

"You can't leave her. She will die here."

"If we stay, we will too! Now keep your hands clear of the flight controls. I'm getting this jet out of here."

The aircraft commander pushed on top of his foot pedals to release the small jet's parking brakes. "Call ground control," he told the copilot. "Get clearance out of here."

The copilot didn't move. Reaching across the cramped cockpit, he grabbed the aircraft commander's shoulder, his grip tight as steel, the adrenaline surging through him and adding strength to his fist. "If we go now, we will live. But what will we have to live with, knowing we deserted her? She trusted us enough to come here. Is this really what you want?"

The aircraft commander hesitated, both of his hands on the yoke. The airplane vibrated beneath him, the engines humming in the night heat that seeped off the hot Saudi sand.

"Please, sir, I'm begging you to think this thing through. If we leave her, she is dead. Even if our U.S. fighters might shoot the Ares down, they still would kill her."

The pilot shook his head and swore.

ARES TWO
FORTY-EIGHT MILES NORTH OF MECCA

Jesse's aircraft screamed forward as fast as it could possibly go with one good engine in afterburner and the second, without igniters, set at military power.

Flying through the darkness, he quickly scanned his system function displays. Besides no afterburner on one engine, he had also lost half a dozen radar-absorbing panels on his jet, which meant he would light up on radar like an airliner in the sky. Worse, he had no defensive systems or sensors to help keep him safe, only a partially functioning radar, a cracked windscreen, and several broken panels on his slats. The aircraft had been bombed little more than forty-eight hours ago!

But he had a working laser.

Was that enough?

He didn't know.

Everything depended on his locating the other Ares. Of course, the target was invisible to radar, which meant he had to find it with his eyes. A black aircraft. In the dark. It was like trying to find a pin in a haystack in the middle of the night.

But he knew where the Ares was heading, the approximate route Ray would fly to get there, and the approximate altitude. Ray would stay high and go slow, not wanting to leave a sonic wave behind him that would reveal where he was. And he would have to approach from the northwest, right where Jesse was.

And Colonel Ray hadn't hit the target yet, which meant he had to be . . . somewhere almost . . . straight off . . . his nose.

He glanced around him. The moon was high now and the stars had come out. Then he pushed both throttles, demanding every ounce of energy from his jet. The fuselage vibrated with a high-speed buzz, the result of the missing panels, as he strained to peer through the dark. The moon was only half full but clear and white. The stars were bright, and at sixty-seven thousand feet there were a billion more of them than could be seen from the ground.

If he could just catch a glimpse of the aircraft, just a flash of the moon bouncing off the top of its wings, Jesse knew he could take him. If he could find Colonel Ray, he could kill him.

But he was running out of time.

KING AZIZ ROYAL PALACE
MECCA, SAUDI ARABIA

The king of Saudi Arabia stared at his personal aide and gulped like a stranded fish out of water. "The American secret fighter is out there?"

"Yes, my *Sayid*."

"How far away?"

"Not far, sir. Somewhere between forty and ninety miles. The Americans have warned us, but they don't know where it is!"

"Forty miles! Are you kidding! That leaves us—"

"Barely seconds, sir."

The king staggered back. "And they think he is armed with a nuclear warhead?" His voice was soft, his head swimming.

The aide nodded and pulled his shoulder, directing him to the door. "We've got to get into the shelter." He pushed his master toward the elevator in the hall.

All of the king's palaces had been configured with an emergency shelter and command post in the basement, but none of them were hardened for a nuclear bomb. Still, they had to get down there. What else could they do?

The aide pulled.

The king swore bitterly, then disappeared through the door, leaving Petrie surrounded by half a dozen guards.

They looked at her awkwardly, then went toward the closed door. Not being part of the king's emergency contingent, they had nowhere to go.

ARES ONE
TWENTY-THREE SECONDS FROM THE BOMB RELEASE POINT

Ray stared, a sudden look of fear and desperation on his face. He gulped in disbelief, a drop of sweat rolling down the left side of his ribs.

The other Ares! It was up here!

How did they fix it? Was it ready to hit him with its laser?

He *hadn't* destroyed it!

Who was piloting the other Ares?

Jesse—yes, it had to be Jesse. And he was coming after him!

He heaved, his mind racing, every thought coming with perfect clarity as he considered what to do.

Thirty-four seconds on the bomb run. No time to reprogram his computer. He had to hit the release point or the warhead would not eject from the jet.

Thirty-two seconds now and counting.

The other pilot was behind him. Well within laser range.

Thirty seconds now and counting.

Too much time to sit there like a target flying straight and level through the sky! Thirty seconds was a lifetime—no, a death time. Aerial combat was measured in fractions of a second, not in full seconds, and certainly not in anything more than ten!

If he continued, he would die; it was as simple as that. Jesse would hit him with his laser.

He would not get his bomb out.

He had to turn around and fight him or he would be dead.

His defensive counter system growled angrily in his ear. He swore, then grabbed the control stick, rolled the aircraft on its wingtip, jammed the stick back with as much force as he could stand, then held his breath against the onslaught of the g-forces as the jet rolled into the tight turn. The blood drained from his head. The aircraft pulled to six g's. His vision tunneled and he strained against his abdomen, grunting and pressing against his diaphragm to force the blood to return to his head. He felt a light buzz in his ears, then rolled off on the stick.

He was focused and intent now.

Kill the other pilot. Complete the bomb run. Nothing mattered more than that.

ARES TWO

Jesse threw his radar across the sky. It didn't matter if the other pilot could detect him now, with the missing RAM panels, he would find him anyway, and he wanted Ray to know, at least to think, that he was in position to fire his gun. So he swept with his radar but kept his eyes outside, always searching.

Above fifty thousand feet, the sky was clear as outer space. Deep black and dazzling. Brilliant stars. Nothing moved. No obstructions. No shadows. It was like being on the edge of the universe and staring into the center of the Milky Way. Ray had to be out there, somewhere straight off his nose, maybe a few degrees left or right.

Then he saw him. A flash in the moonlight. A dark, deadly shadow passing in front of the stars.

He adjusted his radar.

Another flash across his windscreen. Yes, that was him!

Jesse had counted on Ray's arrogance and played on his pride, hoping the fool would roll his wings up to him.

And yes, now he had him.

"Come on, baby!" he cried.

ARES ONE

Ray rolled the jet, but while it turned, he kept his eyes inside the cockpit. He paused and locked the countdown on the weapon, storing all the information into flash memory, switched over his avionics to air-to-air mode, then brought up his radar and flashed it across the sky.

There he was! The other pilot was coming at him! Time to blow him from the sky.

ARES TWO

There! Jesse got it. The idiot had powered up his radar. What a fool! Arrogance could be a good thing in the cockpit, but there was a price to pay. With his radar sweeping, Ray was a flashlight in a dark room, shining his light to look for Jesse while illuminating himself. Jesse's avionics system growled, a low buzz in his ears. It sounded almost angry, like a dog getting ready to attack. The designers knew the psychology behind air-to-air combat and had designed the angry growl as a manipulation to pump more adrenaline into the pilot's veins.

Jesse slammed through the switches on his radar, getting a lock on his gun. A second passed, the mirrors moved, and the generator powered up. Another second. He sucked in a breath, knowing Ray would be doing exactly the same thing. It was a race now to the trigger. Who was better with this weapon? Who could fire first?

The status light on his Helmut-Mounted Display switched from red to yellow. He held his breath for green.

Then he reached down and pressed the transmitter switch on his radio. *"Gun Riders, target is twenty-one DME, three-ten radial. Say again, target twenty-one miles, three-ten radial off the bull's-eye. You are free to fire now!"*

Ray waited for his status light, his finger on the trigger of his gun. His radar locked Jesse up, feeding the coordinates to the fire computers, adjusted the mirrors, generators ready to—

Then he heard it; *"Gun Riders, target is twenty-one DME, three-ten radial . . ."*

The colonel froze. Jesse had brought his buddies. He wasn't out there alone.

The light on his HMD slipped to green and he fired his laser gun.

Jesse felt his aircraft shudder and he knew that he had been hit. His laser status light flickered green and he fired his gun even as he screamed into his mask. His fighter reeled as his laser shot a beam of light hopelessly off target, then cut short. Behind him, sparks from tearing metal, a flash of light, a crunching noise, then a crushing tuck-and-roll as his aircraft began to spin and fall from the sky.

The Saudi F-15 fighters climbed from underneath the dogfight. They had also sensed the radars. They locked up the stolen Ares.

Ray's defensive system screamed in his ears. Missiles inbound! Almost directly below him! Coming right at his guts, straight up from the darkness, like a shark attack. He couldn't see directly below him. Jesse knew that, of course, and had set up the other fighters to come at him from the only place he couldn't see them or directly fire back. His gut tightened up as the defensive system warnings sounded in his ears. "*Fox Two! Fox One! Fox Two! Fox One!*" the recording announced in an absurdly calm voice.

He rolled. Fox One and Fox Two. Radar and heat-seekers missiles. He cut off his own radar and pulled, slammed both throttles into full afterburner, spouting dual bursts of flames from the back of his engines, and pulled into a turning dive.

He had to get his nose on the missiles. Had to get them face to face. Had to get his belly away from their radar-guided systems, for the bottom surfaces on his wings flashed back way too much radar energy. It was the only place they could detect him—from directly above or below.

Jesse had set him up. He cursed his old friend again.

He pulled—the turn was tight, bottomed out at 59,400 feet—then let the nose drift toward the dark earth until he was pointing straight down. Down toward the missiles. Eight or ten coming at him. He saw their dull yellow tails, the heat from their engines lighting up the sky. He pointed his nose toward them and pulled his power back. Face up to the missiles. Engines idle. No IR energy to guide them. Every particle of radar energy scattering around him, flying off into space, none of it returning to guide the missiles to him.

They wobbled, tried to find him, then scattered through the sky.

Some exploded. Some drifted earthward, their fuel gone. None of them continued tracking.

Then he saw others coming at him and his defensive system growled again in his ear: "*Fox One. Fox Two.*"

He had to find and kill the fighters that were shooting at him.

He brought his radar up. There. Forty-two thousand feet. Eight point two miles to the west. Looked like . . . four F-15s.

He brought up his laser and fired. One . . . two . . . three . . . The laser fired until they all were gone.

Mecca was off his right now, almost thirty miles away. The lights glittered, a perfect round bowl of illumination against the utter emptiness of the desert.

He was still pointing straight down, almost falling, his engines still at idle, passing through forty-seven thousand feet. He pulled and turned the aircraft, hauling the nose past the horizon, higher, higher, pointing at the moon. He pushed up his throttles and turned toward the target again.

Climbing again.

Back to altitude.

Where was the other Ares?

Should he chance it? He flashed his radar again and looked north.

Pieces scattered. They were falling. No IR return on his sensors. No heat sources in the sky.

The other Ares was gone.

METRO 37
KING KALID PRIVATE AIRPORT
MECCA, SAUDI ARABIA

The palace was located less than eight kilometers from the king's private airport, normally a five-minute drive.

The driver made it in less than two minutes, sometimes hitting more than a hundred miles an hour.

The single black SUV screamed across the tarmac toward the waiting aircraft, its tires belching gray smoke as it screeched to a stop.

Two Saudi security agents jumped from the front seat. Three scrambled from the back. Petrie followed. As she ran toward the U.S. aircraft, her eyes darted upward, searching the night sky. The door to the aircraft was dropped into place as she ran toward it and scrambled up the narrow stairs. The five Saudi agents followed her into the aircraft, their eyes wild, their faces tense and scared.

"Go! Go! Go!" Petrie screamed as she scrambled through the door. "You have a few minutes, maybe seconds, to get this jet out of here!"

The copilot looked back into the cabin. "Who are they?" he cried.

"Forget them. They're with me. Now get this jet off the ground!"

The aircraft started moving before the door even closed. Turning sharply, it accelerated down the taxiway, maneuvering behind a row of royal jets.

Inside the cockpit, the aircraft commander jammed his engines up to full power. He wasn't going to taxi to the runway when the taxiway would do.

Seconds later, the aircraft lifted into the air.

ARES TWO

Jesse fought the controls. His jet lurched. He spun, pinned against the side of his cockpit by the force of the g's. He jammed both of his throttles into afterburner to stop his descent, but it only accelerated the spinning, and he brought them back to idle and pressed his back against the eject seat.

He should get out. He was falling. Completely out of control.

He reached for the ejection handles, then pulled his hands back.

No. He would not quit now. He *couldn't* quit now. He still had a chance.

He glanced over his shoulder, straining against the g's that were throwing him against the side of his seat. The force of the spin threw him violently forward, then back, and his neck muscles snapped. The aircraft spun. Images flashed through the front of his cockpit. Moon. Stars. Ground lights from Mecca. Moon . . . stars . . . ground lights from Mecca . . . the dizzying cycle repeating itself every second. Spinning like a top. Falling out of the sky. He jammed his flight controls. They were worthless in his hands. The Ares was a monster when she was out of control. Unforgiving. A wild bull. Once in a spin, there was no way to regain control. No rudders. No elevators. His ship was falling apart.

He didn't have any more options.

He thought about the eject handles again as he strained to breathe.

Gritting, he wrenched his neck to look behind him. The skin of his aircraft reflected in the light of the moon. The twin vertical fins on his tail were gone. Nothing but little stubs of broken metal and composite material protruded upward from the rear of his jet. Another few feet and the laser would have cut through his cockpit. And his fuel tanks. And cut off his wings.

He centered the control stick, neutralizing the control surfaces on his wings to give the flight computer fly-by-wire system a few seconds to analyze the dramatic change in airfoils.

He cursed as he waited.

And continued to fall.

ARES ONE

Ray swept his radar one more time, convinced the other Ares was falling out of control, then shut his radar down.

His mind flashed. Major James. A good kid. He meant him no harm. In fact—and this made him shudder—in some ways Jesse reminded him of his son. But he was stupid enough to try and stop him. What choice did he have?

Leveling off at 62,000 feet, he turned back toward the target. Shoving his throttles forward, he headed for the bomb line again. Breaking through the speed of sound—no reason to pretend anymore that they didn't know where he was—he accelerated quickly, turned over to bomb-nav mode on his avionics package, then gave his computers control of his aircraft.

The countdown started again. Sixty seconds. Barely enough time to update his position to the internal navigational systems on the warhead, barely enough time to spin up the internal gyros, confirm the codes, and arm the warhead again, but he didn't care anymore; he wanted the warhead out of the bowels of his jet. He wanted it over and to head out to sea. If he didn't hit the target just exactly, it didn't matter anyway. A few miles, a few thousand feet, what could it matter with a nuclear bomb?

He raced toward the center of Mecca, brought his throttles back to slow down so he wouldn't blow off his bomb bay doors, then waited, holding his breath for the final countdown.

ARES TWO

Jesse allowed the aircraft to stabilize in a flat right-hand spin, nudged over the nose to help it level it out, then jammed in opposite stick and slammed in the right engine to counterbalance the spin, and waited. His Helmet-Mounted Display altimeter clocked down through twenty-eight thousand feet. More than thirty thousand feet of altitude lost in fifty seconds! The spin slowed. He almost had it. He let the nose fall toward the ground. As the aircraft began to move forward, the flight controls started to react to his commands, the air moving over them giving him better control. He brought up both engines, giving him equal thrust once again. One hundred knots. One twenty. One fifty knots. He pulled the nose up and lifted. He was flying again.

He took a grateful breath. The avionics were adjusting for the loss of his vertical flight controls, helping him control the aircraft through the moveable slots on his wings and elevators. The aircraft continually yawed, his nose rolling around the center axis like an amusement park ride, but he could control it if he took it easy. And moved everything *very* slowly. And didn't demand very much from the jet. He nudged the throttles forward and his nose drifted right. A bit more right throttle and then it evened out.

He had control—if just barely—and he stroked his broken jet.

Knowing Ray would have climbed again, he pointed his nose toward the sky. He only had a few seconds to find Ray before he released his bomb. He brought up his radar, powered up the laser, and started searching for the Ares.

Ray was up there. He was going to get him. This fight wasn't over yet.

Twenty seconds. Ray ran through the final checklist one more time. He was ready.

He didn't care what was below him or behind him; he would not break off the bomb run. Any threat, it didn't matter.

Ten seconds. Bomb bay doors opened up. A gentle rush of air as the spoilers slipped into the slip stream. He took a breath and held it. Five seconds. Four. Three. He almost cried with relief.

Two.

One.

Say good-bye to Mecca.

He felt a sudden *thump!* The aircraft lifted.

And the nuclear warhead fell away from the jet.

The warhead was roughly constructed, crude in both design and manufacture. But although it wasn't made for precision, the firing mechanism was as solid as anything mechanical could be; the enriched material was pure, and the internal avionics as reliable as an old wind-up watch.

As the warhead fell, it turned down, its nose pointing earthward, the steering fins moving just a fraction of an inch to keep it stable as it fell. It accelerated to terminal velocity very quickly, then swished downward through the night. Blackness was all around it, but below it there was light. The bright and burning lights of Mecca. It aimed for the city center, for the Holy Mosque, for the Rock.

Fifty thousand feet above the flat earth, the final arming mechanism kicked in.

And that was it. It was over.

Nothing could stop the nuclear explosion now that final arming was complete.

Jesse's radar screen was blank. The Ares could not be seen. He searched, knowing it was up there, while he nursed his aircraft toward the starry sky once again.

Then he saw it, a sudden pop on his radar, a quick flash on his screen as Ray's spoiler doors descended into the slip stream to cushion the release of the bomb.

Jesse cried in his mask. No! No! He was too late! Ray was ready to drop his weapon. He only had five or six seconds to stop him. He aimed his laser desperately. Eight seconds until the generators and computers were ready to fire! He couldn't wait.

He manually fired his laser gun.

He watched on his radar. There was another target now. His radar flashed again.

Another target. This one tiny. The nuclear bomb fell through the sky.

His mind froze in fear and crazed emotion.

The warhead was falling now, toward him.

He would die in the explosion.

Along with a quarter million other souls.

Ray felt his aircraft lurch beneath him. For a second he thought that one of his bomb bay's doors had blown off. But the vibration got worse, feeling like a hammer against his head. The Ares lurched again, this time so violently that his teeth jammed, biting off the tip of his tongue. His mouth filled with blood and he cursed in pain. He started spinning. The aircraft bucked. Smoke began to pour into his cockpit. He was on fire. A Christmas tree of lights began to blink on his warning and status displays. Generators. Hydraulics. One of his engines spooled down. Oil pressure. Fuel pressure. Without the generators, his laser was now worthless.

It took him a second to figure it out. Then he cursed again, splitting blood.

Jesse had shot a hole through his jet!

He looked down in a rage, searching for Jesse's Ares. He cursed and he cried, knowing he soon would be dead. Without his gun, he couldn't get him. And his jet was breaking apart. He'd never make it to the Gulf. He was falling now, descending in a flutter like a dry leaf from a tree. His aircraft was barely controllable.

The he saw the other Ares right below him.

His mind raced in savage fury.

He was going to die now.

But he would kill Jesse too.

Jesse watched the bomb falling on his radar and felt a violent sickness inside, estimating how long until all those innocent people died. It was like watching a nightmare. The monster was coming and he couldn't run. He could see the bomb fall . . . falling toward him . . . passing through his altitude. Barely two miles off his nose. His radar tracked it perfectly, a tiny dot on his screen. Close enough to touch it. Almost reach out and touch it . . .

So close he could almost hit it—

He could hit it with his gun!

Stupid man! It was so obvious!

He almost screamed with frustration. He had the world's most powerful radar. It could track the falling warhead. He had a working laser.

He could shoot the falling warhead.

Spinning with his finger, he rolled his curser over the tiny blip on his radar. He locked it up, fed the aiming computer. It counted down, the generators fired, the mirrors moved, focusing the energy.

An invisible light cut through the falling warhead and it quickly broke apart, sending a thousand tiny pieces of cold debris to fall through the night.

Jesse watched in awe, his heart racing, his mind spinning. Then he cried in relief.

He had killed it.

Ray aimed his falling aircraft, barely keeping it under control. He had no engines now, but the emergency generators still allowed him to fly. Falling, spinning, tumbling from the air, he saw the other Ares below him and aimed. At a thousand feet, it flashed before him, a shadow in the night. He maneuvered his crumbling aircraft toward it, aiming for the cockpit, then closed one eye.

Five hundred feet. Half a second.

He smashed into the other jet.

The flash was so quick and so close that Jesse never understood what hit him. It took more time for the image of the approaching Ares to go from his eyes to his brain than for the falling aircraft to tear his crippled fighter apart.

The world exploded around him. And then he was blind.

FIFTY-TWO

The Ares slammed into the side of his wing, sending Jesse's aircraft tumbling through the sky, wing over wing, nose low, upside down, then around one more time until he was nose-high once again. The cockpit exploded around him, slamming his head and cracking his helmet like a gray ostrich egg. The force of the onslaught seemed to rip his organs from his chest, and though he didn't know it yet, he was already bleeding inside from the crushing force of the crash. Blinded, barely conscious, hardly able to breathe, he reacted out of instinct, reaching for the ejection handles tucked by the sides of his thighs. He felt them. He grasped. He lost them. He tumbled. He reached for them again, pulled the ejection handles, and was jettisoned out of the crippled jet.

A blast of air. The pressure of the wind on his face, folding back lips and skin until they almost peeled. The bitter cold. Gasping for air to fill his lungs. Bitter cold. Deadly cold. Blackness. He pushed it back. It swirled, then merged around him, turning everything black.

He fell, his head limp, his arms flailing.

The parachute opened. He drifted earthward, his head still resting on his chin. He hit the ground with a jolt but never woke. Lying in a heap on the desert, he moaned with his face in the sand.

Ray's aircraft disintegrated all around him. Fire. Heat. Pressure. Unbelievable sound and pain. It hurt from his feet to his brain. The cockpit smashed into his legs, severing bone and flesh completely. The metal pushed farther up, crushing into his lap, breaking both of his femurs and his ribs. The cockpit separated from the aircraft, escaping most of the heat, then tumbled and spun through the bitter cold atmosphere. He was alive. And he was conscious. He felt every tremor, every pain. Every blast of heat from the exploding jets seemed to singe into his brain. He reached for his ejection handles, but the pneumatic lines had been severed and the explosive charges that would drive his seat out of the broken cockpit were completely destroyed.

He remained strapped in the eject seat and crumbling cockpit. He screamed as he fell until the cold frosted his lungs. He drifted into blackness until the thicker air at the lower altitudes brought him back to consciousness again.

Opening his eyes, he squinted against the onslaught of the wind. He saw the ground lights coming at him and he started screaming again.

Then he impacted the Arabian Desert that he had hoped to turn into glass.

AIR FORCE ONE
OVER THE NORTH ATLANTIC SEA

The president was so exhausted he could barely keep his head up. His hands trembled with fatigue and he felt as if he might collapse. Still, he focused on Edgar Ketchum, his eyes weary but alive.

"The choppers have him?" he demanded anxiously.

"Yes, sir, they do. U.S. Air Force MH-60 rescue helicopters located his beacon in the desert. He has been recovered and is en route to the USS *Reagan* in the Gulf. They will stabilize him in the ship infirmary, then move him to the medical facility in Germany."

"But he is okay?"

"He's alive, sir. That's all that we know."

"I want more than that. I want to know now!"

"He's alive, sir. That's a start. He's pretty beat up. Apparently Colonel Ray intentionally crashed his aircraft into him, but yes, from what they are saying, it looks like he's going to live."

The president sat back and nodded. "And the young woman?"

"She's on her way back here. She should land within the hour."

Abram nodded, then waved his hand. "I need some sleep now," he said.

"I understand, sir. We all do."

Ketchum turned and left him, shutting the president's private office door.

The president heard the door shut, then lay his head on his desk. He slept like that for two hours, then stood, removed his clothes, staggered to the couch, and fell asleep once again.

LANDSTUHL REGIONAL MEDICAL CENTER
LANDSTUHL, GERMANY

Three days later, a cold front blew through central Europe, dropping the temperatures and bringing a cold, misty rain.

The military hospital at Landstuhl was by far the largest U.S. medical facility anywhere outside the United States. A web of tangled corridors and rooms, many of them off limits to civilian personnel, it was an intimidating structure, but especially for her.

So she moved slowly, reading the signs at each corner, until she found his room. There she took a deep breath, touched her hair, then pushed open the door.

The curtains were drawn and it was almost dark, but she could still see his outline under a thin sheet on his bed. His eyes were closed, and she hesitated, standing like a statue by the door. She stared at his messy hair and tan skin, then took a silent step back. Lowering her eyes, she reached for the door once again.

"Where you going, Petrie?" Jesse said as he rolled onto his side with a smile. "You can't leave me already. I've been waiting for you!"

NORTHERN MECCA DESERT
SAUDI ARABIA

The sun rose over the blazing desert. The flies came out and the wind picked up, turning the air dry and gritty and unbearably hot.

The body was almost entirely covered over with sand now, leaving only the left hand and the lower portion of his legs exposed. But the sands always drifted in the desert, and with the morning wind already blowing, they would drift a lot today.

By midmorning, Colonel Ray's corpse was completely covered in gray sand. By nightfall, the broken pieces of cockpit and ejection seat were completely covered as well.

EPILOGUE

CHINESE MILITARY HEADQUARTERS COMPOUND
DOWNTOWN BEIJING, PEOPLES REPUBLIC OF CHINA (PRC)

The two men sat across from each other, both of them smoking and sipping scalding tea. They hadn't seen each other since the luxury villa in Turkey, a period of only two days, but already that seemed a long lifetime ago. Both men were Chinese, though one of them, the foreign agent, had spent most of his time stationed at Chinese embassies throughout the Middle East. Ostensibly, the younger man served as a private contractor to the embassies in Iran and Kuwait, but everyone in the intelligence community knew his real masters were the military officers that ran the Sixth Bureau Ministry *of State Security* for the PRC.

The thinner officer, at one time the youngest colonel in the Chinese Special Forces before moving over to the Sixth, was as bold and ambitious as any man alive. The entire Ares operation had been not only his idea, but for going on almost five years it had been the primary focus of his life. Every piece, every move, had been planned out by him. A master chess player, capable of winning on the international level, he knew how to plan ahead, how to be patient and deceive, how to set a trap and then wait for a weak and unsuspecting prey.

The older man, the fat one, the Chief of the Sixth Bureau Ministry of State Security stared at his protégé. "We were so close," he muttered simply. "So close, I could taste the victory on my tongue."

The army officer only nodded, a bitter look of frustration on his face. He was crushed with disappointment. No, that wasn't a strong enough description. He felt almost dead.

So close. He cursed bitterly.

The older man, his only master, gently placed his hand on his arm.

"We almost did it," the younger man whispered, talking mostly to himself.

"We almost started a war that would have brought them to their knees. They would have fought each other for the next hundred years. And while they were concentrating on each other, spending all their resources to keep the other in check, we would have grown in great power."

The general nodded in sympathy. Yes, he shared the disappointment, but he had lived a little longer and was willing to take a broader outlook on their failure.

The younger officer cursed, his shoulders slumping. "A few more seconds . . ." His voice trailed off in rage.

"You should not underestimate what you have accomplished," the general said. "Look at what you've done here. No, we didn't start the Great War between the nations, but you have ratcheted up the tension between them to an unbearable degree. They hate each other even more now, if that is possible, and they trust each other even less."

The officer looked up, his dark eyes still in flames. "We almost started a war between the U.S. and the entire Muslim world. After they had destroyed each other we could have reigned supreme."

The general huffed, pulling a long drag on his smoke, then pressed his lips as he thought. "It isn't over," he offered simply. "There will be other opportunities. We will try again."